GERMLINE

GERMLINE

The transference of genetic information from one generation
of an organism to the next through the sex cells.

GERMLINE

Julia Melanie Miller

Dear Vanessa,
Take a journey into the
post pandemic world
of GERMLINE and stay
safe!

Julia Miller 2020

Cover image of the Riley Graves
at Eyam in Derbyshire, Great Britain,_
courtesy Alamy (BFKG9X)

Published by
Forty South Publishing Pty Ltd
Hobart, Tasmania
www.fortysouth.com.au

Printed by
McPherson's Printing Group
Melbourne, Australia
mcphersonsprinting.com.au

Dedicated to my parents
Miriam and Henry Priestley

PROLOGUE

Eyam, Derbyshire, England
August 1666

The stench of death hung in the air. Elizabeth Hancock closed her eyes and clenched her teeth as she squeezed the sodden earth within her fists. Mud oozed from between her fingers. Rain began to fall, mingling with the tears trickling down her grimy face. Sobbing, she pressed her cheek to the ground, trying to sense the buried girl. She lay there, still and cold, as the fog rolled in across the moors, smothering the village as if wanting to end its misery.

The sound of her children's voices had begun to fade. The details of their faces had melted away. Rolling onto her back, Elizabeth raised both arms and cried out to the Lord.

'Why 'as tha kept _me_ alive? Why 'as tha takin' _all_ that 'av luved so dear?'

There was naught left for her here. No mouths to feed. No faces to wash. No man to wrap her thighs around.

She was completely alone.

Elizabeth was determined to leave this godforsaken village. She would steal away in the dead of night, across the moors to Sheffield. It would take a few days. No matter. She *would find work and start afresh. She would ensure that the bairn in her belly had a chance.*

Elizabeth had tried to leave yesterday, but Marshall had stopped her. As she scurried up the hill, he'd caught her and pinned her to the ground.

'Get the fuck off me,' she'd screamed, biting and scratching at him with her filthy nails. He'd kept hold of her wrists and tried to reason with her.

'Tha knows that tha can't leave 'ere, lass. None of us can. It's 'ard, I know, but we 'av all agreed to stick it art.'

Once her body relaxed, Marshall had gathered her in his arms and carried her home. He'd drawn the curtains, lit a candle and stoked the fire, before returning to his wife and their sick boy.

That was yesterday. Tonight would be different. She would leave and never return. Marshall wouldn't stop her this time. He had dug four graves today. She had watched him in the distance from her attic window. Tonight, he would fall into a deep slumber. Her slender fingers moved to her stomach. She stroked and caressed her womb, then began to weep as she gathered together some food and treasured possessions.

Melbourne, Australia
March 2074

1

Ellen Hancock leaned into the shower cubicle and flicked on the mixer. She sighed as she sat down to remove her shoes, then dragged herself up to peel off her clothes. Standing naked, she caught sight of her refection in the mirror. Her waist looked thicker. Too many carbs … not enough exercise. Steam swept across the glass and the image vanished. She wished her memories of today's shift would vanish. Her stomach churned and her head ached. She had become a doctor to heal people. Today she had failed and … her period was late. Ellen glanced down at her wrist. The specified time had passed. She turned her concentration to the test strip as two pink lines came into focus. Desperation flooded her body. She was pregnant. How had she let this happen? A wave of nausea engulfed her. Slumping to her knees, she grabbed hold of the cold porcelain toilet bowl and vomited.

'Are you all right in there, Ellen?' Rob called through the door.

Rob Davies was the friend of a friend. He'd moved in for a couple of weeks, just until he found a place. That was a year ago.

'I'm fine,' she replied, wiping her mouth with the back of her hand. 'I just had a rough shift.'

A rough shift? Is that how one describes a shift where you watch a four-year-old girl die as her mother looks on with fear in her eyes and hope in her heart? Yes, it was a *fucking* rough shift, but it was also tragic and soul destroying. Tonight, a beautiful little girl lay dead in the morgue. Little thing never stood a chance. Her body was covered with black spots that hadn't disappeared when Ellen pressed them. Meningococcal. New strains emerged each spring. Vaccination programs fell behind. Deaths were inevitable. Ellen's brain was etched with the image of the mother with an unresponsive child in her arms. Thrusting her head back over the bowl, Ellen violently expelled more stomach contents. The acidic stench of the vomit ran up her nostrils and she retched again.

She paused for a moment to catch her breath then stood up, brushed her teeth and stepped into the shower. Only then did she allow herself to cry. As her sobbing intensified Ellen leaned against the tiled wall. The last thing she needed was to bring a child into this world. A world packed with superbugs. No partner. A dying mother. The timing couldn't be worse. The pregnancy was a complication she could ill afford. Yes, she was well aware how it had happened. For once in her life she had let her desires override her inhibitions.

2

Thirty-eight-year-old Ellen Hancock had been born in Newark, New Jersey. Until his retirement, her father Harold had been a botany lecturer at a local university. He was responsible for designing the largest and most successful communal garden in the state. Prior to her illness, Ellen's mother Beatrice had taught music, giving piano lessons to the local kids. Beatrice's services were popular. She didn't send out accounts and the word had spread. Ellen had one sibling, James, an architect. Her parents had adopted him when ongoing fertility issues prevented Beatrice from having a second child.

Ellen's love of biology began as a child, ignited by her grandfather, Henry Hancock. The retired science teacher was a kind, patient man who spent hours teaching her the skills of observation. Learning contextually was his method, not in a classroom where nothing was quite connected to the real world. He encouraged her to perform experiments. She would record her findings in a logbook and together they would arrive at conclusions about life on Earth. Her logbook, now tattered and worn, remained a treasured possession.

Ellen's continued fascination with science led her to study medicine. She was an outstanding student and graduated with first-class honours. Two years later Ellen emigrated to Australia to take up a position at King William Hospital in Melbourne. The posting was the opportunity of a lifetime, with intriguing clinical cases and cutting-edge technology. She was in her element, in a captivating country with plenty of space, clean air, delicious food and a relaxed lifestyle.

Then, in 2064, an avian flu virus, AV64, caused the final collapse of ailing health systems across the globe. Over the preceding fifty years there had been numerous microbial outbreaks, but none compared to the one in 2064. For two years a worldwide pandemic raged; millions died. There was no successful antiviral treatment for AV64 itself. To exacerbate the problem, antibiotics had finally stopped being effective, causing survival rates to plummet. In a return to the era before penicillin, one in three people died of infection. Despite extensive research, the microorganisms were winning.

Traditional emergency departments could no longer safely manage a diverse patient case mix. It seemed ludicrous to risk placing a patient with a potentially contagious disease into any casual contact with others while awaiting diagnosis. The twenty-first century health system was no longer fit for purpose. Hospitals that could not be redesigned and decontaminated were demolished and a new health system emerged.

Ellen had never fallen ill despite working in what medics called the 'dirtiest' hospitals. She didn't put her continuing good health down to luck alone. She believed it was also due to her rigorous adherence to the World Health Organization's 'Standard Precautions'. She now worked in one of the drive-through emergency 'Health Hubs', located in the Melbourne CBD, next to Spencer Street Station.

Health Hubs reduced cross-contamination by keeping clients and medical staff separated. Once assessed at a Hub, patients could be treated on site or stabilised and transferred to specialist hospitals. People with infections went to different hospitals from those requiring surgery. Maternity hospitals ensured healthy pregnant women and newborns weren't exposed to disease. Cancer patients undergoing chemotherapy were kept away from contagion, their suppressed immune systems too fragile to withstand a secondary onslaught. Regardless of the primary reason for health presentations, the infectious status of a patient remained the most important factor in deciding where they were treated. Protection of the human herd far outweighed the rights of the individual.

Architecturally, Health Hubs resembled old motorway toll-booths. The Melbourne Hub had twelve drive-through treatment bays. One doctor and a robot controller were allocated to each side of a bay. In times of high demand, both sides of a bay would be operational. Staff worked from a base located directly above their allocated bay.

A triage nurse practitioner was shared between four bays. They analysed the incoming patient data from emergency vehicles and consulted with doctors. Each doctor and robot controller performed remote medical and minor surgical interventions as required, with little or no direct patient contact. Staff communicated with triage and patient via CCTV. Additional storeys linked all the bays, allowing staff to move freely between bays and floors. These floors housed staff bases, pathology labs, medical stores, pharmacies and diagnostics. A helipad was located on the roof, next to a central lift shaft.

Health Hubs were works of art compared to hospitals of the early twenty-first century. They were designed as carbon-neutral 'green' buildings, with solar panels and wind turbines collecting and storing energy in the batteries hidden inside the support structures of each bay. Standing as tall as the building and disguised as rock sculptures, these also redirected wind gusts and provided shade. A range of colourful succulents grew in pockets on the outer walls and on the sloping roof, softening the building's clinical atmosphere and cooling the air.

Members of the public could phone or hail one of the driverless hovercraft ambulances that roamed the streets, parks and shopping complexes. Oval in shape, the highly manoeuvrable vehicles could accommodate two patients lying side by side, or one patient lying down and three seated. Each was equipped with parobots: robot paramedics, spherical in shape with multiple sensory receptors and four retractable appendages. Two parobots between them could lift 190 kilograms.

Parobots retrieved, carried and loaded patients through the side-opening winged doors. Once a person entered a hovercraft, the parobots' primary function was to maintain life by immediately commencing the screening and assessment process. They hovered over and around the patients, scanning, administering intravenous fluids and medications. Parobots could undertake a range of life-support interventions, including defibrillation. Observational data including temperature, blood pressure, respiration and heart rate was relayed to the receiving Health Hub.

The impersonal nature of the new health system was its main disadvantage. Robots and androids replaced people whenever practicable and conversations between patients and health professionals were undertaken via CCTV and intercom, rarely face to face. The system—though less than ideal—was necessary, as health workers were a scarce commodity.

The health workforce had decreased by forty per cent during the 2064 pandemic. Health workers had either been killed by the virus or simply stopped coming to work. Making work environments safer had been essential to regain staff confidence, and this had required an increased reliance upon technology.

3

Ellen arrived at the Health Hub the following evening around seven and was assigned to Bay 5. Not feeling enthusiastic about the forthcoming shift, she wasn't pleased to see that Jane Brown had been allocated as her triage nurse practitioner. The seventy-one-year-old was burnt out, with a personality that Ellen felt better suited a cactus. The tracks of Jane's life choices were etched onto her face. Ellen concluded the bad ones had won.

'I wish she'd retire,' Ellen said under her breath, knowing that her colleague couldn't afford to. She forced a smile and said 'Evening,' to Jane, who grunted without lifting her eyes from the computer and continued to type with one finger.

Tonight's robot controller was Abdi Deng. Ellen liked working with this third-generation Sudanese Australian. He was young and enthusiastic and had a perfect smile like the ones in toothpaste ads. Abdi took his work seriously but still liked to have fun. Ellen found him highly skilled; Jane found him annoying. *If I can stop Jane killing Abdi before the shift is over, that will be an achievement*, she thought. Ellen raised her hand and threw a smile in his direction.

'Hi, Ellen honey,' he responded. Abdi was amusing himself by trying to balance a vomit bowl on an enviro-bot's head using a robotic arm.

'Grow up, Abdi,' Jane said as a hovercraft tracked towards them.

Abdi stuck out his tongue at the camera in response, just as the ambulance entered the screening portal.

'What's the problem?' Jane's gravelly voice echoed through the vehicle intercom.

The woman's voice quivered as she replied, 'I feel really unwell.'

'Mmmm ... well ... screening does show that you have a high temperature ... forty degrees ... blood pressure is also high ... respiration rate normal ... no rashes ... glands not swollen. Do you have any other symptoms?'

'I have a headache, a sore throat and my nose is running,' she said with a forced cough.

'Okay, you have viral symptoms so most likely you have the flu. Did you have the ten-strain flu vaccination this year?'

'No ... err ... I forgot.'

Jane let out a sigh then continued, 'Well, I recommend that you have the Fluvax next year, there's little we can do for you tonight if you have contracted the flu. Stand by while I upload your chip data.'

Wrist-implanted health chips provided direct physical monitoring and access to a person's medical history. The e-health data was stored centrally within the Australian Medical Data Analysis Tracking Corporation tower, known as AMDAT Tower.

Jane reviewed the woman's chip data and consulted with Ellen before reactivating the intercom.

'According to your medical history, Ms Williams, you don't have any known allergies. Doctor Hancock recommends that you have an immune system booster, along with paracetamol to lower your temperature. This should make you more comfortable.'

Thirty seconds of silence passed as Jane typed, one key at a time, into the woman's chip before speaking again.

'Please respond to the question on your chip.'

The woman looked down at the screen on her wrist as the text scrolled through.

Do you consent to the administration of an immune system booster with paracetamol? Please select 'Yes' or 'No'.

She pressed 'Yes' with her index finger.

Her fingerprint was authenticated and the consent for treatment filed in her e-record. Jane then droned off a set of instructions, much like a well-rehearsed script.

'Proceed to Bay 5; the staff will administer your injection. The doctor recommends that you drink plenty of fluids and stay in bed. Monitor your temperature and take paracetamol before it reaches forty degrees. Do not take more than eight wafers in twenty-four hours. Seek further medical treatment if there's no sign of improvement in seventy-two hours.

'Do you have paracetamol wafers at home?'

'I don't know.'

Jane sighed again. 'I'll dispense some, just in case. You'll receive a pharmaceutical account that must be paid within seven days to avoid interest. Have you got that?'

'Yes.'

'Health authorities will be notified that you have an unidentified virus and need to isolate yourself. Will you be staying at your current residence in Toorak tonight?'

'Yes,' Ms Williams replied.

'Please make sure you go straight from here to Toorak.'

'Okay.'

'Do you have food at home?'

'I do; I shopped yesterday,' she said, expecting the operator to be pleased with this response.

Jane's eye rolling signalled she wasn't.

'Not great for anyone who has come into contact with you, but at least there's no reason for you to stop on your way home, is there now?'

'I guess not.' Ms William's face dropped and her left eye gave one nervous twitch.

'Your employer will be notified that you can't attend work for at least the next seven days.'

'Okay.'

The hovercraft proceeded forwards into Bay 5 and the roller door slid closed. The woman stepped out of the vehicle and seated herself in the tall cylindrical stainless-steel treatment pod. On the large monitor she could see Abdi smiling. He asked her to roll up her right sleeve. The robot arm swung into action, using laser sensors to locate the precise position, before injecting the woman.

'Thanks, ma'am,' Abdi said.

The woman exited the treatment pod. It immediately closed and hermetically sealed. Within seconds the internal sterilisation process was completed. A hatch opened to the left of Ms Williams, displaying a packet of paracetamol wafers.

'Please take the medication. I hope you're feeling better very soon.'

In complete contrast to Jane, Abdi's tone was warm, and the woman smiled for the first time since her arrival. She stepped back into the hovercraft. The rear roller door slid open and the vehicle passed through. Once Ms Williams was delivered home, the hovercraft would be decontaminated and return to service roaming the city streets. As the vehicle turned the corner out of sight, Abdi pressed a button and two enviro-bots (one with a vomit bowl on its head) commenced the final Bay 5 clean-up. Abdi laughed. Jane snorted.

The second patient was a woman with leg ulcers, who was unable to walk. The hovercraft docked, the winged door lifted and the patient's stretcher glided out sideways until it touched the treatment zone wall and locked on. Abdi smiled and introduced himself to Ms Hayes, then proceeded to expose her wounds using robotic arms. Ellen watched and assessed for treatment. The woman didn't have a high temperature, so there was, as yet, no systemic infection. Ellen decided on manuka honey–infused gum pads on two of the sores and maggot therapy to eat away the necrotic flesh on the third.

Research had identified twenty species of maggots that were effective in wound healing, distinguished by the different speeds with which they ate flesh and the unique antimicrobial properties of their digestive secretions. Ellen selected rapid-eating black fly larvae, which produced lower acid levels that better suited delicate skin.

Abdi liked performing maggot therapy. With a one-finger zip motion across her lips, Ellen signalled him to lose the grin. Jane was watching his every move and Ellen didn't want any unnecessary friction. Jane was easily agitated. She had already turned an ominous shade of scarlet. *Increasing the age pension to seventy-two was ridiculous*, thought Ellen.

Abdi used robot control to clean the wound and to attach the maggot sack and honey gum patches. The woman was treated and on her way within twenty minutes. The enviro-bots recleaned Bay 5.

The night was becoming hectic. A helicopter had just airlifted two stabilised trauma victims to Prince George's Surgical Hospital when a scuffle broke out at the outer perimeter entrance to the Health Hub. Tex, the security guard, could be observed on screen attempting to placate a dishevelled, agitated young man who had approached the boom gate on foot. Ellen was on her break. She noticed the action on Camera 2 and turned up the volume.

'I'm sorry, mate. You aren't chipped, so I can't let you through,' Tex said. 'You can only receive treatment at a Health Hub if you're chipped. Surely you know that?'

'I really need help. You have to help me. Please, please help,' he begged.

Ellen zoomed in the camera. She estimated the young man was around eighteen to twenty years old. He was dressed in grubby camouflage gear and was sweating profusely. His eyes darted rapidly from side to side in a paranoid manner. She put down her mug and activated the intercom.

'Hey, Tex, I think he's psychotic. He appears to be responding to visual or auditory hallucinations. Check out his eye and hand movements. I'll come down and assess him.'

'You know that's not allowed, Ellen.'

'What did you say? Sorry, Tex, I can't quite hear you. I'll be there in a minute.'

Jane heard Ellen, rolled her eyes and, frustrated, threw both her hands in the air. Abdi grinned; he enjoyed any action. Ellen pulled on a gown and gloves, left Bay 5 and, in the cool night air, walked to the main entrance.

With an open, non-threatening stance, Ellen approached the youth and asked him his name.

'Storm … Private Storm Carter' he replied as he grabbed her hand. Tex moved in to assist, then stopped as Ellen raised the palm of her free hand, signalling that she was okay.

Ellen reassured Storm that he was safe and that she would help. A VR headset was dangling by his side.

'May I?' she asked him as she reached to detach his VR equipment. Storm nodded and let go of her hand.

Ellen attached herself to the gear, pulled on the headset and started the program. In an instant she was transported to the middle of a battlefield. Blue-black clouds swirled all around her. Purple and white shards cut through the sky. She looked down and found herself holding a weapon. Her feet were ankle deep in thick grey mud. Orange steam hissed from wormholes in the ground. She heard a whistling sound and looked up to see a thin silver disc hurtling towards her. Ellen instinctively shut her eyes and dropped to the ground. Gunfire echoed to her left. An explosion came from behind. She slowly opened her eyes, stood up and looked around. It was some sort of alien attack. Hideous creatures with multiple appendages were ripping soldiers apart. Yelling … screaming … crying. Bodies lay everywhere. She turned to her right. One of them was savaging the soldier next to her. The man cried out then dropped to the ground as his head was torn off. The creature propped then turned and began moving towards her. Ellen dropped the weapon and started walking backwards. She began to whimper then screamed as an appendage reached for her face. The screen froze. YOU HAVE DIED, flashed in red. GAME OVER. RESPAWN IN 5 ... 4 ... 3 ... Ellen pulled off the mask, leaned forward and grabbed hold of her knees.

'You okay?' Tex asked.

'Just give me a moment,' she said, holding up her hand. There was a pause before she stood back up and spoke.

'Okay ... so now I know why kids become so disturbed from playing these war games. It should be illegal to market this rubbish.'

Ellen pulled Tex aside.

'That poor kid has probably been fighting in VR for days and become so immersed he can no longer distinguish fantasy from reality. He's developed PTSD. I'll sign the mental health paperwork. He's not chipped but he only looks about ... err, seventeen, don't you think?'

Tex glanced up at Storm and nodded.

'I'll state that he lacks capacity. My request for assessment will get him admitted to Broadmarsh VR-detox facility for at least seventy-two hours. They'll transition him back to reality. Beats me why people can't be happy in the real world.' She walked back to the young man.

'You're okay, soldier,' she reassured him, making a snap decision to work with his delusional state of mind. 'The battle's over and you're safe. I think it's best if I transfer you to the field hospital for treatment. Okay?'

Still trembling Storm nodded his approval. Not that she needed his consent, as she intended to certify him.

Ellen walked Storm inside the perimeter fence of the Hub and motioned to him to lie down on one of the transfer gurneys reserved for self-presenting patients. 'I'll give you something to help you relax,' she said. Using her penjab, Ellen administered a rapid-acting sedative and then sat down on the bench next to him.

The night was still; the temperature was rapidly cooling. Despite the lights of the city, the stars of the Southern Hemisphere were clearly visible to the young man, who had stopped trembling and was now gazing skywards.

'Look, there's the planet Arrakis,' he said in a whisper, then rolled over and closed his eyes. Ellen looked across at Tex and tried hard not to let out a giggle.

'Can you contact transport and arrange the transfer to Broadmarsh for me? He'll need an escort.'

'Will do,' Tex replied.

Tex was a large man with a red beard and moustache. He reminded her of an actor in the old Viking series she had watched with her dad as a teenager. Most people followed his instructions without argument, not wanting to find out what would happen if they refused. In reality, he was a big softy. He also made the most convincing Santa Claus she had ever seen.

The evening continued to unfold with a range of cases: a five-year-old boy with a tiny toy stormtrooper helmet stuck high up his left nostril that Abdi removed with tweezers; a teenager with acute asthma and a man in his fifties with chest pain that turned out to be indigestion. The Health Hub was a safe and efficient medical model.

The clock was approaching midnight when another group was triaged to Bay 5. A middle-aged couple and an elderly gentleman were sitting in a row on one side of the hovercraft, a young boy lying on the stretcher opposite. The boy's leg was broken—an open fracture. Preliminary scans and chip data checks showed that three of the vehicle occupants—Samuel, a five-year-old, and his parents— were related but the older man was not chipped. From his age, Ellen guessed he was the boy's grandfather.

The parents and their son had no identified infection 'triggers' and were Gold Class Health members. The additional fees entitled them to personal interaction with Health Hub staff. Ellen put on her personal protective equipment and entered the Bay 5 treatment zone to undertake the assessment. Sam's stretcher had locked on to the treatment wall. The two men stood nearby while his mother tried unsuccessfully to comfort her son. Ellen introduced herself.

Sam's mother's eyes were red from crying. Her name was Louise. His father, Dale, had a blank expression and his forehead glistened with sweat. *Shock?* thought Ellen. The pale-faced elderly gentleman was indeed Sam's grandfather Francis. He looked familiar to Ellen, but she couldn't quite place him.

'The triage nurse tells me your son has taken a tumble down a flight of stairs—and on his birthday, of all days,' Ellen said. 'Not a great way to end your birthday, is it Sam?' Sam didn't answer and continued to scream. He was in severe pain and required immediate surgery to clean and close the wound.

'I told grandad not to race him down the hotel stairs, but he wouldn't listen and now this has happened,' said the mother with a flick of her hand.

'Well, Louise, at least it's his leg, not his head,' Sam's grandad replied.

Sam's father didn't comment.

He's really stressing, thought Ellen as she smiled at him reassuringly.

Ellen gave Sam a shot of morphine, cleaned and covered the wound and placed his leg in an inflatable sterile splint. She notified the helipad flight deck and arranged an immediate medevac to Prince George's Surgical Hospital. Within fifteen minutes the pain relief had begun to take effect and, with his leg now supported, Sam was comfortable and ready for transfer—via the patient lift—to the helipad. Ellen would personally escort Sam (another bonus for Gold Class). His grandad would travel with them on the journey, which would take around ten minutes. His parents would follow.

Cleared for take-off, the helicopter rose into the clear Melbourne sky. It flew higher than the glowing Health Hub symbol—two red H's crossed at right angles—then banked to the left. The buildings and streets below danced with lights, as the edges of the 'intelligent' roads released their captured solar energy to the night.

Sam's grandad turned to Ellen.

'Will he be okay? He's my only grandchild. We … that is … Louise and Dale, lost their beautiful daughter Rosie two years ago from pneumonia. Children are very precious. The world has lost so many. I just don't know what I …' He paused, as he realised Sam was listening and composed himself.

Ellen broke the silence. 'We're doing everything we can for young Sam, Mr Stuart.'

'Please call me Francis; there's no need for formalities. I'm just so very grateful for your help.'

'It's my pleasure, Francis,' Ellen said, glancing at him with a smile as a wave of nausea rose in her throat. She pushed the thoughts of her pregnancy from her mind and focused back on the task at hand.

In the distance they could see the large red lion insignia of Prince George's. Beneath them, an array of solar-powered billboards advertised the latest products. It hadn't taken long for entrepreneurs to take advantage of pandemic fear, selling pills, potions and lotions with claims that could rarely be substantiated. Immune system tonics, miracle cures, designer foods and even designer babies were all on offer. In reality, most of these products didn't sell anything but hope, yet these days, hope was a valued commodity.

The helicopter landed and they were met by two attendants. A sedated Sam was transferred onto a gurney and, after reassurance from Ellen and a kiss from his grandad, wheeled into the preoperative suite. Ellen and Francis were not permitted to enter the operating theatre. They were escorted inside to a health-deck cubicle, where they could choose to watch the procedure on screen.

The closed theatre was circular in shape with large glass windows that provided perfect vision for the robot operators and their assistants located outside. The eight robotic appendages weaved and rotated in all directions as they undertook the work of four theatre staff. The surgery progressed without incident, but Ellen knew the quality of the procedure wasn't the main issue. Post-operative infections required months of antibiotic treatment. Even then, many patients died. Prince George's was one of the best hospitals in the country, so Sam's chances of recovery without infection were better than most.

Sam's parents arrived and joined them. He was now in recovery and his family continued to watch his progress. Crisis over, Ellen encouraged everyone to have a hot drink and talk. Mental illness was rife in the community, anxiety and depression being the most prevalent. PTSD had engulfed a world in which random terrorist attacks and viral outbreaks were the norm. No-one could be sure of anything anymore. Public fear was palpable.

As the group chatted, the layers of fear and anxiety around the day's events fell away. Everyone grew calmer and the colour returned to Francis's cheeks. Even Sam's father, Dale, joined in the conversation. Ellen hoped for a good outcome. After a brief visit with a sleepy Sam, the family returned to their hotel. As hospitals had such high infection rates, Sam would be discharged as soon as possible, to be cared for at home by community androids.

Ellen hailed a driverless cab. She swiped her e-cab card that prepaid the fare before the door slid open. It was eight in the morning; she just needed to sign off at the Hub, then cab home. She flipped back the seat and closed her eyes. The overtime this week would be useful, as she had splurged on some new genealogy texts. Dad would be envious.

Her father was currently on an extended trip to England. He had returned there to trace their family history after unexpectedly inheriting a cottage in the Derbyshire village of Eyam. Hiking the

Peak District had always been on his bucket list, so he believed fate had now intervened to ensure this outcome. Divorced, with his children both adults, there was nothing to stop him fulfilling his dream.

4

Ellen punched in the code to her apartment and the door slid open. In the dim light she tripped over the robot vac that was caught on the doormat and landed hard on her knees. The crash and swearing that followed woke up Rob. He came out of his bedroom, bleary eyed in his Victorian Vipers footy shorts.

'Sorry,' he said, yawning and stretching both arms above his head. 'I meant to put Ruby back on her charger when my mobile rang. I forgot all about her.' He turned and loped back to his bedroom.

Typical, thought Ellen.

Zoe, her new housemate, was up and dressed. She peered around her bedroom door, spotted Ellen's bloodied knee and dashed to get the first-aid kit.

'Let me assist you, Doctor Hancock,' Zoe said, in a pretending-I'm-already-an-official-medic tone. 'I need to clean and cover this wound *stat*.' Zoe was the daughter of Ellen's best friend Georgia.

'We are now sisters,' the two Grade 1 girls had announced to their parents. They had decided on this course of action after their friends Caitlin and Carol had returned from the summer holidays and declared they were sisters. (Ellen and Georgia didn't understand the girls had become stepsisters.)

Ellen had remained friends with Georgia throughout their school years and had been her bridesmaid when she married Frank. Ellen provided emotional support when they were undertaking fertility treatment at a clinic where she worked one summer. Georgia and

Frank's infertility journey came to an end with the birth of a beautiful healthy baby girl, Zoe Elizabeth Ashmore. Tragically, Frank died of leukaemia when Zoe was five. He had finally lost his lifelong battle with cancer, but not before his dream of parenting a child with the love of his life was realised. True to form, Ellen swooped in to help her 'sister' and Zoe navigate the crisis. Georgia had suffered from anxiety ever since.

Zoe had just turned eighteen. She was intelligent and beautiful—a tall, slender girl with clear skin, crimson lips, green eyes and long dark wavy hair. From an early age, Zoe had set her sights on a career in medicine. Auntie Ellen believed she had inspired this career choice, although Georgia was not pleased with her daughter's decision.

'Are you sure this is what you *really* want?' her mother had asked. 'Medicine is a dangerous occupation. Just think about all those horrid bugs!'

Regardless of her mother's concerns, Zoe couldn't be swayed. When she was offered an AMDAT scholarship to study medicine in Melbourne she was thrilled. Georgia only earned a meagre living as a photographer: Zoe's scholarship was the break they needed. Moving in with Auntie Ellen was an added bonus.

Using tweezers, Zoe wiped antiseptic swabs across Ellen's cut knee before applying two layers of non-stick gauze. She was reaching for a third when Ellen intervened.

'I think that will do, Zoe. Great job, but I'm starting to look like I need some stamps and a post box.'

'I just want to practise wound-dressing techniques,' Zoe said, giggling as she surveyed her work.

'Finish with that Qwik Dri waterproof spray, please, darling. I want to take a bath.'

Ellen's breakfast routine consisted of fresh fruit, muesli and yoghurt, which she followed with meditation. She was rostered off for the next two days. Zoe joined her.

'What do you have planned today?' Ellen asked as she crunched on her organic fruit and cereal.

'Today should be good. The scholarship group are meeting at AMDAT Tower to be chipped, followed by a full tour. We'll have access to some of the research labs and this afternoon is our first lecture. Oh! And we're being assigned to research teams, based on yesterday's test results ...' Zoe paused. 'I just wish I knew someone else on the course.'

'I'm sure you'll make friends in no time at all. Give yourself time to adjust. Just concentrate on today and enjoy the tour.' Ellen recalled the hot summer's day when she had stood in front of AMDAT Tower's huge glass conservatories for the first time. She had been totally mesmerised by the exotic butterflies fluttering among the tropical flowers. 'I look forward to hearing all about it, particularly those bats.' Ellen exposed her top teeth and grinned like a vampire.

Zoe wasn't amused. 'I think bats are disgusting, gross, creepy creatures. I plan to keep well clear of them.'

Ellen chuckled at this reaction. 'Well, you'll need to toughen up if you think bats are gross. As a medic you'll see far worse than those little mammals.'

'Anyway,' continued Zoe, 'enough about me; how was your night shift? You look pale.' She screwed up her forehead. 'You didn't bump your head just now, did you?'

'No, I didn't bump my head, but I am stuffed. I don't like night shift much and right now I feel spacey from lack of sleep. Feels like jetlag. I'll be okay, just need sleep.'

'Eeew, I don't think I'll like night shift then; I hated jetlag.' Zoe glanced at the wall clock. 'I have to get moving,' she said, jumping up and placing her bowl in the dish steamer. 'Please try to get lots of sleep. Put in some earplugs, use your eye mask and close the window to keep out the noise. That should all help.'

'Yes, Mom,' Ellen replied. Zoe leaned forward and kissed her on the forehead, then grabbed her backpack and strode towards the door. 'Bye, see ya tonight.'

Such a delightful young woman, living in this crazy world, thought Ellen. Zoe reminded her of a naive young Georgia, who was always too trusting. Georgia had once given her bank details to a non-existent charity—'Save the Purple-shelled Snail' or something equally implausible. Her bank account was emptied the next day. Ellen had made protecting Zoe, and building her resilience, a priority.

With breakfast finished, Ellen selected the latest Gingers soundtrack, ran a bubble bath and threw in some sprigs of dried lavender. As she climbed in, the warm water enveloped her body and she felt her muscles start to relax. She slithered down until her head was submerged and she held her breath for a moment before re-emerging. As usual, her thoughts drifted to her last shift. She shuddered as she recalled the VR experience. Why would anyone design such a game? And why was Sam's grandad Francis so familiar? As she soaked, her tension eased and the thoughts faded. She lay there until the water began to cool.

Climbing out, she rubbed herself dry and slipped on a cream lace nightgown. She went into her bedroom and lit a candle. A large patchwork cushion leaned against the wall in one corner. She pulled it into the centre of the room and sat cross-legged, wriggling until she was comfortable. Then she began settling her 'mad monkey' mind, breathing in and out slowly and methodically, counting each inhalation and exhalation.

One ... two ... three ...

Meditation was routine since she turned to Buddhism a few years earlier, although Ellen didn't consider herself a great Buddhist. For a start, she was too judgmental, her own internal dialogue being the main offender. She reminded herself that the path to perfect enlightenment was a continual work in progress. Ellen made a mental note to be more tolerant of Jane in the future. *Who knows what she has been through?*

Around ten minutes passed before the sound of an incoming vid-link call pulled her back to reality. Ellen was tempted not to answer;

however, it was Georgia, so she accepted the call. Georgia was looking pale and drawn. She was always stressing about one thing or another, so that in itself wasn't unusual.

'Is Zoe okay?' Georgia blurted out, before even saying hello to her best friend.

'Well, hello to you too, Georgia,' Ellen replied. 'Of course she's okay. I just had breakfast with her and she's left for AMDAT. Did you try her mobile? No point, I can see it's in the charging dock. Anyway, what's up?'

'Well, do you remember Sally and Eric? They had fertility treatment around the same time as Frank and I did.'

'Yes, of course I remember them. Can you just get to the point?'

'Why are you so grumpy?' Georgia asked.

I must try to be more patient, thought Ellen. *She is my best friend and she's missing her daughter.*

'Sorry for snapping. I'm just tired. I was on duty last night. Go on. Tell me what's happened.'

'Well ...' Georgia paused before continuing. 'Their daughter Kasey has gone missing. No-one has heard from her in twenty-four hours. Sally and Eric are frantic.'

Just then Ellen heard the door slam. An exasperated Zoe called out 'Forgot my mobile; can't do without it today. I'm going to be sooooo late.'

'Don't go, Zoe. Your mom just called with some news,' Ellen said, before turning her attention back to Georgia.

'Try not to worry, Georgia; it won't help the situation, and fretting could put your blood pressure up. It'll amount to nothing, I'm sure of it. Kasey is probably upset with her parents and off somewhere with her friends. I bet she shows up soon enough. I'll call you in a couple of days. Right now, I really need to go to bed.'

Ellen had decided not to tell Georgia about the pregnancy. She didn't want anyone sending her on a guilt trip if she decided to have an abortion. Georgia adored children, and would have loved more of her own. Georgia viewed abortion as murder. The decision wasn't that clear-cut for Ellen. She, and perhaps the baby, could end up like her mother. It might be best if the baby was spared that possibility.

Ellen left Georgia and Zoe to talk. She put on her eye mask, climbed into bed and sank into the soft mattress. Grizzlepuss, her fat, flat-faced ginger cat, lifted his head to acknowledge her presence, then went back to sleep. Even with earplugs in, she heard Rob close the front door as he left for work. With the faint sound of chatter in the background Ellen drifted off to sleep.

Rob rode swiftly along a city bike track. Cycling was a fast, cheap mode of transport and it kept his middle-aged body fit. A clear cloudless sky heralded another hot Melbourne day as the heatwave continued. The CBD was a different place since the banning of private vehicles within a five-kilometre radius of the old GPO on the corner of Bourke and Elizabeth Streets. Hovercraft and driverless cab lanes had been installed on one side of the iconic Melbourne tram tracks, cycling and walking lanes on the other.

The greening of Melbourne was well underway. All buildings were required by law to devote thirty per cent of their surface area to vegetation. Vertical succulent gardens were a popular choice on government buildings. Hotels often preferred climbing roses or wisteria. Café garden walls frequently included herbs and other edible plants. Insects, birds, skinks and snails could be observed grazing on the lush greenery. Trees and natural-fibre sails provided plenty of shade for pedestrians and cyclists. The air felt cool and smelt fresh.

AMDAT Tower loomed in the distance, casting shadows on the surrounding streets. It was an architectural masterpiece of steel and glass rivalling many great buildings. Deep purple flowers framed each of the tower windows as the bougainvillea wove its thorny tentacles around the steel columns and into every crevice.

Rob got off his bike, folded it and entered the foyer. The entrance still intrigued him: a lobby extending through twelve of the tower's forty-three floors, with two large glass conservatories attached on either side. Before heading for the lift, he took a deep breath, paused and looked up. The first conservatory was full of rare plants and insects, including butterflies and moths. From the exterior of the building, the public could, by day, view the colourful butterfly display. The second conservatory was dedicated solely to bats. Each evening, at feeding time, people strolling to nearby restaurants and theatres were treated to a spectacular display of bats flying in and around their artificial cave system gorging on moths. Every animal and plant in the two conservatories had been bred for medical research purposes.

Rob had worked for AMDAT for a year. When AV64 caused Medicare—the previous public healthcare system—to finally collapse, privatisation was viewed as the best solution. AMDAT was poised ready to take over. The Australian Medical Data Analysis Tracking system was designed and ready to become fully operational. The AMDAT Corporation offered a new healthcare model, which included excellent microbial stewardship, fairer surgical waiting lists and the latest technological advances.

While this new system was fully funded, it came at a price: the loss of personal privacy. If you wanted free public health treatment, you had to consent to being chipped.

Chips were the brainchild of Daniel Grant, the scientist who founded AMDAT along with his billionaire father-in-law. The chip was a tiny device which was inserted into a person's wrist and continuously analysed their blood. A crystal display provided information to its wearer.

Whenever a person travelled across state borders, visited medical facilities or came in contact with government agencies, their chip data was uploaded, via the chip's wi-fi, to AMDAT's databases. Blood composition, including levels of alcohol, nicotine and drugs of all kinds, was monitored. This information was accessible on request by authorities, mainly within Health and Justice. A continuous signal emanated from each chip allowing AMDAT to trace and track the wearer's movements via their twelve digit code. Tracking a person without authorisation was a serious matter.

The chip technology was a closely guarded secret. World governments, devastated by unrelenting viral and bacterial outbreaks, welcomed this new way forward. They paid a fortune to AMDAT to install the chip technology in their health systems. As a result, AMDAT had established headquarters in many capital cities throughout the world and was expanding each year.

Human rights campaigners had tried and failed to prevent chipping. AMDAT lawyers were the best in the country, while the federal government could no longer fund Medicare and needed a viable alternative. The problem for the rights campaigners was that everyone was being treated equally. Adults didn't have to accept a chip; it was their choice. Children automatically received healthcare without being chipped until they turned eighteen. Individuals who lacked 'capacity' also received free healthcare and, in certain cases, could be chipped with the consent of their guardians. The law required all prisoners and migrants to be chipped.

The younger generation didn't care. Avid use of social media platforms had left them complacent. The benefits of free healthcare offset any concerns about AMDAT owning their personal health information. People who chose to pay for private treatment or who didn't want to be monitored didn't sign up. The rest consented to be chipped in droves.

AMDAT made billions from analysing the continuous flow of health data, previously only attainable via ethical research. Chip data expedited medical research outcomes and Australia now led the world in scientific innovation and pharmaceutical development. A cure for one type of dementia had been the first big breakthrough.

A single tablet broke down protein amyloid plaques in the brain into a substance that could be safely absorbed by the body. Thousands upon thousands of people who had been locked inside their heads came back to life, back to the families they loved and the places they had forgotten. Overnight, the burden of dementia on the health system was reduced. How could anyone argue with a corporation that had delivered such a sensational outcome?

Rob showered and changed into his AMDAT biosuit, then stuffed his clothes and backpack into his locker. Monday was always spent processing the latest batch of eighteen-year-olds. Today was particularly hectic, as regional universities were providing free travel to AMDAT Melbourne. If you wanted to be chipped, you had to travel to the nearest capital city. No exceptions.

Tasmanian, Western Australian and Northern Territory residents were the biggest abstainers. Tassie had become known as the organic hippy state with many people never travelling to Hobart to be chipped. Western Australia was home to many large surfing communities who generally boycotted Perth. The highest population of unchipped adults was located in the Northern Territory, due to the number of townships remote from Darwin and a large Indigenous population, who remained highly suspicious of chipping.

Rob settled into his cubicle and turned on the biometric machine. He pressed the NEXT CLIENT button, then looked up to see a familiar face come through the door.

'Hi, Rob,' Zoe said, smiling and breathing hard from running to keep the appointment.

'Hello, Zoe,' Rob replied, at first somewhat surprised to see his young flatmate. 'I completely forgot you were orientating with the scholarship group this week.'

Zoe smiled. 'I must say that I'm glad to see a familiar face. I'm quite nervous about getting chipped. It's all a bit scary.'

'No need to be scared. Just relax. I'll take good care of you.'

'So, what do I have to do?'

'Well, first you have to give written consent to undertake a full range of procedures including biometric eye and fingerprint scans, DNA profile, full blood count and permanent insertion of a health chip.'

'Any risks?' she asked.

Rob peered over his reading glasses. 'Didn't you read the paperwork given to you on that clipboard you're holding?'

'No, sorry; Mom called and I was running late. Only read as far as the bit that mentioned a rare polymer allergy. I don't know if I have any allergies,' she said, screwing up her mouth and nose.

'No problem,' Rob replied, 'I'll test you for the polymer allergy before we start. I just need some of your saliva in this tube,' he said, placing it under Zoe's mouth.

She spat twice into the tube.

'If the liquid doesn't change colour within sixty seconds, you're cleared for the chip insertion. The procedure is incredibly safe.' Rob paused. 'Looks like you're clear to go,' he said, giving the test-tube contents one final swirl.

Zoe finished reading the informed consent document, signed it and handed it back to Rob.

'Take a seat.' Rob directed her towards a padded red swivel chair with the AMDAT monogram in gold lettering on the back. He adjusted the chair to make her comfortable and then slid the biometric eye scanner directly in front of her face.

'Now, place your chin in the rest and lean your head forward until it just touches the bar. Take in a deep breath, sit completely still and hold—five, four, three, two, one—breathe out and sit back.'

The machine whirred and clicked loudly.

'Now, place your hand onto the scanner, ensuring your fingers are around the bars in the same configuration as the hand outline. Hold still.'

Five seconds passed before the machine beeped.

'Now remove your hand and replace again.'

This process was repeated three times until every minute detail of Zoe's handprint was mapped and recorded.

'Roll up your left sleeve and place your arm through the plastic shield and onto the guide plate.'

Zoe didn't expect the metal plate to feel warm. Three clamps extended out from the sides and held her wrist in place, while a robot arm cleaned and anaesthetised the procedure area, then extracted a small vial of blood. Zoe watched with fascination as the chip was inserted.

When finished, the clamps released her arm and folded back into the shield walls. Rob asked her to remove her arm from the device. A small screen was now visible on her wrist in the same location where watches were once worn.

'Wow,' she said, as if someone had just given her a new piece of jewellery.

'It doesn't hurt either.'

'It will be a bit sore when the anaesthetic wears off, only for about twenty-four hours or so. Similar to a vaccination. I'll activate it for you; just give me a second.' He began typing into his computer as he continued to speak, 'The chip has high-tech features, including gathering fitness and nutritional data like the old Fitbits your grandmother probably used as a teenager. It also keeps perfect time and can take high-resolution images that you can download and edit.'

'It's on! … This is sooo exciting,' she said.

Rob showed Zoe how to operate the chip, to scroll through and access some basic data. He activated the fitness program. Everyone was encouraged to improve their health to reduce their personal burden on the health system. Zoe was quick to grasp the main features. Like most young people, technology was central to her life. After about ten minutes the session drew to a close.

'Thanks, Rob; you're the best. Catch you at home tonight,' she said as she rose from the seat to leave.

Zoe made her way down to ground level to the designated assembly point. The tour was due to get under way and most of the students in the first group had already gathered. As she approached them, she felt butterflies in her stomach. She didn't know anyone; everything was unfamiliar and so different from home. Her mouth went dry. *I should have brought my water bottle*, she thought. For a brief moment she missed her mother. Then she recalled that Ellen had said it would take time to adjust. She took in a deep breath and thought about what the scholarship meant for her future.

Working for AMDAT was one of the most secure jobs in Australia. One day she could become a member of a research team and make her own positive contributions to world health systems. Securing a scholarship was a good first step. A blonde-haired girl glanced in her direction then walked over to her.

'Hi. I'm Sarah from Sydney,' she said with a smile.

'Zoe, from New Jersey; pleased to meet you Sarah,' she replied with a nod.

'Well, you have come a long way, haven't you? Your finals results must have been amazing,' Sarah raised her eyebrows in anticipation of a reply.

Three loud sharp claps summoned their attention. The tour guide had arrived and introduced himself as Nigel. He welcomed them all, outlined a few housekeeping matters, reminded them to attach their name tags, then began his overview of AMDAT. Zoe wasn't able to continue the conversation with Sarah. *She seemed forward and a tad nosey anyway,* thought Zoe. *I do need to make new friends, though. Sarah might be nice when I get to know her.*

The tour began on the Level 40 viewing deck that encircled the tower. A cloudless sky ensured uninterrupted 360-degree views of the city and surrounding suburbs. Everyone was very excited. They chatted among themselves and tried to locate familiar landmarks. The panorama was breathtaking and Zoe's hair tossed about in the wind. She smiled as she surveyed the city of Melbourne—her new home.

Nigel pointed out a three-metre-wide brass compass that was attached to the side of the tower and asked them all to choose one of the twenty-five telescopes.

'To view key landmarks just point your telescope north, south, east or west,' he said. 'The lens will automatically focus and identify the location for you.'

Zoe swung her telescope towards the east. She could see waves crashing onto white sand, two kids flying a kite, a toddler paddling in a rock pool. She read the text along the bottom of the screen: *St Kilda beach*. She moved the telescope slightly and lowered it. A stand of tall deciduous trees came into focus. Colourful blooms were visible beneath a tree canopy. Birds on the grass and ducks on a lake: *Royal Botanic Gardens Melbourne* noted the text.

Zoe felt so privileged to be in this beautiful city. Life couldn't be more perfect ... or ... could it? Some of the young men in the group were cute. Maybe it was time for that first romance without her overprotective mom hovering. Zoe loved her mother dearly, but being an only child had its pitfalls: no siblings to move the focus away from her. *I'll message Mom heaps,* Zoe thought. *That way she won't get worried.* She felt more relaxed having made that commitment. Now she could concentrate on enjoying herself.

Nigel's voice interrupted her thoughts.

'All glass in AMDAT Tower is bulletproof,' he said as he pointed out the top-floor penthouse on Level 43 where the reclusive founder of AMDAT lived. Daniel Grant was worth billions and visible security guards supported the advanced—and invisible—systems that ensured his privacy and safety.

'AMDAT is not popular with everyone, you know. The threat of espionage and terrorism is very real. Levels 42 and 41, directly beneath the penthouse, are also off limits. Level 42 is where Professor Lambert has his apartment. It's also where Doctor Grant's personal laboratory and medical emergency centre are based. Level 41 is vacant and contains a sophisticated laser security system second to none.'

'That's sounds like overkill?' Zoe heard one student comment.

'More like paranoia,' said another.

I think Mom would be impressed, thought Zoe. Georgia had installed a high-tech security system at their home.

Nigel led them down to the AMDAT boardroom on Level 39. In the centre of the room was a long rectangular table made from Huon pine inlaid with other rare timbers.

'Some of the timber used to craft this table came from tree species that are now extinct,' Nigel said.

'How did they become extinct?' asked Sarah.

'Wood chipping and bush fires caused by global warming … mostly,' he replied.

Nigel encouraged the students to feel the surface of the table and try to identify five different types of wood as he continued to speak.

'The Australian division of the World Health Board conducts hearings at this very table—surgical waiting list disputes and capacity hearings, to name a couple.' He pointed out the holo-conferencing systems. 'These systems are designed to reduce unnecessary air travel and ensure that board members have instant access to extensive global networks.'

They continued their descent via an enclosed spiral staircase that wound around the building's exterior. Nigel held the fire door open and counted each person as they passed through. The staircase was engineered utilising the ancient castle technology of interlocking stone steps with a cantilever lip system. Each step overlapped with the previous one. They appeared to be floating. Zoe found the experience both exhilarating and daunting, as if at any moment the stones could give way and send her plummeting to the ground. The rush of adrenaline made her already dry mouth even drier.

On every floor, scientists could be seen hard at work. Nigel outlined the research domains of the corporation, counting each one on his fingers as he spoke.

'AMDAT focuses on five key domains: monitoring of microbial outbreaks, development of new antibiotics and vaccines, improvement of the human immune system, chip data analysis and embryonic enhancement.'

Hope I'm in the antibiotics and vaccines domain, thought Zoe. She had made it her number one choice on the application form. There was not long to wait now. At two in the afternoon, all the students would assemble in the main lecture theatre, receive the results of yesterday's examination and be assigned to a research team.

On the fifth floor a data analyst noticed something unusual.

'The DNA analyser must be faulty. A result just came through with strange DNA coding. Take a look.'

'Yeah, that *is* weird. There are three sets of DNA and two sets of mitochondrial DNA instead of one.'

The two operators stared at the screen with blank faces.

'It doesn't appear to be an error either.'

'No, it doesn't … Call the supervisor; the sample must have been contaminated.'

'We probably need to delete the entry and recall the client.'

'What's the problem?' asked the supervisor.

He peered over their shoulders to gain a better view of the screen, which showed a blood sample containing two sets of mitochondrial DNA extracted from a female.

'Must be a procedural error … I'll arrange the recall myself.' He jotted down the name and address on his e-pad. He then leaned forward and punched a couple of keys, deleting the record. 'I'll contact the client personally,' he told them. 'I'll also check with the operator who extracted the sample. They must have breached protocols and caused contamination.'

The supervisor returned to his office, locked the door and tapped four digits on the secure internal com system.

'Sir, the female you've been expecting has been chipped.'

'Are you sure?'

'Yes, positive: right age, three types of DNA. Everything matches.'

'Has her DNA record been deleted?'

'Yes, I'll replace it later tonight with another sample. The error will appear to have been corrected via a recall.'

'Good, handle this without delay.'

'End call,' Daniel Grant told his phone, then continued pacing as he waited for his personal physician to administer his lithium dose. He could afford to have his dosage titrated daily to ensure the therapeutic level was precisely maintained, no more and no less than his body required. He wanted at all costs to avoid another full-blown manic episode and to maintain good kidney function. He didn't want to be hospitalised under the Mental Health Act ever again. *Fuck the psychiatrists.*

Daniel suffered from bipolar disorder. The illness ran in his family: his mother, Annette Ward, had also been bipolar. Daniel never knew his father. When he was sixteen, his mother had consumed illicit drugs washed down with vodka and jumped off a bridge in Hobart to drown in the cold waters of the Derwent River below. He hated Tasmania. Before ending her life there, Annette had dragged her son all around the country in her endless search for love, moving states frequently to pursue some new romantic interest she had met online.

'This is it, Daniel—this is the one—a new father for you!' she would exclaim with all-too-familiar optimism.

Annette was a very attractive woman and each new man would at first be highly attentive. Promises of forever and cheap love tokens followed, perhaps a ring or a necklace or, on occasions, even a puppy or kitten. Once her mental illness emerged the relationships all ended the same way. Within a short time, the fighting would start, along with the foul language, drinking, drugs and domestic violence.

Daniel would try to assist his distressed mother, but she always refused to go to the police, for fear of being placed into another mental health system. Eventually, they would be tossed homeless into the streets.

This dysfunctional lifestyle had been the pattern of Daniel's childhood. His mother was too emotionally unstable to maintain a relationship. Despite having access to solid psychiatric medication regimes, she frequently stopped using her prescribed meds and reverted to self-medicating with alcohol and drugs.

Moving states made it easy for Annette to avoid mental health systems. Each state had its own Mental Health Act, so jurisdictions could do very little once Annette had fled across a state border. She would simply invent a new alias and disappear. That was, of course, in the days prior to chipping. No-one could hide anymore, once chipped.

On the final occasion, she had met another narcissistic arsehole online. She always chose abusive men—Daniel knew that his mother had been abused as a child. When she was drunk the truth of this abuse would come pouring out of her. Daniel didn't want to hear the details, but that didn't stop her. He only agreed to move to Tasmania to try to keep her safe. He'd been undertaking a minder role for years but this last time he really didn't want to leave Melbourne and change schools yet again.

Daniel could recall the day his mother died as if it were yesterday. She was as high as a kite from some drug the boyfriend had supplied. He had tried to gain assistance via the local helpline, but none was forthcoming. When his back was turned, she had slipped away into adjoining bushland. Daniel had hunted for her on his own for hours and eventually reported her missing. He explained to the police that she suffered from bipolar disorder. When he mentioned she used illicit drugs they were less interested and just quizzed him as to why he wasn't in school.

Later that evening, the police made contact and informed him that a woman matching the description of his mother had been captured on surveillance footage. Daniel tried, without success, to control his anxiety as he drove with the female constable to the Hobart Police Station to view the footage. The constable glanced in the rear-vision mirror at the red-haired teenager, clenching his jaw and wringing his hands as the beads of sweat on his forehead glistened in the headlights of each passing car.

In the comms centre, Daniel had stood silent next to the tall blonde constable as together they reviewed a single frozen screenshot. He could recall the sensation of his heart pounding in his chest. It was racing so fast he imagined it might burst free of his ribcage like one of those creatures in the ancient *Alien* movies.

The woman captured on the flickering black-and-white screen was a dishevelled mess. Mascara smudged clown-like around her eyes and down her cheeks. Her clothes were filthy and torn from making her way through the bracken and blackberry thorns that grew near the Tasman Bridge. It was a face all too familiar. It was her.

'I'm sorry, Daniel, but the next piece of footage shows that she jumped. We haven't located her as yet, but she fell from the highest section, so we aren't hopeful of a good outcome.' Constable Bond had a kind face and her concern was genuine.

Daniel felt completely numb. He knew how her story ended. He closed his eyes and imagined her stepping off the bridge rail. He slid to the floor of the police station and curled into a ball. He had failed to save his mother. What sort of loser son was he?

So Daniel hated Tasmania. He would never venture there again. Why didn't the fuckers come and help him when he called? Why didn't the fuckers ever believe children of fucked-up parents? Silently he hoped all Tasmanians would never get chipped. Perhaps they would all die out from contracting a deadly disease, or be permanently disfigured by facial tumours like the Tasmanian devil. He knew that these were ridiculous notions, yet imagining the demise of the state's entire population somehow made him feel better.

Later that same night, Daniel returned to his mother's boyfriend's house. Johnno was intoxicated, sitting on the couch watching footy. Empty beer cans and pizza boxes littered the floor. Daniel checked the whereabouts of Johnno's dog before grabbing the unsuspecting man by the T-shirt and giving him two hard punches to the face. He split his lip and knocked out a tooth. The pit bull terrier barked and yanked on his chain as Daniel continued yelling and pummelling his master's body, releasing on Johnno every bit of anger for every man that had ever abused his mother.

Breathing hard, Daniel headed for the door.

Johnno screamed out after him, 'I should have let me fuckin' dog eat youse two loonies.' Then he grabbed his mobile and managed to dial triple zero before slumping to the floor.

Luckily for Daniel, Johnno's injuries weren't serious. Nevertheless, he landed himself a two-year stint in the state's youth detention centre and remained there until he turned eighteen.

The majority of the detention centre staff were bastards. They were rude and lacked empathy. Daniel determined within the first week that they were a pack of fucking arseholes. Middle-aged psychiatric nurses Brian and Cecile—a married couple—were the worst. They took every opportunity to needle the boys they disliked, denying them access to snacks, drinks, phone, internet, the games room and anything else that made their sad lives bearable. They were unhappy, nasty little power trippers. The boys nicknamed them Mr and Mrs Burns after the miserly 1980s *Simpsons* character.

By the end of their shifts, at least two boys could be heard scream-ing and banging on the seclusion room doors. Daniel was one of these boys most of the time. He became a key target when one night he tripped Cecile as she waddled past him with a tray full of the residents' food nicked for the staff. The boys had all laughed as she splattered to the floor; her long flowing black dress up over her head displaying her granny bloomers.

Cecile never forgave Daniel and was hell-bent on revenge, resulting in him spending time in seclusion whenever she was rostered. Daniel only had to look at Cecile the wrong way and she would call a Code Black and lie through her rotten teeth as to why he needed seclusion. Resisting a five-man take-down was pretty much impossible. Daniel would fight and struggle, but it only made things worse. Occasionally he landed a blow or managed a satisfying bite or scratch.

Cecile was just a fucking ugly old hag. Closest thing to a real witch he had ever seen, with wrinkled, pale waxlike skin, a long large bent nose and a top lip that curled like a cartoon character's as she spoke. He vowed to settle that score one day.

Fortunately, the diversional therapist at the facility took an interest in this anger-driven youth. He had the one thing the other staff lacked: empathy. He recognised in Daniel an intelligent kid who'd never had a chance and began to mentor him.

With Steve's encouragement, Daniel began online courses. He became so obsessed with education he barely slept and read text after text. In fact, signs of bipolar disorder were already evident, if anyone had cared to notice. He excelled in biology, physics, chemistry and maths. When he sat the final Year 12 exams, his scores of one hundred per cent in biology and chemistry didn't go unnoticed.

The Australian Innovation Foundation for Disadvantaged Adolescents offered him a place at Melbourne University, with accommodation and finance, for the duration of a bioengineering degree. He seized the opportunity and so, on his eighteenth birthday, gave the finger to Tasmania and moved back to Melbourne.

7

'Here's your lithium, Dan. I've reviewed your twelve-month kidney function data. It's excellent,' said Vaughn, Daniel's private physician and closest friend. They had been friends since university, and he was one of the few people Daniel trusted. Daniel could never understand why celebrities, with all their billions, ended up dying well before their time, when they could have afforded the best medical care in the world. Vaughn titrated all of his medications. Daniel wasn't taking any chances. He rarely drank and had never smoked or used illicit drugs. His mother had demonstrated the end result of that lifestyle.

'Thanks,' he said, tossing the pills into his mouth and washing them down with beetroot juice. Daniel was standing on the balcony of the penthouse apartment. Through high-powered binoculars, he was observing the tour group on the viewing deck below. 'I've just been informed that the female has arrived safely on the premises. I did tell you that she would find the scholarship offer too good to refuse. She's an intelligent girl, so should easily meet the course demands.'

'Guess you were right again, Dan.'

'Wonder which one she is? Here, have a squiz.' He handed Vaughn the binoculars.

'They all look so young; I don't remember ever being quite so fresh-faced.'

'*You* weren't,' Daniel said.

'There are some gorgeous looking females. Are you sure the selection panel picked them on their exam results and not their body measurements?' he said, as he continued to observe the visual feast, moving the binoculars to ogle more effectively. 'I should have some fun lecturing this year, if these specimens are anything to go by,' Vaughn continued, smiling in a predatory way, recalling how much fun he had with last year's intake.

'Pervert,' Daniel said. 'We weren't ever fresh-faced naive kids; we had seen way too much of the seedy side of life.'

Vaughn was the eternal bachelor and although Daniel didn't approve of his womanising, he left him to it. He was, after all, the closest thing to a brother he had ever known.

'By the way, Gum called when you were in the shower. She asked me to let you know our project is on schedule. She expects the New Jersey clean-up to be completed very soon. Gum has always had your back, Dan; she's one loyal friend.'

'I agree, very loyal, but it's that dash of crazy that worries me.'

⑧

Daniel Ward, Vaughn Lambert and Gum Lin had been drawn together at university by their pure genius and dysfunctional, traumatic childhoods. 'Birds of a feather flock together' could have been coined with this trio in mind. Dysfunction was their normal. Abuse was their teacher. They were the three campus leftovers that didn't have 'normal' families to go home to during the semester breaks. No visits from favourite aunties or money deposited to their bank accounts on Christmas and birthdays. It didn't take long for them to gravitate towards each other amongst the crowd of also-rans. The traumatised are drawn to trauma like a magnet.

It only took one semester for them to realise they had their scholarship money, brains as big as small planets and each other. That was all they needed. Together they became obsessed with money and power but wrapped it in a 'save the world' package for their lecturers and benefactors. Gum could look quite sweet in a dress leading a tutorial, but from the day she graduated her naked legs were never seen in public again. Vaughn could charm his way into any girl's underpants … and he did … quite frequently. Daniel didn't know the meaning of 'impossible'. Nothing was impossible if you focused on the problem and worked twenty-four hours a day, seven days a week until you found the solution.

Together, the three non-biological siblings became a powerful combination: Daniel the bioengineer, Vaughn the medic and Gum the computer expert. All graduated with first-class honours from Melbourne University and all lacked a moral compass.

Between them they cleaned up the university prizes, and following graduation they used this prize money, plus more won from gambling, to holiday together in the USA. Once the money ran out, they gained cash via various cons. Card counting was a speciality; they would hit a casino, work together, then leave town the next day. They were careful not to be greedy or go back for seconds.

Daniel had his first full-blown manic episode on the trip, following many late-night drinking binges. They had gone their separate ways for two months to explore different states and Daniel failed to arrive at the designated rendezvous point. Despite Vaughn and Gum's best efforts to locate him, he remained missing for a further month.

Vaughn and Gum eventually tracked Daniel down in a New Jersey psychiatric facility. Vaughn persuaded the psychiatric team to discharge him into his care and brought him back to Melbourne to recover. To cover up his mental illness and gain a fresh start, Daniel changed his surname from Ward to Grant. Laser eye surgery meant that he no longer required glasses and once his red hair was dyed a dark brown, Daniel Ward was essentially erased.

The chip was the first of this dynamic team's projects. Daniel developed a prototype chip by moving the Fitbit concept from external physical monitoring to internal blood analysis. He developed a new kind of bioplastic tubing, through which blood flowed. The tubing continuously cleaned itself, in the same way as the body naturally cleanses veins and arteries. Gum designed the chip's functionality and Vaughn developed the robotic insertion technique.

In the beginning the trio had no approval or money to launch the project, so they made plans to gain the government's attention and secure finance. First, Gum hacked into digital medical recording systems, to highlight the health system's security flaws and force state health ministers to examine alternatives.

Daniel's personal health records were the first Gum deleted along with all his social security files. She changed his name from Ward to Grant on his passport, driver's licence and university transcripts. Gum also had fun with the health records of Cecile and Brian. She amended their records to include sexually transmitted diseases and changed both their blood groups. Bring on a need for a blood transfusion, and it would be game over for those two.

Daniel and Vaughn worked on securing funds. They purchased designer clothing and hired a Porsche. They made a point of being seen in all the right places, even if they had to gatecrash. Vaughn was handsome, outspoken and flamboyant, using flattery and his skills as a con artist to gain his desired outcomes. Daniel was also handsome, but more aloof than Vaughn. Medication levelled his mood somewhat, giving him an air of mystery.

After a few false starts, the pair gained the attention of Margaret Stuart. She was a plain young woman from a wealthy family and Vaughn had no interest in her. Margaret was not interested in Vaughn either, finding Daniel much more intriguing. He acted less interested than most of her admirers, which she found refreshing as well as challenging. It wasn't long before she began falling for him, despite her father's objections. The romance grew and the harder she had to work to maintain Daniel's attention, the more obsessed with him she became. Margaret had a science degree and was totally fascinated by Daniel's biotech inventions and visions for the future. She convinced Daddy to provide the funds for a pilot chip project. For her, Daniel was 'the One'.

Kenneth Stuart could not persuade his daughter to change her mind. He was unable to find out anything about Daniel's past and this troubled him.

'My mother was born in Australia but died when I was a teenager,' Daniel had told Kenneth and Margaret. 'We were part of some witness-protection scheme, relocated to New Zealand. That's why there are no records. I was only three—too young to remember my real name or in which state we lived. When Mum died, I was placed with a family. Once I turned eighteen, I was brought back to Australia.'

Kenneth felt Daniel's story was too far-fetched to be real; however, despite going to great lengths, he couldn't prove it to be false. With reluctance, he agreed that Margaret and Daniel could marry, but not before insisting on a watertight prenuptial agreement. Daniel and Margaret were married in a lavish ceremony on Hamilton Island on the Great Barrier Reef. Vaughn was their best man and Gum assisted with security. AMDAT was founded a few years later.

Daniel didn't love Margaret; she was just the means to his endgame. He doubted he had the ability to love anyone. Margaret was, however, a useful commodity, if not his ideal wife, and he treated her kindly. Margaret adored Daniel and just wanted him in her bed every night, even if he was frequently too tired to make love. Daddy's money was endless as long as Margaret remained happy. Daniel appointed her as one of his research scientists.

The corporation's launch plans had gone better than expected with the outbreak of AV64 and the collapse of world health systems. AMDAT was given the green light to commence trial-chipping consenting adults. Within two years, seventy per cent of the Australian population were chipped and the continuous data stream was being utilised to reduce catastrophic viral outbreaks and cure rare diseases. The AMDAT Corporation was viewed as the saviour of the human race.

⑨

'Better go, I have a hearing this morning,' Vaughn said to Daniel. 'Some overweight alcohol-dependent politician that thinks he's more entitled to a liver transplant than the rest of us. Claims his life is essential to governing the country and wants to move up the waiting list. I suppose the usual financial incentive will be on offer if the board decides to grant him the transplant. The offer had better be good.'

'He'll also need to stay clean for at least six months to jump the queue, whatever he gives us,' Daniel said, now watching the tour group via CCTV. 'We can't risk upsetting the masses.'

The twelve Australian board members were assembled around the highly polished table admired just a short time earlier by the tour group. The Darwin delegate was having trouble connecting. Her holo-projection was quite unstable. The quivering image and bursts of static delayed the proceedings. She decided to excuse herself until the tech experts fixed the problem. Judge Baron was the chair of the board, with a casting vote if necessary. There was no right of appeal from a board decision.

Behind the panel a huge screen displayed the surgical waiting lists of all Australian states. The digital display, continuously updated courtesy of the endless stream of chip data, looked much like a stock exchange. Theatre lists displayed in a vibrant green were only locked in seventy-two hours prior to the actual surgery.

The first item of business was a Victorian application. The client's lawyer spoke first.

'Mr Barnett has applied to be expedited on the waiting list for a liver transplant, Your Honour. He's offering an annual research donation of ten thousand dollars per year into alcoholism for the term of his life, in the hope of assisting other people with alcohol issues similar to his own.'

Peanuts, thought Vaughn. *An insulting offer!*

AMDAT's lawyer rose to speak.

'Your Honour, Mr Barnett's twelve-month chip data shows that his blood is rarely free of alcohol, his nicotine levels are continuously high and he has unmanaged high blood pressure. Apart from these factors, he's moderately obese and the chances of him surviving the operation are slim. Can we afford to waste resources on a person with such limited future potential?'

'Mr Barnett has agreed to modify his lifestyle over the next six months in order to reduce his nicotine and alcohol intake and lose weight, if he's given a firm date for the procedure,' his lawyer stated.

The AMDAT lawyer responded swiftly.

'Your Honour, I simply *cannot* support this application. Waiting lists are managed nationally, to ensure that those with capacity take full responsibility for their lifestyle and subsequent health issues. Waiting lists have built-in consequences for a reason and the current system is fair. This board can't risk undermining the system for one individual. We would be risking chaos. Furthermore, my learned friend knows full well that firm surgical dates are *never* given.'

Mr Barnett's lawyer continued 'My client is needed for the urgent review of the Victorian ambulance system. The review is due at the end of the year and he has undertaken some groundbreaking work. It's essential he finishes this project.'

Not sure how he achieved groundbreaking work. His sick record shows he only attended work sixty per cent of the time in the last year. He's just another lazy government prick, thought Vaughn.

The AMDAT lawyer smirked, tossed his head back slightly at his opponent's last comment and responded, 'I'm sure there are others who could complete this work just as effectively. I believe this is simply a smokescreen to achieve the end result of a transplant to which he's clearly no more entitled than anyone else who has abused their body for years.'

The judge raised his hand. 'I think we have heard enough. The board will now vote. Those who support Mr Barnett's application please raise your hand.'

Only two hands appeared.

'Raise your hands if you do not support the application.'

Nine hands were raised.

'The application is denied.'

Judge Baron turned and spoke directly to the client: 'Mr Barnett. You're well aware that chips are reset annually, giving you the chance to modify your lifestyle. Clean up your act and you'll automatically move up the waiting list, just like everyone else. You have to realise that personal health is, in the majority of cases, an individual's responsibility. This board owes it to the rest of society to reward those who make an effort to stay healthy and deter those who abuse their bodies and then expect the public health system to fix it for them. That irresponsible health model is long gone. The decision of this board is final. This case is now closed.'

The next case was based in Perth. The judge peered over his glasses and paused before speaking.

'I hope that this application has more merit than that last one. Professor Lambert, I suggest the Victorian division pay more attention when reviewing applications. That hearing was a complete waste of this board's time.'

Vaughn smiled and nodded at the judge.

Baron needs to go, he thought. *Car accident? ... Home invasion ... new little virus perhaps?* He'd think of something.

Outside in the corridor, the politician conferred with his lawyer.

'I'm sorry, but with this new judge, it's getting increasingly harder to push cases through the board, even with the promise of large donations. I suggest you do clean up your act and we can give it a shot in six months.'

'I'll be dead by then,' he replied.

10

A loud crack of thunder woke Ellen. A flash of lightning filled her bedroom, followed swiftly by another deafening boom. The storm was close. She remembered sitting on her father's knee as a child and counting the seconds between the flash of light and the thunderclap, to estimate the distance of a storm.

'Every second means the storm is a mile away,' he would say.

They would count together as he snuggled her close: one, two, three, four, five, six, seven, eight, nine, ten then *boom.*

'You see, sweetheart, the storm is ten miles away from our house, and you are very, very safe.'

Those were the days when she always felt safe. No man had ever been quite good enough for Ellen. No man was as good as her father. There had been a few, but only a couple had come close. The first was her childhood sweetheart Patrick O'Connor. Ellen couldn't remember a time when she hadn't known Patrick. Their mothers, Beatrice and Claire, had been good friends and the two toddlers had played together, attended the same childcare centre and the same schools. For a few years in junior high they drifted apart, but once they passed through the girls-are-yuck and boys-are-smelly-gross-creatures phase, they became sweethearts. They spent hours together listening to music, gaming at the VR precinct, hiking and camping with friends and, of course, exploring each other's bodies—at every opportunity. Eventually they became lovers.

Patrick and Ellen made plans to one day marry and have four—no, five—children, two boys and three girls. He would join the police force and she would study medicine. Their future was sorted. All the boxes ticked! Nothing and no-one would stand in their way. And then—it happened. Beatrice Hancock was diagnosed with an incurable genetic disease. A disease her daughter could be carrying. The foundations of Ellen's life crumbled.

Ellen became sure of only one thing. If she was going to die prematurely, she had to compress her life and live in the moment. She told Patrick she needed space. Time to think. He didn't understand. He became insecure, needy, smothering—and eventually, she pushed Patrick away.

Ellen was preoccupied with her studies when she met her second love interest. A Doctor Dawson had invited her to work at his IVF clinic across the semester break. It was there on one hot summer afternoon that she crossed paths with Daniel Ward. He was just what the young woman needed—a handsome, carefree, outgoing Australian who didn't mention settling down or starting a family. Instead, he talked of travelling to exotic places and get-rich-quick schemes. He had a full head of deep auburn hair and an attitude that matched its intensity. Ellen was intrigued by him from the day they met. He knew she was smitten with him, and deliberately made her blush by asking very detailed questions about the sperm donation process. The following day he came into the clinic and asked her out to dinner. The relationship lasted for six long unforgettable weeks.

Daniel introduced her to new sexual experiences, which she embraced, despite her conventional upbringing. He was spontaneous and adventurous, though at times over the top. He enjoyed making love in places where they might get caught. At first, she felt uncomfortable, but, as the weeks passed, her suggestions became just as risky as his. They made love on park benches, under bridges and once in the ladies' change room at her local gym. She could still recall quite clearly the feel of his lips and his warm breath condensing on her neck, his fingers caressing her breasts and the long slow build-up to an almost overwhelming climax. The look on the faces of the half-dressed women as they scurried out past them was priceless. Daniel blew them a kiss and they all seemed too stunned to respond. Needless to say, Ellen's gym membership was cancelled.

That blissful summer was almost nineteen years ago. Daniel had disappeared from her life as suddenly as he had entered, almost as if she had imagined him. One day he was there, the next she could find no trace of him. No goodbye text. He didn't answer her calls and left no forwarding address at the hostel. He had vanished. Ellen just had to accept that for him, their relationship had been a holiday romance and nothing more.

Her friends believed her continued obsession with the mystery Australian was simply an excuse not to commit to any future suitors. There were plenty of dates and short-term relationships, and Patrick never quite exited the picture. Ellen was an attractive woman. She appeared, however, to be married to her job. Only a couple of her closest friends knew the truth about her mother and the real reason she was reluctant to commit or start a family.

Ellen rolled onto her back. By the light streaming through her bedroom curtains, she estimated it was around four in the afternoon. A glance at her chip display confirmed it was. Suddenly the nausea swept in and she remembered her pregnancy. Her state of denial couldn't go on much longer. She knew it was time to face the family skeleton. Her slender fingers moved to her stomach and she began to cry.

11

Three months earlier, Ellen had needed to travel back to New Jersey to assist her brother James to dispose of the family home and their mother's unwanted possessions. She would also visit her mother, whom she hadn't seen for five years. On the one hand she felt guilty about not visiting more often, but on the other she knew there was little point, as her mother would not know her and she, Ellen, would walk away as distressed and confused as ever. Guilt, she reminded herself, was after all a very narcissistic emotion. The timing of the trip meant she could attend her college reunion, a glimmer of light in what was, for the most part, to be a dismal visit.

International air travel was no longer readily accessible to the general population: only the rich and healthy travelled the globe. It was a costly process ensuring passengers didn't transmit diseases between each other and between continents. Following the outbreak of AV64 only a handful of international airlines remained in operation. In Australia, Qantas dominated.

Qantas operations were reduced, but the airline had survived due to the implementation of advanced microbial control systems. Spacing between seats had been increased to minimise personal contact and specialist air conditioning installed. Passengers were screened for elevated temperature and other signs of illness. Carry-on luggage was banned, cargo-hold contents were fumigated and androids replaced human flight attendants.

Face masks were worn during flights, every breath being drawn through an antimicrobial solution. The filtering system made masks extremely effective. Companies had made millions from the sale of streamlined comfortable personal protective equipment including masks. Leading fashion houses ensured this everyday necessity had become a status symbol among the rich and famous—custom masks sported gemstones and gold leaf.

These extreme measures were taken after air travel spread the AV64 virus worldwide in just three months. As the pandemic unfolded, few survivors could forget the horror streaming live across news channels and social media platforms.

It all began with news footage of a poultry farm in the southern USA. In a twelve-hour period, six workers had died from an unknown virus. Footage of charred chicken carcasses being bulldozed into mass graves and the poultry processing plant being razed to the ground did not at first raise undue concerns. The farm was later identified as ground zero.

The world began to take notice when a clip emerged of a passenger detained on a plane displaying the same symptoms as the poultry workers. The man begged to be allowed to disembark to seek medical assistance. He could barely breathe. In the background fellow passengers could be heard coughing and crying.

Frustrated relatives began posting footage of planes lying idle on tarmacs with their loved ones detained on board. Armed guards surrounded the planes as health workers decked out in biosuits boarded to assess the threat.

The most troubling footage came from a Johannesburg airport. Passengers were filmed activating emergency exit slides in a vain attempt to escape, only to be gunned down by snipers as they ran across the tarmac.

The blame game continued as a plane in Russian airspace mysteriously exploded after requesting permission to land to deal with a medical crisis. When it was revealed that eighteen passengers had become critically ill during the long-haul flight, rescue teams refused to approach the wreckage.

Scientists eventually isolated the deadly virus. A disease quite common in poultry had mutated and passed directly to humans— probably a result of raising chickens in overcrowded conditions while relying on prophylactic antibiotics. Chicken consumption in the USA had increased from 28 pounds per capita in 1960 to a staggering 115 pounds by 2060. The obsession with eating huge quantities of fried chicken had cost the world dearly. As worldwide health and travel systems collapsed, the real world resembled an apocalyptic Stephen King novel.

For over five years, only essential air travel took place. Business in 2074 was mainly conducted via holo-conferencing, rather than risking travelling to meet in person. Mixed reality could place committee members in the same room, in real time, without all of them being physically present. Quarantine or 'Q' precincts sprang up next to airports. These proved to be very successful as biological border-control facilities.

Ellen made her way through the terminal, her face mask firmly in place. Her ID was verified via her chip, as was her temperature: normal. Her bag was weighed and placed on a conveyor belt destined for the fumigation point. Although Ellen was flying economy, her flight to Newark was still costing her six months' salary. Before AV64, the same flight would have cost only a couple of weeks. Luckily her living expenses in Melbourne were low and her job paid good money for high-risk duties. Ellen didn't expect the journey to be a pleasant one, but at least she would be celebrating her thirty-eighth birthday with her closest friends.

Sleep eluded her on the flight. Even several glasses of champagne didn't help; planes were so noisy. Every time she felt sleep enveloping her, turbulence would toss her neck around and make her head throb. Ellen was glad to disembark at the other end, pass successfully through the infection-screening and customs portals and enter the Q precinct.

12

All international travellers were required to reside in Q precinct for fourteen days. Only then, if they remained symptom-free, would a country grant them entry. This quarantine restriction extended an international return trip by at least one month. If a person developed an illness in Q precinct, the time would be extended, or they could be denied entry and deported. Some people found themselves trapped in Q. Trapped in limbo, Q-ites, as they were named, were unable to progress or go back. Once they ran out of money, penniless and now homeless, it was rumoured that these people were transferred to remote islands in the Pacific. Despite these perceived risks, the robot cities of Q thrived. Accommodation and entertainment industries had arisen. Entrepreneurs promoted the quarantine period as a holiday, rather than an imposition. The first time Ellen passed through Q Newark she had found the place fascinating.

'Artificial intelligence is everywhere,' she told her friends. 'Everyone is isolated. You don't have any physical contact with any other humans, yet surprisingly, there was so much to do I didn't feel lonely. Economy rooms are very small, but they are crammed with the latest technology. Virtual-reality portals allow you to access a wide range of experiences. Q even has its own e-sports team, but I failed their audition. Oh! and holograms suddenly appear at all hours trying to sell you stuff. They even sell sex. Some of the male androids on offer are very good looking. I must admit I was tempted. I heard that as many as five hundred men die in Q precincts each year from shagging themselves to death. Android females can apparently go all night.'

Everyone laughed.

'It's true … they even have a medical emergency team made up of androids and—I'm not kidding—there were code blues called every … single … night.'

'What's the food like?' Georgia asked.

'It's okay, considering it's mass catering,' Ellen said. 'You can order gourmet meals, but they cost more. Watching the robots delivering meals is quite amusing. One night a robot dropped my tray and the food went flying. Of course the robot didn't care and just set about cleaning up the mess. About an hour later they sent a customer service android. He … it … was very handsome. He apologised to me then offered me a choice of two items, ugg boots or a private hour with him.'

'Which did you choose?'

'The ugg boots,' she replied.

'Oh, Ellen,' her friends had said in unison.

'I know … always regretted that decision … but sex with an android wasn't something I'd planned on doing. He looked so real. It freaked me out a bit—and I still have my ugg boots!'

This was the third time Ellen had been through Q and the novelty had worn off. Having a good rest was her main goal. To maintain her fitness, she participated in VR exercise sessions. The rest of the time she binged on the latest episodes of the hit series *Terror Plots* or took virtual tours to far-off places. Antarctica was a favourite; she loved penguins. Ellen also vid-linked with her friends; Georgia took her virtual shopping for a new gown and accessories to wear to the reunion. The dress designer scanned her 3D body image to ensure the correct fit. The gown would be ready and waiting for her.

For many, the weeks in Q were a welcome retreat from a fast-paced society that did its best to suck out your lifeblood. The world had become a cold, hard place compared to the first half of the twenty-first century. People thought they had it tough then, with terror attacks, unemployment, the second global financial crisis and the ever-present threat of war. They had no idea that what was to come would be worse than anything they could imagine. Money cannot buy health, and without health there was little happiness.

13

The days flew by and Ellen looked and felt refreshed when she stepped into the sunlight. It was winter in New Jersey and her warm breath was visible as it mingled with the chilled air. Quite a contrast to the Melbourne summer she had just left behind. It felt good to be home. She'd forgotten how much she missed the familiar accent and the aroma of lobster cooking in nearby restaurants. The sound of ice and snow crunching beneath her feet was something she hadn't really noticed before.

She caught an e-cab to Georgia's house, where four of her friends and Georgia's daughter Zoe were awaiting her arrival. They had cooked a sumptuous feast, complete with her favourite Tasmanian bubbly. As Ellen passed through her old friend's doorway, she detected the unmistakable fragrance of garlic and basil. Georgia's signature lasagne was on the menu.

It was clear to all who visited Georgia's home that she was artistic. Each room was arranged with unique objects that she had either collected or crafted herself. The lounge room fireplace was especially remarkable. Georgia had carved intricate acorn and oak leaves on the mantel surround. The detail had been enhanced by the ageing of the wood. It was as if the years had airbrushed the carvings with a brown-black hue.

The crackling log fire heated a room already overflowing with the warmth of Ellen's friends. One by one they greeted and hugged her. It had been a decade since she had seen Caitlin and the reunion brought tears to the eyes of both. She was sad to learn that Marni, another of her schoolmates, had died following a burst appendix: a subsequent infection had failed to respond to antibiotic treatment. Death touched everyone these days.

Nevertheless, the small group ate, drank, chatted and laughed. They all had families of their own and Ellen enjoyed looking at their albums and listening to stories about the intervening years. In turn, they were intrigued by Ellen's continued commitment to work in the field of medicine at such a dangerous time. They wanted to know all about her work at the Health Hub and any new men in her life.

They asked if she had tracked down Daniel Ward, her Aussie heartthrob, believing he was the reason she'd moved to Australia. They were disappointed to discover that the love story didn't have a happy ending and that Ellen had no idea what had happened to him. Their paths had never crossed and she hadn't heard from him again.

It was around two in the morning when the last friend left. Zoe went to bed, leaving Ellen and Georgia alone. Georgia began cleaning up.

'Come … sit down by the fire and leave the washing-up until the morning,' Ellen said, patting the couch next to her.

'Okay, I'll just pop the baking dishes in the sink to soak.'

'Thanks for arranging tonight. I really didn't expect such a welcome; it was wonderful. I can't believe how well Caitlin looks.'

'Well, she did have a facelift, you know, despite the risks. She's married to a cosmetic surgeon and he takes good care of her. He's one of the best operators in the country. They're fabulously wealthy.'

'Well, she doesn't look her age, that's for sure, but I don't agree with any unnecessary surgery.' Ellen's voice rose to a higher soapbox pitch, mingled with a slight hint of disgust as she continued. 'Millions of people are undertaking facelifts, eye lifts, tummy tucks and breast implants, and most of them take prophylactic antibiotics. The obsession with physical beauty has accelerated antibiotic resistance by at least twenty years. Antibiotics rarely work anymore. It's a shame for the patients that really need them.'

Georgia raised her eyebrows at Ellen's response.

'Just as well you look good without surgery then, isn't it?' she replied, smiling at her friend, hoping to lighten the mood.

'Sorry,' Ellen replied. 'That was a bit intense, but I have to care for children who die from simple infections, just because the world has few effective antibiotics. I see the family grief firsthand, and for what?' Ellen shook her head. 'Vanity, nothing but pure vanity.'

Ellen popped open another bottle of champagne. The cork just cleared Georgia's head and hit the wall behind her with a thud, causing them both to burst into laughter that melted away the last remnants of tension.

'With all that stress, it's a wonder you look so great for your age, Ellen. Perhaps not having a husband or children has helped,' Georgia continued, attempting to move the conversation in a different direction. 'Once you have a baby you never sleep soundly again. You remain on constant alert. When Zoe was little, even the slightest whimper from her room would wake me.'

'Well, she was a real miracle baby and she's your only child, so I'm not surprised about that.'

Georgia was much shorter than Ellen and carried a little extra weight around her midriff. She felt and looked older than her thirty-eight years. The death of Frank had shattered her life and in many ways she'd never recovered. It seemed strange to her that Ellen avoided family life, the one thing that she had held so dear and missed so much.

'Do you regret not marrying and having a family?' she asked her friend.

Ellen sighed, 'I didn't until recently and my career was all that I needed. But I can foresee a lonely future. I really love your Zoe and I'm excited about her coming to live with me. I guess it's not too late to have children. I do have frozen ova at the IVF clinic, extracted when I was working there. If I met the right man, I could be tempted. But Georgia, you know the problem I face. I can't even consider such a step until I know my future.'

'Well, why don't you just get tested? Then you can move forward with your life; you can't leave things much longer. You're heading towards forty. If it's going to happen the symptoms could start soon.'

'I just can't face it; if I'm found to be positive, then I've little to look forward to. Anyway, can we leave this topic tonight? I'm going to Manor Hall to visit Mom tomorrow and I have to face reality then. I don't want to spoil tonight.'

A cheeky grin moved across Georgia's face. 'Okay … well, to change the subject, are you looking forward to seeing Patrick at the reunion?' she asked. 'He's now one of New Jersey's finest detectives, you know.'

'Yes, I know; we do keep in touch. He's very intelligent, so that's not at all surprising,' Ellen replied.

'Some say he could be the next police commissioner,' Georgia added.

'That's impressive.'

'And,' Georgia continued, 'he's still single.'

'Haven't you given up on that match by now?' Ellen mumbled, as she drained the last drops of champagne from the crystal flute.

'Never,' said her intoxicated friend. 'Oh, I know that it's late, but please, please, try on your new dress.' Georgia left the room to fetch the garment without waiting for Ellen's response.

The two old friends giggled like schoolgirls as Georgia zipped Ellen into the gown. The two-toned dress was simply divine. The strapless bodice was deep purple velvet, low cut—to show off her neat breasts—and fitted snugly into her waistline. The fine floral beadwork on the bodice glistened in the firelight. The full skirt contained several layers of a paler shade of purple chiffon that floated as she swayed from side to side. A side slit designed to show glimpses of one leg completed the picture. It fitted Ellen perfectly. She looked beautiful.

'Patrick will love it,' Georgia said.

'Stop it,' Ellen said, although she hoped that he would.

'Oh, I nearly forgot.' Georgia opened a small parcel. It contained a matching purple fascinator with detachable ornate facemask, adorned with miniature peacock feathers. She placed it on Ellen's head as the finishing touch. The college reunion was going to be fun.

The two old friends cracked open another bottle of champagne. Ellen undressed and started to climb into her pyjamas by the fire, while Georgia put the gown and fascinator away in Ellen's bedroom. On her return, the sight of her friend's bare legs made her giggle.

'Oh, my God, I'd know those legs anywhere,' she said. 'They still look like they belong on a chicken.'

'Well, you can't talk,' said Ellen, hiccupping. 'You're still titless.'

They drank, chatted and reminisced about their school days for a further two hours. Georgia made fun of Ellen's hideous purple spotted pyjamas and Ellen made jokes about Georgia's latest attempts at male nude figure pottery. By now the fire had grown dim and Ellen reached towards the wood basket for a log.

'Don't bother,' Georgia said. 'We're going to bed in a minute. Throw on a few of those champagne corks; that will liven up the fire while we finish our drinks.'

Before Georgia could stop her, Ellen tipped the full bucket of corks on to the red-hot coals. They caught fire instantly and began to crackle and flare. The flames lapped higher and higher into the chimney. Suddenly, a dull roar could be heard overhead. They both looked up towards the ceiling, then back to each other. At what appeared to be the same moment, they both realised the chimney was on fire.

'Shit!' Georgia screeched, jumping off the couch, 'I knew the chimney needed sweeping.'

Being quite intoxicated, their first instinct was to throw what remained of the champagne on the fire. That did absolutely nothing, except fill the room with smoke, making them cough. Ellen rummaged in her handbag for her mobile and dialled 911. A neighbour had beaten them to it and, although it seemed like an eternity, it wasn't long before six firefighters were dragging their hoses onto the roof of the house and dousing the flames. Ellen and Georgia looked a sorry sight, covered in soot.

Zoe had been woken by all the screaming and was now sitting on the couch enjoying the action in her usually boring home. Auntie Ellen had certainly livened things up. Amid all the commotion, there was a knock on the front door.

'I'll get it,' Ellen said and rushed to open it. She flung the door open so hard it crashed into the small hall table. Ellen made a grab for the vase of flowers as it wobbled about, just managing to save it, and then looked up to find herself face to face with Patrick dressed in his ceremonial police uniform. For a brief moment they both said nothing; just stared at each other, until eventually Patrick spoke.

'Is that you, Ellen? I thought you were arriving tomorrow.'

'Well, you know what thought did,' Ellen slurred. 'Buried a feather and thought it would grow a chook.'

'What did you say?' Patrick said looking quite perplexed.

'Oh! Did I actually say that out loud?'

'You look … er … well,' Patrick said, staring at her purple spotted flannelette pyjamas and soot-mottled face.

'Well, you look really hot in that uniform, I must say,' she replied, cringing as the words tumbled out. 'Don't tell me, I said that out loud too, didn't I?' Then she hiccupped.

'Hi, Patrick,' Georgia said, deciding she needed to rescue Ellen. 'Come in, come in; join us for a drink.'

'No thanks, I've already had my limit of alcohol tonight. I was just on my way home after a police function, when I noticed the fire brigade at your place. I decided to check to see if you're okay.'

'Well, as you can see, we're all fine,' Georgia reassured him.

'Ab...so...lu...tely ... fine,' Ellen added.

With a grin Patrick replied, 'Well, I think you had better call it a night; you both seem to have had quite enough to drink, don't you think?'

'Yesh, Detective,' Ellen said, standing up straight and giving him a salute.

Patrick continued to be amused by his ex-girlfriend's smashed behaviour.

'I'm looking forward to seeing everyone at our reunion.'

'Me too—it should be a great night,' Georgia said, winking at him and cocking her head stupidly in Ellen's direction as if she had suddenly developed a nervous tic.

'And, don't forget that we need to confirm a time for your birthday lunch Ellen.'

'Yesh, we do,' she replied.

'Well, I'd best be off.' Goodnight—or should I be saying good morning?' he said, glancing at his chip. 'Take care ladies.'

Patrick paused then stepped forward and gave Ellen a quick hug. He then turned and left. Ellen closed the door behind him. Then, with both hands covering her face, she slithered slowly down the back of the door and slumped in a bundle on the floor. *How embarrassing.* She looked ridiculous, spoke like an Aussie bogan and had drooled over the uniformed Patrick like an idiot, calling him 'hot'. Georgia and Zoe couldn't stop laughing. Ellen eventually joined in. What else could she do?

The firefighters packed up and made sure all electrical appliances were turned off, before encouraging the two intoxicated women to go to bed. The best friends would both have one hell of a hangover in the morning.

14

Ellen's brother, James, collected her from Georgia's the next afternoon. Not surprisingly, she had a bad headache and was wearing dark sunglasses.

'Rough night, sis?' James asked with a grin. Ellen just moaned as she carefully climbed into his car, keeping her head as upright as possible, as if she suffered from a spinal disorder.

The siblings had a great deal of catching up to do, apart from making the final arrangements to empty and sell the family home. James still lived in the home on the outskirts of town. He had recently announced his engagement to his girlfriend, Joanne, and they had started to build a smaller modern house. Ellen had gone to school with Joanne's older sister, so knew her family quite well and approved of the match. Not that James needed anyone's approval at thirty-three.

The drive to Manor Hall was as beautiful as she remembered. The sprawling complex was set high on a hill, away from prying eyes. The buildings were surrounded by lush gardens that were nourished by unusually warm air currents. The grounds were immaculately maintained, with large deciduous trees and an undergrowth of fuchsias, camellias and rhododendrons.

The large man-made lake sparkled in the sunlight and her nostrils were filled with the smell of pine. One could hardly expect to find a more tranquil place, with such a sad, yet essential, purpose. James dropped her at the front circle; they had decided she would cab home to allow for whatever time she needed alone with their mother.

Ellen was greeted at the hall entrance by Doctor Ingrid Fischer, who ushered her into a small neat office. She was a short, rotund woman with large features, high cheekbones and grey hair pulled into a large tight bun from which hair didn't dare try to escape. Ellen had always felt she would be better suited as a villain in a James Bond movie than running a nursing home.

'It's great to see you again, Ellen. I can't believe it has been five years since you last visited your mother,' Doctor Fischer said in her strong German accent.

'I know. I turn thirty-eight next week: nearly middle-aged. Where do the years go?'

'Well, I turned sixty-three last December. Time just accelerates each year, I fear.' Doctor Fischer paused for a moment as if reflecting on the past before continuing. 'Tell me now, dear Ellen, how is marvellous Melbourne? Doubt I'll ever visit there again, not with the current state of travel.'

'It's better than it was a few years ago. I'm enjoying working in the Health Hub; the model makes it far safer than traditional emergency departments and I love all the advanced technology. AMDAT has really reshaped the health system.'

'What about your love life—have you found that special someone?'

'Nah, too busy for love … I do have a cat, though; Grizzlepuss is good company. I also share my apartment with an AMDAT employee and Zoe Ashmore received an AMDAT scholarship, so she's travelling back with me when I return home.'

'Wonderful news! Georgia must be so pleased; she had much to contend with after the death of Frank. That was a real shame. She'll miss her daughter, though. How do you think she'll cope with Zoe living on the other side of the world?'

'It'll be hard. She is somewhat of a helicopter parent, but I think it will do them both good to spend time apart. Georgia plans to move to Melbourne later this year or early next. She just has to sell the house and her photography business before she leaves. We will probably invest in a larger apartment close to the Health Hub where I work. House sharing is the only way to go. It's too expensive to live alone.'

'Don't forget that you still have enough time to have your own family, Ellen. Have you reconsidered genetic testing? I presume you have frozen ova that can be genetically screened and implanted so the window of opportunity remains open?'

'Yes, I have ova stored here in Newark. But no, I still can't face being tested, not at the moment. Too much is happening right now career-wise and I don't have a partner. I realise it must seem like a stupid decision to you, but I prefer not to know if one day I'm to become neurologically impaired. I can't prevent the inevitable, so why know now? I have no plans to marry or have any children, so I'm not hurting anyone … am I?'

'Only yourself, I fear, Ellen. You'd make a great mother and many men would love to be your life companion. It seems to me that you have locked your heart away. You may be worrying unnecessarily. Think of what you may be missing out on if you're negative to Huntington's?'

'I admit it would be good to know if I'm clear. I promise I'll give it serious thought during my stay.'

'Promise me that you really will give the decision consideration. I can arrange the specialist DNA test personally, and always remember I'm here to assist and support you whatever the outcome. I've known you since you were a teenager and I care about you, Ellen. You're part of the wider Huntington's community, even if it's something none of us chose.'

'I know, thanks.'

'Now, let's focus on the real reason you're here today. Before we visit your mother, I need to prepare you for what you're likely to observe. Beatrice is barely eating and can no longer control any of her physical movements. Her speech has been replaced by groaning sounds that you may find distressing. She is unlikely to recognise you and may even respond to you with fear or aggression. You'll need to be strong, Ellen. This visit won't be pleasant.'

Beatrice Hancock was in the end stages of Huntington's disease. Ellen could clearly recall the dreadful day she had sat with her father and James as a much younger Doctor Fischer explained her mother's diagnosis and what the family could expect.

'Huntington's is a cruel genetic neurological disorder. The disease is inherited, not transmitted. If a person carries the gene and they have two children, each child has a fifty per cent chance of inheriting the gene. This does not mean one out of the two will inherit the gene; both could inherit it, or conversely neither.

'As occurred in your mother's case, sufferers appear quite normal until around the middle of their lives, when they begin to display mental and physical disabilities. Personality changes frequently make employment and family life increasingly difficult.

'Eventually, speech is lost and normal movements are replaced with uncoordinated, uncontrollable actions. Essentially, a person with Huntington's becomes a shell of their former self and can no longer function normally in society. As the disease progresses it will be very distressing for you all to watch her deteriorate.'

Ellen dreaded the thought of finding out she carried the gene. She couldn't imagine any disease eating away her brain function.

Beatrice had no idea that she was a Huntington's carrier until the irritability and irrational intolerance began in her mid-forties and she received the tragic diagnosis. She had required IVF treatment to become pregnant with Ellen. Four years later they adopted James, so he wasn't biologically related.

Ellen had never been tested for Huntington's. She had made up her mind long ago that if she ever had a child it would be only via IVF using her own stored DNA-screened ova. She was determined to do her part to eradicate this crippling disease from her family lineage. Ellen rarely spoke of Huntington's to anyone, preferring to ignore it.

Doctor Fischer and Ellen made their way to H wing, through immaculately carpeted and painted corridors in which hung splendid works of art, donated by relatives of the residents, past and present. Her mother was in one of eight secure suites, arranged in an octagonal design, with a central nurse station. From the nurse station, three staff could view all eight residents, while still retaining privacy between patients.

Ellen entered her mother's suite with Doctor Fischer and the primary nurse. It was a sad sight that awaited her. Beatrice was dressed in a jumpsuit made from material designed to resist her constant tugging. The zipper was sewn into the back of the garment, out of reach. The room was sparsely furnished, containing two vinyl-covered foam chairs and an adjustable bed set thirty centimetres from the ground. Was this to be her fate? Was her recent intolerance towards her work colleague and friend the first sign of changes in her personality?

As Doctor Fischer had warned, Beatrice appeared not to recognise Ellen; in fact, her presence seemed to spark irritation. She groaned more loudly and her movements became jerkier. She appeared more distressed. Perhaps this response was itself a sign of recognition? Ellen tried to touch and soothe her, but the agitation increased until the staff suggested that it would be best if she retreated.

Ellen was visibly shaken by the experience and spent the next thirty minutes observing her mother's behaviour from the nurse station. She discussed with Doctor Fischer the inevitable end of her mother's life. Ellen didn't intend to travel back to New Jersey for her mother's funeral; she would attend by holo-conference. It was simply too expensive and unsafe. Today was the time to say final goodbyes to the person who gave birth to her and nurtured her into a young woman although, in essence, that person had died years ago.

With all the care arrangements in place, a teary Ellen said goodbye to the medical team. As the cab drove her down the tree-lined driveway for the last time, she began to sob. Despite encouragement from Doctor Fischer, she had declined the offer of DNA testing, preferring to stay in her current state of ignorance. It was now over to her brother James, who held their mother's enduring power of attorney, to continue to look after her needs. It began to rain as a red-eyed Ellen looked back at the beautiful old building. The cab rounded the bend and it disappeared from view.

15

'Sit still, Georgia,' Ellen mumbled with her mouth full of hairpins. 'I can't fix your hair with you Facelogging.' Ellen was attempting a hairdo that Georgia had chosen from a step-by-step guide to salon-quality hairstyles. DYI guides to undertaking various tasks at home had increased in popularity; they reduced social interaction, thus lessening the risk of contracting diseases. She stepped back and admired her work in the mirror.

'There, that looks pretty good,' she expressed with satisfaction, completing the hairdo with a liberal dose of hairspray.

'That's nice,' Georgia cooed, 'you could have been a hairdresser.'

'Wouldn't go that far,' Ellen replied.

Once dressed for the reunion, the two old friends stood side by side and admired each other. Georgia programmed her camera and captured the scene, which she immediately uploaded on to Facelog. They felt, looked and smelt fabulous. The e-cab arrived and they were soon on their way. As they alighted from the cab and walked towards the school hall, the sound of one of the hits of their school days blasted through the air. Georgia and Ellen linked arms and spontaneously joined in the chorus.

Only sixty-five of the original one hundred and two in their college year were attending the event. Some had died in the pandemic of 2064 and others couldn't afford the time, expense or risk of travelling. Late cancellations had also occurred. It was now an offence to attend a social gathering if you were infectious, even with the common cold. The days of turning up to functions and passing on your germs were gone. Nevertheless, everyone who attended seemed determined to have a good time.

Entering the hall was a surreal experience, like being transported back to those teenage years when worries were few and friends abundant. The reunion committee had done a fantastic job, replicating the decor from images of their original graduation dance. It was the same venue, after all, and although the furnishings had been renewed, structurally the building had changed little.

There was something quite eerie about meeting former classmates over two decades later. They were essentially the same people, but wrapped in different packaging. Ellen had kept in touch with some; others she hadn't seen since graduation. Naturally, everyone had aged. *Look at the eyes,* she told herself. *Windows to the soul remain a constant.*

The boys, in particular, were less recognisable; most with extra weight and an array of facial hair, and some were completely bald. Most of the girls also appeared to have gained weight. Except for Clara, who still looked anorexic. She was shaking her head and holding up the palm of her hand as the canapés and nibbles circulated through the room.

Most of the nerds still looked and sounded nerdy, although a couple of beautiful people that Ellen didn't at first recognise turned out to be among the nerdiest of all. One, Blake Stanthorpe, was now the most handsome man in the room; a group of women had gathered around him. He was a wealthy bank manager and had travelled from Nova Scotia to attend the function. *Probably combining a parental visit like me,* Ellen surmised.

Patrick was standing near the bar table with Tony Scallioni. The two had been inseparable at school and now worked for the same police department. They were engaged in conversation with a woman whom Ellen didn't at first recognise. Unexpectedly, she felt pangs of jealousy. How ridiculous: Patrick was not her boyfriend anymore; it wasn't college. Strange how the brain could be tricked into reliving an earlier time, just by the decor and company.

The woman turned out to be the once skinny and plain Lauren Miller, now no longer skinny or plain—indeed, she was very attractive. Lauren was now a circus performer. A trapeze artist, no less, and her figure highlighted the benefits of daily high-intensity exercise. Patrick and Tony seemed engrossed in conversation with her.

'She's quite the successful novelist as well,' Georgia said, noticing Ellen staring in their direction. 'She writes detective novels. I've read a couple; they are very good. None of that needy heroines and handsome heroes rubbish. In my opinion, Lauren Miller is the complete package.' Georgia resumed sipping her punch, then, as she observed Ellen still staring at Patrick with Lauren, she added, 'feeling a bit jealous are we Hancock?'

'No … not in the least,' Ellen replied, as her cheeks coloured. An unconvinced Georgia giggled.

The evening didn't take long to warm up and the intervening years melted away. Everyone joined in the dancing, drinking, eating and chatting. Old friends and foes reconnected, discussing days long gone, as well as current careers and family. Even a few teachers had made the effort to attend. Ellen's old biology teacher discussed at length AMDAT and the Health Hub model. She was clearly proud of her former student. A great time was had by all and, for the night, the state of the world was forgotten.

Patrick danced a few sets with Lauren, before Tony tapped him on the shoulder. He thanked her and then made his way over to Ellen.

'Care to dance?' he asked, holding out his hand.

Ellen smiled and walked forwards with him onto the dance floor. As he moved in closer, she smelt his aftershave—'Kouros'. Ellen had bought Patrick his very first bottle of Kouros. Since then, whenever she smelt that fragrance, she thought of him. Tonight, she didn't need to think of him. He was here, with her, just like old times.

Patrick and Ellen danced and chatted for the remainder of the evening. They were comfortable in each other's company; it was as if the years spent apart had never happened. The time flew by quickly and it wasn't long before it was early morning and the lights were dimmed for the last dance. Patrick pulled Ellen close and she could feel her heart beating within his firm grip. *A life with Patrick would be very simple to imagine*, she thought, as they swayed gently from side to side. The song ended and spontaneously everyone clapped and cheered and began saying their goodbyes, swapping contact details and promising to keep in touch.

Patrick offered to share a cab home with Ellen and Georgia, which they happily accepted. Lauren looked a bit miffed. *She probably had her own plans for him,* thought Ellen as she observed Lauren watching them leave.

The cab pulled into the curb outside Georgia's home. 'Coming in for a nightcap?' she asked.

'That would be great, thanks.'

The three friends sat together drinking and remembering their school days.

'Do you recall the time we put the principal's car for sale online at a bargain price?' Georgia asked.

'I do,' Patrick replied. 'Ms Ramsey had to keep leaving our classroom to take personal calls and we didn't get our math test done because of all the interruptions.'

'That's right' replied Ellen. 'Then you took an image of the test on her desk and we worked out all the answers.' Patrick nodded then added, 'Ms Ramsey couldn't figure out how Georgia—the worst math student in the class—got the highest score.' They all laughed.

'What about the time Ellen lit incense on top of a cupboard behind the world globe. Mr Frank had no idea where the smell was coming from. Georgia started freaking out as Africa was being slowly singed off the face of the planet.'

Georgia giggled, 'I think Home Economics lessons with Ms Linton were the best. Remember the day she was dishing out chocolate and mixed nuts ready for us to make rocky road. The boys kept munching them all down, then telling her she hadn't given them any?'

'Oh … that's right,' Ellen replied. 'She went bright red with anger didn't she, and the veins in her neck bulged as she yelled, *if you boys don't stop eating your nuts, you'll have none left.* Half the class fell off their stools laughing. It took the poor thing a while to catch on what had happened. I can still visualise the perplexed look on her face.'

'God we were awful to our teachers,' Georgia said.

'Nah—we were just normal kids,' Patrick replied.

The reminiscing and drinking continued until Georgia decided to call it a night, leaving Patrick and Ellen alone. They were sitting on the couch in a room lit only by the glow of candles. It wasn't long before Patrick slid closer and placed his arm around her bare shoulders. Ellen didn't resist his advances. He tucked a lock of hair behind her ear and gently kissed her cheek. She turned to face him, and they stared lovingly into each other's eyes. Ellen always felt safe with Patrick. She felt at home with this man, her childhood sweetheart, but she had never been able to commit to him. Primed with alcohol and enjoying the company of her dear friend, Ellen decided to stop worrying about the future. *I'll be back in Melbourne soon enough. What harm could it do to just live in the moment?* She smiled and leaned forward until her lips touched Patrick's. Then they began to kiss—slowly at first until the heat spread through their bodies and the passion intensified. Patrick moved to her neck. He licked and kissed her softly, nibbling her earlobes as she began to moan. It wasn't long before she made a snap decision. She stared into his eyes, then stood up, took hold of his hand and led him to her bedroom. He didn't resist.

After making love, Patrick and Ellen lay snuggled in the candlelight enjoying their *petite mort*. He stroked her face and ran his fingers through her auburn curls. Patrick was in awe of the girl he had always loved, who was now such a beautiful woman. The relationship that had simmered on and off for so long had, once again, reached boiling point.

'Why can't you stay here and not return to Melbourne?'

'Shhh,' she uttered sleepily, 'tonight has been wonderful, just enjoy.'

Have you decided where you want me to book for your birthday lunch? He asked.

Ellen didn't reply; she had fallen asleep and begun to snore. Patrick smiled to himself them snuggled his body down next to hers.

He woke around dawn, to find their bodies still entwined. He carefully untangled himself, climbed out of bed and got dressed. Before leaving, Patrick stood and watched Ellen sleeping ... the rise and fall of her chest, the bunch of curly hair on the pillow, the cluster of freckles perched on the end of her nose. He smiled, then leaned down and kissed her on the forehead. Ellen murmured and then rolled on to her other side. The first rays of sunlight were dancing through the lace curtains of Georgia's home as Patrick walked home.

16

The shafts of sunlight could barely make their way through the dirt-stained windows of their mother's attic. The dust was so thick it was as if snow had fallen through the roof onto the discarded items jam-packed within. A large brown wolf spider, unused to intruders in its world, retreated from its web into a crevice.

'God, it's dusty up here, James,' Ellen said spluttering.

'Here.' He handed her a mask.

'I doubt anyone has been in this back section of the attic in thirty years,' Ellen said, as she pushed a few boxes aside and made her way further through the piles of junk. 'I think Mom must have kept everything. Look, here's your baby car seat, and this old trunk is full of her old clothes. They have to go back at least fifty years. My God, she had a very neat little waistline, didn't she?' Ellen said, holding a pair of bright yellow trousers against her own, much larger, midriff.

Just then, her foot fell through a rotted floorboard and she squealed with surprise rather than pain.

'Ouch! I'm stuck, James. Quick, help me out before I fall right through the ceiling.'

'Hold still,' James said. He carefully moved the jagged piece of board from around her foot, before trying to lift out her leg. 'It's wedged on something,' he said, unable to see exactly what was wrapped around her ankle.

'Be careful,' Ellen said. 'I don't want to break the skin if I can help it.'

He reached his hand into the ceiling cavity and pulled out a small metal tin with a piece of string that had become entangled with Ellen's shoe. Her foot came out with it.

It was an old Nabisco biscuit tin. Inside was a collection of their grandmother's birthday cards, along with a piece of cross-stitch, about the size of a lady's handkerchief. The material, which appeared to be linen, was yellowed with age. The edges were torn and tatty. The fabric was much older than the tin.

Although the colours were faded, Ellen could just make out a cross-stitched letter and number in each corner. The initials *E. H.* with six small black crosses and one large black cross were clearly visible in the centre. Beneath the *E. H.* was a sailing ship with the name *Kent* embroidered on the bow and another set of initials, *H. H.* Ellen couldn't quite make out the year; was it 1677?

'It couldn't really be seventeenth century—wouldn't have survived, would it?' James asked.

'It's probably a nineteenth-century cross-stitch sampler,' Ellen said. 'A girl would embroider it to depict the story of her relatives. She would learn various stitches at the same time, so a sampler served a few purposes. *E. H.* … they're my initials, and *H. H.* are Dad's.'

'I wonder where it's from?' James asked. 'I guess we'll need to ask Dad; he might know. It's probably his mother's. Can't ask Mom now, anyway, can we?'

Ellen continued, 'Might be worth getting the sampler dated; it looks pretty old. If the *H* does stand for Hancock, then it's definitely been passed down Dad's line, not Mom's. She was a Fletcher.'

'Do you mind if I take this back to Melbourne with me?' she asked.

'No, you're welcome to it.'

Ellen placed the sampler back into the tin, put it to one side and continued to sift through the remnants of her family's life.

Clearing the home was proving to be an emotional rollercoaster. Ellen felt as if she was a supporting actor in a silent movie. The raw naked truth of her family's life flashed in and out of her mind like a slideshow as each box, letter and package was opened. Her parents had kept love letters, exam papers, essays, artwork, medals, certificates, trophies marking achievements and successes. With each find, she was tossed uncontrollably into a sea of memories like a ship with a damaged rudder. Some memories were comforting, others just plain confronting.

Ellen found the names of her two best girlfriends, Georgia and Caitlin, etched inside the door of her old wardrobe. Loose photos were scattered throughout the home. Ellen gathered them all and made plans to sort, restore and digitise. Stored in the attic was every small electrical appliance from at least the last forty years. Most were now useless; they included an array of heaters, computers, cameras, radios and cooking appliances. It was a total mess—disgusting really.

'James, you and Dad could have tackled this mess before now. Why didn't you?'

'I don't know,' he said defensively. 'I guess I just didn't want to touch their stuff and, since the divorce, Dad rarely comes near the place. Mom's illness and irrational anger left him shattered. He pretty much walked away with nothing. I told him not to bother coming home if he didn't feel up to it. Anyway, don't start blaming either of us; you just took off to follow your dreams. Did you expect me and Dad to handle everything?'

Ellen paused, 'Okay, let's not argue. We just need to accept that this mess needs sorting and get the job done. I'm really sorry that I wasn't here to help more.'

It took a solid two weeks to empty the home. A second-hand dealer bought some of the furniture and a local collector was happy to take the electrical goods away to sort, salvage and recycle whatever he could. A cleaning company whizzed through the place in no time. Fumigation and a lick of paint in a few key rooms and the place was finally ready for sale.

'I hope a family buy and love this house as much as we did, James,' Ellen said as they stood side by side watching the real estate agent hammer in the *For Sale* sign.

'It does need work, but it has potential,' he replied, as he turned and put his arm lovingly around his big sister's shoulder. 'I miss having you here. Do you think you will ever come back?'

'I love Australia now, James. It's my home—the lifestyle and weather are fabulous. I'd be too restless here these days. Hopefully, when the world beats all these bugs, you and Joanne can come for a visit.'

'I'd like that,' he replied, squeezing her shoulder affectionately.

Ellen had lunch with Patrick on her birthday. He was such a kind, supportive and caring friend. Sleeping with him had probably not been the greatest of ideas, as it had clearly offered him renewed hope. The way Patrick looked as he sat opposite her today made her feel guilty. But how could she be expected to make any plans with him when she didn't know her fate? DNA testing could clear her, but a positive test would be devastating. Patrick and Georgia were on the same page regarding Ellen taking the genetic test. *Just get on with it!*

Patrick's mother Claire had eventually told him about Beatrice's illness. When Ellen ended their relationship, her son had been so distraught that she felt it might help him to cope. She encouraged him to let Ellen sort herself out—to be patient. If Ellen was destined to become his wife, she would. In the meantime, he should concentrate on his career, date other women and just have fun. For the most part Patrick didn't think of Ellen, but whenever he was in contact with her, his strong feelings resurfaced. Today was no different.

Patrick had visited her in Melbourne in 2063, just prior to the pandemic. Ellen had been home to Newark once since then and they always kept in touch. Today he sat listening to her Hub tales. Her face, full of the expressions he adored … mannerisms still quirky. Despite the time apart and distance between them, he still loved Ellen Hancock. *Does she love me?* he wondered. Patrick decided to test the waters.

'You seem to have enjoyed being home' he said.

'Other than my visit to Mom, everything has been great.'

'Even the night of the reunion?'

'Of course! It's always lovely to see you Patrick.'

'We did a bit more than see each other Ellen. Making love to you has always been special. Perhaps you should come home. Share my bed more often.'

Ellen sighed. 'Look Patrick, I still don't know where my life is headed.'

'If you took the test then maybe you would,' he replied, frustrated.

'I know that you mean well, but I'm just not ready?'

'Will you ever be ready? I can't wait forever you know.'

'I've never asked you to wait at all—have I?'

Patrick stared at her for a few seconds then stood up and started putting on his coat. Why had he expected her to respond any differently? Their relationship had always been on her terms. Why was he so surprised? Ellen avoided any commitment or decisions around her personal life, including him. He felt used. Ellen stood and moved towards him for a goodbye hug.

He held up his hand to stop her 'Don't,' he said, then added, 'take care of yourself Ellen. Have a safe trip home.' As he walked towards the restaurant door, he thought, *Perhaps it is time I let go and move on. Maybe I should give Lauren a call.*

The holiday slipped by quickly and it seemed no time at all before a teary Georgia drove Ellen and Zoe to the airport to begin their journey to Melbourne. They would spend two weeks in adjoining rooms at Tullamarine Q Precinct, and then Zoe would start her new career with AMDAT.

'Take care; don't forget to dress warmly and eat properly,' Georgia said.

'It's summer in Australia, Mom; stop fussing,' Zoe replied. 'Auntie Ellen will look out for me.'

'She had better. You're the most important person in the world to me. I can't believe my little princess is all grown up and moving away,' Georgia's eyes flooded with tears for the umpteenth time.

'I'll be okay, Mom. I *will* look after myself and I'm going to work for the safest and best health corporation in the world, after all.' Zoe paused. 'Please try not to worry. Bye. Love you. Talk soon,' she said as she exited the vehicle.

Zoe blew her mother one final kiss, then turned and began attaching her mask as they walked towards the first screening portal. Only passengers with valid boarding passes could enter an airport terminal. The journey from Newark to Melbourne on a routine flight would take around eight hours.

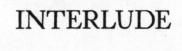

INTERLUDE

Eyam
August 1666

The journey from Eyam to Sheffield would take Elizabeth Hancock three to four days. Eleven miles as the crow flies—fourteen by road. But she really had no choice. If a peddler or gypsy recognised her, she would be sent back—or suffer a fate far worse. Her best option was to journey on foot across the moors. Travel by night and rest by day—less chance of being seen—more likely to succeed.

Elizabeth looked down at her red swollen finger. A splinter of wood from the spade peeked through her translucent flesh. She had tried to dig it out with a needle, but it was in deep. She would just have to wait until it festered. Wait. That's all she seemed to be doing today: waiting. Waiting for one thing, or another. Now, as she looked out of her cottage window, she was waiting for her God. He had begun to wash his sky with tones of pink, blue and grey. Once he finished it would be twilight. Twilight—the time caught between day and night. Her John called it limbo light.

'Neeither one, nor t'uther,' he used to say. John's mouth didn't say anything anymore. Her eyes filled.

On the floor at her feet was a hessian sack. It held a loaf of bread, a pot of dripping, a crock of pickled onions, a lump of cheese and a flask of ginger beer. That should be enough.

Earlier in the day, Elizabeth had rummaged through her clothing.

'Nowt much 'ere worth keepin',' she had mumbled to herself. To save carrying the garments, she had tried wearing layers. That idea had been abandoned—too heavy and restrictive. The discarded rags now lay in a bundle by her chair.

Elizabeth peered out of the window. Marshall had gone. His spade stood upright—abandoned near a freshly dug grave. Tomorrow it would be filled. As she looked skyward, the light suddenly dimmed. God had finished, it was time to leave. She picked up the sack, flung it over her shoulder and then made her way up the hill towards Mompesson's Well. Two large stones lay in the grassy field nearby. They had been drilled with holes that were now full of vinegar. In the dim light she could just make out some coins glinting on the bottom. Coins that tomorrow should be exchanged for food. Fruit, vegetables and meat that her neighbours needed to survive. Elizabeth wasn't a thief, but today she became one. Reaching into the vinegar she grabbed the coins and shoved them into her pocket. Dropping her head in shame she mumbled, 'Forgive me father, for I 'av sinned.'

Elizabeth paused for a moment and then stepped up to the boundary—that invisible line that enclosed her village. The line wasn't real. It was all in her mind. There were no guards. No fences to climb. No gates to open. Elizabeth stared down at the soil, as if at any moment, a hand might reach out of the ground and grab her ankle. Taking in one deep breath she leapt across. Elizabeth didn't look back. With her eyes fixed on the horizon she began to run. In a few days—God willing—she would be with her son.

This is the rate thing to do, she told herself. The rate thing fa' me and the rate thing fa' me babbie. Then she hurried into the stand of elms and her silhouette gradually merged with the evening shadows.

Melbourne
2074

17

When Professor Vaughn Lambert entered the lecture theatre, the deafening chatter gradually died down, until everyone was silent with their gaze fixed upon him. He oozed confidence and moved gracefully. His body language was captivating and his smile mesmerising. Zoe studied him closely. She knew he was forty-two years old. He was slim, and she guessed about 185 centimetres tall. His skin was tanned and clear, his white teeth perfect, and he obviously exercised regularly.

Zoe glanced in Sarah's direction. She was grinning stupidly and looking at Lambert as if she was viewing a god. She turned her concentration back to Lambert as he raised both his hands upwards and outwards in a welcoming gesture that reminded her of an evangelical preacher and began to address the group.

'Welcome to AMDAT. You've all earned your position within this corporation and hopefully you will find your niche and have a long and rewarding career. Yesterday, you completed an examination designed to allocate you to one of the five speciality research groups. I'm not going to apologise for the length and intensity of the test. It's very important that your area of expertise is matched to your intelligence, psychological strengths and resilience, as well as your specific area of interest.

'The five research domains are well known to you all, and by now, you should understand the importance of them to the overall improvement of health systems, not only within Australia but around the world.'

Professor Lambert clicked his autopen and the five domains appeared inside coloured spheres, circling around him. His presentation of each research domain was quite theatrical. He reached his hand towards the circling spheres and summoned them towards him. One by one each sphere took centre stage then grew enormous until every minute detail could be clearly seen by the group. He briefly outlined each one to the students, who were by now fully engaged with this spectacle. Music composed especially for the occasion enhanced his performance. It was as if the group were attending a rock concert rather than a lecture.

Sphere 1 displayed a detailed map of the world circling around and above them. Lambert pointed out the current viral outbreaks in South Sudan, China and Mexico and went on to outline how the chip tracking system functioned to better manage global pandemics.

In Sphere 2, images of prominent scientists of the past and present appeared along with their groundbreaking antibiotic and vaccine discoveries.

'AMDAT is focusing on identifying natural replacements for antibiotics, just as Alexander Fleming identified penicillin mould in 1928. Plants can't go to the doctor when they need to be healed, so analysing how they promote healing is a key focus.'

Some of the group nodded in agreement.

'We're also investing in the synthesis of antibiotics by analysing and copying their chemical makeup.'

Sphere 3 focused on the improvement of the human immune system.

'In my opinion, our bat project is the most exciting research to date.' He then paused, threw his head back and raised his arms high above his head, just as an enormous flock of holographic bats flew from the roof of the auditorium and descended on the unsuspecting students. The group began to scream, duck and weave. A couple of the boys who were obviously very familiar with holographic projection sat grinning with their arms folded, watching the others waving their arms frantically in the air trying to beat off the swarm of flying mammals. Eventually the entire group realised they weren't real and calmed down. Lambert continued to further explain AMDAT's bat project.

'Bats carry a raft of diseases harmful to humans without becoming ill. They have fantastic immune systems that remain switched on continuously, without causing tissue damage. The human immune system only activates when it is required to fight an infection—thus limiting damage to tissues. When bats fly, they increase their basal temperature, which no doubt plays a role in their immune defence systems. Humans also increase their basal temperature when faced with a bacterial or viral attack; however, this does not happen on a daily basis as with bats.' The holographic bats began to disintegrate, crumbling into millions of sparkling silver-grey particles, then slowly fading away.

Lambert motioned Sphere 4 into centre stage where a display of the known benefits of chips moved in and out of focus. Live streaming of the nation's chip database was then displayed. This data was usually only available to AMDAT executives and the group were blown away watching the information continuously updating in front of their eyes.

'You're already aware of the benefits of live chip data streaming and collection. AMDAT uses this data in many ways, one of which is to track and monitor the benefits of prescribed medications. Continuous data analysis has enabled dosages to be refined to precise therapeutic levels, saving millions of dollars of waste and reducing the toxic side effects of incorrect dosing.'

The last research area was the most controversial. Sphere 5 contained 3D footage of people with inherited diseases. Most inherited diseases had been largely eliminated throughout the course of the last century. Next, the current, as yet unresolved, illnesses were graphically brought home to the group with examples of deformed fetuses.

'Embryonic research has allowed AMDAT to identify faulty human genes and to perfect gene clipping. The editing of genes can eliminate many genetic disorders, thus alleviating unnecessary suffering and premature death. Embryos that have been genetically corrected can be implanted via IVF and result in healthy viable children for couples with an otherwise high risk of birth defects.'

Professor Lambert continued, 'Twenty-five of you have been allocated to each domain and will work with the head researcher on key projects. Two days per week you will attend the required medical lectures at Melbourne University. The medical degree will take you an additional two years to complete. However, you'll be paid a generous salary throughout this time.

'Each week, we will meet to share and discuss ideas in an informal, relaxed environment. These meetings will occur every Friday afternoon and include refreshments. Networking and getting to know each other on a personal level is vital for you all to feel connected and supported. Some of the best ideas have emerged from these informal gatherings. Please make every effort to attend, as I'm quite sure you'll find these sessions most worthwhile.'

The five head researchers had been seated in the front row throughout the presentation. They now rose from their seats and stood beside Lambert. He introduced them one at a time, along with their area of expertise. The one that sparked the greatest interest was Margaret Grant, Daniel Grant's wife. A buzz of anticipation slowly grew within the group.

'Before you get too excited, I'll allocate you to your group.' He pressed a key on his computer and asked everyone to focus on their chip. A personalised message scrolled through. Zoe looked down to view hers.

Congratulations, Zoe Ashmore; you have been allocated to AMDAT Group 3: Improving the Human Immune System, headed by researcher Margaret Grant. Do you accept the challenge?

Bats! I have to work with filthy bats! thought Zoe.

'I'm in Group 5—embryonic enhancement,' Sarah squealed loudly.

Lucky you, thought Zoe.

By now the atmosphere in the whole room was electric, as each person received their message and responded. Most were ecstatic, but others—like Zoe—less so. One thing they all knew—it was a once-in-a-lifetime opportunity and complaining was not an option. The AMDAT examination had assigned them to the research teams and that was that.

The leaders asked their teams to move to their respective research laboratories for a more detailed orientation. Zoe rose from her seat and made her way to Level 12, along with the other twenty-four Group 3 members.

18

To maintain a high level of security, entry to the bat conservatory was accessible only from Level 12. The habitat was designed like a series of large caves made from synthetic material that resembled stone, shaped into huge boulders that weighed next to nothing. Plants and lichens covered the synthetic stone surfaces. The light, temperature and humidity were all maintained to optimise bat health and fertility.

'You will be working closely with the bats,' Margaret said, 'so your first lesson is how to safely handle them. AMDAT's bats are infected with many of the rarest and most deadly pathogens known to man. We're continually examining the mechanisms that prevent the bats from becoming ill and dying, but this makes them very dangerous for researchers.

'We change the bat species approximately every three years. Unfortunately, the bats used in research are too infectious to be released into the wild. Once the research is completed, they're destroyed. The conservatory currently houses the common bent-winged bat, found in caves throughout Victoria.

'I can't emphasise enough that the use of personal protective equipment is vital. You must wear the correct overalls, headgear and gloves whenever you enter the bats' domain or handle them, even if they have been anaesthetised. It's not unknown for a bat to wake up halfway through a procedure and we wouldn't want anything to happen to any of you, would we?'

The perplexed group shook their heads in agreement. Zoe didn't feel comfortable at all. She would have much preferred to have been allocated to any of the other groups.

A female researcher named Kerrie began to demonstrate how to correctly attach the safety equipment. This included a headset with a camera relay system to enable monitoring and recording of all who entered the bat zone and the tasks they undertook.

'Now it's your turn,' Margaret said. 'Let me see how well you can gear up. Oh, and by the way, all your clothing is named, as it has been designed especially for you based on your 3D profile.'

Everyone moved to find their lockers. They were arranged in alphabetical order, so Ashmore was in the first bank. A couple of young men—Oliver Adams and Charlie Black—had lockers on either side of Zoe's. They both said a polite hello.

Once the group were prepared, Margaret led them through the safety airlock, into the bat zone and down an internal staircase to a series of platforms with one-way mirrors. From the various platforms they could view the bats in their artificial habitat undertaking all aspects of their daily life. A distinct odour of wild woodlands was blowing through the air-conditioning ducts above their heads, instantly transporting Zoe back to Lake Inawendiwin Girl Scout Camp.

Margaret continued the briefing: 'If you look carefully, you'll see most of the bats are sleeping. Over here, you can observe some bat babies; these are called pups.'

'Ahhh,' they all murmured. Babies are popular whatever the species. *Even bat pups are cute* thought Zoe—*all pink, scrawny and hairless.*

'Note how the hairless pups clump together on the roof of the cave to keep warm. They hang on tightly with their claws. If they do happen to fall, they will die. Bats are mammals, like us, so using bats for research is similar to using mice, quite close to humans in a genetic sense. Mice are generally preferred as they're safer to handle. Any questions?'

'What would happen to me if I did get bitten?' a sweaty-faced Charlie enquired.

In a very matter-of-fact manner, as if she was perhaps responding to an enquiry about a fleabite, Margaret began her blunt scientific explanation.

'Well Charlie, that really depends on your personal immune system. AMDAT's three bat colonies have been deliberately infected with AV64, Ebola or mutant strains of the bubonic plague. A bite would most likely cause an illness that would kill ninety per cent of the human population but, as we have seen in all outbreaks around the world, there is always a percentage of humans that survive.

'AMDAT call these survivors "super immune" or "SIs". SIs are very important to researchers, as they carry a range of disease-protective codes in their DNA. Crack these genetic codes and embryos can be engineered to be resistant to specific diseases. That's the area of research that Group 5 are working on.

'In essence, Charlie, you simply can't afford to get bitten, as you could become seriously ill, or even die. There are many other professions with this level of personal risk, such as microbiologists and nuclear physicists. If your line of work contains dangers, then mitigating the dangers safely and effectively becomes a key skill.

It's paramount that you take care whenever you handle the bats. The vaccinations that have been developed to date will be provided to this group, but keep in mind that these only assist your body's immune system; they aren't completely effective. Any further questions?' she asked, surveying the stunned faces of her research group as they processed the potential dangers of their new workplace.

The afternoon continued with Margaret explaining her research in greater detail. At four o'clock she dismissed the group for the day.

Back at their lockers, Oliver asked Zoe if she wanted to go for a drink before heading home. She was a bit surprised, not being used to such requests, but quickly composed herself.

'I'm only eighteen; I can't legally drink until twenty-one.'

Her accent gave her away.

'You can in Australia,' Oliver said with a grin, realising he had a cleanskin on his hands.

'Well, thanks for asking. Not today, but another time, perhaps. My auntie is expecting me home for dinner.'

Oliver is quite cute, she thought to herself as she watched the tall blond young man walk away.

Zoe made her way down to the foyer. A security guard directed her to use the secure rear exit to avoid a group of protesters that had gathered at the front. She could see and hear them shouting and waving banners. The target of the demonstration appeared to be embryonic research. They were chanting loudly, 'AMDAT should not play God', 'Ban gene clipping', 'Human DNA is sacred', 'Embryos have rights' and 'Embryos can't consent'.

Zoe wasn't sure how she felt about these issues, having never before been confronted with such ethical dilemmas. She paused to observe the group. They were diverse in gender, ethnicity and age, some around her own age group and a few quite elderly. Two of the younger women were carrying babies and a couple of toddlers were running between the protesters' legs, unperturbed by the commotion, as if they had grown up in that environment. An elderly dark-skinned woman dressed in colourful clothing seemed to be leading the group.

The security guard suggested she leave before any violence erupted, apparently not an uncommon event at AMDAT. *I guess it goes with the territory of cutting-edge science,* she pondered as she walked towards the rear of the building. Suddenly she felt a hand in the small of her back.

'I do hope the protesters haven't scared you Zoe? It is Zoe isn't it?'

Zoe turned around to see Professor Lambert standing next to her.

'Yes, that's right. I'm Zoe … Zoe Ashmore.'

'Well Miss Zoe Ashmore, let me walk you outside just to make sure you stay safe.'

'Before she had a chance to reply, his hand returned to her lower back and he guided her out the rear exit and across the street.'

'There, you should be quite safe now' he said. 'No doubt I'll see you tomorrow.'

'I guess so,' Zoe replied. She smiled uneasily at him and then turned and walked away.

Oliver was waiting for his tram when he noticed the interaction between the pair. The pretty American student was now heading his way. Someone should warn her about him. Lambert's womanising was well known in student circles, but Zoe wasn't from here, was she?

'Are you okay?' he asked. 'You looked a bit uncomfortable just now with the professor.'

'I'm fine,' she replied, not wanting to appear weak. Oliver wasn't convinced.

'Well, let me know if he bothers you. He has a bad reputation with female students you know. You need to be careful.'

'Thanks for caring Oliver, but I assure you I'm fine.' She gave him a warm smile and then continued on.

Zoe enjoyed the walk home. The shortest route wound through the local parks and gardens, past terrace houses and the modern structures cleverly designed around them. The thunderstorm had now passed over the city, leaving it washed and refreshed. She felt so lucky to live right in the middle of the city. Ellen's apartment was small but cosy, and the communal spaces throughout the city provided plenty of places to relax and enjoy nature.

As she strolled past the Footy Precinct, she could hear voices coming from within. Large screens continuously displayed the main oval, on which the athletes and their children were having an informal kick. Smaller screens adorned the stadium walls, allowing the public to view the athletes and their families undertaking all aspects of their daily lives. Once principally a sporting competition, AFL—the Australian Football League—was now the most popular live reality TV show in Australia. Players were paid millions to live and work in the spotlight for the duration of the footy season. Female teams competed from October through to March and male teams from April to September.

AFL was smaller than it used to be. Following the pandemic, most competing states now had only two football teams. Tasmania was the exception, with only one team. The territories didn't participate.

Rob had explained to Zoe, while they watched a match on TV, that all team members and their families moved into the Footy Precinct at the start of pre-season training and remained in lockdown until the Grand Final. Footy Precinct was a small isolated community, a bit like an Olympic village, with its own school, shops, medical centre, warehouse hydroponic vegetable gardens and synthetic meat factory. Rob also explained that the precinct grew enough vegetables to supply the local hospitals and prisons as well as the AFL community. AFL was pretty big in Australia: she needed to choose a team to follow if she wanted to really assimilate. Rob followed the Victorian Vipers, which had been formed from the remnants of half the old Victorian teams including Geelong, the team his grandfather had idolised; perhaps that was the way she should go.

19

Zoe arrived home to find Ellen cooking synthetic chicken and tarragon balls with lemon-zest risoni, one of her favourites. It smelt delicious and she realised just how hungry she was. The unexpected shock of being allocated to the bat research team had made her lose her appetite completely, but now she was starving.

Ellen had papers scattered on the lounge room floor. She had been researching the provenance of the embroidery sampler she'd found in her mother's attic. Having received confirmation of its age from the local museum, she had determined that it was a replica in a nineteenth-century style, but only about sixty to seventy years old, not the real thing. Ellen had called her father, who confirmed that the Hancock family had originated in northern England and he had found a reference to Hancocks living in Derbyshire.

'Dinner smells divine, Ellen. Have you discovered anything new today?'

'Well, the *Kent* is the name of a ship that left England and sailed to New Jersey in 1677. I can't find any Hancocks on the passenger manifest, but the list doesn't contain anyone who boarded at Hull in the north of England, so that's the most likely explanation.'

'That's interesting; I must ask Mom if she knows anything about where the Ashmore family originated.'

'Come, eat.' Ellen motioned her towards the table, where she had dished up a steaming hot bowl of the risoni topped with a good portion of grated parmesan and cracked black pepper. Zoe tucked in eagerly.

'This is so yum. You must teach me how to cook it. I could eat it every day,' Zoe mumbled with a full mouth.

Ellen smiled.

'Now tell me all about your day. Did you get placed in the antibiotic-development research group like you hoped?'

Zoe's face dropped and she put down her fork.

'No, I have to work with horrible, dangerous, stinky bats.'

'Oh … Surely, it can't be that bad? Can you request a change?'

'No, the examination results were used to allocate us; decisions are final. I guess I'll just have to get used to the horrid creatures. I certainly don't want to be seen as a failed scholarship holder; so many people would give anything to be in my position.'

'Well, at least you have the right attitude. Just try to stay positive.'

'I'll try. Anyway, I don't want to think about it. Can I just enjoy dinner? Let's see what's on the news. There were some protesters outside AMDAT Tower as I left; they might get some coverage.'

Ellen selected the World News channel. The death of a Mars colonist was the lead story. It was the third reported death in the crew that had departed Earth in 2059, five years prior to the pandemic. Scientists hadn't yet determined the cause of this latest death. The woman's friends and family all commented on her bravery and how sad they were to lose her. The small colony was, not surprisingly, also distressed by another unexpected death. Her Mars family had nothing but glowing praise for the talented scientist.

The news reporter continued: 'Judge Baron, of the World Health Board, has been shot and killed while leaving a local restaurant this afternoon. His bodyguard was critically injured. Police are interviewing persons dissatisfied with recent decisions of the board. Anyone who saw a black car leaving the crime scene is asked to contact police. Judge Baron will be sadly missed. He is survived by his wife and three sons.'

'His poor family—I hope the bodyguard makes it,' Zoe said.

'Sounds like a professional hit to me,' Ellen replied.

The AMDAT protest story was next. Professor Vaughn Lambert declined to speak to the media, relaying a message that he was unavailable due to the new student intake. He would release a press statement at a later date.

The news bulletin was interrupted with a breaking story from New Jersey. An eighteen-year-old woman had been found dead in a local park. In the last seventy-two hours four other women of similar age had also disappeared. The camera focused on Detective Patrick O'Connor, who explained that, as yet, no clues had emerged. Ellen's face flushed seeing him and she felt pangs of guilt about the baby growing in her belly.

Patrick was answering questions fired at him from a large squad of journalists.

'Do the police think they might be dealing with a serial killer?'

'Although the young woman died in what appear to be unusual circumstances, we can't be certain until we have the autopsy report. The death may be unrelated to the missing women, so speculation is premature. At this point in time, we remain hopeful that the four women will be found safe and well.' The words coming from Patrick's mouth told one story; his facial expression suggested something else. He was clearly worried and looked like he hadn't slept properly in days.

'Poor Patrick,' Zoe said. 'He looks exhausted.'

'Do the police have any solid leads?' asked another journalist.

'Not as yet. We're focusing our investigations on possible connections between all five women. Other than their age and the fact that they were all living and studying in the same geographical location, we're trying to determine if they have anything else in common.'

'Could the four missing women be together?'

'That's highly unlikely,' Patrick replied.

'To obtain proof of life, has a court order been approved for AMDAT to track the specific location of the girls' chips and determine if data is still streaming?'

'Yes, it has. AMDAT have already attempted to track their chips, but it turns out only the deceased woman had been chipped.'

'The other four weren't chipped?'

'That's correct.' Patrick continued. 'This is one of the most troubling aspects of the case and why we believe their disappearances are in some way linked. The girls can't be tracked.'

Images of the four missing women were then broadcast and Zoe was shocked, as the faces of two former classmates, Kasey and Alice, appeared on the screen, along with two others she didn't recognise. Patrick then confirmed the name of the deceased young woman as Bridget Patterson as an image of another of Zoe's friends, dressed in her prom gown, filled the screen. Within a few seconds Zoe's mobile began to ring and Ellen's vid-link screen started beeping. It was Georgia.

When Georgia saw Zoe sitting next to Ellen, she began sobbing with relief.

'Mom, I'm okay. I'm safe here and, whatever is going on over there, I'm in a very safe place, right here.'

Georgia could barely speak, she was so upset. 'Darling, Bridget is dead and Kasey and Alice are both still missing. Someone is clearly targeting girls your age. Why them? What's going on?'

Zoe's eyes began filling with tears as she continued to process the information. Ellen hugged her to give what comfort she could and just listened as mother and daughter tried to come to terms with the news. Five minutes of emotional turmoil passed before some composure returned to the conversation. Ellen spoke first.

'Look, you need to put your heads together and think what is different about these girls that a person might want to harm them. Zoe, you know three of the girls. Any ideas what might be happening?'

'No,' said a still teary Zoe. 'They're just like me, finished school and planning a career. Bridget and Alice were both going to university and Kasey had started an apprenticeship as a hairdresser. I can't think why anyone would want to hurt them.'

After a short pause Zoe spoke again: 'They were all very attractive. Perhaps someone couldn't take no for an answer.'

'That's a good thought,' Ellen said. 'Can you recall if they had the same boyfriend at school, or someone you noticed was interested in them?'

'I'll need to think about it,' Zoe said, sniffling. For the next ten minutes they threw possibilities around. Ellen eventually left mother and daughter to talk. Grizzlepuss was hungry and becoming impatient, wrapping his deep red bushy tail seductively around her legs and meowing loudly.

'You're a very chatty cat. Come on, boy; let's get you some tucker.'

20

Shards of sunlight and the long shadows they produced signalled the end of another hot Melbourne day. Margaret Grant leaned over Zoe's lab bench to closely observe her bat dissection technique. The group needed to understand bat anatomy fully before they could begin work as qualified researchers.

'Good job, Zoe; you have great dexterity, most impressive.'

Zoe's anxiety around the bats had lessened over the last month and, surprisingly, she had even started to warm to the little mammals. She was not keen that they had to kill twenty-five bats for today's dissection lesson. However, Maggie (as Margaret had asked her group to call her) had reassured them that the colony needed to be culled, because the artificial environment didn't contain any natural predators.

It was Friday afternoon and the usual gathering would be underway in less than an hour. Just as Vaughn Lambert had predicted, these sessions had proved most interesting. Each week, one group member would present key aspects of their team's work to the others. Zoe had quite taken to drinking alcohol, in moderation, and enjoyed a few glasses of wine with canapés each Friday. There was nothing cheap about AMDAT.

Zoe photographed the final stages of the dissection process for her lab report and then began to clean up.

'How are you settling into life in Australia?' Maggie asked.

'Surprisingly, very well. The people are friendly; I've made new friends here and at uni. Kobi seems really nice and we have lots in common.'

'How are you holding up with the death of your friend Bridget and two of your other former schoolmates still missing? It must be very stressful. I'm sure your mother is pleased you're in Melbourne, out of harm's way.'

'Yes … it has been a stressful few weeks and Mom is very glad I'm in Melbourne. I attended Bridget's memorial service via holo-conference, thanks to AMDAT letting me use their facilities. That was very kind. I couldn't have afforded the money or time to travel home.'

'That was the least we could do, Zoe; you're part of the AMDAT family now.'

'We haven't had any news of Kasey and Alice as yet, so we remain hopeful. But it's been nearly a month.'

'Well, let's not give up hope just yet. Throwing yourself into your work is probably the best distraction.'

'I guess. Keeping busy is helping me, and no other girls have gone missing, so that's something. There, my lab work is completed for another week,' Zoe said with satisfaction. She carefully wrapped up the blood-soaked bat remains and placed them in the contaminated-waste incineration bin. She just needed to throw her outer gear into the laundry chute before hitting the shower block.

'I think you're handling the stress remarkably, considering you've only been in the country for a few weeks. Try to stay positive; that's all you can do at this stage. Run along now and enjoy the gathering. Have a great weekend and I'll see you on Monday.'

'Cheers, Maggie, and thanks.'

Zoe arrived at the meeting just as Sarah began reading her group report. Strands of her long blonde hair fell loosely on the lectern as she spoke clearly and confidently with an unmistakable Australian twang.

'Human embryonic enhancement is very controversial. You're no doubt aware that a protest group has been camped at the front of the building for weeks. Despite the ethical and moral issues, our group have begun working on gene-editing exercises using mouse embryos and we intend to use human ones in the near future.'

Utilising digital film, Sarah went on to describe the latest gene-editing software.

'CRISPR, or Clustered Regularly Interspaced Short Palindromic Repeats, is the adaptive immune system that bacteria use to protect themselves from viral attack. It is the means by which bacteria detect viral DNA, seek it out and destroy it. Bacterial cells achieve this via the protein CAS-9 seek-and-destroy function. When CAS-9 finds the virus in the bacterial DNA, it chops it out, precisely like a pair of scissors. The cells repair themselves but leave a calling card that automatically recognises and destroys the virus in the future. Using this new edition of CRISPR software we can now easily and cheaply copy what bacteria do naturally. Our ancestors used to write books in longhand—word by word. If they made a mistake, they painted over it with white paint or wrote everything out again. CRISPR software is similar to the invention of word processing. Just as we can now cut and correct a word in a document, so we can now cut and correct errors in human DNA. We have a software program that can recognise a particular DNA sequence, cut to delete the sequence, then manipulate the repair to suit the end goal. It's that simple.

'Monkey, mouse and bat DNA have all been successfully used in CRISPR experiments. A limited amount of human embryonic research has been undertaken for quite some time. Global conversations continue, but currently the World Health Organization has stipulated that all embryos used for experimentation must be destroyed—hence the controversy. Personally, I'm glad they are destroyed. I wouldn't want to meet a tall six-armed man with bionic vision, a swag full of weapons and a bad attitude.'

The audience laughed.

'AMDAT are asking for female student volunteers to donate two fertility cycles of their own ova towards our research project. As a reward, AMDAT will screen and store, for free, fifty per cent of your best ova and only use the lower-quality ones for research. Screening of your ova will also enable you to discover more about your DNA and any potential genetic abnormalities. I've already signed up and commenced the injections to control my ovulation cycle. It's really quite exciting and great that I don't have to pay the usual harvesting and storage fees, which can be as much as thirty thousand dollars. Please give careful consideration to this request and let me or anyone in our team know if you decide to proceed.'

Sarah's impressive presentation concluded. The students gave her a hearty round of applause and the noise level increased as everyone went back to drinking and socialising.

Zoe was chatting and drinking with her new friend Kobi. As usual, Kobi was dressed in colourful vintage clothing that complemented her figure. With deep blue eyes, olive complexion and waist-length black hair streaked with silver, she stood out from the crowd. A kind and confident girl with strong opinions which she aired frequently, Kobi had sensed that the young American needed a friend. By the end of the first week the two girls had gravitated to each other and a solid bond had begun to form.

'Donating ova for experimentation is not a decision to be taken lightly,' Zoe said to Kobi.

'I agree. I'm not keen on any form of unnecessary hormone therapy, either,' Kobi replied. 'We're both young, so there's no rush to harvest and freeze our eggs. I'll freeze mine when I'm twenty-five but not before.'

'Why twenty-five?' Zoe asked.

'Well, I'll be old by then,' Kobi replied.

Zoe laughed.

Kobi and Zoe continued to discuss ovum donation as they sipped champagne. Neither noticed Vaughn moving towards them. Suddenly

Zoe sensed someone standing next to her. Vaughn was standing so close she felt quite uncomfortable. His aftershave smelt strong and not that pleasant. Much too spicy.

'You would have beautiful eggs, Zoe,' he whispered in her ear. 'You ought to seriously consider this generous offer.'

She felt his hot breath condensing on her neck and her skin began to crawl. He also smelt strongly of alcohol and, with her personal space invaded, she replied, 'Yes, I will,' without much consideration. Anything to make him move away.

'Can I get you another champagne?' he asked.

'Yes ... Thanks.'

Sarah came over to join them, although Zoe felt it was Vaughn that Sarah really wanted to be near. No matter, it made him move his attention away from her at least.

'Excellent report, Sarah; you seem to be enjoying your research,' Vaughn said with a smile.

'I'm enjoying the work very much, Professor; I'm glad the report met with your approval.'

Vaughn moved in closer to Sarah and lowered his voice, although Zoe and Kobi could still hear their conversation. 'Care to have dinner with me again tonight?'

'That would be great,' Sarah replied.

'I'll send my car around at, say, seven?'

'Great, thanks.'

Vaughn then left to get Zoe's drink.

Sarah turned her attention back to Zoe and Kobi. 'How are those bats going, girls? I think you're so brave, working with infected animals.'

'Not really, we take every precaution to ensure our safety,' Kobi said.

'Well, I couldn't do it.'

'Sarah, do you think it's a good idea to mix socially with Professor Lambert?' Zoe asked.

Sarah gave a scoffing laugh. 'Mix with Vaughn socially? I've already fucked him, darling. You're so naive, you little New Jersey princess; you have much to learn. If you want to get ahead, Zoe, you have to use all your assets and I don't just mean those big brains inside that pretty head.'

'What if you were to get pregnant?'

Sarah stared at Zoe with a perplexed expression. 'Haven't you heard of contraception, Miss Priss? You're more naive than I thought. I have absolutely no intention of getting pregnant but, even if I did, who cares? Vaughn is worth millions; I'd never have to work again.' She tossed her long blonde locks, stared incredulously at Zoe with her vibrant blue eyes, shook her head in disbelief and walked off.

Well, my first instincts about Sarah were right, thought Zoe. *She is very nosey, and forward, and I can now add bitchy to that list.*

Sensing Zoe was hurt, Kobi offered some advice to her new friend: 'Girls like Sarah aren't worth worrying about, Zoe. They're selfish and don't care who they trample on to get ahead. Don't give her a second thought.'

'Hi, girls.'

They turned to see their research teammates Oliver, Charlie and Felix. The five were fast becoming good friends, although Zoe seemed oblivious to the fact that Oliver and Felix both found her attractive and constantly competed for her attention.

Vaughn returned and handed Zoe her champagne. He deliberately kept hold of the glass, forcing their fingers to touch, lingered a moment, looked directly into her eyes, then smiled and walked away. She thought he was rather handsome, but he was old enough to be her father and that made his attentions quite creepy. Sarah was welcome to him.

'Need to watch that one, Zoe; I think he has the hots for you,' Oliver said. 'Rumour is he sleeps with the best-looking women in every year group, but never makes any type of commitment.'

'Nice to know you think I'm one of the best-looking women,' Zoe replied.

Oliver blushed.

Sensing his embarrassment, Zoe put her hand on his shoulder. 'Thanks for looking out for me, Ollie, but he's clearly old enough to be my father.' Nevertheless, the attention of such a powerful man had heightened her curiosity.

Charlie offered his opinion: 'Well, I don't trust him. In fact, there's a great deal about AMDAT that doesn't make sense. With predators like Lambert, it can't be quite the squeaky-clean corporation everyone wants us to believe.'

'I agree,' said Oliver. 'Did anyone else notice that at the rear of the bat atrium there's a well-concealed set of locked steel doors? Barely visible.'

'No, I didn't see them. They're probably just fire exit doors' said Zoe. 'Why don't you ask Maggie what they are for and where they lead?'

'Fire doors wouldn't be locked Zoe and I shouldn't have been back there, so I'm hardly going to ask Maggie, am I? The doors are well disguised behind a curtain the exact same colour as the wall. I came across them when I was looking for the storeroom. I expected to find a great view, but it was a set of doors, not a window.'

'*Oh!!!!* … Ollie has found a mysterious secret bat door,' Charlie said with a grin.

'Could it be where Batman and Robin live?' Felix asked, feigning surprise.

'Maybe you two need to cut down on the comics,' Kobi said, shaking her head.

'You are both being mean,' Zoe replied, not wanting Oliver to feel put down. 'Show me where it is later, Ollie. I'd like to see it for myself.'

21

Ellen was on her final day off and was due back on shift that evening. She had spent the day researching her family history while attempting to manage the now unrelenting nausea naturally, with ginger and lemon tea. With the help of her father she had traced the Hancocks' lineage from New Jersey all the way back to the small village of Eyam in Derbyshire. It appeared that some of their ancestors did sail to Jersey on the *Kent* in 1677.

Harold had found a brief reference to a Henry Hancock in the plague records of a local parish. Apparently, young Henry had visited Eyam with his mother and older brother, just prior to leaving on the *Kent*. He was only ten years old at the time.

Harold's recent inheritance of a cottage in Eyam came about when an international company specialising in the location of obscure beneficiaries had made contact with him. They offered to reveal the details of their search and requested a fee of one hundred US dollars. Harold thought it was a scam. Four months later his curiosity became overwhelming and, scam or not, he paid up.

Much to his surprise, the details of the inheritance were forthcoming. A distant cousin with no other living relatives had died and left him her property. Harold was reluctant to leave Beatrice, but James assured him he could handle things. Ellen also encouraged her dad to take a deserved break. That was eight months ago, and he was now thoroughly enjoying living in his cosy cottage. Whenever the weather was fine, he hiked in the stunning hills and dales, collecting and cataloguing plants. When the weather was poor (as it frequently was in England) he enjoyed reading by the open fire. Working with Ellen to map the Hancock family tree was providing great satisfaction to them both.

Patrick had been calling Ellen's apartment for the last two hours and she hadn't accepted his calls. The noise was distracting Rob.

He was on a rostered day off and trying unsuccessfully to watch a movie on the big screen. Ellen was becoming increasingly annoyed with them both: Rob for urging her to take the call and Patrick for his persistence. Ellen hadn't made up her mind if she was going to keep the baby and she didn't want the complication of Patrick finding out. The vid-link beeped again and this time he left a message. He sounded rather desperate, which for Patrick was unusual. He wasn't easily ruffled.

'Ellen, it's obvious that you're avoiding me. I need to speak with you. Not about "us", not that there is an "us". I need to ask you some questions about the fertility clinic you worked at as a med student. It was razed to the ground overnight and all electronic patient records have been destroyed. Seems no-one backed up the files. The police believe they have found a link between all five girls and I have Bridget Patterson's autopsy report. Please call.'

'Autopsy report—that sounds confidential. Why is he involving you?' Rob asked.

'He must think I can assist with the investigation because of my medical knowledge. He isn't a gossip. We've known each other for years and he trusts me to be discreet.'

Nosy sod, Ellen thought. *Rob is always getting calls at odd hours and I never stick my nose into his business.* She decided to call Patrick back from her room to give them some privacy.

Patrick's vid-link screen only beeped once before he picked up.

'At last,' he said with a sigh of relief. 'What took you so long?'

'I'm a busy person, Patrick. Can you activate your camera, please?' she said rather frostily.

'I can't ... it's ... errr ... broken. I spilt wine on it last night. Although I wish I could see your beautiful face as well.'

Ignoring the last comment, Ellen continued, 'How do you spill wine on a wall camera? On second thoughts, never mind. I really don't need to know. What do you need to speak to me about that's so urgent?'

'Are you alone? Are you sure no-one is listening?' he asked.

Ellen rose from her bed and peered down the hall, then closed and locked the door. 'I'm in my bedroom. Door's locked. Why all the cloak and dagger?'

Patrick continued, 'The investigation has reached a dead end. I think you just might be able to help.'

'Have you solved the young woman's murder yet?' Ellen enquired.

'It wasn't a murder.'

'Really? Then what do police think happened to her?'

'A blood clot blocked a major artery.'

'She was very young. Did she have a pre-existing medical condition, or did something else occur?'

'Medical condition. She had a blood-clotting disorder. Coroner's report states that her right carotid artery was completely blocked. She was taking the contraceptive pill. Apparently the pill can cause the formation of blood clots.

'That's correct' Ellen agreed. 'A small percentage of women form clots when taking hormone therapy like the pill. The clots can be fatal if they block a major artery in the lungs, heart or brain. Then Bridget wasn't murdered after all?'

'No. The case is all but closed.'

'Any trace of the other four girls?'

'No trace whatsoever. All leads so far have been dead ends.'

'What is the common link you mentioned in your message?'

'It appears that all five girls were conceived by mothers who underwent fertility treatment at the clinic you worked in as a student.'

'Really? That's an interesting coincidence.'

'I don't believe in coincidences, but it is a solid connection and the best lead we have so far,' Patrick continued.

'Well, I haven't worked there for years. I don't see how I could possibly help?'

'Well, the four missing women were all conceived during the year you worked at the clinic.'

'No way … well now, I have to agree with you that it's too much to be just a coincidence.' Ellen paused to think for a moment and then continued, 'I still fail to see what value I can add to this situation.'

'Well, for starters, you have a very good memory and Zoe Ashmore was born via IVF later that same year, so maybe you can remember some of the details of the others.'

'That's right, she was, but it's a very long time ago, Patrick.'

'Are you sure you can't remember anything? The missing girls and Zoe were all part of the controversial cytoplasmic transfer experiments that were banned in 2002, then recommenced by Doctor Dawson decades later without approval.'

'Ahhh, yes. You're right. I do remember those original experiments. There were only seventeen babies born using that technique in New Jersey in the late 1990s, and another fifty or so were born at fertility clinics around the world. In 2002 the Food and Drug Administration withdrew funding and banned the procedure. The babies all ended up with mitochondria from two different women in their genetic code. Years later, Doctor Dawson disregarded the ban and undertook more cytoplasmic transfers. Zoe was conceived via this method. She also has two types of mitochondria in her genetic code.'

'Good; you're remembering. I thought that you would.'

'What specifically do you want me to try to recall?'

'Well, in order for you to help me find a way out of this puzzle, I need you to cast your mind back to that summer when you worked at that clinic and think like Houdini.'

Houdini. She hadn't heard that word in years. It was the secret code word that Patrick used to warn her if something was wrong. It signalled that he was in some sort of trouble from which he needed to extract himself like a magician. Patrick hadn't used the code word since they were teenagers, and even then it had only been for insignificant things like his mother loitering near his bedroom when they were chatting on their mobiles. They weren't kids anymore, so using it now meant that something was really wrong—and probably not insignificant. The spilt wine on the camera hadn't sounded plausible. Patrick sounded like he was carefully choosing his words. Why had he deliberately used their old secret code word now? Was he trying to alert her? Perhaps someone was with him. Perhaps he was under duress. Trapped. That would explain his continual calling, not like him at all. She decided to stay calm and listen to what else he had to say.

'Go on,' she said. 'Explain to me exactly how you think I can help?'

'Correct me if I'm wrong, but Doctor Dawson ran the fertility clinic until he was forced to retire after being exposed for undertaking unauthorised cytoplasmic transfers. Once the scandal broke, his medical licence was suspended and his clinic sold. He retired a broken man and never worked again. He died a few years back.'

'That's all correct, although I believe the clinic was purchased and reopened within six months. There's a frozen ova and sperm storage facility attached to that practice that's quite a lucrative business.'

'Can you recall if Doctor Dawson kept any other records aside from the electronic database at the clinic? Any hard-copy patient files perhaps? I recall your job that summer consisted mainly of front reception and managing patient records.'

'It did, but can't you ask Mrs Jarvis, his old receptionist? She was with him for thirty years.'

'No, she died in a traffic accident a week ago.'

'That's terrible. What happened?'

'A hit and run on a crosswalk. They haven't tracked the car down as yet. Number plates had been oven-baked black, so the registration wasn't captured on the nearby CCTV.'

'What an awful way to die,' Ellen said with genuine concern. 'Well, she obviously can't help you.' She paused to think for a moment. 'What about his practice nurse at the time? Nina. Now what was her surname? Kay. That's it: Nina Kay?'

'Died of AV64 two months ago.'

'What? I didn't know that there had been a fresh outbreak in Newark?'

'It's a bit of a mystery, but she must have been in contact with someone who was infectious. The authorities are currently looking into her movements over the last six months but haven't as yet pinned down the infection source.'

'That's really worrying,' Ellen commented.

'I know, but I try not to dwell on outbreaks; it's just too depressing. So,' he said, giving an audible sigh and pausing for a brief moment. 'I'm afraid, Miss Houdini, you're the only one left that might have some knowledge about any additional hard-copy files.'

There was the code word again. Ellen paused to think. She remembered that Doctor Dawson did keep a large personal ledger. It was unusual for a doctor to keep records in that format and to take them home each day. The ledger was set out like a birthday book rather than a diary that only lasts a year. In it, Doctor Dawson kept a record of each live birth written in code. He used letters and numbers to represent the parents, donors and subsequent children—not unlike the coding still used today—so he was adamant it wasn't a problem taking it home, as no-one else could interpret it.

Towards the end of his career, he sent personalised birthday cards to the children he had helped create. His wife helped him to organise and send all the cards on time. With her assistance he rarely missed a birthday. Zoe treasured her cards. She kept them in an album and had brought them with her to Melbourne. In many ways Doctor Dawson must have felt like a father figure to these children.

Intuition told Ellen something was wrong. Patrick had used Houdini not once but twice, as if he was making sure she heard and recalled the meaning of the word. Until she could see Patrick's face and make sure he was okay, she was not telling him this important piece of information. She thought of a way to determine if he was in trouble. She would wait until the conversation was winding up, then test him with some false info that only he would detect. She needed to know one way or the other. For now, at least, she decided to withhold her knowledge about the patient ledger. She proceeded with a lie.

'Well, he did keep some hard-copy patient records, but these were all converted to digital computer records when I was there. In fact, I helped to convert them and to shred all the paper files. If the computer and backup systems are gone then the information is lost. I'm absolutely certain that, in this case, the clinic was fully converted to digital patient-record keeping.'

'Well, the records must be all gone, then. Can you let me know if you remember any specific names or other information?'

'Yes, I will, but I have such a poor memory when it comes to names.' She was lying; her memory was excellent.

'Thanks, anyway, for confirming what I already suspected. I thought it was a long shot.'

'Patrick, you said the fertility clinic is destroyed. What about the separate building next door where the freeze chambers are housed?'

'Gone, all gone. Everything was destroyed. A gas explosion appears to be the cause of the fire. It spread to the houses on both sides. Sparks ignited several gas lines and blew the place sky high. There's nothing left.'

This news shocked Ellen. She momentarily lost her breath then gasped loudly. If the freeze chambers were destroyed, then so were her stored ova. Patrick heard the gasp.

'Are you all right, Ellen?'

'I had my ova stored at that facility.'

'Oh.'

'It's not just me,' she continued. 'There will be many others whose dreams are now completely shattered. It's a tragedy.'

Her hands instinctively moved towards her stomach. It seemed strange that just as all her ova were destroyed, she found herself pregnant at thirty-eight. Patrick was a pretty special man. Perhaps this baby was simply meant to be?

'Patrick, I'm really sorry to cut you short, but Miss Houdini really needs to get ready for work. It has been nice hearing from you. Please give my regards to your brother. I haven't seen him in years.'

'I'll pass on your greeting to him and thanks for your help; I really appreciate it.'

Patrick didn't have a brother. His answer showed that he knew she had worked it out. He was not alone, and he was in trouble.

'Sorry I can't remember anything that might help, but it has been nineteen years. Take care and bye for now.' Ellen deactivated the screen.

22

Patrick was secured to a dining chair with four electronic devices, one on each ankle and one on each wrist. His left eye was swollen, his lip split and bloodied. He looked up at the two masked women and wondered how the hell he was going to extract himself from his current situation.

'Good work, Detective,' said one of his captors.

'That wasn't so hard, now, was it?' said the other. 'You did a good job. Let's just hope, for your sake, that your love interest is telling the truth.'

'She will be. Ellen is one of those highly ethical people. I doubt she could lie even if she wanted to. Can I please have some water?'

The second female picked up a mug of water and threw it in his face.

Bitch.

He studied the two masked women carefully. He needed to be able to recall as much detail as possible if he stood any chance of a future arrest.

They were around the same height—quite short, he guessed five feet. Their accents were Australian, yet their thick smooth black hair seemed Asian. They were both slender. The skin visible on the arms of one was pale. No visible freckles or age spots. He could see a tattoo, but only about ten centimetres of it, not enough to determine the design. It was a mix of maroon, black and vibrant blue.

'We're going to leave you now, but we will be watching your every move. Stay away from Doctor Hancock, otherwise we will be forced to eliminate her. Stop digging into the clinic fire. Wind up the investigation as soon as possible,' said the tattooed woman.

She reached over and activated all four devices. Digital clock faces appeared and a countdown commenced.

'If you stay completely still, the devices on your arms and legs will automatically deactivate and release you in an hour's time. If you tamper with them, they will start heating to two hundred degrees Celsius and cause extensive burns. You'll probably need your hands and feet amputated—if you survive the trauma, that is. Have I made myself perfectly clear?'

'Crystal,' he answered.

She wound strong gaffer tape tightly across his mouth and twice round his head. The two women then went into his kitchen.

He heard at least two other voices, male. That must have been how he was overpowered. The women wouldn't have been able to handle him on their own. He didn't recall much—just being grabbed from behind, then a strong smell of chloroform as he drifted into unconsciousness. They must have entered during the night and were waiting inside as he went naked to the bathroom the next morning. He hadn't stood a chance.

His only hope was Ellen. He knew she had realised something was wrong—but what could she do from the other side of the world? He badly needed a piss. He'd been secured for hours already. He decided he couldn't hang on any longer, so he just let it go. What a relief. He would just have to sit there and hope that the bitches were telling the truth about the devices. He had never seen anything like them before. Highly sophisticated. Whoever was behind this clinic fire meant business—though what business he had no idea.

Ellen sat on her bed wondering how she could help Patrick from the other side of the world. What should she do? Call the Newark Police Department from Melbourne? They would think she was a complete nut. She could call Georgia, but she would probably faint if she asked her to help. *Think Ellen; come on, think.*

Frustratingly, nothing inventive came to mind. It would have to be Georgia, but she couldn't risk calling her from home; her vid-link might be bugged. She would go into work right now and call Georgia before her shift started. She jumped up, grabbed her coat and bag and ran into the street to hail a cab.

Ellen went directly to one of the Health Hub communications labs and dialled Georgia's number. She answered straight away—*thought she would, with Zoe being in Melbourne.*

'Hi, Ellen; is Zoe okay?'

'Nothing wrong with Zoe, but I do need your help. I think Patrick is in some sort of trouble. I just need you to listen.' She explained everything she knew.

'But if he's in trouble and I go around there or call the police then I might do more harm than good.'

'I agree, so you need to pretend to be doing something else.' Ellen paused momentarily to think. Georgia could almost hear the cogs in her brain turning. 'I know. You can pretend to be selling raffle tickets.'

Ellen suddenly felt hopeful that Georgia could safely find out what was going on at Patrick's home. At least they were now developing an action plan, not sitting around biting their nails. Ellen continued to direct Georgia how to proceed.

'Take a basket of goodies and park around the corner from his home. Approach his house on foot—it's the first one on that strip. Even if they are watching, they won't know that you haven't been to any other houses.'

'Who are *they*?'

'I don't know who *they* are,' said Ellen, raising her voice in a frustrated manner. 'Just suss out Patrick's house. If no-one answers at the front, try the side and then the back. Look in the windows as you go. See what cars are in the driveway. Use that covert camera gear you have for creative film work.'

'Slow down, Ellen; you're talking so fast I can't think,' Georgia pleaded.

Ellen didn't have time to waste making Georgia feel more comfortable, and only slightly modified the rate of her speech. Patrick's life might be at stake, after all.

'Can you set the micro-camera up to stream live to my mobile?' she asked.

'Yes, that's the easy bit, but I can't go around there. I'm just too scared,' Georgia said as her teeth began to chatter—from fear rather than cold.

'Look,' Ellen paused then began pleading her case very slowly and calmly. 'Zoe might be next. She was born after IVF at the same clinic in the same time period—so clearly there's a link. You don't want anything to happen to her, do you?' Ellen's words and sentences suddenly accelerated as if she had taken some pep pills. 'You just need to do it. Go right now, Georgia. Stop thinking about how scared you are. Take an anti-anxiety pill if need be and just get right on over there,' she demanded, flicking her right hand in the air.

For the first time since she left America, Ellen felt incredibly frustrated that she was not in Newark so she could deal with this issue personally. Maybe Patrick was more important to her than she realised. The thought of Patrick not being there for her anymore made her feel quite panicky. She increased the pressure on her friend.

'Georgia, I need to tell you something. I'm pregnant with Patrick's child. You need to help him for all our sakes.'

'You're pregnant, Ellen?' she replied, somewhat taken aback. 'Why didn't you tell me?

'Because I'm not sure if I'm going to keep the baby, Georgia, and I knew you'd make a fuss, all right?'

'Oh, you have to keep the baby, Ellen. You can't seriously be considering killing an innocent child.'

'I knew you'd make a fuss and I was right, wasn't I? Look, can we discuss this later. If you don't help Patrick and something bad happens to him, the baby won't have a father anyway, will it?'

Silence reigned for a few seconds as Georgia processed the torrent of information and made a decision.

'Okay, okay. I'll do it for my Zoe and you and Patrick's baby. I'll have a shot of sherry. That should be enough; I need a clear head. The camera gear is ready to go; I used it only last week. I'll activate it to live stream to your mobile as soon as I can. Just give me five minutes to get it ready.'

Ellen's words slowed again, as she reassured Georgia. 'Good girl. That's the spirit. I know you can do this. Just think of Zoe and don't think of what might happen. I'll watch and call the Newark Police from here if things start to go pear shaped.'

Georgia grabbed her large cane shopping basket and crammed it with packaged goods, including wine, chocolates, biscuits, a couple of ornaments and a stuffed toy. She put on her coat and attached the camera brooch to her lapel, before jumping into her vintage Mini.

Patrick lived only three blocks away. She would approach the house from Smith Street and park around the corner. Once parked, she activated the camera to live stream to Ellen's mobile and checked the connection with her friend. Ellen gave her the thumbs up.

I must be fucking bonkers, Georgia thought as she scurried down the sidewalk, looking all around her as if she was a paranoid raccoon.

There was nothing unusual happening in the street. In fact, the whole street was exceptionally quiet. Patrick's car was parked in his driveway. Not unexpected. She approached his front door and knocked a couple of times. She could feel her heart pounding in her chest and thought her blood pressure must be way up, as her head was thumping and her cheeks were burning hot.

No-one answered the front door. She walked slowly down the side garden path, making sure she captured the interior of each room with the camera. She hesitated for a moment before knocking even more loudly on the side entrance door.

No answer.

By now she was breathing so hard and fast that her fingers started to feel numb and tingly. She was hyperventilating and blowing off too much carbon dioxide. Ellen had taught her that if she didn't have a paper bag to breathe into, she should hold her breath and the tingling would stop.

Georgia began to hold her breath, only taking shallow breaths when her brain forced her to. The tingling subsided. It was working. She moved to the rear of the house and knocked on the back door. Again there was no response. If anyone was inside, they clearly had no intention of acknowledging her presence.

She continued to peer into the rooms, filming as she went. When she looked into the lounge room, she saw Patrick. He was gagged and tied to a chair. Georgia dropped to the ground and crouched there, terrified. He had blood on his face. For Christ's sake, what had she got herself in to?

Ellen saw Patrick as well but now, due to Georgia's slumping to the ground, all she could see was foliage from the bush where she was hiding. Georgia sat still and just listened. Her heart was beating rapidly and her increased breathing rate was again producing tingling. There was no sound coming from within.

After a few minutes she composed herself, stood up tentatively and peered through the window at Patrick. Their eyes met and Patrick motioned her, the best way he could, with his head and eyes that it was safe to enter. She tried to open all three doors. They were all locked. None of the windows were unlatched. Finally, she picked up a large white rock from the succulent garden, closed her eyes, turned her head away, then smashed the laundry window and unlocked the back door.

Ellen was frantically observing the action. She was stunned, having never expected such a scene. Georgia moved swiftly across the room to Patrick and reached to remove his restraints. Then she spotted one of the digital screens counting down with thirty minutes and ten seconds remaining. Patrick eyes grew wide. He shook his head and mumbled as loudly as he could from under the gaffer tape until she backed away.

Reaching to remove the gaffer tape he nodded his approval. The tape was stuck fast in his hair and she had to use scissors to cut it out.

'Thanks, Georgia; now move over there away from me. Can you get me a drink of water, please? On second thought, make it a scotch; might be my last.'

'I'll have one as well,' Georgia replied. 'What's that smell?' she said, sniffing the air. Then she noticed his wet pants and the puddle on the floor. 'Oh.'

'I couldn't hang on, sorry.'

'God, Patrick, what are those things attached to you?'

'Supposedly, they're only heating devices that won't activate if I keep still. That in mind, we won't take any risks. In twenty minutes, I want you to go outside and down the street. The last thing I need is for you to get hurt as well as me.'

Georgia was wringing her hands and then combing her fingers back through her hair. 'What do you want me to do? Shall I call the bomb squad or something?'

'It's okay, Georgia. I don't need you to do anything. Finish that scotch and have another. Pour me another one too, please.'

She continued to carefully pour the liquid into his mouth in small enough amounts to ensure he didn't jerk his body or cough. When his thirst was finally quenched, he continued.

'The reality is … I'm not sure who to trust. Tony is on leave. If the devices do deactivate, then we don't have to involve anyone just yet. If not, I'm going to detail what happened for you to tell Tony. Can you get a pad and pen from my study?'

'I won't need to write anything down, Patrick; I'm recording everything.'

'Are you now? Even better.' He was impressed. This was a big step for Georgia.

'Ellen is watching too. She planned the whole thing, called me from her work.'

Patrick smiled. 'She's clever as well as beautiful. I knew she would think of something. I think everything will be okay, Georgia; we just need to sit out the next twenty minutes. Can you bring Ellen up on my vid-link so I can talk to her?'

'You really love her, don't you?'

'Yep, I do, though it has never done me an ounce of good.'

Georgia didn't mention the baby. She wasn't sure if Patrick already knew or not, but it wasn't her place to tell him.

Georgia activated Patrick's screen. Ellen had brought Tex, the Hub security guard, into the room as a witness and explained everything. When she couldn't start her shift as planned, she knew he would cover for her by making it a security issue and placing a guard outside the communications room. Patrick looked terrible and both Ellen and Tex were stunned. They certainly didn't expect this outcome.

The four of them discussed possible scenarios for the clinic's destruction and what might have happened to the missing girls.

'If someone wanted the girls for a specific purpose, then they're probably still alive. Bridget's death was natural causes, after all,' Ellen said.

'It was and it wasn't,' answered Patrick.

'What do you mean?' she questioned.

'Well, I didn't tell you everything, because I didn't want those two fucking women to know how much I had really discovered.'

'Okay, well, tell me now.'

'Bridget's autopsy appeared to be completely normal. No sexual assault. No drug or alcohol usage. No trauma of any kind. The clot lodged in her carotid artery was definitely the cause of her death, but what is most puzzling was the state of her ovaries.'

'Why, what was abnormal about her ovaries?'

'They were completely shrivelled, like a woman who had gone through menopause.'

'Maybe she was born like that and no-one knew until now,' Georgia replied.

'That's what the coroner documented in his report, but it sounded suss to me. When I spoke to her mother, she said that Bridget had a normal menstrual cycle. When she had appendicitis last year, they scanned her lower body to finalise the diagnosis, as ovarian cysts cause similar pain. I've seen copies of the scans, Ellen. She had two very normal looking ovaries last year. In fact, she was midway through her menstrual cycle and about to ovulate. The scan clearly showed the swollen follicles. How does a young fertile woman become fully menopausal in a year? It's just not possible.'

'I don't know what to say, Patrick. It does sound implausible. I've never heard anything like it.' Ellen paused to think for a moment. 'Unless, somehow, all her ova had been harvested?'

'How and why would that happen?' Georgia asked.

'I don't know, but we might be on to something. You need hormone therapy to harvest ova, and if it was being administered to Bridget, then the clot might have been an unexpected side effect.'

'There are millions of women who would donate their ova for free. Why abduct someone just to harvest their ova?'

'You're presuming she didn't agree to the harvest procedure,' Ellen replied.

'A young woman with her future ahead of her surely wouldn't agree to the harvesting of all her ova,' Georgia added.

'Removing all the girl's ova might not have been the intended outcome.' Patrick added, 'We might never know what that poor girl did and didn't consent to.'

Ellen nodded then replied. 'Whatever has occurred, we do know that the coroner's report stating that Bridget was born with shrivelled ovaries is clearly wrong. Why didn't he check with her family doctor, or, even speak with her mother? It smacks of a cover-up, or outside interference—and just look at the lengths being taken in order to silence you, Patrick.'

'Or, it could just be plain incompetence,' added Georgia.

'Unlikely,' replied Patrick. 'I suspect someone intimidated the coroner to deliberately omit certain details from the autopsy report. Somehow, they discovered I was involved, hence the current situation.' Patrick glanced down at the device on his wrist. The countdown had reached five minutes.

'It's time for you to leave, Georgia.' He instructed her to go down the street and to keep filming in case the devices detonated. He told her that if he was killed to only talk to Tony Scallioni. 'Show him the film footage. Only Tony,' he stressed. 'Just say "Houdini"; he'll know what to do.'

'Okay', Georgia said with a puzzled expression. She shrugged her shoulders, kissed him on the forehead and wished him good luck. Then she left through the front door.

Ellen spoke up on hearing the word 'Houdini' for the third time in a matter of hours.

'"Houdini" reminds me that I have to tell you something that I held back when we spoke earlier.' She quickly explained about Doctor Dawson's clinical patient ledger. Patrick agreed this information was important and asked her to contact Tony Scallioni and give him the details if he couldn't.

Patrick then turned his attention to Ellen. He stared longingly at her for the next five seconds then spoke.

'I love you, Ellen. I've always loved you and I'll love you until the day my heart stops beating. Promise me that you'll think of me fondly and that you'll always look after yourself.'

Ellen's eyes pooled with tears.

'Patrick, don't be silly. You're not going anywhere.' She paused for a few seconds before continuing. 'I need to tell you something.'

'Well, you'd better make it quick.'

'I'm pregnant.'

'And you're telling me that now?'

'Yes, I'm telling you now.'

'Impeccable timing, Ellen.'

'I know, and I'm sorry. The baby *is* yours.'

'I presumed that, otherwise you wouldn't be telling me.' He felt happy and a bit pissed at the same time.

The countdown had now reached one minute.

'I love you too, Patrick; I just can't do anything until I know if I carry the Huntington's gene. The baby will also need testing if I'm found to be positive. Please forgive me for not telling you before now.'

'You have done nothing that needs my forgiveness. Just take care of yourself and look after our baby.'

The pooled tears began to trickle down Ellen's face. She had been trying to hold herself together and be strong for Patrick's sake but hadn't succeeded. She felt so incredibly guilty and frightened for what the future held. What if she and the baby both carried the Huntington's gene? What if Patrick died today?'

Ten seconds remained: *10 ... 9 ... 8 ... 7 ... 6 ... 5 ... 4 ... 3 ... 2 ... 1 ... 0*

The four devices stopped, unlatched and released Patrick. He let out a long sigh and then stood up, rubbing his wrists and smiling at them. Ellen and Tex both smiled back and started cheering. Suddenly Patrick heard a ticking noise coming from the kitchen. Fucking cruel bitches had planted a bomb to coincide with his release.

Georgia heard the blast before she saw the flames leaping metres into the air. She had called the fire brigade as she left and told them there was a fire at Patrick's address. Couldn't hurt, could it? If the devices didn't blow up, then it would be simply seen as a hoax call. If they did blow then the fire would be extinguished more swiftly. The crew arrived just seconds after the blast. The police and ambulance arrived a short time later. Georgia just stood there paralysed, too shocked to move.

In Melbourne Ellen and Tex saw Patrick's face change from elation to fear and then he turned and moved out of sight. They heard a loud noise. The vision on screen appeared to melt into a mix of black, yellow and red, a bit like old celluloid film when it catches alight. Then the connection failed. Tex and Ellen were speechless. She felt sick, numb and weak. The last thing she saw was Tex's face as she fainted.

Georgia had captured the explosion above the rooftops on her camera. She was now crying, shaking and pacing up and down the street. She just couldn't believe it had come to this. It didn't take long for the scene to be crawling with emergency vehicles and onlookers. The firefighters couldn't approach the house immediately; the heat was too severe. Patrick could never have survived.

It would take three hours to put out the flames. An accelerant had been used and the gas mains had blown. The intensity of the fire made her wonder if there would even be any remains left to find. She felt sick at the thought of the beautiful, kind, generous, caring man she was talking to only a few minutes ago being reduced to ash. She grabbed the bottle of medication from out of her handbag and downed two tablets.

The police were making their way through the milling crowd speaking to witnesses, trying to determine exactly what had happened. Georgia looked up to see a man and a woman pointing in her direction.

'That's her, officer. She had a large basket with her when she went around the back of the house and nothing when she came out the front door.' It was the neighbours who lived directly opposite Patrick.

A police officer headed towards her. She turned in the opposite direction and was attempting to shove her way through the dense crowd when he grabbed her arm.

'You had better come with me,' he said, and began reading Georgia her rights. She was by now so shocked and anxious, everything seemed to be moving in slow motion. It was unreal, like a bad dream. She was clearly dissociating. It happened when her anxiety became overwhelming. He placed the cuffs tightly on her wrists then held her head down as he shoved her into the back of the police vehicle.

At Newark Liberty International Airport, Gum Lin signed the declaration that the AMDAT cargo jet was only carrying frozen biological material that didn't pose any quarantine risk. The plane was owned by AMDAT and used to carry cargo between Melbourne and other destinations around the world. The pilot couldn't disembark. He basically lived on the plane for a three-month rotation. The plane only carried cargo, no passengers, so there was no need for the usual fourteen-day hold in Q precinct.

Gum and Susie waited by the edge of the road outside the airport perimeter until they observed the plane take off safely. Gum tapped on her computer for a couple of minutes then made a quick call to finalise a financial transfer. Finally, she checked the AMDAT database and confirmed that Patrick O'Connor's chip was no longer transmitting, before turning and kissing Susie passionately on the mouth. She needed a sexual release, always did after an incident. This, however, was very different. It was the first time she had used her skills to kill someone, a police officer no less, but a man—and they were all the same.

Gum had last seen her own father many years earlier. He had come home around midnight, drunk and in a foul mood. Her mother had placed his dinner on the table, yet by then the meal was overcooked and the rice clumped together. He had taken only one bite before hurling the plate of food at his wife's head. She successfully ducked as it splattered against the back wall where the five-year-old Gum stood watching. With teeth clenched he sauntered slowly and intimidatingly towards his wife and spat the remaining contents of his mouth in her face.

'What the fuck do you call this shit?' he yelled.

As the bashing began, her small-framed mother had no means of defence and Gum was too little to help. She tried to stop her father by hitting him on the ankles with her toy broom. He just swatted her away, as if she was a fly. It took only two blows and her mother lay quivering and bleeding on the kitchen floor.

He turned as if to leave and, for one brief moment, daughter's and mother's eyes met. Both were filled with the same sense of relief that the assault was almost over. However, on reaching the back door, he propped then turned. He pushed little Gum roughly to one side and approached her mother. One well-aimed kick to the head from his metal-toed boot and his wife breathed her last.

Gum never set eyes on her father again. She had received a letter from the prison that he had been taken by the pandemic and they were very sorry for her loss. Loss? Good riddance, more like it. Because of him she had spent years passing from one foster home to another. Years of abuse by foster brothers, foster fathers, carers and other supposed do-gooders. She complained. No-one listened. No-one cared. Nobody believed her. She was just seen as a little Asian troublemaker and moved on.

Killing the cop was in some ways like finally killing her father. As the mechanisms clicked open the detective must have felt the same relief that she and her mother had felt as her father had headed for the door, only to find that there was another bomb timed to match his release. The detective would have felt a sense of relief, then, on hearing the bomb—a hopeless realisation of what was to come. Just like she had done, as her mother's spinal cord was snapped and her world changed forever.

Vaughn and Daniel would not be pleased with this outcome. It was not the brief she had been given. She had gone too far this time and she knew it.

'I need to think of a way to ensure Daniel and Vaughn aren't blamed for my actions,' she said to Susie. 'Something that only gets released when I die.' Susie, Gum's partner in both life and crime nodded. Gum was satisfied with her plan, all she needed now was her extreme tension released. She couldn't wait until they returned home. She flipped back the leather seat of the black Mercedes sports car, pulled up Susie's jumper and sucked hard on her nipples. God, she smelt and tasted so good.

23

Oblivious to the events occurring on the other side of the world, Zoe was enjoying the usual Friday-evening bash. Charlie and Felix had dressed up as Batman and Robin to give their research group presentation and had everyone in stitches. Even Oliver, although he knew they were taking the piss out of him. Vaughn Lambert was preoccupied on his mobile at the back of the room and Sarah was particularly twitchy, glancing frequently in his direction. Probably the hormone therapy she was taking. They had warned it made some women moody.

Zoe had declined the offer of AMDAT ova harvesting and storage, preferring to take care of her own eggs, thank you very much. When Zoe told Ellen about the offer, she was surprised that AMDAT were banging an egg-harvesting drum.

Zoe had consumed about three glasses of wine when Oliver beckoned. By now she was quite tipsy. 'Come, I'll show you that door,' he said. Oliver slipped his hand into hers and gave her a warm smile. She looked up at him as they realised they felt the same way about each other. Feeling elated, she squeezed his hand tightly and went with him. They ran up two flights of stairs and down a long corridor. 'It's just over there,' he pointed. 'Wait here, I need to pee. Be back in a minute.'

Zoe walked towards the curtain and pulled it aside. Sure enough, it was a very well-concealed double metal door. There was no handle.

It was activated solely by a PIN pad on the wall. She tried a couple of combinations. Naturally, they didn't work. Suddenly a hand went across her eyes. Oliver being silly, she thought. She heard a combination being punched into the pad then the person pushed her inside. She started to feel frightened. If it wasn't Oliver who was it?

From the sound and motion, she realised it was a lift and it had been activated. In a few seconds the door opened, and Zoe found herself in a luxurious apartment.

'Welcome to my apartment, Miss Ashmore. I presume this was the destination you were after?'

She turned to see Vaughn Lambert.

'I think we should go back down to the meeting,' she said nervously.

'You obviously wanted to see what was up here, and now you have,' he continued.

Sensing her fear, he paused and immediately softened his tone to one as smooth and silky as liquid chocolate.

'Why don't you just relax, Zoe? You're a very beautiful young woman,' he said, moving in closer and running his fingers through her long dark locks. 'I specialise in making love to beautiful women.'

She stood motionless, paralysed, with shivers running down her spine. She was quite unsure how to respond to this man. Eventually, she found her voice.

'*Please* let me go back to the meeting.'

His impatience began to ooze out again, even as he tried hard to hide his frustration with her.

'You shouldn't have been snooping around my apartment lift entrance if you didn't want to come up here with me, should you?'

'I'm really sorry. Oliver and I just wanted to know where the concealed door led, that's all.'

'Ahh, young Oliver.' He paused. 'Haven't you and Oliver heard the saying "curiosity killed the cat"?' he said, lifting her chin with his index finger and forcing her to make eye contact with him. Sensing her fear, he once again softened his approach.

'Relax. Enjoy the view. It's one of the best in Melbourne. I do find you very attractive but I'm not going to hurt you, Zoe. Why would I? Loosen up, have another drink.'

He poured a glass of champagne and handed it to her. Although she felt glued to the spot, she knew she needed to keep calm. Zoe recalled the female detective who spoke at her college about unwanted sexual advances, after one of the students had been the victim of a date rape. The girl had sustained serious head injuries inflicted when she fought off her assailant. It had shocked the whole school community.

'Your main aim in any tricky sexual situation is to stay alive. If you can't safely extract yourself from the situation, staying alive is more important than anything. Non-consensual sex, although a terrible ordeal, won't kill you. An angry, pissed-off assailant might. Think before you act and make staying alive your top priority.' Zoe hadn't given any real thought to the meaning of this advice. She believed herself to be savvy enough to avoid a sexual predator, yet here she was. Zoe felt sure Vaughn wouldn't kill her, but he clearly wanted to bed her. Surely she wasn't going to find herself fighting for her life. Then again, what if that was where she was headed—should she fight, or should she just be compliant? Zoe found herself wishing she had examined alternatives before now, asked more questions, discussed the issue with her friends and family but … that moment had passed. She made the decision to try and talk her way out of this current dilemma. Hopefully, in this instance, that would be enough.

She sculled the drink and asked Vaughn again if they could go back to the meeting.

'In a few minutes,' he said, smiling. 'What's the rush? Just look at that *view*. Spectacular isn't it?'

Zoe walked over to the window and looked out across the city as if showing genuine interest. After a few moments she began to feel woozy. The drink must have been spiked. The room began to spin and her vision began to blur. The situation felt surreal, as if she was in a dream. She became unsteady on her feet and leaned against the glass.

I need to sit down, she thought as she began breathing heavily. Zoe staggered across the room towards the large white leather lounge, sat down abruptly, leaned to one side then slumped backwards.

Vaughn left her for five minutes until the drug took full effect, then lifted her onto his king-sized bed. He carefully began removing her clothing, kissing and licking her body as he exposed each part.

Hadn't he been very patient with her? Hadn't he been extra kind? Zoe was nothing but a little prick teaser. She had resisted his advances for weeks now and he could stand it no longer; he just had to have her. *A girl needs to learn that flirting has consequences.*

Anyway, with Rohypnol on board, she wouldn't remember much. He would use a condom then douche any traces of him off her body. He had done this before. She wasn't the first student to reject him. He would claim it was consensual. He hadn't lost a court case yet, and he wouldn't lose this one. For now, he just wanted to enjoy fucking this perfect body. He hadn't had a virgin in a long time. He was determined to enjoy her. The drug would make her compliant and that was all he needed.

Oliver had returned to the hallway to find Zoe gone. He waited, thinking she had perhaps gone to the toilet as well, but five minutes had now passed. She must have got cold feet. He decided to go back to the meeting. He scanned the room: she was definitely not there. Vaughn Lambert was also nowhere to be seen, and that raised Oliver's concerns even further.

Over the past few weeks Vaughn had made his intentions towards Zoe perfectly clear. Whenever Oliver broached the subject Zoe just passed Lambert off as a bad joke. Oliver really liked Zoe and today his feelings had been reciprocated. Where the hell was she?

He decided to ask Maggie for help. She seemed genuinely caring and was no doubt aware of Lambert's predatory behaviour. He couldn't think of anything else to do.

'Have you seen Zoe?' he asked her.

'A while ago, I saw her talking to Felix,' she replied, somewhat uninterested.

'I'm really worried about her. I went with her to check out the door behind the maroon curtain.'

'You mean the private lift door?'

'I guess. We didn't know that's what it was.'

Maggie's interest was suddenly sparked.

'I left her there and now she's gone.'

Maggie started to scan the room. She didn't say anything, but Oliver suspected she was looking for Lambert.

'I'll go and look for her. You stay here,' she said and pushed her drink into his hand. 'I'm sure she's fine.' She strode off while dialling a number on her mobile.

'I think Lambert has Zoe in his apartment. I'm on my way; meet me there.' Maggie took the flights of stairs two at a time and sprinted down the corridor. She pulled the curtain aside and punched in the code that summoned the lift to Lambert's apartment.

She arrived just in the nick of time. Zoe was lying naked on Vaughn's bed and he was standing over her, dressed only in his shirt, pulling on a condom.

'Stop, leave her alone.'

'Piss off, Maggie; mind your own business.'

'Come on, Zoe, get dressed. Let's go back to the meeting.' Zoe didn't respond. 'God, Vaughn, have you drugged her?'

'She's … just … *drunk.*'

'She's more than drunk; she's clearly drugged. Put your clothes back on. I'm not letting you rape her, you bastard.'

'Fuck off, Maggie. You don't tell me what to do.'

'Get dressed,' said a male voice. They both turned to see Daniel Grant standing in the doorway.

'What is this?' Vaughn asked with both hands open wide and palms faced upwards. 'You two have never cared about my sexual antics before. Why now?'

Maggie walked over and covered Zoe's naked body with a throw rug as Daniel continued.

'You know Zoe is special. That's why we've brought her here. I understand that her unavailability makes her even more sexually desirable to you, Vaughn, but you have to stay away from her. Do whatever you want to anyone else—but not Zoe.'

'I don't see how me having one good fuck can spoil our plans! She isn't going to agree to her eggs being harvested for research purposes anyway.'

'We know that would have been the easiest solution, but Maggie and I have another plan to gain her cooperation. Anyway, can we all stop talking? She's right here with us, even though she appears to be unconscious.'

Daniel continued, put his arm around his wife and lowered his voice to a whisper. 'Please don't push this one, Vaughn. You know I never interfere in your sex life, but this is different. We can't risk a scandal that might focus any media attention on Zoe. This little stunt of yours will be difficult enough for us to cover up.'

Vaughn was really pissed off. He was the brains behind AMDAT, after all, but Daniel's marriage to that ugly rich bitch had marginalised his status. Daniel saw himself as the boss, and now the two of them believed they had the right to control him. Daniel had it coming. He needed to knock him off his pedestal, but now wasn't the time. Vaughn would be covert and clever when he finally sought his revenge. He started putting his clothes back on and glared at them both before looking down at the unconscious teenager.

'Now what?' he said, staring at the sleeping Zoe. His penis was still hard and he felt highly frustrated.

'Go back to the meeting Vaughn. Maggie will stay with her and try to smooth things over.'

As Vaughn walked towards the lift, Daniel called out, 'Make sure everyone sees you.'

Zoe heard glimpses of conversations. People seemed to be arguing but she couldn't hold on to any of the information for very long. The jumble of words floated like bubbles in the air that burst and vanished before she could catch them. Where was she? She had felt her body being tugged and touched but felt too tired to open her eyes to see what was happening. Things then went quiet and she fell into a deep sleep.

'Put her clothes back on and I'll move her,' Daniel said, turning his gaze away from the girl.

Maggie began dressing Zoe but was having difficulty.

'Can you give me a hand here?' she asked.

'You're doing fine on your own,' he replied without looking up. Then he turned his back on them both and gave a dismissive wave in the air.

Why is he acting so weird? Maggie wondered, as she continued to struggle with the blouse buttons. Eventually Zoe was dressed, and Daniel carried her via the lift to their penthouse apartment. Maggie put her in one of the guest-room beds and sat next to her with a glass of wine and a good book. It was going to be a long night, but she was determined to stay by Zoe's side until she woke.

Oliver saw Lambert return to the meeting and grab a drink. He looked flushed and agitated. He went over to talk to him.

'Have you seen Zoe?' he asked.

'What's it to you if I have?' Vaughn replied frowning.

'Well—I'm her boyfriend,' Oliver blurted out.

'She didn't mention a boyfriend.' He looked Oliver up and down and then spoke. 'Anyway, Zoe seems like the type of girl who would prefer a man to a … *boy*!' Vaughn grinned at Oliver then walked off. *What a complete tosser,* thought Oliver.

By now the meeting was winding up. Several of the students including Felix and Charlie had already left. Oliver waited around for Maggie to return with Zoe but she didn't. He hoped that wasn't a bad sign. About ten minutes later his mobile buzzed. It was a text from Maggie:

Zoe is with me. She's very drunk and I've put her to bed in our guest room. She's completely fine. I'll get her to call you as soon as she's able. Have a good weekend. Cheers Maggie.

Oliver felt relieved. He didn't trust Lambert, but he did trust Maggie. She wouldn't be lying to him. He responded with simply: *Thanks.*

Oliver would just have to wait to speak with Zoe. Find out what happened and who was involved. Lambert was a powerful man with even more powerful friends. Oliver needed to have evidence of inappropriate behaviour before he took action. In the meantime, he would be more vigilant, and never give Lambert a chance to be alone with his Zoe.

Sarah had cheered up remarkably now Vaughn was by her side. He was being quite loud, clearly wanting everyone in the room to know where he was. *Fucking buffoon,* thought Oliver. After about fifteen minutes, Vaughn left in a fanfare of laughter with a now more cheery Sarah on his arm.

24

Now that Ellen had regained consciousness, Doctor Muriel Spencer was undertaking a quick body scan. Tex had called for medical assistance when Ellen fainted. He had tried to catch her, but she'd hit her head hard on one of the sharp corners of the stainless-steel bench. Once Muriel arrived, Tex left the room to give them privacy.

'I presume you know that you're pregnant?' Muriel asked as she concentrated on the screen, peering over the reading glasses balanced on the end of her nose.

'Yes,' she replied. 'I'm nearly four months. I know the exact date of conception.'

'Right,' said Muriel, raising her eyebrows.

Ellen suddenly remembered Patrick and the explosion and sat bolt upright. Her head immediately began to spin.

'Steady on,' Muriel said. 'I need to check you out; lie back down. You've had a serious bump as well as a nasty shock. Tex told me that you were talking to a friend when there was a fire at their home, and you fainted. It that correct?'

'I'm not exactly sure what happened. The screen melted and the connection failed. Where's my mobile? I need to find out if my friend is okay.'

'Your mobile's over there. I know you're anxious to check on your friend, but first I need to check you. I'll be as quick as I can with your assessment and then you can make that call.' Muriel scanned Ellen's chip data. 'Your blood glucose levels are a bit on the low side.'

'I forgot to have dinner. I came in early to call Georgia. I have a low glucose threshold, so that doesn't help.'

'Who's your obstetrician?'

'I haven't chosen one yet.'

'Mmmm, well, in that case, while I have you here, do you want me to do a more thorough ultrasound to see how you're progressing?'

'That would be good, but first I need to make that call.'

Ellen's mobile call to Georgia went straight to message bank. 'Damn!'

'No luck?' Muriel asked.

'No. Look, can you do something else for me? Can you test me for Huntington's?'

'Huntington's?' Muriel said as wrinkles formed on her forehead.

'My mother is in the late stages of Huntington's back home. I've never been tested. It's time I was. I have to decide what to do about my baby. If I'm positive I will need to have the baby tested too. I will abort if we're both positive.'

Muriel was more than just Ellen's colleague; she was also a friend. She felt that Ellen wasn't fully considering all the options. Had she even stopped to consider the perspective of her unborn child, or whether a short life could be better than none at all? Muriel decided to step over the doctor–patient boundary and speak her mind.

'That's a pretty drastic step to take, Ellen, and you have really left it a bit late to abort. Does it really matter if your child is positive for

Huntington's? They can still have forty years—or more—of good life rather than none. What if your mother had chosen to abort you? Would you have preferred that outcome?'

Ellen looked crushed and began to cry. Muriel realised that she had been rather blunt. 'Sorry, I'm getting a bit carried away. It's not really any of my business; your decision to make entirely. Let's just hope the test results are negative so that it doesn't come to that.'

Still crying and now shaking, Ellen tried to explain. The words and tears tumbled out rapidly in a cascade, as if someone had suddenly unlocked and opened a cupboard crammed full of the plans, fears and regrets of a lifetime.

'I had planned to only have kids using screened ova and IVF. But that plan is stuffed, as the clinic where my ova were stored has been destroyed. And now I'm already pregnant.' Ellen's sobbing increased and Muriel held her until her distress eased.

'Hey, let's not get ahead of ourselves; you're obviously quite fertile without any fertility intervention. I'll do the test, get the results and we can take it from there, okay, sweetie?'

'Okay,' Ellen said, still sniffling.

Muriel checked her out thoroughly. Everything seemed okay. Ellen watched as Patrick's child—their child—bounced around happily inside her womb. Because of her, he or she would never know their handsome, intelligent father. Why had it taken so long for her to realise that she loved Patrick? Why had she wasted her life avoiding commitment? Now that he was gone, she could admit it. *I love—or rather, loved—him,* she corrected herself. How could she have been so cruel, not telling him about their baby sooner? She had been uncaring and selfish and now she could never fix what she'd done. She began to cry again.

Muriel sent a tissue sample for DNA testing. She would know the results in a few weeks. There was only one lab left that tested for Huntington's and that was in Germany. The genetic disorder had now been eliminated in Australia via gene editing and IVF. Muriel advised Ellen to stay at the Health Hub overnight. As long as all her neurological observations remained stable, she would drop her home in the morning when her shift ended. Tex would sit with her overnight.

Due to the mild concussion Ellen had to stay awake. She switched the screen to TV mode and they settled in for a long night. The explosion at Detective O'Connor's house was already on the World News. The authorities said it was believed to be a deliberately lit fire that caused a large gas explosion. Tex and Ellen knew that wasn't what had happened. The fire was so severe that the search for his remains could not begin. Then they were both shocked to see a close-up of the prime suspect, Georgia, being manhandled into the back of a police car.

Ellen's mobile began ringing and she answered it, hoping it was Georgia. It turned out, however, to be Rob calling to let her know that Zoe would be spending the night at AMDAT. Her research team leader, Margaret Grant, had left Ellen a message to make sure she didn't worry. Zoe had drunk too much to walk home safely.

'God, I've let Georgia and Zoe down as well as Patrick. It's all just one big fuck-up. I just want this day to end,' she said to Tex. 'Please make it end.'

Tex took hold of Ellen's hand.

What a cluster fuck, he thought.

25

Georgia sat in the police interview room waiting for the interrogation to begin. It was nothing like the interview rooms in the detective shows she liked watching—all dim with a two-way mirror and high barred windows. In fact, it was light and airy with brightly coloured walls, carpet and large windows that framed a good view of the river below. A polite young detective named Melanie had brought her a box of tissues, a cup of coffee and a chocolate brownie.

Despite all this positive attention, Georgia was still in shock and couldn't stop shivering and crying. She had refused to speak until her lawyer arrived and then she said she would only tell her side of the story to Detective Scallioni. She hadn't spoken to Ellen. Georgia was only allowed one phone call and she used that to contact Jim Garcia, her family's lawyer. She presumed Ellen had no idea she'd been arrested on suspicion of blowing up Patrick's home.

It took an hour for Jim Garcia to arrive and a further hour before Detective Scallioni could be located. He was on leave, but had seen the fire at Patrick's house on the news and didn't hesitate to come in, especially with Georgia's arrest and her insistence that she would only talk to him. He had known Georgia since high school and knew she was incapable of such a crime. Nevertheless, he needed to get the whole story and remain both impartial and professional. Tony sat himself down directly opposite Georgia and Jim.

'Georgia, I need you to stop crying and speak to me. Tell me why you're insisting that you'll only tell me what happened?'

'That's what Patrick told me to do,' she sobbed. 'He said he didn't trust anyone but you and that if the house blew up, then I was to tell you everything I knew. He also said a word.' She paused trying to recall the code word. '"Houdini"—that was it: "Houdini".'

'So he knew the house would blow up?' Tony asked.

'Yes and no,' she replied.

'Not sure I'm following you.'

'Patrick just said that if it did blow up, you'd know what to do. That you would remember your pact—whatever that means.'

Tony knew exactly what it meant. 'Please continue,' he prompted her.

'Well, I have proof I didn't blow up his house.'

'What proof do you have, Georgia?' Jim asked.

'I can't show you without my coat.'

'Why do you need your coat?' asked Tony.

'I just do. Please ask them to bring my coat.'

Tony sent for her coat.

Georgia removed the brooch and carefully unscrewed the mechanism.

'Can I use your e-pad, please?' she asked Jim, still sniffling and wiping her nose on the back of her hand. Jim passed her the box of tissues, followed by his device.

Georgia inserted the memory card and activated the program. The raw footage began to play. Jim and Tony watched as she bumbled around outside Patrick's house and garden, knocking on doors, looking into rooms, falling into a bush.

'This footage is very clear Georgia,' Jim commented.

'I'm a professional photographer.'

'A rather good one it seems,' added Tony.

They came to the part where she smashed the laundry window, then watched as Patrick interacted with Georgia telling him to show Tony the footage. 'Show him the film footage. Only Tony,' he stressed. 'Just say "Houdini"; he'll know what to do.'

For the next few moments Tony sat in silence. He was thinking how to handle the situation and what to do next. Finally, he spoke.

'I'll keep the original card as evidence and make a copy for you Jim. The more pressing issue, however, is what to do with Georgia.' He paused before continuing. 'It's very unfortunate that the news footage of your arrest has already been released. Jim and I know that you're innocent, but the perpetrators now know there's a witness. Criminals don't like witnesses. They'll be wondering what you know, what you saw, who you spoke with. You may be in danger if they feel the need to silence you. We must keep you safe.'

Jim nodded, 'I agree.'

Tony continued, 'You definitely can't go home. I think we should keep you here at the police station for at least the next twenty-four hours. By then the fuss will have died down and the press will have moved on to another story. Once that happens, we'll relocate you.'

Georgia looked dazed as the sedatives continued to cloud her thoughts.

'But you know I'm innocent, so why can't I just go home?'

Tony explained again. 'It might be safe for you to return home, but it might not. We don't yet know why Patrick was targeted. Until the investigation uncovers a motive, or we make an arrest, we have a duty to keep the only witness we have safe.'

Tony continued, 'It's hard to say how long this investigation will take, but I'll get you moved to a more comfortable safe house as soon as possible. If the investigation drags on for too long, we might even need to consider a temporary change of identity.'

'Safe house, change my identity,' Georgia parroted. 'No, surely not! This can't be happening.'

Jim turned towards Georgia.

'You need to calm down Georgia and listen to me very carefully.'

'It appears that you have become inadvertently mixed up in something that could be more dangerous than any of us realise. I suggest you seriously consider Detective Scallioni's proposed course of action, even if it means a temporary change of identity. I don't really see how you have any other choice. You trusted Patrick, and Patrick trusted Detective Scallioni.'

After a few moments Georgia looked at Jim, nodding as she spoke.

'Okay, but are you sure this is the best way to handle this situation?'

'Yes,' Jim said before turning and speaking to Tony. 'One week in a safe house Detective, then we will review things. In the meantime, can you make sure Georgia has everything she needs?'

'Most definitely,' Tony replied, smiling at her.

A puzzled expression moved across Georgia's face.

'If you want me to change my identity and go into hiding—why can't I go to Melbourne? I was intending to move there eventually anyway.'

Tony leaned forward and pointed to her left wrist. 'Why aren't you chipped, Georgia?'

She shrugged her shoulders. 'Dunno. Too scared of needles and creepy robots,' she replied.

Tony looked at Jim. 'The best solution might be to organise a temporary change of identity. Georgia could be chipped in her new name and relocated to Melbourne.'

'I just want to be with Zoe and Ellen. If I have to be chipped to do that then I will.'

'Do you realise what a temporary identity will mean, Georgia?' Tony said. 'For an unspecified time period you won't be Georgia Ashmore anymore; you'll be a different person. For as long as the investigation takes you can't live at your home or contact anyone other than Ellen and Zoe. We can't even specify a timeframe. It could take months or even years. It's a big decision for anyone, Georgia—but a decision that could ultimately save your life.'

Georgia just wanted to be with Zoe, even if she had to arrive with only the clothes on her back. But she felt scared and confused. Tears filled her eyes once more and she started to shake.

'B-but what will happen to my home and all my possessions, then?' she asked.

'Well you could either close your house down until the investigation concludes, or you could give my firm the power to pack up and store your belongings and liquidate larger assets like your house and car. The firm would deposit the funds into an Australian bank account once you open one in your new name.

'Detective Scallioni and I will need to liaise with the Australian Federal Police and immigration. We will need your visa fast-tracked and gain approval to transfer your money into the country.'

'That sounds reasonable,' Tony said. 'What do you think, Georgia? Are we all in agreement that this is the best way forward? A new identity for you—some assets stored and others sold?'

'I need more time to think,' Georgia replied. 'Can I just have a few days to think it over?'

'I can only give you twenty-four hours,' Tony said. 'Talk things over with Jim and make your decision tomorrow. In the meantime, I need to move ahead with your formal police interview.'

Georgia nodded.

'During this interview, Georgia, I want you to just say "No comment" to everything that might reveal what really happened. Whatever you decide, we need to maintain this charade to keep you under arrest.' He turned to Jim, 'If you can interject to ensure she stays on track that would be good.'

'Are you ready for your interview?' Tony asked.

Georgia nodded again.

'Good.'

Tony left the interview room and returned a short time later with Melanie. He had explained to her that Georgia was highly anxious. Tony turned on the recording device and began the interview.

'Time: 2.00 pm on March 31st, 2074. This is an interview between Detective Tony Scallioni and Ms Georgia Ashmore. Also present: Detective Melanie Hunter and Mr Jim Garcia. As you're aware, Ms Ashmore, I'm investigating a fire and explosion at the residence of Detective Patrick O'Connor and his disappearance. I believe that you were the last person to see him. I must advise you that you have the right to remain silent and to refuse to answer my questions. Anything you say may be used against you in a court of law.'

'What were you doing at 35 Hill Street today?'

'No comment.'

'Did you see or speak with Detective Patrick O'Connor?'

'No comment.'

'We have two witnesses who observed you going around the back of his house then coming out the front door around thirty minutes later.'

'Nosey neighbours.'

'Steady, Georgia,' cautioned Jim.

'So you admit you were there?' Melanie cut in.

'No comment,' Georgia said, getting back on track.

'We already know you were there Ms Ashmore—the 911 call came from your mobile—how do you explain that?' Melanie asked.

Georgia was taken aback, as she realised the emergency call had placed her at the scene before the explosion. She quickly composed herself and said, 'No comment.'

'This is pointless,' Tony said with a feigned look of frustration. 'Take her back to the cell to give her time to contemplate her future and whether she's going to cooperate and tell us exactly what happened. Interview terminated at 2.04 pm.'

What a strange interview, thought Melanie. As they left the room, she looked at Tony, hoping he might tell her what was going on, but he didn't speak.

'Sir, I really think Ms Ashmore needs a mental health assessment,' Melanie said. 'She shook all the way through that interview. I don't feel comfortable locking her in a cell. She could be a suicide risk.'

'I agree. Could you arrange for the assessment? Oh, and Melanie, could you place Ms Ashmore in the largest available cell. Keep the door open and allocate someone to sit with her.'

'Okaay … but that's a bit unorthodox. Do you think that's really necessary?

'Just trust me—it's all *very* necessary.'

26

Zoe woke around midday on the Saturday. Her head was pounding as each heartbeat sent blood surging through the arteries in her neck. Her mouth was dry, her tongue furry and she felt nauseous. She eased her body upright, trying to figure out exactly where she was. Her head wobbled; it felt as if it wasn't properly attached to her body anymore. She looked down at her clothing. Her blouse buttons were not aligned and her bra was loose—fastened on the wrong hook.

Zoe scanned the room. The bed was enormous; she decided it must be a super king. The penthouse was exquisitely decorated. Lots of black and polished steel fixtures, softened with luxuriously thick cream carpet and brocade curtains with deep blue-black tasselled tie-backs. The views through the huge glass panels were stunning, even better than that from the AMDAT viewing platform. Maggie was sleeping in the chair next to her. She must have fallen asleep reading. A book was open, lodged awkwardly between the chair and a bedside table; her glasses were hanging off her nose at quite a peculiar angle. Zoe took a few moments to look around and try to remember what had happened and why she was there.

The harder she tried, the less she recalled. It reminded her of being in an exam when you're so nervous you can't snatch the answers you know must be circulating in your brain. *Sit up straight, relax and breathe deeply; the answers will come,* Auntie Ellen had explained. She decided to give it a go.

Zoe sat up straight, breathing in deeply. *God, my head hurts,* she thought, when suddenly the wedged book fell to the floor, startling her and waking Maggie, who took a couple of seconds to orientate herself.

'Good morning, Zoe,' she said, straightening her glasses, picking up the book and snapping it shut.

'How did I get here?' Zoe asked.

'It appears that you had a little too much champagne and when Vaughn was showing you the view from his apartment you passed out. He called me to come and help and, as it turned out, Oliver had asked me to find you, so I was already on my way.'

Despite the deep breathing Zoe couldn't recall what had happened. She could only remember Oliver asking her to wait in the corridor. The next thing she remembered was Vaughn offering her a drink in his apartment and feeling woozy.

'I think my drink might have been spiked.'

'Oh no, you just drank too much, darling, that's all,' Maggie said, as if trying to convince herself as well as Zoe. 'Haven't you ever been drunk before?'

'No,' she paused. 'I haven't.'

'Well, I guess it does feel similar to being drugged. Your head spins and you can't stand up or walk straight, which is exactly what happened to you.'

'How did I get here, then?'

'Daniel and I brought you up here to sober up. We thought it would be best for you to sleep it off in a safe place.'

'Someone has touched my clothing?'

'That would be me. I considered undressing you and putting you in a nightie, but in the end, I just loosened a few bits of your clothing.'

Suddenly, Zoe remembered that Ellen could be looking for her and that, if she had told her mother she hadn't come home last night, Georgia could have had a heart attack.

'My auntie and my mom will be so worried,' she said.

'It's all okay, Zoe; I couldn't get in direct contact with your Auntie Ellen, so I left a message with your flatmate Rob.'

'So she knows I was drunk?'

''Fraid so. Don't worry about it, Zoe. Most young people get drunk when they first discover alcohol.'

'Even you?'

'Even me, and more than once.'

Zoe suddenly recalled that Vaughn had covered her eyes and pushed her into the lift. Maggie was being nice, but she could be covering for him—because of his friendship with her husband perhaps? Zoe had read about Vaughn Lambert's relationship with Daniel Grant in the *Times*. 'Like brothers,' the article had said. They were one powerful duo. She didn't know much about Daniel. Vaughn, on the other hand, had a bad reputation when it came to the ladies, but apart from a bad headache she felt okay. Maybe nothing had happened.

Regardless, Zoe began to consider options to distance herself from Vaughn. She could transfer to Melbourne Uni, but then she wouldn't be paid a salary, she wouldn't see quite so much of her friends and she might be labelled a dropout. That would *not* be good for her career. Zoe was also really enjoying her studies and was quite invested in the bat research program. Maggie was an excellent teacher. Zoe decided that she needed to talk the incident over with Ellen and Oliver; there was a great deal at stake.

Her thoughts were interrupted by an android entering the room, pushing a food trolley. The breakfast choices included muesli, Greek yoghurt, fresh fruits, corn fritters and warm pancakes with maple syrup and ice cream. All the food looked and smelt delicious.

Maggie had given her two painkillers when she woke, and these had eased her headache somewhat. Despite the nausea she was hungry; she hadn't had any dinner last night. Maggie said that eating was the best way to deal with the raw stomach of a hangover.

'I must admit, I am hungry.'

'Well, tuck in, young lady. After breakfast, I have someone I want you to meet.'

With breakfast over, Zoe showered and changed into some fresh clothes that Maggie provided. She was now sitting waiting for the visitor, whom she suspected would be Daniel Grant. After all, she was in his penthouse. Maggie had gone to fetch the surprise guest. Sure enough, Daniel and Maggie entered the room a short time later.

'Zoe, I want you to meet my husband, Daniel.' Zoe stood up and smiled. He was not at all what she had expected. He wasn't that tall, being around the same height as Maggie. His hair was dark brown and he had a bushy unkempt auburn beard. He seemed withdrawn—or was he just shy? Maggie sat down next to her and Daniel sat opposite.

Maggie spoke first.

'We have a proposition for you, Zoe. Daniel and I have been unable to have children naturally. I had ovarian cysts in my teenage years and, after several operations, I was left infertile. We've decided the time is now right to have a child via IVF but, as you can well imagine, we have to choose our egg donor very carefully. I—that is, we—would love you to be our egg donor. You're such a beautiful, intelligent girl with great morals. I've been observing you closely for weeks, and just know you're the right one for us.'

Zoe was speechless. These were two of the most powerful people in the country and they had chosen her to be their egg donor.

Daniel began to speak.

'We realise that you will need to carefully consider your decision. Because of our high profile we're asking you not to discuss our proposal with anyone, as it could make you a target for kidnapping or unwanted advances.'

Zoe wasn't sure what to say. On one hand she was stunned, yet she was also quite flattered. She had been emphatic about not donating ova for research purposes but quite a few of the girls in her group had said the process wasn't a big deal. Anyway, wouldn't she be helping an infertile couple to conceive a child? Maggie had been so good to her—but after last night, could she be trusted? Had Maggie covered for Vaughn? Then again, Maggie did have AMDAT's reputation to consider, didn't she?

After a minute had passed Maggie spoke, 'I can almost hear the cogs in your brain turning Zoe. What do you think? Would you consider donating your ova to us so we can start our family?'

'It's a lot to process,' Zoe replied. 'Just exactly what would you need me to do?'

'Well, we would simply like to harvest some of your ova. To achieve a live birth by IVF we need around eight high-quality embryos. With you being so young, I expect we could extract the number of ova we need in, say, one cycle.'

'That doesn't sound difficult,' Zoe replied. 'I really do need to think about it though.'

'Of course,' Daniel replied. 'Sleep on it. Take all the time you need.' Then he paused and added some incentives. 'Obviously we can't pay you for your ova, but in return, we will buy you your own apartment in Melbourne once you graduate—nothing too showy. We wouldn't want to draw unnecessary attention to you, but something really nice and fully furnished, of course. Maggie tells me that your mother wants to move to Australia. Perhaps we could pay for her relocation costs?

Anyway, you think it over and let Maggie know when you've made your decision. In the meantime, please remember that you can't tell anyone what we've discussed here today, not even your close family or friends. Infertility is a very private and personal issue.'

'I understand,' answered Zoe. 'I promise I won't say a word to anyone.'

✕✕✕

Later that afternoon Oliver came to Ellen's apartment. He was so relieved to have Zoe back safe and well. On seeing each other they spontaneously hugged, then, as their hold relaxed, they pulled apart, looked at each other, smiled and kissed for the very first time. Zoe kept her word and didn't discuss the Grants' proposition with anyone. She made her decision the following week. Zoe's innocence and naivety, coupled with her inability to say 'no' to a reasonable request, her empathy for the childless Maggie and the temptation of a significant monetary reward that would bring her mother to Australia, led her to agree. It was a decision she would live to regret.

27

Tony Scallioni arrived at what remained of Patrick's former home, which was now a crime scene. Forensic officers were already in attendance, placing tape barriers and erecting temporary screens around the house perimeter. The murder of a police officer was a serious business.

Tony surveyed the scene. The damp, smouldering ruins looked eerie in the moonlight. All that was left was Patrick's large safe standing defiantly amongst the charred remains. In a way, the safe symbolised his friend. A strong, solid man who had handled every challenge life threw at him without defeat, until now.

Tony recalled the day Patrick bought his safe. He had bought a similar one a few months earlier. In their respective safes, they kept their guns, passports, cash and other private documents. 'Bet it's where you two keep your porn collection,' their work colleagues had joked.

The safe idea had germinated when they were young police officers fresh out of the academy. Both had attended robberies where safes had been skilfully opened and the contents stolen. They were determined to own safes that could not be so easily cracked. Tony's Uncle Alfonso had been a petty crim in his youth. He had taught the young Tony the art of safe cracking, and Tony passed the skill on to Patrick. They had both became quite adept.

According to Uncle Alfonso, safe cracking did have a legal side to it. He had assured them that his current line of business was totally above board. Alfonso only cracked safes where someone had died and taken the combination with them to the grave. Safes that were forgotten, abandoned inside buildings, much too large to move without a crane, or those occasionally surrendered to family members, police, insurers or estate lawyers who sought his practical expertise.

Tony and Patrick had quite enjoyed the art of safe cracking, so when Tony's dad helped them to build their new homes, they had both decided to install large antique safes. Their safes were useful and had unique design features. Both of them had come from old bank branches. Tony and Patrick liked to tell their friends and family about the folklore and legends that surrounded their respective safes. The yarns about Mafia bank robbers and Bonnie and Clyde, although very entertaining, were all bullshit.

Their safes could only be cracked by extensive drilling. Both were of a similar vintage and required three large keys used in a specific sequence to open the complex mechanism. This type of mechanism provided an early type of security system for banks.

Three different bank employees—usually the manager, accountant and one other—would each have a key; each key was kept in a different location. This meant that all three of these employees had to be present on the bank premises with the keys before the safe could be opened. Thieves could not intimidate the bank tellers to open a safe because they simply couldn't achieve that aim. Patrick and Tony had their respective keys copied and each of them held copies for the other.

Tony recalled the day Patrick's concrete slab was laid. The large crane had drawn a crowd as it lifted the safe into place. The sheer weight of the object had ensured the legs dug deep into the wet cement. It was to become a permanent fixture and that had never been more evident than it was today.

Tony walked over to the safe and brushed off the ash with his gloved hand. The metal casing was still warm. He then walked to the bottom corner of the block and into a small hothouse full of cacti. The plastic panels of the hothouse facing the fire had partially melted. He stood motionless, closed his eyes and listened.

The night was quite still. He could hear music, a dog barking in the distance, someone shouting words he couldn't quite make out. The frogs at a nearby pond were croaking loudly. He continued to listen. That's when he heard it: a quiet low humming sound. Houdini was on.

28

At the end of her shift, Muriel collected Ellen to escort her home. Her hourly neuro observations had remained stable throughout the night. They shared an e-cab and discussed her predicament.

'Ellen, I want you to take some time off. I checked the human resources system and, as I suspected, you have excess leave, in fact 950 hours. Way over what an employee is allowed to accumulate.'

'I took leave only last month.'

'Not enough to be well rested, and now you have a baby on the way.'

A baby on the way. Ellen never thought she would hear that phrase—not in relation to herself, that is. It sounded nice; it sounded exciting—something to really look forward to, a little person in her life. Why was she even letting herself think this way—or was Muriel right? Did she really have the right to deny a child forty good years, just because it might end badly? Would she have preferred her mother suctioned her apart, limb by limb, and then flushed her away down an abortion clinic drain?

Ellen suddenly realised that, whatever the test results, she was going to have this child. Patrick's child, the child they should have enjoyed together as a little nuclear family, in a little suburb, with a white picket fence and a shaggy dog that might bark at Jane if she ever came to visit. Not that she would ever invite Jane over. Or she just might; it would be a very Buddhist thing to do, wouldn't it? Why was she babbling? Had the bump on her head sent her simple?

Muriel suddenly interrupted Ellen's thought bubble with an interesting thought of her own.

'Why not take the opportunity to visit your dad in Eyam while you're still able to travel? You could stay for a few weeks. The rest would do you and the baby both good. You know that you won't be able to leave Australia once the baby arrives. With the high child mortality rate these days, it's best not to mix kids until they have completed all their vaccinations and that takes several years.'

'Okay, I will,' Ellen replied, without any hesitation.

Muriel couldn't believe how quickly Ellen had processed the idea and, thinking she was simply fobbing her off, continued trying to convince her.

'Go for a well-earned holiday and see your dad. He isn't getting any younger and the world isn't getting any safer. It's harder to raise a child than ever before. The next few years will be challenging.'

'I agree,' Ellen said. 'I'll go, as soon as I sort out a few things.' By a few things she meant Georgia being under arrest and Zoe's overnight drinking binge.

'Good,' Muriel replied. 'All sorted.' She looked over at Ellen, who seemed decidedly pleased with herself. *Well, that was easier than I thought,* mused Muriel.

29

Georgia needed to be transferred to a safe location as soon as possible. Jim Garcia made contact with Ellen and outlined the plan. Georgia's new name would be Anna Taylor and she was now a distant cousin of Ellen's, no relation to Zoe Ashmore. She would be arriving in Australia shortly. Ellen and Zoe were not to try to make any contact with her, no matter what happened in the next two weeks or how worried they became. They would both just have to be patient and wait for 'Anna' to make her own way to their apartment. Jim re-emphasised that there were to be no calls to Q precinct during the quarantine period. No discussions with anyone else about these arrangements. It was essential they both maintained absolute silence.

Well, this will be a first, thought Ellen. *Georgia gets lost in large shopping centres, let alone travelling alone from New Jersey to Melbourne.* Anyway, for once her friend would have to draw on her own resources. Ellen outlined the plan to Zoe. Once Georgia— Anna—arrived safely and was settled, Ellen would leave to visit her father. Ellen was relieved to have everything organised. Life seemed to be settling down. All Ellen and Zoe had to do was start thinking of Georgia as Anna. Ellen would have to give Rob notice to vacate her apartment. Georgia—Anna—needed his room.

Her father was very excited about the upcoming visit. He was keen to show his daughter Derbyshire and had a few surprises pertaining to their ancestry waiting for her, including some locals he was eager for her to meet. He was acting quite mysteriously.

30

'Anna Taylor' flew out of Newark Airport the following week. Android companions were only provided for business and first-class passengers. Tony had convinced the police department that supplementing Georgia to upgrade her ticket could be the cheaper option, especially if the investigation proved lengthy. Safe houses were expensive. Tony was pleased with the outcome. He couldn't imagine Georgia surviving Q precinct without someone to keep her distracted and on track. She was simply too anxious and disorganised.

Everyone, including Georgia, knew that entering Q precinct was not without its risks. She had heard the rumours about Q-ites and was convinced she was going to be one of the unlucky ones. The thought of being dumped on a tropical island to slowly starve to death was making her feel quite twitchy. Georgia inspected the chip on her wrist. It itched. She felt the glands in her neck and checked her temperature for the umpteenth time. Surely this thing had infected her with something horrid? The chipping process had been ghastly. She had passed out halfway through, just as it was being inserted. Apparently her collapse had caused quite a commotion: no-one had fainted at that facility before.

Georgia had drunk too much champagne on the flight to Melbourne. She had slept little and was overtired and restless. She was now sitting at Q precinct entry portal at Tullamarine Airport, undertaking her entry interview. Georgia glanced across to the wall mirror. Brown eyes stared back at her. She barely recognised herself. Contact lenses hid her dark green eyes. She looked thinner in the face—*must have lost weight*. She liked her new hairstyle. *Never thought soft blonde would suit my complexion,* she thought as she fluffed up the sides. She decided the pixie cut was flattering. *Not sure about the floral summer dress, though—nothing like what I would usually choose. Do I look younger? Yes, I think that I do.*

Sitting directly opposite her, behind a glass panel, a neat-looking woman who reminded Georgia of a school principal was efficiently entering her answers to a range of what she considered to be stupid questions. The responses were supposedly designed to enhance her overall business-class Q experience. Georgia was finding it difficult to concentrate and couldn't stop fidgeting. She just wanted to get to bed as soon as possible.

'Do you drink coffee or tea?'

'Both.'

'Do you prefer hot chocolate or cocoa at bedtime, or some other beverage?'

'Hot chocolate.'

'Do you prefer to take baths or showers?'

'Showers.'

'What is your favourite colour?'

'Blue.'

'Are you heterosexual or part of the LGBTQIA community?'

'Heterosexual.'

'Do you prefer tall, short or average-height men?'

'Tall.'

Do you prefer men with blond hair and blue eyes, auburn hair with green eyes or black hair with brown eyes?

'Well, actually, I prefer black hair with blue eyes.'

'That's not one of the options,' the woman said, glaring at her as if at any moment she might throw something. Please choose from the available options.'

'Black hair with brown eyes,' Georgia replied, pulling a face at the woman's curt response. She must have climbed out of the wrong side of the bed this morning.

'What is it with all these silly questions, anyway?' she asked.

'Trust me,' the woman replied, taking off her glasses and staring Georgia straight in the eye. 'Once you've been in Q for a few days you'll be glad that the experience has been tailored for you and that you don't feel like climbing the walls or even killing someone.'

Doubt that will happen, thought Georgia, *all I want is to be with my Zoe and I'd walk across hot coals or broken glass if I had to.* Q precinct couldn't be that bad.

'Do you prefer vaginal, oral, or anal sex, or combinations?'

'Oh! Now, let me see. Actually, I like it every which way,' Georgia said, pouting her red-lipped mouth as if she were Marilyn Monroe. She was getting somewhat impatient, irritable and a bit silly. Being tipsy wasn't helping either.

'Do you prefer your meals warm or hot?'

'Hot—just like me,' Georgia replied.

Why do I always get the pissed ones? The woman thought to herself, before sighing and moving on to the next question.

'Do you like pure cotton sheets or polyester-cotton blend?'

'I like red satin, actually' she replied with smirk and a tilt of her head.

'Well, that's one variance we can accommodate.'

'Do you prefer soaps or gel products?'

'Don't care.'

'I need an answer.'

'Okaaaay … gels.'

Questions about food and entertainment preferences went on for a few more minutes. Finally, the woman finished typing into her computer. A swipe card and remote control came out of a wall slot on Georgia's side of the window.

'Please take your swipe card and android remote, Ms Taylor. Your android also works by voice control. It's entirely up to you which method you chose. Your suite will be ready for you in approximately ten minutes. Take a seat just over there until your escort arrives. Oh, by the way, I'm the last human you will have contact with until you exit Q.'

A short time later, the robot escort was opening the door to her compact Q suite. Fingers crossed it would only be her home for the next fourteen days. On entering, Georgia grimaced as a strong smell of eucalyptus, masking a harsh disinfectant, momentarily took her breath away. It had clearly just been fumigated.

The walls were decorated in swirling shades of blue. The colour was being projected from behind the walls and was not permanent. *So that's how they accommodate endless variation in taste,* she thought. The queen-sized bed was made up with red satin sheets; Georgia giggled as she pulled back the duvet. She heard a rustle in the kitchenette. A tall, handsome android with black hair and brown eyes came into the lounge, carrying a cup of coffee and a large chunk of carrot cake coated with lemon butter icing.

'Hello, Ms Taylor; may I call you Anna?'

'Please do,' she replied. 'What should I call you?' she asked, quite amused.

'I am Dario, your companion for your stay in Q. I'm here to fulfil your every need.'

Georgia looked him over. She had seen androids before, but his model was amazingly lifelike. She'd heard that some people found androids too realistic and creepy. 'Uncanny valley' was used to describe this phenomenon. She didn't find him creepy. He was really quite attractive. He was obviously one of the latest models.

A few years ago, one of the many companies producing androids had developed a new plastic-human cell substance called 'plasticell' which had revolutionised the synthetic skin industry and made their androids almost indistinguishable from humans. They had placed thousands of their next-generation androids in childcare centres, nursing homes and disability services. The androids were employed in human positions, undertaking tasks such as cleaning and gardening as well as assisting clients with activities of daily living. The androids 'earned' human salaries, the money being deposited directly into bogus bank accounts, all owned by the same company. Everyone was fooled.

At the end of each working day, the androids were programmed to return to various houses scattered across the city. One house could accommodate as many as one hundred androids, all standing upright. No need for liquids or food, just a power supply to recharge. It was a very profitable enterprise, until the high fuel consumption of the houses was investigated and the scam exposed.

By law, all androids now had to have their make and model number tattooed on their left wrist in the same place as humans had health chips installed. This ensured that androids could be easily identified. New regulations had also been introduced, specifying the allowable ratio of human to android workers. Georgia had noticed Dario's tattoo when he served her afternoon tea.

She was now studying the android remote. She remembered the woman saying that voice control was also available. Dario was currently set on afternoon-tea mode. She pressed the *Learn My Features* button. Dario immediately began a presentation on his capabilities, which were quite extensive. They included every card game imaginable and a range of board games including chess. He could also play a full suite of computer games, but they didn't interest her. He could sing any type of music—he sang a few bars. Then he picked up the Spanish guitar and plucked a few notes. He could converse in any language about anything and everything. He could cook, clean and organise the apartment. Lastly, Dario assured her, he was an adept lover. At which moment Georgia felt herself blush.

Dare she even try out the lover mode? He was pretty gorgeous, even if he wasn't human. It had been quite a while; in fact, she could barely recall the last time she'd had sex. Perhaps in a few days, when she was used to him, she might give it a whirl. After all, she had never had a one-night stand, she thought, laughing to herself. Dario would definitely not kiss and tell.

'What would you like to do now, Anna?'

'Well, Dario, how about a game of good old-fashioned poker?'

'Okay, do you want to shuffle and deal?'

'You can start,' she said with a smile. 'I want to watch your hands in action.'

Dario went to locate a deck of cards. He returned moments later to find Georgia curled up asleep on the couch. He covered her with a blanket then stood himself in the corner and activated standby mode.

31

Ellen and Zoe attended Patrick's memorial service by holo-conference. It was a heart-rending affair. There were too many friends and colleagues to fit into the small local chapel and his mother Claire had to be supported by her husband as she walked in. Ellen broke down during the montage. She was in several of the images. There was a shot of Patrick behind the wheel of his first car with Ellen in the passenger seat. Another showed him playing volleyball on the beach with Ellen cheering from the sidelines. They were in the school drama production of *Hamlet* together. He had escorted her to prom night.

Ellen realised that she'd taken Patrick completely for granted. Any future they may have shared was now gone. She had behaved like a stupid, selfish woman.

If only I could go back in time, get tested for Huntington's and just get on with loving him, she thought. But Ellen knew the past could never be changed. Just like everyone else, she would have to live with the consequences of her life choices.

That evening, despite being pregnant, she drank champagne and ate a whole tub of coffee-flavoured ice cream. Zoe and Rob had to stop her finishing the bottle and, once she passed out on the couch, they helped her into bed. Zoe woke in the early hours of the morning and could hear Ellen crying in the next room. She was still sobbing two hours later. Unfortunately her best friend Georgia—or rather, Anna—was still in Q Melbourne.

Zoe seemed happier, more settled and excited about seeing her mother. Rob was reluctantly moving out tomorrow. They had explained to him that Ellen's cousin was visiting indefinitely and they required his room. Ellen and Zoe planned a farewell dinner for him. For main course he'd chosen vegetarian lasagne. For dessert, his favourite was pavlova with bananas, passionfruit pulp and fresh cream. Fortunately, Rob had been able to secure an apartment one floor down from them, so his initial disappointment had dissipated. They all planned to keep in touch.

Following two weeks of sick leave, Ellen had returned to work. As usual, she was rostered to Bay 5 with Jane and Abdi. The night so far had been yawningly slow. Regardless, she was determined to be more upbeat and not let Jane drag her down like a giant anchor. Being a sad sack was not good for her or her baby.

Just as she could feel her eyes getting heavy, a hovercraft approached the triage portal.

'Thank goodness,' she said to Abdi. 'I was just about to fall asleep.'

Jane went into her usual caustic mode, as she assessed the middle-aged woman. Ms Stuart was pregnant but her physical observations were all within normal range. She was not an infection risk. Ellen looked more closely at the camera and suddenly she recognised the client. It was Louise Stuart, Samuel's mother.

Louise was worried about her pregnancy and had been hoping that Doctor Hancock would be available to assess her. Jane was busily explaining that a patient in the public health system could *not* choose their physician at the Health Hub assessment phase. If and when she was transferred to a private hospital, then she could choose whoever she—Ellen cut across the conversation.

'It's okay, Jane; let the craft through. I know Louise and have treated her previously.' That wasn't exactly true, but Ellen believed rescuing Louise from Jane's caustic clutches justified the fib. Ellen pulled on her protective equipment and met the hovercraft.

'Hi, Louise; how is young Sam?' Ellen asked.

'He's okay, thanks to you,' she replied.

'Thanks, Louise, but I didn't do that much.'

'Yes, you did; you cleaned him up beautifully and you gave us hope and lots of "vent" time. We all think you're a saint, Doctor Hancock.'

Ellen blushed. She rarely saw the same patients at the Hub. Even when she did, they didn't have this amount of glowing praise. She quickly changed the subject.

'Well, congratulations on your pregnancy, Louise.'

'You need congratulations too, by the looks of things,' she said, noticing Ellen's now obvious tummy.

'Thanks; it was a bit of a surprise at first but I'm now looking forward to being a mother. Anyway, what's brought you to the Hub tonight?'

'I've been spotting today,' she replied. 'I really don't want to lose this baby; it's my last chance. I lost my little girl, Rosie, you know.'

'Yes, your father told me when we were flying Sam to Prince George's. I'm so sorry.'

'Well, I decided to have one of those designer babies. You know, the ones that are specially engineered to resist diseases? I'm hoping that my new little girl will be able to survive all the usual childhood illnesses without any complications.'

'Who undertook your IVF procedure, Louise?'

'The AMDAT team,' she replied. 'They've been terrific, but I did have an insider advantage. They promised to fast-track me if I agreed to be part of their research project.'

'Do you know exactly what the research is trying to achieve?'

'Not really; just that the baby is a girl and will have a stronger immune system and a much better chance of survival. I lost Rosie, and I just couldn't bear to lose another child.'

'Why don't you contact the AMDAT team to check you out, Louise?'

'I will, but the truth is I wanted to see you again. I trust your medical opinion very much. A second opinion is always good, don't you think? I'm in town with Dad and he doesn't know the baby is designer, so I just thought it would be easier to come here and be assessed to avoid an argument. He doesn't approve of embryo enhancement. He says it's not right to mess with nature. He isn't chipped, as you know. He can't abide the process or the AMDAT Corporation.'

Ellen paused for a moment before responding.

'I guess it can't hurt for me to examine you, just in case you require urgent attention. To put your mind at ease, why don't I do an ultrasound and check how things are progressing? Once I've checked the baby out, we can decide what to do next. I've plenty of time. Not much happening here tonight.'

'Sounds like a great plan to me,' Louise replied.

Ellen and Louise entered a lift that took them directly into one of the diagnostic suites. Louise lay down on the treatment bed and Ellen squeezed a large blob of gel on to her tummy. Louise flinched.

'Oops, it's quite cold. Sorry about that; I forgot to warm it.' Ellen then began to glide the ultrasound wand across her abdomen. 'Everything so far looks good, Louise,' she said.

Ellen captured numerous digital images and ticked off the key points required of an ultrasound for a fetus in second trimester. The list was extensive, and it took around thirty minutes to complete. Finally, Ellen checked the results live streaming via Louise's health chip. Levels of her pregnancy hormones were good. Blood sugar levels normal. Everything checked out except for one small detail: the baby's fingers were much too short. By this time in the pregnancy the digits should have been longer and better defined. All the toes were a normal length, though.

She would tell Louise but reassure her as well. Ellen would also send a report through to Louise's AMDAT obstetrician. They would need to follow it up. She was part of their research program, after all.

'I don't think the spotting is serious, Louise. It was a very small amount, only a couple of drops, and it has now stopped. Your baby does have ten fingers but they are slightly shorter than one would expect for this point in gestation. Still, short fingers aren't life threatening, so I don't want you to worry unduly. Everything else pretty much checks out. The baby is fine. I suggest you go home and rest for a couple of days. I'll send a report through to your doctor.

'Who is your doctor, anyway?'

'Professor Vaughn Lambert. He's been taking wonderful care of me,' Louise replied. *Lambert! I wouldn't let that creep anywhere near me, let alone my lady bits*, thought Ellen. She was sure that she had pulled a disgusted face, but Louise didn't seem to notice and went right on talking.

'By the way, Ellen, my father never stops talking about what a great job you did with our Samuel. He was absolutely convinced that Sam was going to contract an infection and die like our poor Rosie. He really believes that you're responsible for saving his life.'

'Well, that's a nice thought, but it wasn't just me; Prince George's has a very professional surgical team.'

'Dad has become a bit obsessed, really, and determined to invest some of his wealth into the health system. He gets a bit elevated from time to time. His latest plan is to build a hospital in the desert for people who don't consent to being chipped. He thinks being isolated will better protect the general population from contracting diseases. He's been researching and planning nonstop and comes up with new ideas every single day. I'm really quite worried about him. He's getting too old to start another large venture. He works hard enough already.'

'Well, planning can't hurt,' Ellen said. 'He can't really achieve a goal like that—it would take millions.'

'Don't you know who my dad is, Ellen?'

'Yes, of course. You know that I've met him: Francis Stuart,' she answered in a puzzled tone.

'Fran…cis Stu…art,' said Louise slowly and methodically as if she were talking to someone with a severe hearing deficit. 'Doesn't his name ring a bell for you, Ellen?'

'No. Should it?'

'He's only one of the richest men in Australia, Ellen. Kenneth Stuart's estranged brother. Surely you know *him?* He's the founder of AMDAT.'

Suddenly the penny dropped. Ellen had read about the Stuart brothers years ago, but Francis was now much older and stayed out of the media spotlight. She simply hadn't made the connection.

According to the reports, the Stuart brothers were sons of the late Leonard Stuart, who had emigrated from Yorkshire with his parents. In his late teens, he started working in the mining fields of Western Australia. Kenneth and Francis Stuart followed their father into the mining business and purchased several new mineral licences. They found huge reserves of copper and iron ore and became instantly rich. The mining boom days were over but they both remained very wealthy. Kenneth and Francis had argued bitterly when they fell in love with the same woman. She was no longer in the picture, yet the feuding continued. The brothers hadn't communicated in decades. Kenneth went on to found AMDAT and Francis founded the Natural Energy Grid Company (NATGRID) located in former desert mining lease sites around Australia. NATGRID now provided sixty per cent of Australia's renewable energy.

So that's why Francis was so familiar. Underneath the grey beard was the man she should have recognised. It was those eyes, those large piercing green eyes. Quite unusual.

'He lives in the outback on NATGRID East with his second wife, Mindy. My mother died when I was a baby.'

'Oh, I am sorry.'

'Thanks, Ellen, but it was harder on Dad than me, really. I don't remember her. I guess never knowing a parent is sad for any child, though.'

Ellen couldn't help but think that her own baby would never know their father.

'Anyway, Francis and Mindy come to Melbourne quite frequently. They just love Sam so much. Following Rosie's death and the recent scare with Sam, Dad wants to build a hospital closer to Melbourne, near NATGRID East, complete with a specialist children's wing.'

Ellen didn't know quite what to say. She was stunned.

'So, let me get this straight,' she said. 'Kenneth Stuart is your uncle.'

'Yes.'

'So Margaret Grant is your first cousin?'

'Yes, she is … Dad doesn't know that I reconnected with Margaret about five years ago and that this baby is one of AMDAT's new immune system–enhanced embryos. He would be very upset with me, but all I want is a little girl who has a better chance of surviving in a world terrorised by microbes. You can't blame me for wanting that, can you?'

'I'm not here to pass judgement Louise. If you and your husband want a designer baby, then that's your choice entirely. By the way, Louise, everything looks on track. The pregnancy is progressing nicely. Your baby girl appears healthy and she's very active tonight. I'll forward a full copy of my report to Professor Lambert. He can reassess and discuss the short fingers issue with you—I'm sure it will be nothing to get overly concerned about, though.'

'Thanks, Ellen; it has been lovely seeing you again.'

'It has been nice catching up. Give my kind regards to Francis and your husband and of course that young rascal Sam. Oh … and the best of luck with that baby girl when she arrives.'

'Good luck to you as well, Ellen. Are you expecting a boy or a girl?'

'I decided to just wait and see,' Ellen replied with a rather sad smile.

32

For 'Anna', Q precinct business class was turning out to be quite a pleasant experience. She hadn't had a single anxiety attack since she checked in. Dario was largely responsible for making her feel so calm and secure. His programmers had obviously designed him to be kind and considerate no matter what a client said or did. In one way she found him a tad boring. Good looking, but lacking in complexity, as one would expect from an artificial person. The sort of person Ellen described as 'vanilla'.

The end of her two weeks in Q was drawing near. Until today she hadn't seriously considered trying out Dario's lover mode but something in the back of her mind kept urging her on. Ellen had regretted not sleeping with an android. She would have one up on her if she did. Georgia also doubted she would ever go through Q business class again, so this was probably her last opportunity.

Dare I? she thought. *What if he does something weird and I have a panic attack? Guess I could always turn him off.* She turned her attention back to the chess game and made her move.

'Checkmate,' she called out with satisfaction.

'You win again, Anna,' Dario replied.

Only because I have you on primary-school chess mode, she thought to herself. She was certainly finding Dario to be a good companion. He didn't argue with her, just agreed with everything and gave her plenty of compliments. A perfect Mr Nice Guy, but, as Ellen always said, a dash of bad boy makes life much more interesting.

Although she had adored Frank, they still had their moments. She always believed that if a couple never argued their relationship lacked passion. If you're not passionate about your relationship, then you don't ever disagree, because you ultimately don't care what your partner does or says. And that's unhealthy.

It was getting late. Georgia undressed and slipped on her nightdress, then she sat down and began sipping her hot chocolate. She picked up the android remote and stared at the lover mode. Her finger hovered over the button like a moth circling a candle flame. She wondered what Dario would do. She felt self-conscious and a little embarrassed. *He isn't real,* she had to keep reminding herself. *He doesn't have emotions like you do; he just does whatever you ask of him. He won't gossip about you, or tell anyone.* Maybe she would give it a whirl, once she finished the delicious drink he'd made her.

Dario was now busily cleaning and tidying up the suite. In one way he made her sad. He reminded her of the life she used to have with Frank. Frank had adored her and waited on her almost as much as this android did. What would Frank think if she had sex with Dario? Out of the blue she could almost hear him say, 'Take the loving while you can, sweetheart; take it with my blessing.'

She looked down at the remote then moved her fingers tentatively across the device before decisively pressing lover mode. Dario immediately left what he was doing and came over to her. He took the cup of hot chocolate from her hand, then picked her up in his arms, carried her into the bedroom and placed her delicately onto those red satin sheets.

33

'Anna' had been granted entry into Australia and had managed to navigate her way to Ellen's apartment without any problems. She had a strange renewed confidence. Ellen and Zoe thought that she looked great, walking and talking like the new person she now was, Ms Anna Taylor. Zoe had bumped into Georgia in the apartment lift. She had stood next to her mother and hadn't even recognised her. Zoe had jumped out of her skin when the woman standing beside her removed her sunglasses and said, 'Hello, my princess.'

Georgia was now slimmer and quite beautiful. She had a glow that Ellen hadn't seen in years, since well before Frank became ill.

'It's all thanks to Dario,' she had said.

'Who's Dario?' Ellen and Zoe had replied in unison.

Georgia recalled those red satin sheets and simply smiled.

'Remind me to tell you all about him sometime,' she replied, as if she was remembering something both secretive and special.

Ellen remained deeply saddened by Patrick's death. In many ways she knew that she'd let him down, strung him along. He'd been so patient to love her unconditionally for so long, and she had repaid that devotion by using him for her own selfish needs.

Ellen couldn't wait to see her father. She wanted to hold him, to tell him about her pregnancy in person, be with him when she received the Huntington's test results. With a heavy heart she was preparing for her trip to Derbyshire. Despite the ongoing unknowns, Ellen was at least confident that Zoe and Georgia could manage without her. For the first time in years, she felt like those two could actually cope with life. A weight that she didn't even realise was there had been lifted. Rob had promised to keep an eye on the two women while she was away. He was still under the misapprehension that Georgia was Ellen's cousin 'Anna'.

Zoe had revisited the Vaughn *incident* a number of times, hoping to jog her memory.

'Have you recalled anything new yet Zoe—any evidence that we could take to the police?' Oliver asked.

'I really wish I could recall more,' she said. 'But all I remember is Vaughn covering my eyes and pushing me in the lift. I do know that he called me *"beautiful"* and touched my hair and that was creepy. He also gave me champagne which made me woozy. But I did drink quite a lot even before I went to his apartment. I'm sorry but that's it. I don't recall anything else at all. Maybe he didn't do anything to me.

I shouldn't have been in that corridor fiddling with his lift, so perhaps he was just teaching me a lesson.'

'Well I think Vaughn was up to no good when Maggie interrupted him,' Rob said emphatically. If Maggie Grant is covering for him, she won't reveal the truth.'

'I think that under the circumstances we all need to make sure that Vaughn never gets the chance to be alone with Zoe again,' Georgia suggested as the best way forward.

'I agree,' Ellen said, nodding. Tell your circle of friends what's happened. They can help watch your back. Kobi and Aiza also need to be careful. Make sure they take the threat seriously.

Following what was now referred to as 'the Lambert incident', Oliver promised to walk Zoe home on study and meeting days. Georgia frequently prepared dinner to thank him. Everyone suspected that Lambert had spiked Zoe's drink that evening but they had no proof. Even if they could access Zoe's chip data and confirm the presence of a drug, it still wouldn't prove how it came to be in her system. Zoe decided to stay at AMDAT and focus on gaining her degree. She discussed the incident with her close group of friends but didn't tell anyone else.

There appeared to be no new developments around the four missing Newark women. It was a mystery that was not going to be cleared up anytime soon. The news was reporting that the fire at Detective O'Connor's house was no longer considered suspicious. Georgia Ashmore had been cleared of any wrongdoing. Nevertheless, Georgia—Anna—was incognito, starting afresh in her new homeland.

34

Eyam was one of the quaintest places Ellen had ever visited. The village was quiet and peaceful, surrounded by rolling green hills and rocky streams. Nearby towns such as Hathersage were simply delightful. In Bakewell, she especially loved the ducks and ducklings splashing about in the cool water as it tumbled endlessly over the stony weir. The sky was a vibrant blue and the air felt clean and smelt fresh.

The cottage Harold had inherited was snug. Although small and neglected, with plenty of maintenance needed, it oozed character. The five small rooms were configured in a somewhat ramshackle manner, as if each new owner had built on an additional section just to meet their specific needs. There was a lounge, a galley kitchen, two bedrooms and an outhouse bathroom.

Being with her father was comforting, like being wrapped in a thick warm coat on a cold New Jersey day. Ellen had always been a daddy's girl and with a baby on the way their bond was now stronger than ever. Her father had been surprised when a pregnant Ellen arrived on his doorstep. He was less surprised to be told that Patrick was the father, although he was still incredibly sad about the young man's untimely death. An e-mail from Muriel, with test results attached, had arrived during Ellen's stay in Q Heathrow. Harold encouraged her to open the document, but she had decided to wait. 'What's the rush?' she had said. 'Whatever will be, will be. I'll open it before I leave but not right now. I don't want anything to spoil our time together.'

'Okay, but promise me you *will* open it before you go home. I really want to be with you when you do.'

'Promise,' she had replied.

Harold had arranged for Ellen to meet a couple of his new friends the following afternoon. The Greens had invited them both to afternoon tea and asked Harold to remind his daughter to bring the sampler.

Father and daughter linked arms as they strolled down Church Street. The connection felt warm and familiar; it was as if she had returned to her childhood days and was walking with him to school. Ellen was enjoying being lost in the moment when Harold stopped in front of a cottage and she was jerked back to the present.

The small cottage was one of three nestled in a row. They all had neatly maintained gardens packed with a colourful array of annuals and perennials. The scent of the foxgloves, pansies, irises and lavender mingled together in the air, reminding Ellen of a perfume her mother once wore.

Harold explained to his daughter that the centre cottage was where the bubonic plague started its unrelenting destruction of the Eyam community. George Viccars, a travelling tailor, was lodging at the cottage of the widow Mary Cooper. Mary had recently remarried, to a tailor by the name of Alexander Hadfield. It seemed that the plague had been brought to the Hadfield home in a parcel of fabrics and old clothing, sourced from Canterbury and sent via London. On opening the parcel, George found the contents to be damp. When he unrolled the fabrics and placed them by the open fire to dry, fleas carrying the plague jumped free to bite and infect him. He died a few days later, becoming the first reported plague death in Eyam.

The two Cooper children, Edward and Jonathon, fell ill a short time later. Their glands became swollen with pus, they developed a high fever and an unquenchable thirst and were eventually unable to breathe as their lungs filled with fluid. One after the other they died, but not before they had spread the disease to their neighbours, many of whom went on to suffer a similar fate.

Ellen spent time reading the plaques outside each cottage until Harold complained that if she lingered any longer they would be late. He smiled at his daughter as he shook the bunch of cowbells attached to the Greens' well-worn oak front door. Harold was already aware of the story Ellen was about to discover. He was sure she would enjoy this visit and looked forward to watching her response to the tale of the Green sisters.

Miss Irene Green answered the door wearing an old-fashioned floral pinafore. The distinct smell of cooked apples wafted out with her and Ellen began to salivate.

Once she greeted their guests she turned and, in a broad accent, called out, 'Urry up, Edith; they're 'ere.'

The woman was short and stocky with round glasses and grey hair pulled back into an intricate yet loose knot. Ellen estimated she was around seventy to eighty years old. She would have fitted perfectly into any Dickens novel.

Irene smiled warmly and waved her hands in a welcoming gesture as she bustled them both into a small front room. Taking up most of the floor space were two large floral chairs and a matching settee. The mantel was adorned with tiny porcelain animal figurines and an ornate oak clock ticked loudly with each swing of its pendulum.

Tucked beneath the corner window, a small round table was set for afternoon tea. It was decorated with a lace tablecloth, matching napkins, teacups and saucers embossed with pink roses, a small jug of milk and a crystal bowl piled high with sugar cubes. The room reminded Ellen of a museum display. She had no idea such places still existed in a fast-paced world bursting with technology. It was as if time had stood still in Eyam while the rest of the world had passed on by.

Harold grinned as he watched his daughter absorbing this unusual scene. He had enjoyed afternoon tea with the Green sisters a number of times, and now understood his ancestry in greater detail.

'I'm so happy to finally meet you, my dear Ellen,' the old woman said, as she grabbed hold of Ellen's shoulders and kissed her on both cheeks. 'My sister and I have been hoping to have Hancocks come back to our village since we were children, and now we have two of you here—which is more than we ever expected.'

Ellen looked puzzled.

'Sorry, my dear, I must be confusing you. I'll start at the beginning. My name is Irene. My sister Edith and I have lived in Eyam all our lives.'

Just then, Edith entered the room puffing and panting. For one brief moment Ellen thought she had developed double vision. The sisters were identical twins and had it not been for the different clothing she would have been unable to tell them apart.

'This is my twin sister, Edith.'

'That's pretty obvious,' Ellen said, raising both her eyebrows.

Harold's grin broadened.

'I'm just about to tell Ellen our story, Edith, so let's all sit down and get comfy,' Irene began.

'Eyam is known as the plague village, because in 1665 the bubonic plague arrived here from London. In order to prevent the disease spreading to the surrounding towns and villages—'

Edith suddenly cut in and continued the storytelling, '—the townsfolk decided to follow Reverend George Mompesson and former rector Thomas Stanley's plan and cut themselves off from the outside world. The villagers were a God-fearing bunch. They believed their village was struck by the plague because they must have displeased

God. Saving their neighbours through the self-sacrifice of isolation, they hoped, would grant them absolution and ensure them all a place in heaven.'

The dialogue then seamlessly passed back to Irene.

'The plague was highly contagious, so to prevent the disease spreading throughout the neighbouring towns, the Earl of Devonshire, who lived at nearby Chatsworth House, provided food and medicines to the villagers. It seemed like a noble gesture but it was in his best interests for the villagers of Eyam to stay put.

'People from the surrounding towns also left food and other necessities in various locations, including on the stone wall by Mompesson's Well. Once they departed, the villagers retrieved these supplies. To pay for goods, coins were either placed in the running water of streams or in vinegar-filled holes drilled into stone.

'In those days no-one quite understood how diseases spread. However, they worked out that if a person who was well came into contact with a sick person, they often became sick themselves. They also knew that cleaning items with vinegar seemed to prevent disease spreading. Hence the coins in vinegar.'

'The food and clothing supplies kept the survivors alive until the plague had run its course,' Edith piped up. 'By the time the plague burnt out it's estimated that over 259 townsfolk from the 76 families who lived in the parish were dead. In some cases, whole families were wiped out.'

And so the story of Eyam was told by the two sisters, each of whom appeared to know exactly what the other one was thinking. They constantly interrupted and finished each other's sentences, much like an old married couple.

'Isolating the village was an incredibly selfless act. Many of the residents perished who may not have done had they fled,' Irene concluded.

Edith handed a scroll of paper to Ellen. The document contained a diagram of all the households in Eyam, including the number of occupants. A colour scheme depicted whether the people in each house had survived the plague or died. Edith gave Ellen time to examine the document before she unfolded and carefully smoothed flat an old map of the village and surrounding acreage.

'Your ancestors, Ellen, lived on Riley Farm, right here,' Edith said, pointing out the approximate location where the house once stood. 'Elizabeth Hancock, who survived the plague, was your ancestor. Now, show me that sampler; I haven't seen it in years.'

'You know about the sampler?' Ellen asked.

'Well, dear, I did make it.'

'You made it?'

'Yes, my dear. I made it well over sixty-five years ago for a school project.'

'But how did it come to be with my grandmother's personal possessions?' continued Ellen, getting more puzzled with each revelation.

'Well, I sent the sampler to your grandparents, trying to create a mystery, but I never heard back from them. I presumed they either didn't receive it, or they simply weren't interested in their ancestry.' She waved her arms in the air in a manner that signified their perceived lack of interest.

'Well, I'd never seen it before Ellen found it in our attic,' Harold said. 'I don't recall my parents ever mentioning it either.'

'You made the sampler, Edith, so can you please explain it to me?' Ellen asked.

'Most certainly, my dear; but first, I want to know what you have unearthed for yourself.' Edith pointed her finger at Ellen and waited for her to respond.

'Well,' Ellen paused, then began tentatively. 'I believe that the Hancocks immigrated to New Jersey on a sailing ship called the *Kent*.'

'That's correct. We know that at least one did, anyway. Henry Hancock. He was the child born the year after Elizabeth fled Eyam to join her last surviving child, a son, living in Sheffield.' Edith continued to peer at the sampler through an ivory-handled magnifying glass. 'Take another look,' she said to Ellen enthusiastically. 'The letters and crosses in each corner make perfect sense if you join them together.' Ellen studied the corners of the tattered cloth more closely: *E1, Y6, A6, M5.*

'Can't you see?' Edith continued, not quite understanding why Ellen was taking so long to figure out the simple puzzle she had designed as a child. 'The letters spell *EYAM* and the numbers form *1665*, the year the plague came to our village. The *E. H.* stands for Elizabeth Hancock of Riley Farm, and the six small black crosses and the large black cross represent her six children who died from the plague along with her husband who also perished.' Edith's rapid speech paused for a moment, enabling her just enough time to catch her breath before she continued.

'The poor woman had to bury her family all by herself, although Marshall Howe, the local gravedigger, probably helped her. She would have struggled to drag the bodies out of the house and dig seven graves all on her own. From all accounts, Elizabeth Hancock wasn't a large woman and burials needed to occur as soon as possible after death to reduce further infection. The seven souls succumbed to the plague within an eight-day period. That was a lot of digging for one poor grieving woman.'

Ellen absorbed the information for a few moments before a puzzled expression crossed her face.

'If Elizabeth lost all her children and her husband to the plague, then left the village before Henry was born, which of our relatives left Dad his cottage?' she asked.

Irene gave a cheeky grin before she proceeded with an explanation. 'Well, that's just it, my dear. A relative didn't leave him the cottage. My sister Edith did.'

'I'm not following you,' Ellen said. By now she was looking completely perplexed. 'Edith isn't dead.'

Harold chuckled.

'No Ellen, clearly Edith isn't dead … yet.'

At her sister's mischievous comment Edith frowned, pursed her lips and screwed up her eyes.

Irene giggled at her response before continuing. 'Let me explain. We,' Irene said, cocking her head in Edith's direction, 'did everything together and have always lived close to each other in this village. We both found the story of Eyam and the plague enthralling. For many years we ran a small plague museum in Hawkhill Road. We enjoyed talking to tourists about the plague and selling our homemade cakes, biscuits and souvenirs.'

'Oh, that reminds me.' She jumped up and left the room only to return a short time later with a steaming hot apple pie in one hand and a pot of clotted cream in the other. She cut them all a large piece and topped each with a dollop of cream. It immediately began to melt across the sugar-coated surface.

'Eat, eat,' she encouraged them, 'while I continue the story. Visitors to our museum found the story of Elizabeth Hancock incredibly moving. Although long dead and gone she became somewhat of a local celebrity. Tourists always wanted to know what happened to her. Did she find happiness, or did she succumb to the plague like the rest of her family?

'Since we were teenagers, we both remained convinced that your particular line of the Hancock family was the one related to Elizabeth, because there were a number of males in alternate generations named either Henry or Harold Hancock. We decided to try one last time to make contact with the New Jersey Hancocks, but felt we needed something more intriguing to gain their attention this time. We decided that whoever died first would leave their house to a Hancock in New Jersey and try and coax them back to live in Eyam, or, at the very least, visit.

'We were both so excited at the prospect of finally meeting a Hancock that we decided not to wait until one of us died. Neither of us wanted to miss out on the fun. Edith moved into my home because it's larger and we concocted the whole story. We invented the long-lost dying relative and the cottage inheritance just to make the situation seem more mysterious,' she said, wriggling her stubby fingers in the air as if to signify secrecy. 'Your father had already traced the family back to Derbyshire and the rest is history. Your dad now lives in the town which was once the home of Elizabeth, his however-many-times great-great-great-great-great-grandmother.'

'I did tell you that you'd like the tale,' her father said to Ellen, who was still processing this strange turn of events.

Ellen looked from one sister to the other then back to her father. 'So let me get this straight. You two made up the whole inheritance deal just to get a Hancock living back in Eyam?'

'Yes, my dear,' Edith said.

'And didn't it work a treat?' the twins said in unison.

'Anyone care for a cup of Yorkshire Tea?' Irene asked.

Ellen tucked into the delicious apple pie at a rate that was slightly impolite. She hadn't tasted anything so good in a long time. The pastry was crumbly yet moist and the apples were obviously Granny Smiths, cooked to perfection with a minimum of sugar to produce a thick succulent filling. A hint of cloves mingled with cinnamon lingered on the tongue, adding to an already exquisite experience.

'You seem hungry, my dear. Do have another piece. I can see you're eating for two. A new baby Hancock on the way. How exciting.'

The afternoon flew by, with Irene and Edith showing them both a myriad of old memorabilia. They insisted on Ellen accepting a set of books and pamphlets they had left over from their time running the museum. They told her few people were interested in learning about past plagues anymore. Pandemics were no longer just a historical novelty; they posed a real and ongoing threat to the survival of the human race.

At the door, later, the sisters stood close and continued waving until Ellen and Harold turned the corner out of sight. Ellen had promised to visit again before she returned to Melbourne.

Later, in the stillness of the Derbyshire night, Ellen began to sort through the written material while her father sat reading by the open fire. The light of the flames danced around the uneven whitewashed walls and at times the silence was broken by the hiss of evaporating sap.

'Dad, it sounds like Eyam was in fact an inadvertent biological experiment. By isolating the town, every person in the village was eventually exposed to the plague. Those who survived must have had some level of immunity to the illness. Our ancestor Elizabeth Hancock had extreme exposure to the bubonic plague, because she lived with, nursed, then buried seven plague victims without getting sick herself. Her immune system could clearly handle the plague.'

Ellen read into the early hours of the morning. Early in the twenty-first century, a scientific study of living Eyam descendants showed that many of them carried one strand of a mutant gene known as Delta 32. Some carried two strands, one from each parent. She wondered if she carried the Delta 32 gene. Most likely, she suspected.

Ellen woke around five the next morning. Once her thoughts focused on the Green sisters, her mind became too active for sleep. She smiled at the thought of their nonstop banter and their endless enthusiasm for life. A very quirky pair.

As the sun began to rise, she decided to make an early morning visit to the Hancock gravesite. She wanted to reach the Riley Farm site before the township awoke and the sounds of the modern world could intrude. Ellen yearned to gain a feel for the place. She was drawn to pay her respects to the seven Hancocks entombed before their time. She felt the need to capture the scene using all her senses, just as Elizabeth would have done all those centuries ago.

As she made her way up Riley Lane along the well-worn gravel path, the wind gently rustled through a nearby stand of elms. Dew was visible on the ground, heaviest in the regions that rarely saw the sun's rays. Rabbits nibbling on grass tips scurried into the thick bracken when she came too close for comfort.

The gravestones were located in a gently sloping field above Riley Lane. Signage suggested the site was monitored by the local authorities. It was very well maintained. The grass was freshly clipped and the graves were weeded. A low sandstone rock wall had been built around them. It was of no particular shape, though Ellen decided 'oval' would best describe it. To prevent anyone sitting or standing on the wall's surface, the top stones were placed with their pointed ends upright.

Apparently the children's headstones had been moved from their actual gravesites into a grouping around their father John's much larger tomb by a Thomas Birds around 1820. Later, the worn engraving on the headstones had been gouged deeper at the expense of a Sir Henry Burford-Hancock. To this day, it hadn't been established if he was an actual blood relative.

Ellen entered the cemetery through the narrow gap. Large square headstones described five of the children. Their father's tomb was believed to contain the remaining child, a son. A plaque explained that the family members had all died in the space of just eight days from the third to the tenth of August 1666. The ten-year-old girl, Ann, was the last to perish.

Ellen had packed a light breakfast. She rolled out the picnic blanket and cushion on the damp grass, sat down and made herself comfy. The croissant filled with the Green sisters' raspberry jam was most satisfying. She made a mental note to ask Edith for the recipe. The thermos coffee wasn't as good as freshly brewed. However, the location in which it was being consumed made up for any inadequacies.

After breakfast, she lay down and tucked the cushion under her head. The gentle slope provided a prop. It was almost as if she was sitting up. From this elevated position she could observe the township below as it rose to face the new day: a couple of joggers, a Tesco delivery van, a farmer on his tractor. She began to warm up, yawned a few times and, before she knew it, fell asleep.

Ellen dreamed she was hovering above a young woman carrying a small child. The girl looked pale, still and cold as the woman respectfully laid her on a sheet spread open on the ground. She carefully combed and plaited her hair, then washed her small hands and feet before sprinkling her body with pink rose petals. Lastly, she kissed her, not once but on her head, her cheeks, each ear and finally her blue lips. Tears flowed from her frail thin body. Her pain was palpable. She carefully closed the shroud and began sewing the girl neatly within, then began to dig her grave with a small spade.

She had been working for what seemed like hours, when a large man carrying a shovel strolled up the hill and offered her his hand. With his help she rose to her feet and, at his beckoning, sat on a nearby boulder while he completed the dig. He lifted the girl's body respectfully into the grave and carefully began to backfill the fresh hole with soil. The young mother fell to her knees and helped him.

By now her weeping was audible. It was clear that her heart was shattered. Still sobbing she pressed her cheek to the ground, trying to sense the girl beneath. She lay there, still and cold, until the thick fog rolled in across the moors to smother the village as if wanting to end its misery.

Ellen was awoken suddenly by the thud of apples landing near her left ear. As she lifted her head, she heard voices and saw three young lads running away down Riley Lane. *Little sods.*

She packed everything back into her picnic basket. Then, as she walked among the Hancock graves one last time, she recalled the dream. For a brief moment she wasn't sure it was a dream. It had been extremely vivid. From the vibrant colours to the sickly sweet smell that many plague victims were reported to have experienced just before they succumbed. Eerily it was as if she had really been watching Elizabeth bury her daughter Ann.

Elizabeth was a brave woman. How strong she was to keep on living despite suffering from overwhelming grief. She could relate to Elizabeth falling pregnant and then being unexpectedly left without a husband to share the joy and happiness of their new baby. Ellen felt proud of her ancestor. Without her strength all those centuries ago the baby she was now carrying would never have existed. She herself would never have been born. Ellen looked down at her body swelling with the precious but unexpected cargo. Almost on cue the fetus gave a kick as if to say, 'Good morning, Mom'. At that precise moment Ellen knew she'd made the right decision. She owed it to Elizabeth's memory to love and nurture this new addition to the Hancock legacy.

After four wonderful weeks with her father, it was time to face the rigours of the journey home. Ellen carried her suitcase into the lounge room and sat down next to him by the fire.

'I've had such a great time, Dad. I can see now why you love Eyam. Life is just so simple here. I'm almost tempted to stay myself.'

'I only have one regret darling—your mom.'

'You shouldn't regret anything. You were a wonderful husband and you're a terrific father. Your life has been on hold for far too long. It's your time now, Dad. Enjoy.'

'Thanks darling. You and James are great kids. Your mom and I couldn't have asked for anything more.

'So then ... off home tomorrow.' Harold said as he wiped away a tear. Haven't you forgotten something?' Ellen knew exactly what he meant.

Her chin quivered as she proceeded to find and open the email. For a few moments she just stared at the document, then, with a sigh, she opened it. As she began to read, her father reached across, took hold of her hand and closed his eyes.

Ellen Elizabeth Hancock—DNA Test for HD mutation result is NEGATIVE.

Ellen's head dropped and they both began to cry. Laughter burst through the sobbing as their emotions mixed and swirled away all the years of not knowing—years of *what if.*

'Negative,' repeated Harold. 'Our baby girl is negative. Did you hear that Beatrice?'

Melbourne
August 2074

35

Georgia sat smiling at her Black Forest cake as thirty-nine candles flickered on top. It was a large circular cake with five layers and several fat black cherries with intact stalks were poised on the thick cream surface. Rob had joined the celebration. He and Georgia had become quite good friends. In fact, Ellen had noticed some chemistry developing between them. Rob had given Georgia a lovely pair of silver earrings made by his sister Ruth. She was a silversmith who specialised in jewellery featuring native animals. The earrings were tiny ringtail possums that hung from Georgia's earlobes by their tails—most creative.

Ellen, Zoe and Rob sang with great gusto and out of tune at the top of their voices.

'Happy birthday, dear Anna, happy birthday to you.'

'Quick! Blow out the candles; we don't want a bunch of firefighters on our roof,' Ellen said—and they both giggled, remembering that night in New Jersey.

'I don't know,' Georgia mused, 'I wouldn't mind meeting some Aussie firemen. After Dario I'm quite in the mood for more romance,' as she glanced seductively in Rob's direction. Georgia extinguished the candles with one huge breath and then closed her eyes, trying to decide what to wish for. The truth was she now had everything she desired. Living in Melbourne with her daughter Zoe, who was doing very well with her medical studies; sharing an apartment with her best friend Ellen, who was now eight months pregnant and expecting a healthy baby. What a relief it had been to learn that Ellen was not a Huntington's carrier. Her best friend had wasted all those years fretting for nothing.

I know, she thought, *how about some romance for myself and Ellen?* Zoe had that aspect of her life covered with Oliver. He was such a kind young man. She sank the knife deep into the rich chocolate cake then lifted it out and ran her fingers carefully down its sharp edge to gather the caught chocolate and cream before licking them clean.

'Time for pressies,' squealed Ellen like a big kid and handed her friend a square package wrapped in hot-pink paper. Zoe gave her mother a long thin parcel which had a number of smaller ones attached with colourful curly ribbons.

'How exciting,' Georgia said, ripping the paper off Ellen's gift first, with the enthusiasm of a toddler.

'A new camera!' she exclaimed. 'How wonderful! A top-of-the-range solar Canon with a telescopic laser zoom! Oh, Ellen, it has an NLR—no light required function and an optional ATO—this is way too much. It must have cost you a small fortune.'

'You're worth it, darling,' Ellen replied, giving her friend a hug.

'What's an ATO—Australian Tax Office?' Rob asked with a frown.

'No … it stands for add that odour' Georgia laughed, 'Then again, a pic taken in a tax office would probably turn out rather whiffy?' They all laughed.

Zoe's gift was a tripod; a selection of Canon lenses and a can of spray-on-peel-off mood filters. Georgia was thrilled. She hadn't taken any images since the day of her arrest and all her camera gear was in storage.

'I just can't wait to snap some pics,' she said.

'I knew you'd be eager to start clicking, soooo … I've already charged the battery for you,' Ellen said with a smile, as she passed it to Georgia from behind her back.

'You're such a good friend, Ellen; no wonder I love you as much as I do.'

'Hey, Anna, why don't you walk with me to AMDAT this afternoon?' Zoe said. 'You can take some pics in the park on the way and of the AMDAT Tower. If we set off a bit early, I can be your model,' she said, pouting her mouth and posing artificially with one hand behind her ear.

'Great idea! I'll get everything set up while you get organised; shouldn't take me too long with a battery charged ready to go.'

'Well, I must be off,' Rob said as he rose from the couch. 'Happy birthday Ms Anna and have fun taking pics this afternoon.' He gave the birthday girl an affectionate hug and a peck on her cheek. She blushed.

Georgia and Zoe set off for AMDAT, stopping every few minutes to capture images. The day was slightly overcast, which provided a natural filter for photography by reducing harsh shadows. Georgia was a skilled photographer and hoped to set up an online business one day. Her business ambitions, however, would have to wait. Ellen planned to take maternity leave after the baby arrived, and then return to work. Georgia would undertake the childminding and run the household. It was going to be so wonderful.

Zoe kissed her mother goodbye and entered the tower. Georgia stood at the base of the structure, excited by the spectacle towering above her. She sauntered the length of the outer perimeter, zooming in and out with her new camera. She must have taken at least a hundred images. The butterflies were actively flitting around the flowers and even the occasional bat made an appearance. It felt really good to be taking images again. She had forgotten just how much she'd missed operating a camera.

36

Gum turned in the direction of the noise and saw the one-year-old peering out of the window. Little Mika had pushed the red button, causing a blind to start rising. She raced over, picked up the toddler and quickly brought the sunscreen blind back down.

'You need to fix the override switch that controls the blinds, Gum. I can't believe that we have all this technology and you forgot to maintain the program,' Vaughn mumbled, without lifting his eyes from the medical journal he was reading.

'Relax, Vaughn; the windows are tinted. You'd be lucky to see anything through them anyway. I'll check the programming later today.'

'Make it a priority. Mika is getting into all sorts of mischief and we can't be too careful,' he replied.

Mika had been busy playing with her toys when she had deviated from the mat to chase a ball. If you didn't look too closely, she appeared to be like any other toddler. Sensing the tension between Vaughn and Gum, Mika looked in their direction, before dropping to the ground and crawling as fast as she could to the feet of a young woman. Reaching upwards with her arms, she beckoned her to pick her up.

'Cuggle,' she said.

Mika's skin was quite pale in colour and the pupils of her eyes were very slightly misshapen. Her fingers were short and stubby. They were webbed, making it difficult for her to grasp small objects.

'It's time for her hand operation,' said Vaughn, as he observed Mika attempting to unsuccessfully twist the limbs of the toy dinosaur the young woman was holding. 'The excess skin needs to be removed. We shouldn't delay the procedure. She's old enough and it will improve her dexterity. I'll get our resident surgeon to undertake the procedure next Tuesday. It won't be complex. We do need to eliminate the problem, though, before we implant any more embryos. There must be some way to dampen down the external features and still maintain viability.'

'Well, thanks to Daniel and Maggie, we now have Zoe Ashmore's ova frozen and ready to go,' said Gum. 'Those eggs should be far superior to any we've used to date. Hopefully you can undertake less gene editing while still retaining all the positive characteristics.'

'It would be useful if we could test just how robust Zoe's immune system really is before we fertilise the ova though, wouldn't it?' Vaughn commented. The stronger the embryos, the better their final worth.

'Leave that to me,' Gum replied. 'I have a strategy in mind.'

37

Vaughn was not as friendly towards Sarah anymore and he also seemed to be distancing himself from Zoe. The truth was she sexually frustrated him. Vaughn could usually have whatever or whomever he wanted, but in Zoe's case he simply had to keep his hormones under wraps. Forbidden fruit is the sweetest of all and that was certainly the case with Zoe Ashmore.

To distract himself, Vaughn had moved his attentions to Fleur, another very attractive student, who gave the impression that she coped skilfully with his narcissistic personality. Unlike Sarah, she had evidently recognised that being needy wasn't the way to handle Lambert's oversized ego. Zoe had observed that Fleur kept Lambert on the back foot, not always agreeing to do whatever he wanted, whenever he wanted to do it. She was less eager to please than Sarah had ever been. Zoe had witnessed Fleur declining Lambert's dinner invitations, and she always made the effort to maintain positive relationships with the other students.

Zoe was, however, worried about Sarah. She seemed quite nervy, jumpy even. She clearly wasn't coping with Lambert's rejection. Sarah looked like she'd lost weight and her self-confidence had all but vanished. Zoe had watched the deterioration over the last few weeks and felt sorry for her.

'She deserves all she gets,' Charlie said.

'She was a total mean little bitch to you when you tried to warn her off socialising with Lambert, so she's just getting one big dose of karma,' Felix added.

'I don't think that's exactly how karma works,' Zoe replied. 'Lambert is a predator; Sarah was his victim. I might have been one of his conquests if Oliver hadn't sent Maggie to save me.' She cast Oliver a smile and then leaned into his shoulder. 'I think I'll sit with her during the lecture today and I might even ask her to come for a drink with us at the pub tonight.'

Charlie and Felix didn't appear happy with Zoe's plan. They glanced at each other then back at Zoe, hoping to see signs that she was just kidding, but it was clear she wasn't. Oliver smiled at his beautiful girlfriend. *Always putting others first. What a sweetheart.*

Sarah seemed surprised when Zoe slid into the seat next to her. She was, however, appreciative of the company. She was fully aware that she had been bitchy to most of the girls. Now that Lambert had finished using her, she had few friends left. The male students weren't interested in Sarah either. They didn't want a relationship with someone who'd been violated by that creep.

Professor Lambert opened his lecture.

'Today's lecture topic relates to the CCR5 Delta 32 mutation. Delta 32 is the short name for a gene that's found mainly in the descendants of British and European populations. It has been estimated that between twenty-five and sixty per cent of the population died when the plague, otherwise known as the Black Death, spread throughout Britain and Europe in the seventeenth century. We now know that most people who possessed the Delta 32 gene and were exposed to the plague, survived and lived to pass this protective gene on to their descendants. People with the Delta 32 gene have stronger immune systems, useful for fighting a range of pathogens. This gene doesn't specifically protect a person from the bubonic plague. However, it appears to be more prevalent in the descendants of plague survivors.

'Earlier this century it was proven that a person who inherited the Delta 32 gene from one parent was partially resistant to Acquired Immune Deficiency Syndrome, or AIDS, and a person who inherited the Delta 32 gene from both parents was totally immune. The African continent was not contaminated with the plague to the extent that Britain and Europe were. Because the population of Africa had less exposure to the plague they didn't evolve the same resistance, allowing AIDS to devastate this continent in the 1980s. Research has also shown that the Delta 32 gene is virtually absent today in South-East Asian and Native American populations, which the plague didn't ravage.'

When the lecture was finished, Zoe asked Sarah to meet her near the front entrance. Everyone went back to their locker rooms then down to the foyer, where Sarah was already waiting.

'Are you okay, Sarah?' Zoe asked. 'You seem a bit miserable.'

'I'm okay Zoe. What makes you think that I'm not?' she replied unconvincingly.

'Well ... for one thing, Professor Lambert has a new love interest.'

'So what?' she said, as her chin began to quiver.

'So ... how does that make you feel?'

Sarah's eyes pooled with tears and her tough-girl facade began to crack.

'Not too good. I guess you were right Zoe. Go on, gloat all you like.'

'No-one is gloating Sarah. Lambert is a predator—you're his student. In my opinion he's abused his position. Anyway, let's not dwell on him. What you need is a distraction. Take your mind off things. Why don't you come to the pub with us?' Zoe motioned towards her group of friends. 'It could do you good to socialise and I really would like to get to know the real Sarah.'

Sarah's face lit up for a moment then dropped, as if reality had bitten her. 'They won't want me to come,' she said, glancing across at Zoe's friends. Felix's new girlfriend Aiza—a pretty, petite girl with exotic features—had just joined them.

'You want Sarah to come to the pub with us, don't you?' Zoe called out to the group.

'Yes, we'd love her to come,' Oliver replied. Kobi and Aiza gave a thumbs up. Charlie and Felix nodded with feigned smiles.

Sarah reluctantly joined the group. They were sauntering down the narrow laneway towards their favourite pub when Zoe suddenly stopped and began feeling her right ear.

'You okay?' Oliver questioned.

'My earring, I've lost my earring. It must have fallen out when I pulled off my jumper. It's a diamond. Mom will kill me. She bought them especially for my eighteenth. I knew I shouldn't have worn them. You go on ahead. I need to go back and look for it.'

'I'll help you look,' Sarah said, not wanting to be left alone with the group. She was quite aware they weren't relishing her presence.

'I should come with you,' said Oliver. 'Sarah isn't supposed to go into our group's locker room.'

'No, it's okay, Ollie; Sarah can help me. It will only take a few minutes to check. We will stay together. We'll be fine.'

'Well, promise me that you'll stay together,' he insisted, with a frown.

'Promise,' said Zoe, giving him a quick peck on the lips. 'Oh, and buy us a champagne each, please. We shouldn't be long. Are bubbles okay for you, Sarah?'

'Super,' she replied.

38

Zoe punched in the security code and entered Level 12 with Sarah. It was very quiet. Everyone had left for the day. They searched and found the earring near her locker. It must have fallen out when she was getting changed, as she had suspected. Luckily the cleaning crew hadn't yet vacuumed. She didn't find the back of the earring but that could be easily replaced. Zoe placed the diamond into her purse for safekeeping.

They both turned and headed for the door when the lights suddenly went out. It was pitch black. There were no windows in the locker room so they couldn't see anything. Sarah immediately became concerned.

'It's okay, Sarah; just stand still and stay calm. The backup generator should kick in any second now.'

They waited.

Nothing happened.

Zoe could hear Sarah's breathing rate increasing. Her own anxiety levels were also escalating.

'Maybe it's a building-wide power outage. Not to worry, I'll activate the torch on my mobile. I just have to find it.' Zoe began rummaging in her large handbag, feeling for her mobile. Eventually she found it and by the small yet bright beam of light, they again began making their way towards the main door. On reaching the exit they discovered that the door PIN pad had also lost power. They were unable to enter the opening code.

'I don't like this; I'm a bit claustrophobic. Isn't there any other way out?' Sarah asked. 'I'm starting to feel trapped.'

'Of course, thanks for reminding me. There is another way: the fire escape.'

Feeling relieved, Zoe led them towards the back of the locker room. She grabbed the handle of the fire escape and wiggled it. It refused to turn. Her momentary relief turned to frustration and she started pushing the door with her shoulder. It didn't budge. *That's a bit weird*, she thought to herself. *Fire escapes should be exactly that:*

escapes. By now Sarah was having trouble remaining calm. She was becoming quite upset.

'I think my throat is closing over, Zoe. I feel like I can't breathe. No really, I don't think I can breathe.' Sarah began panting so rapidly that she was at risk of hyperventilating and passing out.

Just when Zoe thought things couldn't get any worse, she heard a rustling noise. The noise was familiar. Her spine began to tingle as she realised the gravity of the situation that was unfolding. Somehow the two airlock doors had been opened and bats had accessed the locker area. Zoe felt a wing brush past her cheek and her blood went cold.

'Sarah, keep completely still. Some bats have escaped. It's imperative that we stay calm.' But it was all too late. The minute Sarah felt the warm texture of bat flesh on her face she began thrashing about, hitting the mammals with her hands and screaming hysterically. Zoe's attempts to calm her were all in vain. The terrified bats had begun defending themselves.

Zoe crouched in a corner. She placed both hands over her head to shield her face and sat motionless. Hopefully the bats wouldn't view her as a threat and leave her alone. There was nothing more she could do to help her friend.

In the darkness Zoe's eyes were now useless. She was effectively blind. The adrenaline began surging through her veins and her remaining senses heightened.

She could smell their warm bodies.

She could hear their claws scratching.

She could almost taste their fear.

The guttural sounds emanating from Sarah were enough to tell her the young woman was in serious trouble. Sarah's screaming was bloodcurdling. Zoe began to shake uncontrollably and her breathing rate increased. She felt, and was, utterly powerless.

After what seemed like an eternity the bright fluorescent lights flickered into action. It took only moments for the bats to retreat into the darkness and safety of their habitat. Sarah lay on the floor, quivering and sobbing. From the blood, it was obvious she'd been scratched and bitten. Zoe had also been bitten but that didn't stop her rising and slamming the emergency button as hard as she could.

Within a short timeframe an emergency crew arrived, including Maggie, who was visibly shaken to find two students in such a state. The girls were both taken to Daniel Grant's emergency medical centre on Level 42. Maggie notified Sarah's parents and Ellen, and asked them to come to AMDAT as soon as possible. When Oliver heard what had happened, he also returned to AMDAT.

39

The girls were placed in isolation in the medical emergency room on Level 42. Their wounds were thoroughly cleaned and both were injected with an immune system booster and prophylactic antibiotics. Their chip data was now live streaming on the digital monitors next to their beds. Sarah's blood pressure was abnormally high, which, under the circumstances, was not unexpected.

Sarah's parents, as well as Ellen and Oliver, had arrived at the tower. Ellen had decided to try and find out exactly what had occurred before contacting Georgia. Through the glass barrier, Zoe and Sarah's family and friends did their best to reassure and comfort them. Rather than talk about possible outcomes in front of Sarah and Zoe, Ellen requested that they all move to a private room where they could discuss the incident out of earshot of the distressed girls.

'How has this happened?' Ellen asked angrily. 'Zoe told me the bats could never escape from the bat zone, that it's a secure environment, with a failsafe airlock system.'

'It is,' Margaret said. 'At least it's supposed to be, even with a power failure. Security is reviewing the footage from the lab to determine what happened. We know that the power was cut off to the bat zone and that the backup generator took a couple of minutes to activate, when it should have come online instantaneously.'

'Well, your systems have obviously failed Zoe and Sarah, and anyone else who enters that zone is potentially at risk.'

'We will order a full overhaul. We'll install more backup systems. I assure you, this will never happen again,' Margaret said, sounding desperate.

'Well, that doesn't help Zoe and Sarah now, does it?' Ellen responded, obviously dissatisfied with Margaret Grant's assurances.

'Look,' Margaret paused and took a deep breath, 'I know that you're all very upset and have good reason to be, but we do know that the bats that have bitten the girls are only infected with a pneumonic form of the plague. The bats infected with AV64 and Ebola are in different sections, so at least that's a positive.'

Ellen's face screwed up, as if she simply couldn't grasp the logic or reasoning behind Margaret Grant's latest revelation. All patience was fast draining from Ellen and anger was rapidly filling the vacuum it left behind. Both the pitch and volume of her voice increased.

'Have you completely lost your senses, Mrs Grant? The plague could kill them, so how can you consider it a positive that they might *only* get the plague? Fuzzy logic, Mrs Grant! I thought you were an intelligent person.'

Margaret felt a flush of anger. Due to her power base she wasn't questioned by anyone in the organisation, even if they believed her to be wrong. Criticising Mrs Grant wasn't the way to retain your position within AMDAT. Margaret didn't like this woman's attitude. Who did she think she was, speaking to her in such a manner?

Ellen continued her tirade, 'I demand to see Mr Grant immediately to ensure everything that can be done to help Zoe and Sarah is being done. Someone needs to be held accountable for this incident. You, Mrs Grant, appear totally incapable of handling the situation.'

'We demand,' said Sarah's parents.

Oliver also stepped forwards to display a united front.

'I'll see if he's available,' Margaret said, clearly rattled and not sure what to say or do next.

'He's your husband, Mrs Grant; make him available,' Ellen said, staring her straight in the eye.

Margaret went a bright shade of scarlet. She was fuming. Being Kenneth's only child, she was used to being adored. She did the demanding of everyone else, never the other way around. She tried unsuccessfully to compose herself, then turned and exited via the lift.

Daniel had been working in his private laboratory all day. He was now in the penthouse, having just showered and changed. His hair and beard were still quite damp. Maggie entered the bathroom.

'You look ruffled, Maggs; what's happened?' Daniel asked as he rubbed his hair dry.

Maggie's words blurted out rapidly in a tone that signalled to him just how upset she was.

'We've had an incident.' She drew in a deep breath before continuing, 'Zoe Ashmore and another student, Sarah Baker, have been scratched and bitten by infected bats.' Maggie sighed. 'The woman who is Zoe's emergency contact is hysterical, rude and demanding. Under normal circumstances, I'd have security escort her off the premises. Can you please come down to the medical centre? I don't want to converse with her again. She's being unreasonable and hostile.'

'Okay, Maggs; calm down. I did hear the emergency alarm but thought the problem had been sorted. Now, tell me exactly what happened and how. I need to know everything if I'm going to handle this situation.'

The distressed relatives and friends had been waiting, not so patiently, for Margaret Grant to return with her husband. *What could they be doing?* thought Ellen. *Getting their stories straight,* she suspected. Daniel finally entered the room with Maggie tucked in closely behind him. She was genuinely scared of Ellen, fearing she might even hit someone if she escalated any further. Daniel began introducing himself to the small group. First, he introduced himself to Sarah's parents, then Oliver; lastly, he turned to face Ellen. Ellen was sure he'd deliberately left her until last as a display of power. No doubt his wife had complained to him about her emotional state. Her nostrils flared and her teeth clenched as she waited for Mr Grant to acknowledge her.

For the first three seconds, Daniel looked directly and confidently into Ellen's eyes; then, as he recognised her, he stepped unsteadily backwards, as if he'd been pushed by a pair of invisible hands. Ellen seemed bewildered by this response. Then, despite the passage of years and his changed appearance, she recognised Daniel.

'Daniel Ward?' she mumbled.

'Technically not anymore: I changed my name,' he murmured running his hand back through his hair, as he realised Ellen was about to reveal his true identity.

Maggie was confused. *What was this woman on about?* she thought to herself. *He was her husband; his name was Daniel Grant, wasn't it?*

'And your hair colour—and you aren't wearing glasses,' Ellen continued.

Daniel cleared his throat before responding, 'Hair dye and laser surgery,' whispering in the vain hope that only Ellen would hear.

'Do you two know each other?' Maggie asked, as she surveyed her husband staring at the attractive Ellen Hancock.

'In a different life,' he replied flipping his hand in the air. 'Before you and I were married, darling. I met … Ellen, err … somewhere on my trip to America.'

Ellen tried unsuccessfully to compose herself. Seeing her Daniel was quite a shock. She'd never imagined that Daniel Ward and Daniel Grant could be the same person. On the one hand, she felt a tingle of excitement, wanting to find out everything about him. On the other, she felt angry. Daniel Ward wasn't dead. He wasn't in a lifelong coma or suffering from permanent amnesia. So what excuse did he have for screwing her arse off all summer and then never contacting her again? Daniel was standing right there in front of her, with a smug look on his face, as if nothing intimate had ever happened between them. And, to top it off, he couldn't even remember the city where they had met. Before she knew it, an already overemotional Ellen slapped Daniel's face.

'Security, security' screeched Maggie.

'No need for that,' Daniel said touching his hand to his cheek.

He took in a deep breath and paused to compose himself and then attempted to deflect the conversation.

'I believe congratulations are in order, Ellen,' he said, pointing inappropriately at her baby bump.

Sensing his awkwardness, and feeling rather ashamed of her actions, Ellen acknowledged him with a simple, 'Yes, thanks.'

Awkward silence reigned for a moment before it was broken by Sarah's father.

'Do you think we can get back to the problem at hand, please? Our daughter's life could be at stake.'

'Sorry, of course.' Daniel apologised, and after clearing his throat a second time regained his confidence. He was about to talk about science and that was a subject he was comfortable with at any time.

Just as he began to speak the meeting was interrupted by a security guard.

'Sorry to cut in Mr Grant but there's a woman by the name of Anna Taylor downstairs. She's making a dreadful fuss and demands to be taken to see one of the girls you have up here ... a Zoe Ashmore?'

Ellen looked across at Oliver 'Did you call Anna?'

'Yes, of course.' Ellen rolled her eyes and thought, *shit*.

'Anna Taylor is my cousin. She lives with us. She and Zoe are very close, so I suggest you let her come up and hear what you have to say.'

'Anything to please you Ellen,' Daniel replied.

What the ... thought Maggie as she stared at her husband.

'Bring Ms Taylor up,' Daniel directed the security guard.

A few minutes later, Georgia was led into the room. She shook off the security guard's hand, gave him a filthy look, then went across and stood next to Ellen and Oliver.

'Welcome Ms Taylor. I'm Daniel Grant. I was just about to explain to the group what's happened and how we intend to tackle this very unfortunate incident.' He cleared his throat. 'We know that both girls have been bitten by bats infected with a mutant strain of the pneumonic plague. It's a particularly virulent strain. They have already received an immune system booster and prophylactic antibiotics, so for now all we can do is monitor them closely and wait to see if they develop any symptoms. Fortunately for Zoe, she has been immunised against the plague and, although not a foolproof way of preventing the disease, it should help her own immune system to fight the illness.'

'What about Sarah?' her mother enquired.

'Sarah wasn't assigned to the bat research group, so it wasn't considered necessary for her to be vaccinated against the plague. Sarah should never have had access to the bat zone. She entered after hours with Zoe. She's therefore more at risk of developing the disease. The injections will, however, enhance her natural resistance.

'If either of the girls develops symptoms, we'll manage any subsequent body system failures as they occur. If necessary, we can place them on full life support.'

There was a loud thud as a pale-faced Georgia hit the deck.

Ellen bent down, placed Georgia on her side and began loosening her clothing. 'Why aren't you moving the girls to the specialist infectious diseases hospital?' she asked, as she wrestled with Georgia's belt buckle.

'Protocol,' he replied. 'Because AMDAT research involves the use of dangerous biohazards anyone contaminated in any way must be isolated and treated on the premises. This medical emergency centre is equipped with the latest technology. We have everything we require right here. I have summoned a specialist who will arrive shortly to care exclusively for the girls. If they have contracted the plague, they will soon become highly contagious. I'm confident that the girls will survive, although we'll know more in the next twenty-four hours.'

Daniel was having trouble concentrating. He felt a stirring that hadn't occurred in years. Ellen was as beautiful and as feisty as ever and, although it was completely inappropriate, she had awakened something within him that had long been dormant.

Although still stunned, Maggie didn't miss a thing. Her husband was usually quite dismissive of other females. However, with Ellen, he was showing a softer side and far too much interest. Why had she called him Daniel Ward? What had gone on between these two? Well, Ellen was pregnant, so probably had a partner at home. Whatever their connection, it was a long time ago. She couldn't possibly be a threat to their relationship, could she?

Daniel continued, 'While the girls are being treated, we can accommodate one relative of each in the adjoining suites. These suites are used by researchers for the observation of disease progression. This will allow some of you to stay close to the girls, while staying completely safe from contracting the plague, should they develop it.'

'Thanks,' Ellen said. Her approach had softened. 'That would be really good.' Despite her initial anger, she'd also felt chemistry between them. How could a relationship of only six weeks produce such a strong bond that had lasted all these years? She suddenly felt all hot and flustered.

Oliver noticed the red colour creeping up the skin of Ellen's neck and face. 'You okay?' he asked.

'Yes, I'm fine. It's just a great deal to process, that's all, and it's so hot and stuffy in here, don't you think?' she said, fanning herself with the piece of paper she'd been holding.

'I'm not at all hot,' Oliver replied.

The girls could be viewed through the isolation glass barrier. They communicated with relatives and friends via an intercom. Both girls were calmer. Georgia had recovered from the fainting spell, but she couldn't stop crying. Ellen tried to convince her that Zoe needed a calm mother, not a snivelling mess. Georgia tried deep breathing but she simply couldn't calm down. It was decided that Ellen (as the one with medical training) would stay to support Zoe. Maggie, Daniel and Oliver all thought Zoe's mother, Georgia, was still in America so the decision made sense to them. Sarah's mother, Rowena, stayed to support her daughter.

'I've taken blood samples from the girls, so that I can run the specialist DNA test and check for the Delta 32 gene. This will give us an idea if either of them have any natural immunity. I can test the two of you also,' Maggie offered, turning to Ellen and Rowena.

'I'm not a blood relative to Zoe,' Ellen replied, as she shook her head.

'I thought you were her aunt?'

'No, I'm not a real aunt, just best friends with her mother. So that's what she calls me.'

'That's okay. I can test you for the gene anyway if you like. It's good to have the knowledge and easy for me to manage an additional sample. It's entirely up to you.'

'All right, guess it's worthwhile knowing. I heard about the gene on a recent visit to England and did plan to get tested. So, if it's not too much trouble?'

'None at all.'

Margaret brought over the phlebotomy chair and Ellen's blood was extracted first. The results wouldn't take long to process. By now the specialist medic and her nurse had arrived and begun assessing the girls. For the rest of the evening, the lights were dimmed and everyone was encouraged to get some sleep. It had been a stressful day.

40

With the help of a sedative both girls slept. Ellen had a few hours of sleep in one of the cubicle beds and woke in the early hours needing to pee. The baby was pressing on her bladder, so she rarely made it through the night.

The room was dark. Ellen activated the bedside lamp and, in the dim light, made her way to an adjoining bathroom. She returned a short time later and moved across to the viewing window to check on Zoe. As she peered through the glass, she felt pangs of guilt. She blamed herself for Zoe's predicament. If only she hadn't encouraged her love of science. If only she hadn't encouraged her to accept the AMDAT scholarship offer, she wouldn't be in this mess. Then she recalled her grandfather's view on wishing for a different past.

When a sentence begins with 'if only', my darling granddaughter, best forget it.

Ellen loved Zoe. If anything happened to her, it was doubtful she or Georgia would ever recover.

Lost in thought, she didn't notice that someone was now standing beside her until they spoke.

'Trouble sleeping?'

She turned to see Daniel.

'I guess,' she replied, shifting her gaze back to Zoe as she continued to speak. 'I'm just so worried about Zoe. I couldn't bear anything to happen to her.' She pressed the palm of her hand on the viewing window, as if trying to make direct contact with the sleeping girl.

'I recognise that it's hard not being in control of an outcome. However, if it's any comfort to you, my guess is that Zoe will be okay. Sarah is the one I'm most concerned about,' he said, in a whisper.

'I hope you're right. Not about Sarah, that is,' she added, realising that her comment could be misinterpreted. 'I want them both to be okay.'

'We'll all just have to wait. Nature is in complete control at this point in time. I recognise it's frustrating. However, you're pregnant, so it's not a good time to be stressed. Are you and your husband looking forward to the new arrival?'

'I don't have a husband,' Ellen replied.

'Well, your partner then?'

'I don't have a partner either.'

'Oh, sorry; I shouldn't be prying.'

'Don't be sorry. You're not the first person to presume and you won't be the last.' Turning to face him she continued to explain. 'The truth is this baby wasn't planned.' She looked down and held the bump between both her hands.

'Doesn't the father want to be involved?'

'He can't be,' she replied.

'Well, surely he can't be leaving you to handle the situation all on your own?'

'He can't help me because he's dead,' Ellen said. As the words flowed from her mouth it reinforced the reality that she wouldn't see or talk to Patrick ever again. Her eyes pooled with tears.

'I don't know what to say. I'm so sorry.' Daniel might have been even sorrier if he had realised Patrick's death had been at the hands of Gum Lin.

'Actually, you met him, but you probably don't remember.'

'Did I? When? Where?'

'You two had a scuffle, outside a bar … over me.'

'Oh, that guy; your old boyfriend. He was pretty upset that I was dating you, wasn't he? Did you two get back together, then?'

'Not exactly; just stayed good friends, I guess. Been on and off for a number of years, but I live over here and he lives—lived—in New Jersey. So we both remained free agents.'

'I'm really sorry, Ellen. Facing the birth without the child's father isn't going to be easy. At least you have Zoe and your cousin Anna to support you.'

'Presuming Zoe will be all right, that is,' she replied, glancing back in her direction.

'Would you like a hot milk drink? We can make one in my private office. It's just down the hall. It might help us get back to sleep.'

'That would be good, thanks. I am thirsty.'

The two chatted as they drank hot chocolate topped with marsh-mallows. She apologised for slapping him. He said that he deserved it, but asked to be given the chance to explain. Daniel told her how he'd become ill in New Jersey and been placed under their Mental Health Act, and how Vaughn and Gum had escorted him back to Melbourne, where he had spent a further month in a local psychiatric facility. He had changed his surname and appearance to ensure a fresh start.

'Well, thanks for clearing up the mystery of your disappearance. I still think you could have sent me a message or something. Your whereabouts really baffled me. I checked the hostel where you were staying. I called all the local hospitals and even thought the police might find your body. Eventually I gave up. I also tried to locate you when I first came to Melbourne, without any luck of course. Never thought to look for someone with a different name and changed appearance, did I?' she said glancing upwards.

'I didn't make it easy for anyone to find me. I never wanted to be found. My past had little worth retaining, other than you of course,' he said. 'I literally erased it, along with my appearance and real identity. You'd probably not be surprised to learn how much stigma there is around mental illness, drugs and poverty that follow an adolescent into their adult life. It's a burden I decided to lose in one shake, rather than spend the rest of my life discussing and defending my past. If the press found out, they would have a field day. I know that they were digging around when I married Maggie. They didn't find anything and eventually gave up. Maggie will want to hear the whole sordid truth now.' He leaned forward, placed his hands on his thighs and then looked down at the floor as if contemplating that conversation.

After a few moments he lifted his head, stood up and stretched. 'Anyway, Ellen, we'd better get some sleep. But before you go, I need to clarify something. When I came back to Melbourne, I wanted to contact you. Doctors advised against it. They said that the last thing I needed was a long-distance relationship that could cause me stress. I wasn't cleared to leave Australia, so travel was out of the question. I really regretted losing contact with you but, at the time, I listened to the doctors and believed it was for the best. I now know that I was wrong. But when I finally realised that I needed you in my life, it was too late. I was involved with Maggie and setting up AMDAT. I never expected to see or hear from you again.'

They both looked into each other's eyes. Then spontaneously embraced, holding on to each other far longer than was appropriate.

The camera behind them moved.

41

Maggie had stayed up until the early hours of the morning to complete the specialised blood tests. She was unaware that Daniel had not gone to bed until just before three. It was now seven and, although she had been to bed, she hadn't slept. Maggie was sitting on the chaise lounge near the window, watching the sunrise over the Melbourne skyline. She was lost in thought, clutching a manila folder as if her life depended on it.

Her nose was red from crying and her face was drawn from lack of sleep. Maggie looked down at the folder in her hand and thumbed through the test results for the third time as if hoping they had changed. The truth had always been important to her, but these results were almost unbearable to read. 'Be careful what you wish for,' a friend had once said to her. She had wished to find the truth and now, in the light of a new day, it could no longer be denied. The three pages of results could change her life. Yet only she had seen them. She was the only one that knew they existed. She picked up the third page and screwed it up into a tight ball, before throwing it into the gas flame heater. The paper caught alight and in a few seconds was devoured by the flames. She blew her nose, wiped away the tears and looked affectionately at the husband she adored. Somehow she knew that after last night her world would never be the same. She sat in the quiet until she could stand the silence no longer.

Daniel was still fast asleep, so she coughed and made a few deliberate noises until he began to stir. Eventually he opened his eyes and rolled over to face her.

'Good morning, Maggs.'

'Is it?' she replied, in a somewhat hopeless tone.

'Did I do something wrong, or did I not do something this time?' he responded.

'Perhaps the truth about Ellen Hancock would have been nice. First you fake your true identity and now this.'

Daniel sat up. 'I did tell you the truth yesterday, that I knew Ellen before I married you. Surely I've proven myself as a good husband, so my identity isn't an issue?'

'It proves you're a very good liar, though, doesn't it?'

Daniel shrugged. 'Don't be so quick to judge me, Maggie. If you had been through my childhood, rather than being raised like a little princess, never abused or wanting for anything, you might have done the same. Are you planning on telling your father?' he asked, concerned.

'I'm still thinking about it. Anyway, why didn't you tell me that you'd slept with Ellen Hancock?'

'You didn't ask. And what makes you think that we did? Can you please make me a coffee darling, and then we can discuss this more rationally.'

'Don't "darling" me. Get your own coffee. Try swallowing this instead,' and she tossed the folder onto the bed.

He opened the folder. Before him were displayed the blood results for Sarah and her mother Rowena. Neither carried the Delta 32 gene. The results were also there for Zoe Ashmore, Ellen Hancock and Daniel Grant himself. Ellen and Daniel both carried the Delta 32 gene and Zoe had two strands of Delta 32.

'So you still think you have nothing to tell me?' Maggie said, getting more irritated by the minute.

'Darling, I have nothing to tell you. A high proportion of British and European migrants carry the Delta 32 gene. It's purely a co-incidence.'

'Yes, I thought so too, but it was the way you looked at Ellen.' Maggie paused for a few seconds as if reflecting on their relationship. 'You have never looked that way at me, Daniel.' She paused again. 'Call it women's intuition, or whatever you like, but I made a snap decision to run a paternity test for Zoe Ashmore. It clearly shows that you and that Hancock woman are Zoe's biological parents.' She directed him to check out page two of the test results.

'Good job we aren't actually planning to use Zoe's ova for ourselves, isn't it? That would have been a sort of incest, wouldn't it?'

Her face was screwed up and her lips were being held so tight it was as if they were trying to hold her tongue hostage. She was having trouble containing her emotions, which were escalating with each passing moment. Maggie rose and began pacing back and forth, spitting dots of moisture from the distinctive gap between her two front teeth as she spoke.

'This also means Zoe could make a financial claim on AMDAT. God knows what that will be worth. I'll have to speak with Daddy. He's not going to be happy about this development.'

'Calm down, Maggs; you've got it all wrong,' Daniel said, scratching the top of his head and yawning.

'Unlike you, Daniel, DNA doesn't lie, so it's no good trying to worm your way out of this one.'

'You're just overtired from lack of sleep, Maggs; you aren't thinking logically.'

'Not thinking logically! What do you mean by that?' she snapped.

'We—that is, you and I—already know that Zoe Ashmore has three sets of DNA. That's why we brought her here in the first place. She's a third-generation IVF baby with three human DNA strands and was not conceived in the usual manner.' He paused then added, 'I just omitted to tell you that she was conceived using sperm I donated nineteen years ago.'

'What the ... you knew she was yours and you didn't tell me?'

'Yes, I did, but I thought you might be upset if you knew I was her biological father. With us having trouble conceiving a child, I didn't think there was any real need for you to know that I'd already fathered at least one.'

'What else do you know that you haven't told me?'

'I know that her birth mother is a Georgia Ashmore, but I didn't know that Ellen was the third donor. I swear that's news to both of us.'

'I wonder if Ellen knows. She and Zoe seem very close, and doesn't she call her "aunt"?' Maggie pondered.

'Ellen must know. She would have had to consent to the doctor using her ova,' Daniel replied.

'I agree she would have had to consent to ova donation. The fact remains that most donors remain anonymous. Full disclosure usually only occurs when a child turns eighteen. Ellen told me yesterday that she wasn't related to Zoe. She should have been informed recently.'

'Yes, she should have been informed,' Daniel replied. 'However, the fertility clinic burnt down and all the records were destroyed.'

'Daniel,' Maggie paused and a concerned expression crossed her face. 'What have you done?'

'Look, I simply asked Gum to delete my IVF clinical records and as usual she went too far. I didn't expect that outcome. I thought she would just hack into their digital recording system and delete my records, not blow the bloody place up.'

'I've never understood why you tolerate Gum, Daniel. She's dangerous.'

'Damaged childhoods do that to a kid. Anyway, always remember that without her there wouldn't be a chip. By blowing up the clinic, Gum might have done us a bigger favour than expected. Zoe might never find out her true paternity. Neither you nor I will be telling her, will we, Maggs? If Ellen doesn't already know she's one of the biological parents, she may never learn the truth. And please don't say anything to your father. He really doesn't need to know.'

Maggie, sounding relieved, continued, 'Under sperm-donor legislation Zoe can't make a financial claim anyway, which I guess is something positive. But what will we tell her?'

'The same as we always planned to tell her: that her ova weren't compatible with my sperm, due to an autoimmune disorder, and that the embryos all failed to develop. We will thank her for her generosity and we'll still buy her an apartment and help her mother with relocation costs. She won't be fussed. In fact,' he continued, 'she'll probably be relieved. Gum and Vaughn will be using the ova you harvested from Zoe for their research project shortly, so I suggest we say nothing to anyone. We know that the plague is unlikely to take hold in Zoe, as she has two sets of Delta 32 and has been vaccinated. Sarah's recovery is a different issue altogether.'

Daniel could barely contain his excitement at finding out Zoe was part of him and Ellen. He felt a tingling throughout his body. He wanted to go to her straightaway to find out what she knew, but that was impossible with Maggie's attitude.

42

For the next two weeks Daniel and Ellen met in his private office around midnight and drank hot chocolate. They were becoming close again. They had so much in common. Their conversations flowed naturally; they were never stilted. Both could feel that the chemistry between them was still as strong as it had been all those years ago. Yet neither spoke of feelings.

As Daniel had predicted, Zoe didn't contract the plague. She was staying one more night in quarantine until the final test results were cleared. Really, it was just an excuse to keep Ellen on the premises. Daniel was enjoying their midnight rendezvous.

By now, he was fairly sure that Ellen had no idea that he was Zoe's biological father, although from her closeness to Zoe he suspected that she knew her maternal connection. On the last night Daniel came down to collect Ellen for their routine cuppa.

'You've shaved off your beard and had a haircut. I like it,' Ellen said, as she stepped back and admired the handsome well-groomed man. Daniel looked ten years younger and he was visibly pleased that she had both noticed and approved.

They sat close on the couch, continuing to catch up. Daniel was more animated than he had been in years—quite elevated, really—and this had been noticeable to all that knew him, especially Maggie. He was usually reclusive and often appeared to be depressed. Reconnecting with Ellen had certainly lifted his mood.

'Zoe can go home in the morning,' Daniel said. 'I'm going to really miss our midnight chats. We must keep in touch. I don't want to lose you again.'

'It has been good, hasn't it?' she replied. 'I always wondered what I'd done wrong. I thought we had something so special that it would never end. When you left without any explanation, I lost confidence in myself choosing a partner that was right for me.'

Daniel took her hand and looked into her eyes. Then, although he knew it was wrong, he leaned forward and began kissing her tenderly on the lips. Ellen was aware she shouldn't be reciprocating, yet still grief-stricken from Patrick's death, and feeling so alone, she cast aside all reservations and simply let herself live in the moment. *What harm could it do?*

They kissed and caressed for quite some time. Eventually things became overheated and they both reached the point of no return. He reached to slip off her panties and she didn't resist. He hurriedly removed his trousers. She was heavily pregnant, but neither seemed to care. Ellen was enjoying the closeness and warmth of this man. She had once loved him. Maybe she would grow to love him again. Perhaps Daniel could fill the aching void within her.

'We shouldn't be doing this,' she murmured, 'and yet, it feels so right.'

'Then maybe it is,' he whispered.

Daniel entered her carefully from behind, leaning her over the arm of the couch to accommodate her belly. The act didn't take very long. The foreplay had been extensive and they were highly aroused. In many ways, the sex was rushed and somewhat clumsy, not unusual for two people unfamiliar with each other's bodies. As he began to come, he coaxed her to orgasm by applying gentle pressure to her clitoris with his free hand. They flopped onto the couch, breathless but satisfied.

The camera on the ceiling realigned, then zoomed in to observe them. Neither one noticed. Vaughn had watched the couple with a wry smile as he checked the device was recording. He was quite pleased with himself. Maggie was a plain, boring, entitled bitch and poor Daniel hadn't fucked anything decent in years. Giving him a placebo instead of his mood stabilisers for the last two weeks had worked. Daniel had elevated just enough to act on his undeniable attraction to Ellen.

Vaughn had been monitoring the couple's late-night activities for days and now he finally had hit paydirt. *Perhaps an erratic sleep pattern has some advantages after all,* he thought to himself.

Vaughn's poor sleep cycle had been shaped by his childhood. Thanks, or rather no thanks, to his father he rarely slept for more than a few hours each night. He could barely remember his mother. She died of ovarian cancer when he was five.

His father, Finn, had worked as a security guard by day and supplemented his income by gambling in the evenings. Most nights, around eleven, he would wake up his young son. Vaughn quickly learned not to bother wearing his pyjamas to bed. He needed to be ready whenever his father pulled back the duvet. He would be barely awake as he slipped on his jacket and sneakers and stumbled into the backseat of their car.

Dragged around the car parks of various gambling establishments, he snatched whatever sleep he could until dawn. As the sun rose, Vaughn and his father—and often a lady friend— would head for home through the deserted streets of a stirring city. Vaughn never saw the same woman for more than a few weeks. His father had a saying: 'When a woman starts sweeping the house it's time to grab the broom and clean sweep her out of your life.' Finn used women, and Vaughn had learned early that women were specifically designed to meet a man's sexual needs. Nothing more.

Watching Daniel and Ellen fucking was a powerful aphrodisiac. He returned to his bed, rolled Fleur over and began kissing her neck. He needed a sexual release, right now. He simply couldn't wait until morning. They had enjoyed sex earlier in the evening, so Fleur was wet enough already. He didn't have to bother with any foreplay or whether or not she was fully awake to consent.

Neither Ellen nor Daniel felt guilty in the morning. It was as if no-one else existed and nothing else mattered. They felt alive. Back together at last. Whatever the consequences, it had been worth it. The intoxicating drug of lust had them firmly in its clutches.

Zoe's final test results were all clear. Before escorting her home, Ellen thanked the specialist and reluctantly said her goodbyes to Daniel. Sarah, however, was not so lucky. She had developed the pneumonic plague and remained quite ill, although the medical team remained confident that she would make a full recovery.

Ellen and Zoe would continue to check on Sarah's progress. Ellen intended to use these visits as an excuse to see Daniel. She was enjoying the distraction. It was as if her grief at losing Patrick had taken away her ability to make rational decisions. Every time they met, they were becoming more indiscreet, taking ever-increasing risks. They had even begun to justify their behaviour—completely ignoring the fact that others would get hurt by their relationship. Daniel didn't love his wife anyway. He never had. He'd married Margaret just for her money so he could launch his chip invention. He'd really wanted to be with Ellen, but the psychiatrists had discouraged him, so he couldn't follow his heart. He'd been reclusive and depressed without her and now he was alive again.

They truly believed they were good for each other. Very good. It was amazing how decent people could rationalise unethical behaviour to alleviate their own guilt. Ellen and Daniel had simply convinced themselves that their behaviour was appropriate in the circumstances. Neither could live with the cognitive dissonance that came from thinking any other way.

43

Georgia ran to hug her daughter as she entered the apartment. The young woman glowed with health. Zoe's sense of relief and love for her mother could barely be contained. Her grin was as wide as a Cheshire cat's.

'Glad to have you home safe and well, my darling,' Georgia said. 'Thanks, Ellen, for all your support.'

'No worries,' Ellen replied. 'You know I'd do anything for our Zoe. I also enjoyed catching up with Daniel. We have so much in common, it's refreshing. He even wants me to consider working for AMDAT. I'll fill you in a bit later, though. For now, let's just concentrate on enjoying our beautiful girl.' She smiled affectionately at Zoe.

'Rob's coming over for dinner to help us celebrate,' Georgia added. Rob and Georgia also had a great deal in common and were seeing each other most days.

'These are great, Mom,' Zoe said as she perused the batch of colour prints spread across the dining table. The images were impressive. Georgia knew just how to utilise the light to gain the best from any subject. The AMDAT Tower shots were striking. The perspectives Georgia had chosen were quite unusual. They made the building come alive.

'Perhaps you could sell some of these online,' Zoe continued. 'How large can you blow them up without losing quality?'

'Poster size one hundred by sixty-five centimetres. I just collected one from the printer today.'

Georgia went to her room and returned with a long tube and began unrolling the contents onto the coffee table.

'I haven't even looked at this yet. I left it until you two came home, so we could enjoy the unveiling together.'

The poster was an incredible shot of AMDAT Tower. The afternoon sunlight was casting shadows, giving the building a three-dimensional effect. All the floors could be viewed in great detail. No clarity had been lost whatsoever. Zoe explained to her mother where the access to the bat zone was and described the different activities that took place on each floor. She explained that Level 41 was empty for security reasons.

Georgia ran her fingers up each floor, counting in her head.

'I thought you said Level 41 is vacant.'

'It is.'

'No, it's not. There's a child looking out of the window.'

'It's definitely empty, Mom. You must be looking at another floor.'

Zoe ran her fingers up the tower image, counting under her breath. Sure enough, her mother had been right; there was a child looking out of a window on the forty-first floor. All the other windows on that floor appeared to have drawn blinds.

'That is weird,' Zoe said. 'Perhaps some workers needed to access it for laser faults or something and took their child with them.'

'Take another look, Zoe. It's a toddler, only about a year old. Who takes a toddler to work? Something is not adding up. The floor is clearly not vacant.'

'You're right, it's not. Fascinating.' Zoe paused to examine the child in the window more closely.

Just then there was a knock on the door and Ellen let Rob into the apartment.

'Come and see what you make of this, Rob,' Georgia called out. Rob had a bunch of cream lilies and a box of locally made truffles for Zoe. He grabbed a stubby of beer from the fridge, flicked off the top and then sat down at the table next to Georgia. She pointed out the toddler in the window.

'I don't know what to make of it,' he said. 'I always suspected that the laser security story was a bit far-fetched. That it was probably designed just to scare off intruders. I guess Daniel Grant wouldn't want his medical lab or penthouse to be undermined from below. I don't think it's that big a deal. If you have captured something

AMDAT didn't want you to see, I do think it's safer that we don't mention it to anyone.'

'I'll see what I can find out from Daniel. I'm seeing him next week. I won't let on about the image, though,' Ellen said.

'Zoe is fine. Why do you need to see Daniel next week?' Georgia asked.

'We're friends, Anna; why shouldn't I see him?' she replied defensively.

'He's married, Ellen, and to the daughter of one of the most powerful men in the country. I think you should stay well away from him.'

Feeling somewhat annoyed, Ellen's response was both sharp and swift.

'I think that I'm old enough to decide who my friends are, Anna. Anyway, Daniel has invited all of us to the AFL Grand Final next week. I'm definitely going. We should *all* go. Sit with Daniel in the … *AMDAT Corporate Box*. It will be an *amazing* night.

'I'm not sure sitting with Daniel in any box is such a good idea.' Georgia said looking quite concerned.

'It's just a game of football Anna. What's the harm in that? Anyway, Oliver will want to come and I'm sure Rob is interested in going. The Victorian Vipers *are* playing.'

'Too right I'm interested. I could never afford Grand Final tickets. They cost a fortune. Count me in Ellen. You'll come won't you Anna? It's the chance of a lifetime.'

'If you really want me to I will,' Georgia replied reluctantly. I just believe Ellen's courting trouble, trying to pursue a friendship with that man now that Zoe's medical crisis is over. That's all.'

'For once I agree,' Zoe added. 'Didn't you see the way Margaret looked at you as we left today? She's clearly jealous of your friendship with her husband.'

'Well, that's her problem, isn't it, not mine. If she doesn't trust her husband, she needs to work it out with him. I always do the so-called "right thing",' Ellen said, making inverted commas in the air with her fingers. 'It has got me nowhere in the end. So, for a change, I'm going to do exactly what I want.'

Zoe and Georgia glanced at each other and raised their eyebrows. They sensed a definite change in Ellen. She usually worried about a person's feelings, but in the case of Margaret Grant she clearly didn't give a toss. *Grief dolloped with hormones,* thought Georgia. *Once she has the baby, she won't give Daniel another thought. The relationship won't have a chance to progress and will hopefully die out.* She never for a moment thought that Ellen and Daniel had already crossed the line, and that her concerns for Ellen's safety were completely justified.

44

Tony Scallioni was convinced that Doctor Dawson's missing ledger, as described to him by Ellen, might hold the key to Bridget Patterson's death, as well as the mystery of the other missing girls. The community was becoming increasingly restless at the lack of progress on the case.

The facts weren't gelling into anything that gave him either a motive or any suspects. He knew the missing girls were all from New Jersey. He knew that they all had been conceived using IVF at the now-destroyed fertility clinic. The doctor who undertook the procedures was deceased. None of this information, however, gave him any leads to advance the investigation.

When the police asked for public assistance, Ruby Knox and her mother had come forward. Ruby was Kasey's best friend. Her family had been offline for two weeks and had no knowledge of Kasey's disappearance. Ruby and her brother Rupert had been on a tech-detox with their parents. They had stayed in a friend's cabin and returned home to find their house trashed and all communication devices destroyed. Ruby first learned of Kasey's disappearance when she visited her home to tell her about the robbery.

A distressed Ruby told Detective Scallioni everything she knew.

'Kasey told me she'd met a boy online. She said that he wanted to meet her because she was special—just like him.'

'Did the boy say how Kasey was special?' asked Tony.

'Yes, he told her that God had chosen him, and now her, to help save the world. That AV64 was just the first pandemic wave and that worse was to come. He linked Kasey up to a religious site that talked of the end of the world and the rise of a superior human race. Kasey told me that God wanted to reboot civilisation because humans had become too toxic and were destroying the planet he had created. I told her it was all nonsense and that she should block the site and not meet anyone. The next day Kasey shut down all her social media sites and blocked my calls. We left on our holiday that afternoon and I haven't heard anything from her since.'

Tony and the forensic officers already knew that technology was involved. The missing girls' computers had been examined. They initially appeared to offer some leads, but when the experts opened one particular chat line the screens filled with surreal religious images. The internal systems then collapsed. No-one could start them up again. The hard drives were removed for inspection. It appeared they had heated to an extreme temperature then completely fried. Not dissimilar to Georgia's description of Patrick's restraints, although those mechanisms could never be examined, as they had been destroyed in the blast.

Tony decided to spend the day reviewing the original investigation into Doctor Dawson to ensure that nothing had been overlooked. He made his way to the police department evidence repository.

'Hi, I have a request for the evidence taken from Doctor Dawson's home, please. Case 14765.' He showed the guard his ID and verified his identity via his handprint on the biometric scanner.

'Okay,' the guard responded and went to locate the items, returning a short time later. 'Hope you have a trolley; there are five huge boxes of the stuff,' he said as he placed the first one down on the counter.

Tony loaded all the boxes into his police car. By late morning he was in his office, methodically sifting through each one. He checked every piece of paper, scanning for any information pertaining to the year the missing girls were conceived. He didn't want to overlook or miss any clues, no matter how small.

By midafternoon, he had determined there was no ledger in the evidence boxes and nothing of any relevance to the current investigation. Just correspondence, old appointment books, thank you letters and cards. Where could the ledger be? Could it be at Doctor Dawson's last known residence? He wondered if the doctor's widow still lived there. He grabbed his hat and coat and headed for his car.

Tony parked outside the old Dawson residence and observed the house. It was very run down. The paint was peeling off the cladding and there was water damage around the eaves where the guttering had rusted through. If Mrs Dawson did still live here, she probably couldn't afford to undertake any maintenance. The court cases and subsequent ruin of her husband's reputation must have left them with limited financial resources.

He approached the front door, knocked and waited. The only sound was the rustling of the wind through the leaves of several large deciduous trees. Then, just as he was about to turn and leave, he heard a shuffling sound from within. After a few moments, the door slowly opened. A small elderly woman stared back at him.

'Good afternoon. Are you Mrs Dawson?'

'That depends who's asking,' she replied in an unexpected broad Scottish accent.

'My name is Tony Scallioni. I'm a detective with the Newark Police Department.'

'You don't need to speak so loud and slow, laddie. I'm neither deaf nor stupid.'

'Sorry,' said Tony. He began speaking at a normal rate and volume. 'My name is …'

'I heard that bit. What do you want, Detective?'

'Well, I'm investigating the disappearance of four young women who were all conceived at your husband's IVF clinic. I want to know if you happen to have kept your late husband's personal medical ledger. I think the ledger may be able to shed some light on their disappearance.'

'Now, what makes you think my late husband even kept a personal medical ledger? He did keep an album of all his *babies* if that's what you're referring to?' She smiled sweetly.

'One of the medical students who worked for him about nineteen years ago described it as a ledger. She said it contained confidential patient information—specific IVF details.'

'Oh, and who might this medical student with the loose lips be, then?' she replied sounding quite annoyed.

'Ellen Hancock,' Tony replied.

Mrs Dawson paused momentarily, as if she had pressed the search button on her memory and was waiting patiently for the information to be retrieved.

'Was she that very pretty lassie with beautiful curly auburn hair?'

'That would be Ellen.'

'Yes, I do remember her. Beautiful; unforgettable, really. Fancy her remembering Keith's baby album.'

'Ledger, Mrs Dawson. How about you show me the baby album and I'll see if it looks like the ledger Ellen described.' There was a long pause. Mrs Dawson glared at the detective and didn't speak.

'Alternatively, I could come back with a search warrant and bring a squad of police officers with me to search your home. I'm sure that you would rather not have people rummaging through your personal things.'

Mrs Dawson realised she wasn't fooling Detective Scallioni. She changed her tack.

'I've been expecting the police to come back and search again for records. Only a few people knew about the ledger. Ellen was one of them. Keith took a real shine to that young lassie.'

'Why were you expecting someone?'

'I'm not stupid, Detective. I watch the news. I know that the dead girl and the four missing girls were all created by God with a little help from my late husband. When the IVF clinic's storage chambers were blown up, I concluded that someone wanted to destroy their donated genetic material, their digital clinical records, or both. You know that children receive notification of their biological parents when they turn eighteen. Surely you noticed that all of the girls turned eighteen within a month either side of the clinic fire?'

'No, I didn't really realise the significance of their exact ages. Just that they were all born by IVF in the same year.'

'Anyway, you had better come on in,' she said, peering up and down the street as if making sure that no-one was watching. She herded Tony like a sheep into the kitchen and, in quite a bossy Scottish tone, told him where to sit. Then she continued.

'I knew that I was on the right track when my house was ransacked just prior to the clinic fire. The buggers made it look like a robbery. They stole a couple of ornaments and my great-granddaughter's piggy bank. But I knew what they were really after, as they focused on my husband's study. They had meticulously combed through each and every one of his documents and books. They left one hell of a mess. Ahh, but they didn't find it.'

'Why didn't you report the break-in?'

'I've had enough trouble with the law over the years, Detective, and all I really cared about was the fact that they didn't find his ledger. Keith and I knew we shouldn't have kept it, but it was all he had left. He used it to send all the children birthday cards. When he passed, I continued the tradition. The timing of the break-in and the destruction of the clinic got me thinking. When I crosschecked the ledger with the names of those poor missing girls, it was clear that the two events were somehow linked. It didn't take much surmising to join the dots and come up with a few motives. I was actually planning to hand over the ledger to the investigating team this week. So, Detective, you've saved me a trip into the city.'

'If the ledger was here in the house, why didn't the intruders find it?'

'Well, Detective, if you want to hide something you leave it on display. People rarely see what's right in front of their very noses. Thieves look in cupboards, under things, and in all the typical hidey-holes.'

'Can you get the ledger for me please?'

'Most certainly; I'll do anything to help you solve this damn mystery. The suspense is driving me insane.'

Mrs Dawson rose from her seat and ambled across to a small shelf perched above the stove. A number of cookbooks were lodged in a higgledy-piggledy manner between two marble book ends. She reached up and grasped the one titled *International Cookery the New Jersey Way* and handed it to Tony. Tony started to smile.

'Ellen didn't describe the ledger as a cookbook,' he said.

'It wasn't originally. Keith covered, renamed and hid it when the scandal broke. You're not the first police officer to look for hard-copy clinical records, you know. My husband told everyone everything was digitised, but it wasn't. You're the first person other than me to hold the ledger in years.' Tony opened the thick book and found it full of neatly inscribed pages. Mrs Dawson explained that every IVF birth was outlined, using the dates of conception and birth along with the initials of all sperm and ova donors.

Tony couldn't make any sense of it. He felt that the ledger would hold the key he needed to solve the murders. Yet, now he was holding it, he was not so sure.

'It's all in code. It doesn't make any sense to me at all.'

'That's because you need a decoder,' she said, looking quite smug.

'Is there a decoder?'

'I keep telling you I'm not stupid, but that doesn't seem to sink into your head, does it, Detective?'

She rose again from the table and selected another, smaller, cookery book. This one was titled *One Hundred Ways to Cook Perfect Eggs*. The two books belonged together. She showed Tony how to decode the information. You could determine whether donated ova or sperm was used and whether or not a second female had donated their nucleus or mitochondria. The actual names of live births along with the address and contact details of their parents at the time of each birth were also recorded. The ledger was a virtual goldmine.

'Now, Detective, hopefully this will help the investigation progress a bit faster. The anticipation is killing me. Care for a drink—tea or coffee—and some date and walnut cake before you leave? It's freshly baked this morning and I'd love the company of a handsome young man for afternoon tea. I don't get many visitors.'

Tony hesitated then decided he might glean additional information if he stayed and chatted with Mrs Dawson.

'A coffee would be good,' he said smiling.

'Linda, call me Linda. I have a good feeling about you, Detective Tony.'

She cut two generous portions of cake and buttered them thickly before pouring the drinks.

'Sugar? Milk?' she enquired.

'Just milk.'

They chatted about her late husband and the theories she had about the missing girls. After two pieces of cake Mrs Dawson noticed Tony checking the time.

'Well, Detective, I've kept you quite long enough, but I have just one more question before you leave. How do you know Ellen Hancock?'

'We went to the same school.'

'Mmmm, I see. So you'd know how to get in touch with her then?'

'Yes, I do have her contact details. Why do you ask?'

Mrs Dawson pulled herself awkwardly out of the chair, mumbling 'Bloody arthritis. I just have to give you something before you leave.' She shuffled out of the room, returning a few minutes later with a letter in hand.

'Here, can you make sure Ellen gets this? My late husband wrote it to her. I was instructed to post it after he died, but it completely slipped my mind. I came across it when I was tidying up after the robbery. I posted the letter to what I thought was her home address. It was returned to me unopened.'

Tony looked at the envelope. People rarely sent letters anymore. He certainly didn't. The Newark post only had a weekly delivery these days. The envelope was scrunched and grubby with *Return to Sender* scrawled in red ink diagonally across the front.

'No problem. I'll make sure she gets it. No problem at all.'

'Thanks, that takes a load off my mind.'

Tony stood up to leave.

'Do you mind if I take another piece of this delicious cake?'

'No, not at all.'

Tony picked up a piece of cake and, with the ledger and decoder tucked under his arm, headed towards the door. Mrs Dawson stood up to follow him.'

'Don't get up, I'll let myself out.' He walked a few steps then turned. 'You do realise that I'm considering charging you for withholding evidence?'

Mrs Dawson's smile faded, and her jaw dropped.

Tony smiled and took a big bite of cake, then turned and left.

Tony returned home to start decoding the ledger. He was convinced that the book held the motive for the disappearances within its pages. Mrs Dawson was a sharp old duck. Someone could be covering up their donor identity. Even so, blowing up the clinic seemed a drastic way to achieve that aim, and why was Bridget depleted of her ova and where were the four missing girls? There was a great deal that still didn't make sense.

He decided to cook a stir-fry for dinner. It was nine thirty and he liked to eat late. His usual dinner companion would be joining him shortly. Tony had lightly marinated the synthetic beef-flavoured strips in soy sauce, garlic, ginger, honey and a dash of lime. He selected a Leonard Cohen album and began singing along to 'Suzanne' as he tossed an array of brightly coloured vegetables around in the wok.

Tony heard movement in the attic as the stairs were being lowered. His house guest entered the kitchen.

'Smells great, but don't give up your day job,' he said, referring to Tony's vocals. Tony turned and smiled at his old friend.

Patrick grinned back.

'We have the ledger,' he said. 'Mrs Dawson had it hidden with her cookery books. It's the breakthrough we've been hoping for.'

'Great; we can get stuck in after dinner.' Patrick leaned over the wok and grabbed a piece of the protein. 'Ouch, it's hot,' he said, tossing it around from one hand to the other to avoid getting burnt.

45

Four months earlier, Patrick had been elated as the mechanisms binding him to the chair released. He could see Ellen and Tex jumping and hear them screaming with excitement. Ellen was so beautiful and his feelings for her were stronger than ever. Now she was pregnant with his child, he believed she might just be prepared to give their relationship a real chance.

It was then that he heard the ticking coming from the kitchen. Soft, slow clicks at first, increasing in both volume and rate. It was a familiar sound. Unmistakable to any seasoned detective. He broke into a cold sweat. Those heartless bastards had planted a second explosive device. The cruel bitches intended to give him false hope then kill him anyway. He didn't have time to say anything to Ellen. He just needed to move. He headed towards the safe and leapt into the air, landing to the left of it, directly on the large plastic prickly pear, then disappeared through the floor, as if he was the magician Houdini himself.

He covered his ears and within seconds the ground shook violently above him. Would his panic room hold up, or was the explosion too great a force for the structure to withstand? He'd never expected to use the panic room to shield himself from an explosion.

Despite the thickness of the walls surrounding him, he could feel the intense heat coming through the thick trapdoor. A fire as hot as a furnace was raging above. A small amount of smoke had begun to make its way into the space, curling as if it were a snake seeking refuge. It carried with it the noxious smell of the melted cactus. He needed to get some fresh air circulating fast, or he would suffocate.

He pressed the chip on his wrist. It sprang to life, giving him enough light to find the shelf where some basic provisions were stored. He grabbed a torch, turned it on and located the switch to activate the external ventilation fan. One flick and it began humming. The stale air was quickly replaced by fresh air from the cactus hothouse at the bottom of his garden.

He poured himself a single malt whisky and ate a couple of packets of mixed nuts. He was starving—hadn't eaten for hours. He then sat back and strained to hear what was happening outside. Through the thick walls he couldn't hear any detail. Sirens ... perhaps some shouting ... scraping noises and the occasional bang as something flammable caught alight and exploded.

The wisps of smoke had finally stopped snaking their way into his cramped space and the air smelt fresher. He observed that the metal trapdoor was now red hot and any remaining gaps had closed. It was as if it had been welded shut. That wasn't part of his plan.

To better shield his body from the heat, he tucked himself further under the safe, as far as possible from the trapdoor. He then grabbed a hand towel and poured a bottle of spring water onto it before placing it over his head. He didn't want his brains to cook. Hopefully, Georgia would get his code word to Tony quickly, before his panic room became his coffin. *Problem is, she won't be in any rush; she'll think I'm already dead,* Patrick surmised. To die of starvation wasn't part of his plan either.

Surely Tony would have enough sense to check his panic room. He had one exactly the same, and Patrick would check his—most definitely if there wasn't a body. One last thing. He snapped on the purpose-made lead clasp over his wrist chip, ensuring the wi-fi signal was blocked.

46

Rob, Georgia, Zoe, Oliver and Ellen donned their Victorian Vipers scarves and beanies and headed for the Melbourne Cricket Ground. A sea of fans was flowing through the city as it prepared itself for one of the biggest events of the year. Donned in blue-and-white or black-and-white stripes, with painted faces, tattoos and banners, they sang their team songs and prepared themselves for battle. Grand Finals were the only time the general public were allowed inside the MCG. The few unallocated tickets had sold out within minutes of their release and unlucky supporters had to be satisfied with watching the game on the giant screens that surrounded the outside of the stadium walls, or on TV. Following this final, the competing male teams and their families would move out and the female teams and their families would move in.

The group of friends gradually shuffled their way to the specified entrance. Ellen was feeling a bit uncomfortable. She was due to give birth, but didn't want to miss the opportunity to spend time with Daniel. She shoved her handbag onto the checking table and stood with her arms out as she passed through the body scanner. Her chip was analysed and temperature found to be normal. She walked through the ten-metre-long decontamination tunnel, its light wavelength selected for its effectiveness at destroying surface microorganisms. Finally, a weary looking woman in an AFL jacket handed her a bottle of hand sanitiser and a mask. 'We encourage the use of these,' she said, 'but with no recent outbreaks they aren't compulsory.' Ellen nodded, having already heard the spiel at least twenty times while waiting. *Someone needs to make her a sign,* she thought.

The AMDAT Corporate Box was situated on Level 3 overlooking the Ponsford Stand. The group arrived to find Daniel waiting eagerly. Margaret was nowhere to be seen. He leapt to his feet and greeted them. Georgia introduced him to Rob, who thanked him profusely for the tickets. 'My pleasure,' Daniel replied as he gestured for them to sit wherever they liked, before placing his arm around Ellen's waist and guiding her into the seat next to his. Georgia sensed the intimacy and pulled a sour face. Rob, Oliver and Zoe, on the other hand, were too excited to notice what anyone else was doing. They were soaking up the atmosphere, chatting among themselves and choosing from the list of gourmet snacks, drinks and souvenirs. The pre-match entertainment had already started. A young man with long brown hair, dressed in a green check shirt and light blue jeans, was strumming his guitar and belting out 'Up there Cazaly!'

The food-fest was well underway in the public stands before the first siren sounded. Meat pies, chips and popcorn were the main snacks washed down with beer and cider, just as they had been for years. Synthesised mince was indistinguishable from the real thing these days. Beef farming was less viable in a world that needed to rationalise resources. The younger generation couldn't understand how people ever enjoyed eating huge chunks of dead animal flesh in the first place. To them, charred steaks, and chops cooked on barbeque hotplates until the fat melted and the bones cracked, sounded totally disgusting.

As the players ran on to the field, Daniel explained the background of some. 'Many are sons of former AFL greats, selected under what is known as the father-son rule. Put on your augmented reality masks,' he encouraged them. 'You can gain real-time statistics and personal information about the players throughout the game.' Daniel helped Ellen to attach her mask, but didn't offer to assist Georgia, although she clearly had hers on upside down.

'Here, let me help you,' Zoe offered.

'Thanks, but I think I'd rather just watch the game without this thing,' Georgia replied, pulling it off and shoving it under her seat. Many spectators were like Georgia. They preferred to just watch the players. No headgear. No masks. It was such a treat to be inside the iconic stadium watching a live match for a change.

The match progressed well. First the Victorian Vipers led, then the Western Warthogs took the lead. Goals were frequent and the marking sensational. The roar of a hundred thousand spectators was deafening. Rob's enthusiasm eventually rubbed off on Georgia and, after a couple of ciders, she began to relax. Whenever the Vipers scored a goal, Georgia leapt to her feet and her seat flipped up. When she went to sit back down, she fell to the ground. Following three falls, Rob and Oliver shook their heads in disbelief. They both joked that Anna must be developing early-onset dementia. 'Shuush,' said Zoe as she helped her mother up. 'Don't make jokes about dementia!' She cocked her head in Ellen's direction. Rob and Oliver gave each other a confused glance.

The game was in the third quarter when Ellen suddenly felt a strong pain low down in her pelvis. It felt as if she was about to start a menstrual period. *Am I in labour?* she pondered, as she glanced at her chip to note the time. The pains became more intense and she noticed they were also getting more frequent. Georgia detected something wrong, but Ellen brushed her off, saying she just had indigestion from the two gourmet meat pies she had stuffed down her face. She had no intention of spoiling this special day.

It was a great match, very close, that finally ended in a three-point win to the Victorian Vipers. Their fans were elated, jumping up and down and cheering as the players ran around the field, taking it in turns to carry the Premiership Cup. Two of the players carried the captain on their shoulders. He was retiring at the end of this season, so for him the victory was particularly sweet. Ellen was standing, clapping the captain but not feeling enthusiastic. Her labour pains were now five minutes apart and, as Zoe and Georgia looked at their troubled friend, her waters broke all over her shoes and the plush purple carpet.

'I think I need to go to hospital,' Ellen said, holding her stomach and attempting to smile at Daniel.

'Oh shit, Rob!' Georgia said, nudging him in the ribs. 'Let's get her out of here.'

Rob moved across to assist Ellen, but by then Daniel had picked her up in his arms. Georgia gave Rob her *concerned* look, but he didn't have a clue what for.

Zoe and Oliver made plenty of noise and waved their arms to encourage the spectators to part and let Daniel and Ellen through. They finally managed to get safe passage onto the street, where Rob hailed an ambulance. Georgia went with Ellen in the vehicle. The others stood and watched as they drove away.

Ellen had never ridden in a hovercraft ambulance as a patient before. Being a medic, she had seen the interior of one many times. It was a different experience altogether to be on the receiving end of the health system. A parobot attached leads to Ellen, monitoring the baby's vital signs and relaying the information directly to the Health Hub team. The Hub responded by directing the ambulance to the nearest maternity hospital, St Julia's. There was no need to be triaged at the Hub. Ellen was in the advanced stages of labour.

The vehicle travelled quickly to St Julia's and in no time Ellen was working hard in the labour suite.

'Try not to push until I tell you,' Ellen's midwife, Rebecca, instructed. 'I'm hoping that you don't need an episiotomy, but that means I have to massage your perineum so that it stretches naturally and doesn't tear. Believe me, your future sex life will appreciate both our efforts.'

'Okay,' said Ellen, 'I'll try, but the urge to push is sooo strong. With all this technology, why hasn't someone figured out how to make labour easier? This is simply horrid.'

'You'll be all right,' Georgia said encouragingly. 'Just try to relax and listen to Rebecca. She knows best.'

'Ahhhh … I don't know about that,' Ellen said with desperation, gripping Georgia's hand, as the pain of another contraction flooded in like a tsunami to torture her yet again.

Ellen had decided not to find out the gender of her child when Muriel had scanned her. At that point, she hadn't been sure if she would keep the baby, and knowing whether it was a boy or a girl that she might abort would have made it that much harder.

After hours of labour, at precisely four in the morning, Ellen finally delivered a healthy baby boy. He was perfect, with a strong set of lungs and a full head of dark curly hair, just like his father. The medical team gave him a thorough check-up including routine blood tests. Finally, Georgia snapped an image of the proud mother with her bub and posted it on Facelog. From an AFL victory to the birth of Patrick Harold Hancock O'Connor, it had been a very satisfying twenty-four hours.

INTERLUDE

INTERLUDE

Sheffield
March 1667

E lizabeth went into labour in the tiny room she shared with her son Harold. He had moved from the family farm in Eyam to find work as an apprentice cutler in Sheffield and taken lodgings with the Ashmore family of nine. They lived in the three remaining rooms. The privy was two streets away—shared by the neighbours—and stank. The cobbled streets, with their open drains, were strewn with horse manure and rotting waste. Rats and mice bred unhindered, infested with fleas—the then unknown carriers of disease. Poverty was the norm, hunger a constant, illness, suffering and death routine.

Elizabeth missed her life in Eyam but she couldn't go back. She found work as a charwoman. Elizabeth scrubbed and washed by day and watched Harold burn grubs off the walls of their room by night. The room was always cold. Elizabeth kept her coat on. Her contractions started just as she had finished positioning two clay pots to catch drops of rain. The brown stained liquid was trickling through the slate roof when the first pain swept in. Elizabeth's previous births had been easy, *but she was now older. Her muscles were stiff and her pelvis less giving. Things went wrong quite quickly. Mrs Ashmore recognised the signs and sent Harold to get help.*

'Lizzie's in trouble 'arold. Run an' fetch Fanny. She lives in t' green 'ouse darn second lane on left. Tell 'er that mam needs 'er 'elp. She'll cum. She's a good lass our Fanny.'

Elizabeth's labour dragged on through the night. By morning she had developed a fever. Fanny bathed Elizabeth's head and listened for the bairn's heart by pressing an ear to her stomach. If the baby didn't come soon, she would have to pull it out or they would both die.

In her dreamlike state, Elizabeth had been flung back to her journey across the moors. It was dark and cold. The icy wind bit into her face and hands. The heather with its small leaves and delicate purple flowers bunched low to the ground, as if they were groups of children crouching together for warmth and comfort. She had been travelling for three days and the weather until now had been kind. Not today. The raindrops were full. The storm was close. She counted the seconds between the flashes of lightning and the boom of thunder. Only five. The storm was five miles away—Sheffield less than one. She could see lights up ahead; when the lightning flashed, she caught glimpses of a barn and black-faced sheep. Keep going lass—only one more ridge, she thought to herself, then with her head down she pressed on.

Harold bathed his mother's brow. Her contractions were almost constant. Fanny felt for the baby's head, instead she touched a chin. Fanny had seen this before. Sometimes the head would drop forward into position and the baby would slip out. It was a waiting game—one that didn't always end well.

Seven months earlier, Harold had been surprised to see his wet, bedraggled mother standing on the doorstep of the

Ashmore home. 'I've cum from Bakewell,' she had lied to Mrs Ashmore. 'I was told I'd find me son Harold 'ere.' Mrs Ashmore was less than pleased to have another mouth to feed, yet with the promise of increased rent for the one room, she had agreed to let Elizabeth stay.

As Elizabeth's labour continued the Ashmore children gathered in silence by the fire downstairs. Mrs Ashmore had sent Harold down to join them as Fanny prepared for the final intervention. He sat motionless, listening to the muffled voices and footsteps overhead—calls to 'push' from Fanny—the occasional scream from his mother. Then suddenly the squawk of a baby filled the house. Harold stood up and walked to the base of the stairs. Mrs Ashmore opened the door of his room and called out.

'It's a babbie boy 'arold! You 'av a new babbie brother.'

Harold breathed a huge sigh of relief.

Melbourne
October 2074

47

Daniel knocked on the door of Ellen's apartment. He had decided to personally deliver his gift for her newborn son. He was well aware Maggie would not be pleased if she knew about the visit, but he was past caring. Despite his wealth and power, he'd never been happier than he was since Ellen re-entered his life. He was convinced that she was his true soulmate. They had so much in common. Their relationship was easier than any he had ever experienced. They could talk for hours about science and other topics that would generally bore his other friends. Ellen was so beautiful … and sexy.

Zoe opened the door and was surprised to see her employer Daniel Grant on the other side.

'Hi, Zoe,' he said clearing his throat. 'I've come to visit Ellen and meet the baby. Is she at home?'

'Oh, hello, Mr Grant,' she answered. 'Yes, Ellen is home. Come on in,' she beckoned him in with a wave of her hand. 'I'll let her know that you're here.' Zoe parked Daniel just inside the door and went into Ellen's room, where the new mother was breastfeeding. Zoe closed the door and leaned against it. 'You are not going to believe this,' she said. 'Daniel Grant has come to visit you and baby Pat *in person*. What do you want me to do with him?'

'Bring him in here, of course.'

'What? ... but your breasts are on display.'

'I'm sure he's seen plenty of breasts, Zoe,' Ellen said. 'Please show him in.'

Zoe shook her head and left the room.

Daniel made his way into the bedroom then closed the door behind him before sitting next to Ellen and kissing her on the lips. Baby Pat kept suckling as if nothing had changed.

'How are you?' Daniel asked. 'I've really missed you these past few weeks.'

'Same,' Ellen replied and reached to pull his mouth back onto hers.

They were in the middle of an embrace when Georgia entered the room. She immediately retreated, closing the door behind her. How could Ellen be so reckless? Why would she take such a stupid risk?

'What's wrong?' Zoe asked, turning her head towards Georgia. She sensed her mother also didn't approve of Daniel being in Ellen's bedroom.

'Never mind, it's not important,' Georgia replied, waving one hand dismissively, hoping to delay Zoe's knowledge of Ellen's indiscreet behaviour. 'How about we have some lunch?' she said, glancing across at Rob and raising her eyebrows. He knew something wasn't right.

The three were sitting on the couch watching the midday news and munching on tuna and cheese toasties when a breaking story scrolled across the bottom of the screen.

AMDAT ... student ... unexpectedly ... infected ... with ... bubonic plague.

'Did you catch that news item,' Zoe asked.

'Not all of it,' Georgia replied. 'I only noticed something about an AMDAT student.' They both stopped eating and waited motionless for the text to scroll back around. Zoe could feel her heart pounding.

Could the student be Sarah? Surely nothing had happened to her? She was recovering so well when they visited a week ago. One tense minute passed. Their eyes remained fixed on the screen. The story scrolled back through.

AMDAT student dies unexpectedly after being infected with the bubonic plague.

Zoe was stunned. She began to turn pale and her face crumpled.

'I must tell Ellen,' she said, rising out of her seat and heading towards the bedroom door.

'Zoe, wait. Don't go in there. She has a visitor. I don't think she'll appreciate being disturbed,' Georgia said.

'I'm sure she'll want to know about this straightaway,' Zoe replied, ignoring her mother and barging into Ellen's bedroom. Daniel kissing Ellen was a sight she was not expecting.

Trying to ignore what she had observed and looking up at the ceiling to avoid eye contact, Zoe told them about Sarah's death. By now she was visibly distressed. She was shaking. Her voice trembled and tears that up until now had been pooled in her eyes began to escape. They trickled slowly down her cheeks.

Ellen handed Patrick to Daniel, rose from the bed and pulled Zoe to her chest. The girl was inconsolable. Ellen looked over at Daniel and mouthed, 'What happened? What went wrong?'

'I'm so very sorry, Zoe. This news must come as a shock. As well as visiting Ellen and the baby, I came to let you both know that Sarah developed a secondary lung infection three days ago. She hasn't been responding to antibiotic therapy and I feared that she might not make it,' he explained. 'I didn't expect anything to happen today, though.'

'It's a tragedy that should never have happened,' Ellen said. 'There will be serious repercussions for AMDAT over this incident, Daniel.' Daniel bit his bottom lip and nodded.

Ellen gave Zoe a mild sedative and suggested she rest. Tucked up in bed with a warm drink, Zoe's thoughts began to race. Ellen had just given birth to Patrick's baby and now she was carrying on with Daniel.

What was she thinking? It was so disappointing. Zoe now regretted her decision to donate ova to the Grants. Maggie was showing no signs of being pregnant and Daniel was nothing but a lying cheat. He should have told them about Sarah the minute he arrived. Canoodling with Ellen was clearly his main priority ... not poor Sarah ... nor Maggie. Zoe hoped the IVF embryo transfers had all failed. Perhaps her eggs were gone ... used up. Maybe there would be no baby. That would be the best outcome.

Zoe continued to sniffle as she opened her Facelog newsfeed. The platform was buzzing with comments related to the death of the AMDAT medical student. Everyone was shocked. It appeared this day wasn't getting better anytime soon. Georgia was still watching the newsfeed when a second story broke. This news item was headed 'AMDAT Love Rat'. Suspecting the story would finally reveal Vaughn Lambert's womanising, Georgia called out to Zoe, Ellen and Daniel. 'I think you had all better come out here and see this.'

The five of them sat and watched with enthusiasm that quickly turned to horror. Everyone went silent, as a six-second footage grab of two people having intercourse was displayed for the whole world to view. The faces on the screen were in clear focus. Only the genitals were blurred. Little had been left to the imagination. Ellen and Daniel immediately recognised the scene. It was their first illicit sexual encounter. It had been recorded.

The channel cut across to a live newsfeed outside the front of AMDAT Tower. At least a dozen camera drones were hovering. A number of reporters were demanding an explanation of the student death from a senior executive as well as comments on the newly released 'Love Rat' footage. Head researcher Daniel Grant had been filmed having sex with someone other than his wife.

It wasn't long before Kenneth Stuart and Vaughn Lambert stepped out of the building to face the media pack. Margaret, not surprisingly, was absent.

Vaughn spoke first, reading from a prepared press release.

'AMDAT student Ms Sarah Baker died at ten o'clock this morning from complications of the pneumonic plague. She was infected with a mutant form of this rare disease when another student gave her access to a restricted area known as the bat zone. This was in total breach of AMDAT policies, procedures and protocols.'

Georgia let out a gasp, realising Zoe was being blamed. Zoe turned white, and then ran to the bathroom holding her hand over her mouth to prevent the vomit spilling. The coverage continued.

'Ms Baker was recovering from the plague when she developed a secondary lung infection, for which there was no effective treatment. A specialist team tried all remaining antibiotics but the bacteria that finally took Ms Baker's life was resistant to every one. Ms Baker's family were by her bedside when she passed away. AMDAT pass their condolences on to all Ms Baker's family and friends. All of the systems have been examined and it appears that someone deliberately caused the incident. It was neither an accident nor a system failure. The police will be taking over this investigation and they're confident that the perpetrator will be caught and punished.'

'What about your son-in-law, Mr Stuart?' a reporter shouted.

'How is Mrs Grant coping?' yelled another.

Kenneth stepped forwards.

'I presume you're referring to the ViewTube clip that was released this morning. As you can imagine, my daughter Margaret is too upset to face the media. The death of Ms Baker is, of course, uppermost in her thoughts; she is, however, also quite emotional about her husband's latest indiscretion.'

'Do you know the identity of the woman, Mr Stuart?'

'Yes, it is Doctor Ellen Hancock whom Daniel has known for many years.'

'She looks pregnant in the footage,' said one reporter.

'Is the baby Daniel Grant's?' quizzed another.

'Quite probably,' Kenneth answered. He knew full well that the baby wasn't Daniel's, but was not prepared to miss an opportunity to sully his son-in-law's reputation even further.

'Will Mrs Grant divorce him?'

'That will be up to my daughter to decide. What I can tell you is that under the terms of their prenuptial agreement, Daniel Grant is now in danger of losing everything. The chip technology patent belongs exclusively to AMDAT.' Kenneth peered menacingly into the camera lens and spoke. His expression could barely contain the anger he felt over the betrayal of his only daughter. 'Wherever you are, Daniel, your AMDAT security clearance and system access codes have been suspended. I've arranged for some of your personal belongings to be forwarded to Ellen Hancock's address.' Several media drones immediately flew off in the direction of Ellen's apartment.

'I also need to inform everyone that Daniel Grant is in fact an imposter. He deceived my daughter as well as me. No such person exists. His real name is Daniel Ward. Ward is a very appropriate name, as he was a Ward of the State of Tasmania from age sixteen.'

Two images filled the TV screen, one labelled *Daniel Ward*, a clean-shaven red-headed youth wearing glasses, the other labelled *Daniel Grant*, a more recent one of the AMDAT scientist with his dark brown hair and auburn beard.

Turning his attention back to Vaughn, Kenneth placed a hand on the younger man's shoulder and continued to speak. 'As AMDAT's head researcher, Daniel Ward must be held accountable for the death of Ms Sarah Baker. Therefore, Professor Vaughn Lambert will be replacing him until further notice. Vaughn will take over all AMDAT positions previously held by Daniel as well as completing any of his unfinished research.'

'Where is Daniel Grant now?' asked a journalist.

'If you mean Daniel Ward, I don't actually know. I presume he's with his girlfriend and their new baby.' Before continuing, Kenneth paused and dropped his head, as if examining the pavement as he summoned the strength to look directly at his interrogators, 'Quite frankly, I … we … don't really care.'

He turned and walked back inside the tower with Vaughn, as security guards held back the crowd of reporters. Many were hailing cabs, no doubt headed for Ellen's apartment. A pack of drones could be seen flying in the direction of her apartment, like a swarm of wasps searching for a new nest.

48

Inside Ellen's apartment you could have heard a pin drop. Ellen placed both hands over her face then dropped her head forward into her lap. They all sat in silence for about twenty seconds. Daniel, although embarrassed for himself and Ellen, was also angry. His face took on a dark hue. He could feel that his teeth had clenched, and he felt like punching something or someone.

No doubt Vaughn was behind this latest betrayal. Not only had he deliberately recorded, then released, the footage of him with Ellen, he was most likely the one who had revealed his true identity to Kenneth. Daniel had successfully hidden his past for years and Maggie had promised not to tell. He felt great anger towards Vaughn but in the current company he needed to contain his emotions.

'Well, I didn't see that coming,' he said with a sigh, as he turned to face them all with a feigned smile, as if trying to reassure everyone that the revelation would have little impact on his life.

'Sorry to have placed you all in the middle of this mess. It will get unpleasant with the media frenzy to come, but it will eventually die down. In one way it's for the best, I guess. Not that I expected events to unfold this way. However, our relationship would eventually have been revealed. We are simply meant to be together and now we can stop hiding our true feelings for each other.' He looked over towards Ellen, who nodded her agreement without uttering a word.

Georgia felt overwhelmed with the torrent of information and sat with a perplexed expression and one hand plastered across her mouth. She was simply unable to find the words to comment. So she didn't.

By now, Zoe had composed herself and rejoined the group. A scowl began to form on her face as she listened to Daniel talking of a future with Ellen rather than his wife.

'But what about Mrs Grant and you, and ...'

Daniel quickly interrupted Zoe and, in a firm tone, proceeded to shut her down.

'No decisions have been made about anything at this stage. Let's all just take some time to fully digest what just happened.'

He stared directly at Zoe until he was sure she had processed his message. She had, after all, given her word that she wouldn't say anything to anyone about their IVF arrangement. Fortuitously, almost as if on cue, loud sounds emanating from the street sent their attention in a completely different direction.

On hearing the commotion, Zoe moved across to the window. The street was crawling with reporters. As she came into view, a reporter called out something she couldn't quite make out. A large camera drone appeared from nowhere. It rose to Zoe's eye level then snapped her picture. The unexpected flash caused her to stumble backwards. Rob jumped up and pulled the curtains closed.

'I suggest that you keep away from the windows,' Daniel continued. 'Don't open the door and don't answer your mobile unless you recognise the caller ID. I'm afraid people can be cruel, so all we can do is wait until another news story moves the focus away from myself and Ellen.'

49

Maggie lay on the marital bed. She had cried so much she had few tears left. It was as if her body had gone through an unrelenting drought. She knew in her heart that Daniel was lost to her. One minute she was so angry she hated him and wanted him dead. The next she knew she still loved him and longed to have him lying next to her, as if none of this had ever happened.

She hadn't watched the media conference. Her father promised to visit once it was all over, to let her know the outcome. Sarah's death had sent shock waves throughout the community. Although Maggie knew the dangers of working with infected bats, she had been confident all of the risks had been mitigated. How had such a catastrophe occurred? Had she become so complacent that the real dangers seemed insignificant? Sarah had been a young woman with her whole life ahead of her until she joined AMDAT's controversial medical research program.

She heard a knock on the door. Kenneth peered around and Maggie nodded. He entered with Vaughn. On seeing her father, Maggie teared up. Kenneth sat on the bed and gave her a hug.

'What's he doing here?' she blubbered, looking in Vaughn's direction.

'Now, now, Maggie,' Kenneth replied. 'I know you two don't get on, but under the circumstances you and Vaughn will need to pull together if we're going to survive this crisis.

'Maggie darling, you need to tell us what you want us to do. How should we handle Daniel? Vaughn is happy to take care of anything for you. Vaughn's a good man, Maggie. Perhaps you need to give him a chance. He's far from perfect, but he hasn't let you down like Daniel, has he?'

'He's a womanising bastard, that's what he is.'

'Look, when men are young, many of them go through a highly sexed phase.' He threw Vaughn a look. 'I wasn't a saint at his age either. He'll grow out of it, I'm sure. Your precious husband wasn't much better. He's been lying to everyone about his true identity for years.'

'Who told *you*?' She asked.

'Darling … for the right price, I can find out *anything*. My private investigator uncovered Daniel's identity about two weeks before you were married. By then, everything was planned. The guests were invited, the dress fitted and the venue booked. You were *so* happy that I didn't have the heart to shatter your dreams. Daniel's tale was a pathetic one anyway. I didn't give a jot about him having a dead *mad* mother or him being sent to youth detention. In fact, I was quite impressed that he actually bashed someone—didn't think the weak prick had it in him. Your marriage wasn't a concern. The prenuptial had everything covered and I felt that the identity info could come in handy down the track. I'd say today was perfect timing, wouldn't you?' he looked across at a grinning Vaughn.

'Anyway, I'll ask again. What do you want us to do regarding Daniel?'

'Kill him.'

'I could—but I don't think you really mean that.'

'Well, don't kill him but get him away from that Hancock woman and make them both pay.'

'Are you sure that's what you want?' Vaughn added.

'I'm sure. If I can't have him then nobody can.'

'There may be no turning back from your decision, Maggie. Are you completely sure that you don't want him back and that you want Daniel to be punished?'

'Yes. I don't want him anymore. Make the fucking cheating bastard pay.'

50

Francis and Mindy watched the media circus. He hadn't heard the name Ward for a very long time. His older brother Kenneth hadn't changed. Naturally he had aged. But he was still the same self-centred narcissistic arsehole. Daniel Grant was the brains behind AMDAT and now Kenneth had shafted his own son-in-law just because the young man had been indiscreet. Kenneth had been one of the biggest pants men in Western Australia. What a hypocrite. It was wrong, but not unexpected.

'We should try to help Ellen,' Francis said to Mindy. 'She saved our Sam. Perhaps she could help us set up our new health centre.'

He called his daughter, Louise, who was busily feeding her newborn baby girl.

'Hi, darling,' he said. 'How is my gorgeous little granddaughter Holly doing? I can't wait to see her.'

Louise should have been happy with the comment, but knew that once Francis saw Holly, he would realise what she'd done. Never mind, she had her little girl and, whatever was to come, it had been worth it. Louise answered her father in silly high-pitched baby babble.

'Little Holly is fine, and she can't wait to meet her grandma and grandad as soon as they can visit. When will that be?' she asked, tickling the little girl's cheek with her pinkie finger.

'In a couple of weeks, I'm afraid. I have to visit NATGRID North to supervise the opening of the Queensland flood overflow network. It's taken five years to complete and I'm really looking forward to cutting the ribbon and thanking the workforce for their dedication.'

'It's a fantastic achievement, Dad, but I wish you and Mindy would try to rest more. You're not getting any younger.'

Secretly, Louise was pleased they weren't visiting. It would give her a chance to figure out how to tell her father that Holly was genetically engineered. Professor Lambert had arranged for Holly's minor hand operation to take place earlier than usual. At least her hands would soon look normal.

'Anyway, I was wondering if you had any way of getting in touch with Doctor Ellen Hancock.'

'Not really,' she replied. Louise paused for a few moments to think, before suggesting a possible way forward. 'I guess I could try getting her address via the Health Hub where she works, or at least have someone contact her and she could call me back. I'll try calling, but if necessary, I'll go down to the Hub.'

'That sounds positive, sweetheart.'

Francis outlined the plan to his daughter.

'Great idea, Dad. My guess is Ellen will be up for it.'

51

Tony watched the World News bulletin. The revelation that Daniel Grant was in fact Daniel Ward could drive the investigation in a fresh direction. Both he and Patrick had a fairly good idea why the missing Newark girls had been targeted. There was a strong possibility they had been groomed by a person or persons unknown and then kidnapped. But who had seized them—and where they were now—remained a mystery. Tony was convinced they should focus their attention on the AMDAT Corporation. There had to be a connection. Intuition told him this was no coincidence.

Tony heard the shower running in the upstairs bathroom. Patrick would soon be down for dinner. He knew his dear friend would be shattered at the breaking news of Daniel and Ellen. Tony had lived through the last time Daniel Ward had turned Ellen's affections from him. He clearly recalled Patrick's drinking binges and threats to harm Daniel that he frequently circumvented. The brawl outside the local bar had been the worst. Ellen and Daniel had arrived for a nightcap just before closing time and stumbled straight into an intoxicated Patrick. He had grasped Ellen, thrust her against the bar wall and attempted to steal a kiss. Daniel had intervened and quite a struggle had ensued. Fortunately, Tony and a couple of Patrick's friends had separated them before any damage was done.

Patrick really loved Ellen, but he never quite knew where he stood with her. Tony knew how optimistic Patrick was, now that Ellen had finally proclaimed her love for him and given him a son. He tried to think how he could minimise his friend's shock. Patrick's undercover work had paid off, but his dedication to the police force would be tested if it lost him Ellen.

The ledger had shown the biological parents of the five girls. They all had two sets of mitochondrial DNA. One set was from the same female donor, 'EH'. Cross-referencing with the decoder, Patrick had been surprised to discover that Ellen Hancock's mitochondria had been used in all five fertility procedures. Patrick couldn't recall Ellen telling him she had ever donated ova. He felt this omission surprising, considering they were close and with her knowledge of the current investigation. There was, however, one additional link. The deceased girl, Bridget, was conceived using sperm donated by a 'DW'—Daniel Ward. Daniel Ward, Patrick's rival, was the biological father of two girls, the deceased girl Bridget Patterson and Zoe Ashmore, Georgia's daughter. In the other four cases the biological father and parent were one and the same. The footage exposing Daniel as a fraud could not be ignored. Tony was convinced this was no coincidence.

As Tony chopped the onions and mushrooms for risotto, he could hear Patrick singing in the shower. He had quite a good voice. Tony knew he couldn't prevent Patrick from witnessing Ellen's indiscretion. The news report was airing on every channel; the footage streaming across all social media platforms. The first thing Patrick did each evening was to pour a glass of pinot and catch up on current events. Tony wondered how he could soften the blow, but nothing came to mind. Perhaps all was not lost. After all, Ellen believed Patrick was dead, so she wasn't deliberately cheating.

He glanced across at the letter perched on his mantel. What did it contain? Surely Ellen wasn't involved. Yet she hadn't been upfront about donating ova, had she? The answers could be right there in front of him. He tore the envelope open and walked slowly backwards across the lounge room, reading, before slumping onto the couch. It took him a few minutes to fully process the information. The last thing he'd expected was to find a link between Doctor Dawson, Vaughn Lambert, AMDAT and the missing Newark girls. Tony decided to take a closer look at the contents of the ledger, just in case they had missed something.

Patrick entered the room, combing his fingers through his damp hair. Tony waited until he'd poured himself a glass of pinot, then handed him the letter. Patrick read it and agreed that they should re-examine the ledger.

They checked the ledger from front to back and had just about given up, when Patrick noticed that the back cover was thicker than the front. Tony grabbed a sharp knife and ran it down the edge of the binding. Hidden inside was an envelope. He opened it and tipped the contents onto the table. They consisted mainly of articles about the development of the health chip and research on the human immune system, as well as journal site addresses, e-book references and scraps of paper with scribbled names and contact details. There were also two small coloured images. Tony fetched his high-powered scope viewer and projected the first image on to a wall. The billionaire Kenneth Stuart was pictured with three young scientists, identified as Gum Lin, Daniel Grant and Vaughn Lambert. It was the day Kenneth had pledged his financial backing for the trio to trial their health chip. Tony enlarged each of the people to examine them more closely. It was then that Patrick noticed the tattoo on Gum Lin's arm. It was a serpent, with a maroon and aqua–coloured tail. The tattoo wound up her arm, around her neck and finished with the head of the creature resting on her shoulder, its eyes closed as if asleep.

Patrick had only seen a small portion of his captor's tattoo. Nevertheless, he was convinced that the woman in the image was the same one who had tried to kill him. The second image was of Vaughn Lambert with Gum Lin and a Susie Long—identified as head of AMDAT security. The three were launching AMDAT's new generation security android. The androids were useful because—although unarmed—they could detect the presence of unauthorised personnel. Susie was the same height as Gum with smooth black hair. Patrick suspected she was her accomplice.

Things were beginning to gel for both Patrick and Tony. Daniel, Vaughn, Gum and now Susie were all linked to the investigation in one way or another. AMDAT was clearly involved. No trace of the missing girls had been found in America. Could they be in Australia? With the possibility of the crime crossing international borders Tony involved the FBI. They would need to contact the Australian Federal Police and discuss the case. Checking the flight path logs of AMDAT private jets travelling between Newark and Melbourne around the time of the disappearances was of particular relevance. If the times and dates matched, then the airport camera footage could be checked.

Following preliminary investigations the FBI determined two of their agents would travel to Australia. It was decided that senior detectives Scallioni and O'Connor would be seconded to the FBI and accompany them. Their extensive knowledge of the case made them invaluable.

The four American officers would travel to Melbourne and work with the local authorities to investigate AMDAT's involvement. Patrick hoped the trip would also give him the opportunity to see Ellen and baby Pat. A chance for him to find happiness with the mother of his son before Ellen's relationship with Daniel became entrenched. To maintain his undercover status, Patrick would need a temporary identity. The biggest challenge would be to pass him undetected through Q precinct.

Two days later all the arrangements were in place and Tony called his girlfriend.

'I'm going to Australia on police business. I'll be based in Melbourne. I'm not sure how long the investigation will take. It could be several weeks. I really don't like leaving you for so long. I thought that you could come with me and when the investigation finishes, we can relax and see the sights. I've contacted a friend of mine, Anna Taylor. She lives in Melbourne with Ellen Hancock. Ellen's away at the moment, but Anna would be pleased to have you stay with her while I'm working. Are you interested?'

'I'd love to come. I've never been to Australia. I'll check the weather in Melbourne and start deciding what to pack.'

'Great, touch base soon. Are we still okay for a movie tomorrow?'

'Sure, come over, I've cooked a massaman curry. Always better on the second day.'

'See you then, gorgeous. Nighty night.'

52

Louise called the Hub, but staff would not provide her with Ellen Hancock's contact details or pass on a message. A polite man explained that since the ViewTube footage, there had been an increase in abusive calls. Security had been tightened. Louise was left with no other option than to go directly to the Hub. She caught a cab there and approached the main entrance on foot. There was a large man leaning against the boom gate. She decided to ask him for assistance.

Tex noticed the woman approaching and advanced to meet her. He started his usual spiel, before Louise interrupted him and explained she didn't require any medical assistance.

'I just wondered if you had Doctor Ellen Hancock's mobile number?' she enquired. The man chuckled and shook his head in disbelief.

'You'd better join that queue over there,' Tex replied, drawing her attention twenty metres to his left where a group of journalists and ten hovering drones were patiently waiting, hoping to catch a glimpse of Doctor Hancock if, by chance, she came to work.

'You don't understand. I'm not a reporter,' Louise explained.

'Who are you, then? Don't tell me,' he said, raising his hand in a stop motion … 'Let me guess … mmmm … you're her sister, I suppose?' Tex responded sarcastically, as if he'd spent the entire day listening to ridiculous explanations.

'No, I'm not a relative. However, I do need to urgently contact her, and I'd greatly appreciate your help.' Louise rummaged in her handbag and pulled out a business card.

Tex folded his arms and refused to take the card.

'Look, please take the card and I'll leave. All I ask is that you contact Doctor Hancock once I'm gone and ask her to give me a call.'

Tex didn't respond. He was having a very frustrating day.

Louise continued, 'I'm positive that Doctor Hancock will want to speak with me. My family just want to help her and her baby. That's all.'

'Well, if you're such a great friend, why don't you already have her personal contact details?' Tex asked, raising his eyebrows and smirking as if to say 'Gotcha'. He was not buying this woman's story.

'Look, please just give her a call and tell her Louise Stuart would like to speak with her urgently and pass on my number. That can't hurt anyone, can it? Here, take my business card. Can you please just make the call?'

Tex kept his arms folded.

Louise placed the card on the ground at his feet then turned and began walking away.

Tex picked up the business card. It was matt black with gold embossed text. It looked and felt expensive and had the NATGRID logo stylishly written across one corner. *Couldn't hurt to let Ellen know*, he thought. The woman seemed genuine enough and was well spoken. It was up to Ellen to decide whether to contact her or not.

'I'll consider your request,' Tex called out.

Louise stopped and turned.

'Great, well that's at least something. Thank you, thank you very much.'

Tex decided to make the call. Ellen saw the caller ID scroll through. Tex rarely called her at home. She wondered what he needed to speak with her about. Her face reddened at the thought of him viewing the sex clip. Ellen knew she had to face her workmates sooner or later. She shut her eyes, breathed in and said *Accept*.

'Hi, Louise. I just received your message. Is everything okay with you and your family?'

'We're all fine. It's you we're worried about. Dad would like to help you and has asked me to outline his plan.'

'Okay, well, what does he have in mind?'

Louise talked for about five minutes while Ellen wrote down some details. The conversation was punctuated with quite a few *mms* and *uh-huhs*. Ellen eventually thanked Louise for all her help and ended the call. She turned back to face Georgia, Rob, Zoe and Daniel, who were all waiting in anticipation to find out what the call was about.

'I'll be leaving in the early morning,' Ellen said, as the group hung on her every word. 'I'm hoping that Daniel decides to come with me?' She looked in his direction, raised her eyebrows and smiled.

Zoe stood up abruptly. 'What about me and Anna?' she asked in an exasperated tone.

'It isn't you the media are interested in, Zoe. Once the reporters know that Daniel and I have left the apartment, they'll leave you two alone.'

By the expression on Zoe's face she was clearly not convinced. Ellen continued placating her.

'Look, Zoe. We won't be gone forever. Just until the media frenzy passes and Daniel and I decide on the best way forward.'

'But where are you going?' Georgia asked.

'I can't tell you that at the moment. I'll be in touch as soon as we're safe. I think it's best if you don't know.'

'Oh,' Zoe moaned. 'It sounds so mysterious. I wish we could come.'

'We aren't going on holiday, Zoe. Anyway,' she paused. 'Daniel and I have some planning to do.' She caught his eye and with a nod of her head signalled him to return to her bedroom.

Standing up and placing his arm around Georgia, Rob spoke up.

'You two take baby Pat somewhere safe, Ellen. Don't worry. I'll take good care of these girls while you're gone.'

Georgia blushed as Rob squeezed her shoulder, but she looked delighted.

53

At three the following morning, Daniel and Ellen dressed. Georgia fussed around them like a mother hen making sure they didn't forget anything. Ellen had already fed baby Pat and packed his basic necessities and he was now asleep in a sling tied on Daniel's front. She slung her backpack over one shoulder and her medical bag over the other.

Ellen peeked through a small gap in the curtain to observe the street below. A few reporters could be seen nodding off beneath a street lamp directly in front of her building. The drones were inactive. They sat motionless on the ground like a group of oversized sleeping insects. Drones relied on wi-fi operators, who were most likely sending up zeds from their comfortable control centres.

The couple crept stealthily through the front door of the apartment and into the fire exit directly opposite. They had quite a few floors to descend so they progressed steadily. Ellen checked the time. They had to make it to the forecourt between the museum and the exhibition building by four. She had calculated that it would take around fifteen minutes if they kept up a reasonable pace.

Everything seemed to be going smoothly until they reached the bottom of the fire escape, where the door wouldn't open. It appeared to be jammed from the outside. Daniel handed Pat to Ellen and tried ramming the door open with his shoulder. A deep voice came from outside.

'Steady on. A man should be able to get some sleep in his own bed.'

'Open the door please, mate,' Daniel called back.

'What's it worth to ya?'

Daniel checked his pockets. He only had a flashcard loaded with two thousand dollars.

'Will you open the door for two thousand bucks?'

'Do ya think I'm stupid, mate? Why don't you just piss off and let me get some sleep.'

Daniel pushed the card under the door. The display panel clearly displayed the correct balance. Following a short pause and a 'Fuck, yeah,' the door opened.

'Thanks,' said Daniel. He scrutinised the homeless man dressed in his filthy overcoat, then glanced down at his own designer clothing. They were a bit of a giveaway.

'How about swapping coats with me?' The guy couldn't get his coat off quickly enough.

Daniel tucked Pat back into the sling and hid him under the coat. Its stench wasn't pleasant, but hopefully he wouldn't have to wear it for long. They made their way through the streets and were a block away from the museum when they were suddenly spotted by two media drones. They began swooping down on the couple like magpies.

Ellen and Daniel could hear the sound of a helicopter in the distance and see the beam of light as it searched to locate a suitable landing site. They were on time. One of the drones misjudged a gap and hit Ellen in the face. She fell to the ground, looking up just in time to watch it smash into a tree. The drone dropped to the ground and spun in circles like a giant dragonfly in its death throes.

Ellen sat, momentarily stunned, as a small trickle of blood made its way down one cheek. The commotion had woken Pat and he began squawking. Daniel could hear voices and observed more drones and flashlight beams heading in their direction. He helped Ellen to her feet, linked his arm in hers and encouraged her to keep moving.

By now the helicopter had landed and a figure could be seen waiting for them. When they reached the hatch, a young man helped them on board. Once everyone was safely secured, he pulled the hatch closed and signalled the pilot to take off. The helicopter rose into the night sky. The breathless couple watched the crowd of journalists gathering beneath them gradually reduce in size. Two drones attempting to take one last image for the morning news were hit by the helicopter blades and instantly shredded. The impact caused the helicopter to lean slightly.

Pat's piercing cries echoed throughout the cockpit as the pilot skilfully navigated the helicopter between the buildings and up over the nearby gardens. When they were completely clear of all visible hazards the pilot spoke to them.

'Looks like it's my turn to save you, Doctor Hancock.' Ellen looked up to see the beaming face of Francis Stuart in the cockpit mirror.

'*Oh ... Mr Stuart*, I didn't expect you to pick us up personally,' Ellen said.

'Francis, Ellen. Please call me Francis.'

'Francis Stuart?' Daniel said, taken aback. He looked towards Ellen for an explanation. She pulled down one side of her mouth and then replied.

'Sorry, but I wasn't sure you'd come with me if you knew your wife's uncle had offered us his protection.'

'That's right, son; I'm Margaret's uncle, Kenneth's estranged brother. Welcome aboard.'

'But why would you want to help me after what's just happened?' continued Daniel.

'Well, you're important to Ellen, so that's all that matters to me at the moment,' he replied. 'I don't particularly agree with anything AMDAT does, including that blessed chip you invented, but Ellen sees some good in you, so you can't be all bad.'

Ellen glanced over to Daniel, raised her eyebrows and smiled.

'Where are you taking us this morning?' she asked.

'NATGRID East. It will take quite a while to get there, so relax and enjoy the ride.'

Silence reigned for the next five minutes as they cleared the Melbourne city skyline. The sun was rising slowly, washing the distant hills with soft hues of gold, red and blue. It was breathtaking. The young man who helped them on board had introduced himself. He was Mindy's nephew Dorak.

When they reached the edge of the desert, the vegetation gradually decreased until only the hardy species that could withstand extreme temperatures remained. Dorak began pointing out the NATGRID infrastructure below. Wind and solar farms stretched as far as they could see. The smoky glass panels automatically followed the orientation of the sun, ensuring they soaked up every drop of its energy, which was then stored in giant underground batteries. NATGRID East supplied energy to the whole of south-eastern Australia.

They landed near a large burnt orange tin-clad structure that resembled four huge children's blocks stacked at opposing angles.

'Is this where we'll be staying?' Ellen asked, somewhat surprised.

'Not exactly,' Francis replied. 'I'll take you down to our community. Mindy has your beds ready. You must be in need of a good sleep—

especially that young Pat; he certainly has a good set of lungs and knows how to use them.'

Ellen thought Francis must be kidding. The building wasn't big enough to contain a large family, let alone a 'community'.

As they exited the craft, the hot dry air hit them in the face and took their breath away. Francis assured them that it was still quite cool. Around midday, temperatures would reach into the high forties.

It became clear to them that the block structure was not a residence but the entrance to a large underground facility. They were relieved to enter the building and leave the oppressive heat behind. After passing through two sets of airlocks they found themselves in a spacious lobby. Francis motioned them into the lift and they descended one floor.

The lift doors opened and the group stepped out into a large atrium. Light was beaming through ceiling windows. Francis explained that no heat came through the roof. The windows were quad glazed, with two sets of double-glazed windows and a thirty-centimetre vacuum in between. Tropical plants were flourishing near the lift entrance and a stone water wall gave the space a cool lush feel. The floor was polished concrete and warm to the touch. Floor heating, Francis explained, just to keep any underground damp at bay.

They followed Francis down a couple of corridors into another large room where Mindy was waiting to greet them. She was an Indigenous woman, aged in her seventies, Ellen guessed, but her curly hair was still gloriously dark, sweeping off her face into a thick plait. She was barefoot and wore a robe that resembled a 1960s kaftan.

Mindy offered Ellen and Daniel two separate bedrooms. Ellen said one room would be fine. She explained that it felt like the whole world knew about their relationship, so it seemed pointless keeping up any pretence. They were both happy to toss Daniel's smelly coat in the trash, have a quick shower, feed and change Pat before crawling into bed.

54

Pat's crying woke them around eight. There was knocking at the door soon after; a young woman entered the room and introduced herself as Poppy. She urged Ellen to stay in bed and rest while she changed Pat. It wasn't long before he was suckling contentedly from his mother's breast.

Poppy sat patiently until Pat finished; then she lifted the sleeping bub, burped him and tucked him back in his cot before turning the light out and leaving.

Ellen turned to Daniel: 'If this is how people with nannies live, I could get quite used to it.'

He just smiled. They both snuggled back under the covers for a few more hours of shut-eye.

Pat slept until midday. On hearing his cry, Poppy again entered the room, picked him up and changed him before handing him to his mother. Once again, she sat until he had finished feeding. Pat fell from the breast as if intoxicated. He looked like a little drunken old man.

The intercom buzzed. It was Mindy asking them if they were ready for brunch.

'Will I bring Pat?' Ellen asked.

'No need,' Mindy said. 'Leave him with Poppy; he'll be fine. Make your way outside and turn left. The dining room is fourth on the right.'

Ellen and Daniel showered and changed into fresh clothes before joining Mindy and Francis in the communal dining room. The brunch was vegetarian, with a range of colourful fresh vegetables and pulses.

'This place is wonderful, Francis. It's such a comfortable temperature. How many people live here?' she asked, as she spooned in another mouthful of white bean salad.

'About two hundred,' he replied.

'Two hundred,' she mumbled with a full mouth. 'But from the air I could only see one small building.'

'That was just one of the shaft entrances. After you've eaten, we'll take you both on a tour.'

Over brunch Francis explained that the land on which the NATGRID village was built belonged to First Nations people. Francis and Mindy had negotiated leases in some of the most desolate areas of Australia. NATGRID had started to develop underground communities, using land that was not viable for other industries. NATGRID East was phase one. Four NATGRID villages were now under development, each one self-sufficient. Eventually these would supply eighty per cent of Australia's renewable energy needs.

After brunch they strolled leisurely through the complex. Francis's enthusiasm was contagious. He and Mindy had invested so much of their time and energy in their vision.

NATGRID East consisted of sleeping quarters, communal living areas and work zones. There was a network of tunnels and rooms that had been constructed using recycled natural and synthetic materials.

'These walls look like the inside of shipping containers,' Daniel said as he rubbed the surface with his hand.

'You're spot on! That's exactly what they are,' Francis replied. 'We use containers like giant building blocks. You can create various sized spaces by stacking, welding them together and cutting out the doors and skylights. Only the skylights and entrance shafts are visible from the air. We try hard not to scar the landscape.'

'But how do you stop the heat getting in?' Ellen asked.

'Quad glazing and adjustable blinds. We also use the blinds to control the amount of light that enters.'

They walked past a stone wall with water trickling down the green brown surface.

'Is this your water source?' Ellen asked.

'No, that's just a water feature,' Mindy explained. 'We wanted to incorporate water into the underground space because humans are naturally drawn to it. The stone that water is running down isn't natural stone. Have a guess what it is Ellen. Go on—touch it.' Ellen reached her hand through the water and on to the wall.

'It feels like ... plastic?' she said.

'That's because it is,' Mindy replied with smile.

'So, if that's not your water source, where does the community's water supply come from?' Daniel asked her.

'There is barely any rainfall in this location, so we collect condensation from our hydroponic plant culture and desert condensation pools. That provides us with a reasonable amount. Water is also piped in from sub-artesian basin bores further north and we gather and store water from river systems during floods. We have to be careful not to waste water. Every drop is graded, stored in underground plastic tanks and recycled. A grade, fit for human consumption, through to D grade, suitable only for non-edible vegetation.'

❊❊❊❊

Ellen and Daniel were enthralled by the underground world. Vegetables and fruits were being grown hydroponically in deep vertical shafts made from shipping containers. A young woman named Skye explained the process. 'A conveyor belt rotates the crops throughout the day, providing some natural light for plant growth, with artificial lighting providing the rest. The horticultural process is very efficient. One person can tend each garden from a single platform.' Skye pulled off a few of the dead leaves as one of the pepper berry bushes moved past. 'I'll add these to our compost. No waste,' she said, tossing the leaves into a bucket.

A teenager named Travis showed them through the protein production section where witchetty grubs, caterpillars and other insects were being grown for food.

'We breed crickets in this specially designed sealed room,' he explained. 'Eventually, the population becomes *soo* large that the crickets run out of oxygen and start choking to death.' Travis held his throat as if being strangled and let out a gurgling sound. 'When the crickets fall to the floor and finally stop squirming, we sweep 'em up. My mum sun-dries them and then she grinds them up in a big blender. This produces a protein powder that's used in our food and drink. It tastes great in shakes, but it's a crap colour. I *never ever* drink it in a clear glass.'

'Thanks for that very graphic explanation Travis,' Francis said with a chuckle as he observed the disgusted expression on Ellen's face.

'Travis certainly enjoys what he does,' Daniel said with a laugh. 'In fact, all your employees seem very committed to their work.'

'The people who live here aren't my employees, Daniel. NATGRID could be best described as a cashless commune or enterprise. It didn't start out that way, but we never turned away anyone seeking refuge. Those who are able to contribute to the community do so. All forms of ability are valued, from musician, storyteller, childminder, cook or cleaner through to horticulturalist, farmer and tech expert. Everyone does their bit, large or small, to make the community a success. Take our good friend Mason here. He can turn his hand to just about anything!'

'Mason's one of our originals,' Mindy chipped in, as she gave the grey haired, tall, wiry looking man the warmest of smiles. 'What's your perspective on how our community developed Mason?'

'Like Mindy said, I'm an original,' he smiled. 'I've lived here since the beginning, but I've seen a lot of people come and go. Some are here to find themselves; others feel they don't fit into *normal* society. We don't ask questions and we don't judge. It's that kind of place. The community's always growing. We don't have many rules. Respect everyone, no drugs, alcohol in moderation. Personally, I wouldn't live anywhere else.'

'Is your community specifically tailored to First Nations people, Mason?' Ellen enquired.

'No ... not at all. Families from many cultural backgrounds live here. Those who prefer extended family life and want to avoid the rat race of nine to five find the commune a great alternative. Sharing resources is efficient. We don't all need to own everything we use. But like I said, it's not for everyone.'

Mason's grandson Scout had been reading a book in the same room. He spoke up. 'I love going "upground" with grandad,' he said. 'Sitting around fire pits, cooking, playing music, telling stories, it's great. Sometimes we eat roasted animals and plants. Grandad makes cider and beer on site as well, but I prefer the craft beers.'

'I don't think you should be drinking any beers young man,' Mindy added with a grin.

'Grandad says that one now and again won't hurt me. He says it will put hairs on my chest.'

'Out of the mouth of babes,' laughed Daniel.

'You're both welcome to join in next Tuesday's feast,' Francis added.

'Isn't it far too hot outside for feasting on hot food?' Ellen asked.

Francis chuckled, 'Not at all. Desert nights are actually quite cold. By the way, Louise said she has mentioned my idea for a new health centre to you, Ellen. What do you think of the plan? The one piece of infrastructure we're missing. Good free health care, without people being forced to be chipped. We run quite a successful detox program, but success rates would be higher if we had a specialised medic on board,' he added glancing questioningly at Ellen.

'Well, seeing everything you have accomplished here, Mr Stuart ...'

Francis butted in. 'Ellen, I insist you call me Francis.'

'Okay, Francis, I guess nothing is impossible if you put your mind to it.'

Francis turned to Daniel. 'I'd be happy to use your help on the project as well. Just until you sort out a way forward, that is. No doubt, when the fuss dies down, you'll return to AMDAT. In the meantime, you have a great mind, Daniel. Your thoughts would be appreciated.'

'For the moment I'm just grateful that you've allowed me to come with Ellen and Pat. I'm willing to help you if I can, though.'

'Do you really mean that, son?'

'Yes. Definitely.'

'In that case, I've one question for you. Can you safely remove chips?'

'I'm afraid not. They can be safely removed but it does require a vascular surgeon. My area of expertise is bioengineering. I'd be more than happy to undertake some system analysis for you, though. Might be able to streamline a few of your biosystems and increase your current food production. I'm particularly interested in your underground caterpillar-larvae production and the fish in your aquaponics section are fascinating.'

Francis smiled at Daniel then turned to face Ellen.

'It appears this young man is completely captivated by you, doesn't it?'

'Yes—and I'm so pleased that he is.'

'Come, I want to show you my collection of old technology, and I have a couple of home movies that you might find interesting.'

Francis led the way with Mindy, while Daniel and Ellen walked behind, continuing to chat to people working in the various areas. They came to the recycling depot positioned at the end of the complex. It was a cavernous space with a wide ramp that led up to the surface. Piles of rubbish surrounded the walls on one side and sorting was taking place on the other. Several people were pulling electrical goods apart … stripping them back to their original components of plastic, glass, gold and copper. It was a noisy area, the sound amplified by the addition of heavy metal music pounding in the background.

Francis had to shout to be heard. 'As you know, earlier this century other countries stopped accepting Australia's raw recycled material. The stockpiles grew and governments did little. They buried huge amounts of this waste in desert locations throughout Australia. We recognised an opportunity to do something positive with that rubbish. Our recycling arm only breaks even but more importantly, we're providing employment and restoring the ecology.

'Trent over there likes to call himself a *Garbominer.*' He waved at a man sitting in the cab of a backhoe covered in dust. Wearing a hat, earphones, sunglasses and a scarf tied around his mouth, he looked like a modern-day cowboy. Trent waved at the group, before turning his vehicle 180 degrees and heading back up the ramp.

Francis continued to yell above the din. 'Recycling's a unique job. People don't work in the area unless they like it. I think some enjoy the archaeology—digging stuff up. Others love pulling things apart and figuring out how they work. A few are into restoration—making things useful again. We've also been making building materials out of reinforced plastics. If you get the chemistry right, the resulting bricks, trusses and columns are very strong. They don't rust, break down or need painting. Plastic doesn't break down for centuries. There are tons buried everywhere. We need to find ways to reuse it.'

The tour continued and they eventually reached the museum entrance. Francis leaned in and whispered to his wife.

'Well, what do you think, now that you've met him in person?'

'You could be right,' Mindy replied.

'I really think that I am. Anyway, things will unfold soon enough.'

Francis had gathered a large number of items in what he called the 'museum'. These included early forms of technology long discarded but now restored. There was quite a range of old computers, games consoles, video and CD players, record players, an extensive record collection and old mining tools.

Around the wall were photographs and newspaper clippings relating to mining in Western Australia. They featured the two strapping Stuart brothers, Francis and Kenneth, as well as their father, Leonard. They appeared to be enjoying all aspects of life in the mines. The photographs depicted plenty of partying and gambling as well as hard labouring. Francis and Kenneth were obviously close in those early years.

After they had examined the stories and antique tech, Francis led them to one corner of the room where an old eight-millimetre film projector that had belonged to his grandparents was stored. Next, he rummaged through a large box before selecting three film canisters. Francis opened one, removed the spool of film and carefully attached it to the top slot of the projector. Taking the end of the film, he began winding it around and through various slots then attached it to the empty film spool. The process looked complicated but eventually the reel was threaded and ready to roll.

The footage on the first reel was black and white. It had been filmed in 1972 from the Sitmar Line's Turbine Steamship *Fairsky*. The ship was one of many that carried English migrants to Australia. Relatives were standing on the crowded Southampton dock, throwing streamers and waving.

'There are my great-grandparents,' Francis said, pointing out a man and a woman. The woman was crying. 'My father Leonard is on board with his parents,' Francis explained. 'He was only seven when they emigrated.'

The camera swung round and a young boy holding his mother's hand came into focus.

'My father, Leonard, never saw his grandparents again. By the time he earned enough money for a return passage they had both died.'

Daniel became uneasy as he watched the couple waving from the dock, as their son, daughter-in-law and grandson Leonard prepared to sail to Australia. The image made him sad. Francis changed the reel. The next film, also black and white, focused on the Western Australian mine fields. It was interesting to observe the primitive technology that Kenneth, Francis and their father Leonard had used prior to becoming wealthy. Old cars and trucks could be observed in the footage, along with some interesting shanties in which they had lived.

Francis changed the reel for a third time. This footage, in colour, focused on a visit to the capital city of Perth. A pretty young woman laughed playfully with Francis. She was beautiful, with vibrant green eyes and auburn hair. Daniel went quiet … very quiet. After five minutes of footage had been shown, Francis froze the screen momentarily on a close-up shot of himself and the woman. Then, to prevent the film overheating, he turned the projector off. Silence reigned as he gave the younger man time to absorb and process the vision he had just witnessed.

Ellen wasn't quite sure exactly what was happening, until Francis went over to Daniel and placed his hand on his shoulder.

'It was a shock for me too, Daniel,' he commented. 'I had absolutely no idea your mother was pregnant when she left Perth. Kenneth was jealous of our relationship. One night when I was away on business, he seduced her. I was angry, she left, and I never saw her again. Since then I've only spoken to my brother when I really needed to.'

'Why didn't she tell you?' Daniel asked. 'More's the point, why didn't she ever tell me that my father was still alive?'

'What happened to her, Daniel? Kenneth said in his media conference that you had been made a Ward of the State.'

'Mum killed herself. She jumped off a bridge in Hobart.'

There was a pause before Francis spoke.

'I'm so sorry things worked out the way they did. Annette was a deeply troubled soul. No doubt you knew she had a mental illness of some sort. Abused by her father on top of everything else. She made many poor life decisions, which included sleeping with my brother. I suspect she didn't tell me she was pregnant because she probably thought I might take the baby from her.'

'Would you have?' Daniel asked as tears pooled in his eyes.

'I don't know. I also can't be sure who your father is, Daniel. It could be me or it could be Kenneth. You'll need to undertake DNA tests to confirm whether Margaret is your half-sister or your first cousin. If your marriage turns out to be illegal you will need to get an annulment. Sorry to be so blunt, Daniel, but you just have to look at my father and grandfather to see how much you resemble the men in our family. You're a dead ringer.'

Daniel looked completely stunned. The strong, confident AMDAT executive had been thrust unexpectedly back to his unstable, chaotic childhood. Ghostly images of people from his past floated vividly in and out of his head. He began to feel quite detached from reality, as if he was looking through a pane of glass at someone else's life, not his own. Sensing the young man was in shock, Mindy stood up and turned to Ellen.

'Come on, let's you and I go and check on that young Pat.' She glanced at her vintage watch. 'He must be close to his next feed by now. Let's leave the boys to get better acquainted.'

55

Patrick stared at himself in the mirror. He was barely recognisable. His hair and beard had both been growing since his 'death'. His right arm was now in a lightweight fibreglass cast as if broken, concealing his lead-bound chip. A second chip was now transmitting twenty-four hours of fake data. Patrick appeared to be consuming alcoholic drinks around dinnertime and by the nicotine levels one would presume he was a moderate smoker.

As Tony expected, Patrick had been devastated by the scandalous sex footage. The one thing that had kept him sane all these months was the thought of being with the love of his life, Ellen, and their beautiful baby boy. He had been thoroughly enjoying following the images of young Pat's progress on the Facelog newsfeed. However, that had been short lived. The hateful social media trolls had been merciless. Ellen had frozen her Facelog site shortly after the scandal broke and all postings had ceased.

Doctor Dawson's letter to Ellen had shown a clear link between him and Vaughn Lambert. The AFP had confirmed with the FBI that an AMDAT jet had travelled to Melbourne from Newark shortly after the last girl disappeared. They had checked the customs records for that flight. Gum Lin had verified that the cargo aboard AMDAT Flight 582 contained only frozen biological material. Gum Lin was far from honest: she was almost certainly a criminal. Her declaration could not be relied upon. Footage at Melbourne Tullamarine had also shown Vaughn Lambert and an android personally collecting several metallic boxes. What did they contain that was too important to be moved by the usual AMDAT courier? The AFP and FBI believed the time had arrived to force a wedge into AMDAT's fortifications and crack the corporation's secrets. What was really going on? They were clearly hiding something or someone.

Tony and Lauren travelled to Melbourne on a routine economy flight and arrived ahead of Patrick and the FBI agents. He and Lauren were currently in Q precinct cattle class, where they would receive only the basic necessities. While in Q Melbourne, Tony continued to work on the case and ensure that the undercover arrangements for Patrick were in place.

A few days later Patrick and the agents travelled from Newark to Melbourne via a five-hour hypersonic express flight. Patrick was now waiting in Q Melbourne for the robot to escort him to his allocated suite. The police department had approved a business-class ticket and, after working on the case covertly from Tony's residence for the last few months, he intended to try out all the pleasures Q had to offer.

'Why not?' Tony had insisted. 'You're not committed to anyone and you deserve the break. This is a dangerous mission, pal. Feel free to knock yourself out. Keep in mind that you'll have to pay for your own booze and sex, but the rest will all be at the taxpayer's expense. You can use my credit card details and we can square things up later. Don't go too crazy though, none of that kinky exotic shit, my card does have a twenty thousand buck limit,' he said with a laugh.

Patrick was escorted to his suite, where a female android called Monique was busy making his afternoon tea. Patrick had chosen an android with blonde hair and blue eyes for a change. Something a bit different that didn't remind him of Ellen. Watching Monique, he could visualise her wearing a skimpy negligee. He certainly had plenty to get off his chest. For now though, a hot drink, a shower and a few hours' sleep was far more appealing.

56

Zoe missed the next week of lectures, unsure if she was allowed to return following the assertion that she had placed Sarah in danger by taking her into the bat zone locker room. Maggie had called to reassure her that she was not expelled and that, although she had breached protocol, someone had deliberately opened the bat airlocks and she couldn't be blamed for the incident. She was welcome to resume her studies.

Zoe was now standing in the lecture theatre as the entire group watched Sarah's memorial service. Tears trickled down her face. She was trying as hard as she could not to cry. It was as if she was holding back a flood and every now and again a sob escaped.

Oliver stood on one side of Zoe, holding her hand. Kobi stood on the other side, next to Charlie. Felix and Aiza were in the next row. An image montage to the music of 'Forever Young' celebrated Sarah's short life in a matter of minutes. A beautiful baby girl with curly blonde hair giggled and played with her parents. Family outings, birthday parties, Christmases and school awards nights showed a life full of laughter and fun that had tragically been cut short. The ceremony reminded Zoe of just how precious life is and how she should never take family and friends for granted. She squeezed Oliver's hand as tightly as she could. He responded by squeezing hers back.

Following the memorial service there was afternoon tea, after which a large group of students made their way to the local pub to continue Sarah's wake. As the hours passed, the numbers whittled down until only the usual crew were left. Zoe said she had something important to discuss. She had brought the poster of AMDAT Tower. She unfolded it onto the table and spread it flat, taking care not to knock over their drinks.

'Let's see how observant you all are. What's wrong with this poster?'

Charlie immediately answered, 'Level 41 isn't vacant.'

'What makes you think that?' Oliver asked.

'Well, you're the dark horse,' Zoe interjected. 'How long have you known?'

'I didn't know, Zoe, but you're holding your finger on Level 41 and sounding very mysterious, so I had a wild guess.' He laughed as Zoe gave him a playful thump on his arm.

He continued, 'I've always suspected Level 41 wasn't vacant. The story of the laser beams was most likely just to scare anyone off going there. AMDAT Tower is expensive real estate. Why would they keep an entire floor empty just for security purposes? It always sounded like complete crap to me.'

'Sometimes you're such a smartypants, Charlie. Anyway, you're correct. If you look very closely you can see a toddler in the image.' Zoe pointed to the child peering out of the window. 'Rob said not to discuss the image with anyone, but I don't consider this group to be anyone. Anyway, given the bat-zone incident and Sarah's death, I think we should investigate to find out what's actually happening on Level 41. Why all the secrecy?'

'I agree with Zoe,' said Felix. 'I think we should find out what's going on up there. Any ideas how we can gain access without being detected?'

Zoe continued, 'Vaughn will have access. He probably uses his fingerprint. Biometrics are the most secure,' she added.

'Okay,' Felix paused. 'Just how do you propose we use Vaughn's fingerprints without his knowledge, Zoe? That seems impossible to me, unless we cut them off, or do something equally grotesque.'

'I wouldn't mind cutting that creep's wandering fingers off,' Oliver replied. 'Pass me a knife.'

'Nothing like that,' Zoe responded. 'We just need the right bait.'

'What do you have in mind, Zoe?' Kobi asked.

'Me. Simply put, you need to use me as the bait.'

'No way,' Oliver said. 'That will definitely not be happening.'

'It's the only way,' Zoe pleaded. 'If we plan it properly, then he won't get a chance to abuse me. We just need to lure him into the penthouse lift, knock him out and then use his fingerprint to gain access to Level 41.'

'Oh, that sounds like a really sophisticated plan, Zoe,' laughed Charlie.

'Well, can you think of a better one then, Charles?' Zoe only called him Charles when he annoyed her.

'Cut it out, you two,' interjected Oliver. 'Zoe, you're not to proceed with such a stupid plan. It's ridiculous. Promise me you won't attempt such a silly stunt.'

'Ollie's right, Zoe,' added Kobi. 'Just let it go for now. It's much too dangerous.'

'I guess they're both right, Zoe,' Aiza piped up. 'You only just avoided being hurt last time. If something goes wrong, you might not be so lucky another time.'

'Well, can you all just think about it and see what you can come up with to gain us safe access to Level 41?'

57

The following day, Zoe headed to AMDAT for a lecture everyone was looking forward to. Vaughn wasn't lecturing today, and a noted guest speaker, Professor Henshaw, was presenting his theories on survival of the human species. Zoe was running late again, having forgotten her mobile for the second day in a row.

Just as she was crossing the road, an elderly woman fell, sending her bag and groceries flying. Although Zoe knew stopping would make her even later, she took in a deep breath, remembered she was training to be a medic, and ran across to the woman, grabbing an orange that had rolled in her path on the way.

At first Zoe thought the woman's ankle was just twisted, but from the speed with which it swelled and turned blue-black it was clear that it was very badly sprained or possibly fractured. A couple of young men helped lift the woman to the curb. Her name was Emily. Zoe glanced at her chip. The lecture would be underway.

She dialled triple zero to summon a hovercraft ambulance. Resigned to being late, she sat with Emily and tried to distract her from the pain. A local café owner brought out some ice cubes in a plastic bag with a tea towel folded around them. Zoe placed her jacket around Emily's shoulders and ensured her leg was in a comfortable position before gently pressing the icepack against her ankle.

Oliver glanced at his chip. Where was Zoe? He hoped she hadn't decided to do something stupid, like try to access Level 41 on her own. She was quite a determined girl and she was not happy that the five of them thought her plot to knock out Vaughn and use his fingerprint to activate the lift was ridiculous. She would be here in a minute, no doubt. He turned his attention back to the guest speaker.

'Survival of the fittest is a concept that continually ensures the human species progresses, albeit incredibly slowly. AV64 is just one of many plagues that have swept the earth since the dawn of time, and will no doubt continue to do so into the future. The survivors of AV64 who procreate will continue to pass on their protective genes to their descendants. Young virile students such as you must be ready take up this very challenge.' Laughter echoed throughout the auditorium.

'The human species certainly hasn't evolved much when it comes to sex,' Kobi commented to Aiza, as the males continued to smirk and giggle like a bunch of dirty-minded schoolboys.

Professor Henshaw continued, 'The definition of a species, as you are all aware, is a group of like organisms that can produce offspring that can themselves reproduce. Hybrids are the offspring of two species. Tigers cannot breed with zebras. Monkeys cannot breed with cats. The example that's most frequently used to illustrate this concept is the donkey. If you breed a male donkey with a female horse the offspring is a sterile hybrid, the mule. Mules cannot breed with other mules; therefore, mules aren't a species in their own right.

'Tigers and lions are an exception to the hybrid infertility rule. Tigons are a cross between a male tiger and female lion. Ligers are a cross between a male lion and female tiger. Some tigons and ligers are fertile.'

Oliver checked the time again. Zoe was still a no-show. Maybe she was sick? Not usual for her, yet there's always a first time for everything. He decided to text Anna and Zoe to find out where she was.

'Young man. Are you not interested in the content of my lecture?'

Felix nudged Oliver in the ribs. 'He's talking to you, mate.'

'What?' Oliver looked up.

'Yes, you, young man. I repeat. Are you not interested in what I have to say?'

'Yes, sir. I am ... very.'

'Well, could you do me the courtesy of either leaving this lecture theatre or turning off your mobile and putting it away?'

'Of course, Professor. Sorry.'

Oliver reluctantly turned off his mobile and placed it in his jacket. It would be another forty minutes before he could send his text.

58

The four white mice wriggled and squealed, as if they were aware of their imminent demise. They were being held by their tails in a black-leather-gloved hand, leaving them no chance of biting their captor and gaining freedom. Nevertheless, that didn't stop them trying. Still clutching the terrified mammals, Vaughn continued to observe the action on his bank of CCTV monitors. For the last few minutes, he'd been watching Zoe assist an elderly woman. A smile crossed his face as he determined how he could turn this event to his advantage. He had tried unsuccessfully to separate Zoe from her friends, but since the incident in his apartment, Oliver had stayed close. Today she was alone.

'Saint Zoe is at it again,' he commented to Gum. He glanced at his antique Rolex. 'The lecture will be underway by now. This is the opportunity we've been waiting for.'

Vaughn returned to teasing his five hungry ghost bats. He dangled the mice directly in front of the bat-zone viewing window. Grinning, he released the mice into the complex glass maze. The torment of both predator and prey would continue for some time yet. Four mice and five hungry bats provided great entertainment. However, he didn't have time to enjoy today's food fight. Other prey had unexpectedly become available. He turned his attention back to Zoe.

Gum looked at the monitor. 'Shall I shut down the surveillance system?'

Vaughn nodded without taking his eyes off the young woman. Gum returned to her computer and began typing. Vaughn went across to his fridge and pulled out a small glass vial.

'How much do you think she weighs?'

'Around fifty-eight kilos would be my guess,' Gum replied.

'Well, just to be sure, I'll add a drop extra.'

He pushed the plunger of the injection into the syringe until one small bead of clear fluid squeezed out of the end of the needle.

'Are you ready Vaughn?' asked Gum.

Zoe ran to the lift and pressed *Level 35*. She checked her chip. Would it be too rude to join the lecture now, she wondered? Vaughn was a stickler for time and the guest speaker was the eminent Professor Henshaw.

On reaching her destination, Zoe ran down the corridor as fast as she could before bumping into Vaughn as she rounded a corner.

'Well, well, well, if it isn't Miss Ashmore. You ... are ... late,' he said.

Taking one step backwards, Zoe replied, 'Sorry, Professor. I won't go to the lecture if you think it will interrupt the presentation. I'll go to the library and study instead.'

She turned to find Gum facing her. She moved to walk around her, but Gum stepped sideways, deliberately blocking her passage. Zoe looked from Vaughn and back to Gum as they walked from opposite directions towards her. She knew she was in trouble. Gum grabbed her and covered her mouth as Vaughn injected the contents of the needle. Her body went limp before anyone had a chance to hear her muffled screams.

59

Georgia read Oliver's text and a shiver ran down her spine. Zoe had left as usual this morning. She was both fit and well. She should have arrived at the tower well over an hour ago. Georgia needed to speak with Oliver. Her hand began to tremble as she pressed the call button. Anxiety was already starting to take hold. She took in a deep breath then commenced 'self-talk' in an attempt to stop herself catastrophising.

Zoe would be fine. No doubt she was just being silly, as usual. Overprotective, overly concerned. One of those 'helicopter parents', as Ellen was always reminding her. Zoe wasn't a child anymore.

She was a clever and determined young woman. She was more than capable of looking after herself.

Despite all of her positive thinking, Oliver confirmed Georgia's worst fears. Zoe appeared to be missing. She seemed to have vanished. Not even the staff at the AMDAT Tower reception could remember seeing her. The surveillance system that might have held some hope had been malfunctioning all morning. Georgia decided to call Rob and explain what had happened. He might be able to help.

'Can't you track her chip, Rob?'

'I could, but I'd get caught and it's instant dismissal. Confidentiality around chips is vital for a number of reasons Anna.'

'But Rob, what if Zoe has been taken by the same people that took the other girls? Tracking her chip is the best chance we have of finding her. Don't you understand that this could be time critical? *They* could be removing her chip as we speak!'

'I think you're being overly dramatic. The other girls disappeared in New Jersey. Zoe has only been missing for a couple of hours. Anything could have happened.' There was a pause before Rob continued. 'Look, just in case I think of something, I don't suppose you have Zoe's chip code handy or know where she stores it? I might get the opportunity to run an undetected check of some sort.'

'I do, actually. I know it off by heart: 6780 4783 5713.'

'That's a twelve-digit code Anna. Why would you learn that?'

Georgia's voice rose, both in pitch and volume as she responded to Rob's question. Her reply was quite rude, as if suggesting he was a bit of an idiot not to have realised by now what she was about to disclose.

'Because I'm not Ellen's cousin, Rob. I'm Zoe's mother. I'm really Georgia Ashmore. Why do you think we're so close? Why do you think I'm so worried?' Then she burst into tears. It took a moment for Rob to process this information.

'Wow ... well that explains quite a few things Anna ... I mean Georgia. I did think you were overly affectionate with each other.

Come to think of it, you display the same mannerisms. I also thought it was a bit weird that you knew so much about Zoe when you were Ellen's cousin.'

'It's a secret Rob. I shouldn't have said anything, but I need you to understand why I'm so desperate to find her.' Just then Rob's colleague Mick peered into his office.

'Do you want a coffee, mate?'

'Thanks, that would be good. Latte with one sugar, please.'

Rob suddenly had an idea.

'Hey Mick, I know it's a bit out of your way, but could you get some dumplings as well? I forgot to have brekkie and I'm starving. You know, the ones from Dumpling Land, two blocks away. I'll make it worth your while. Buy you some dumplings and pay for your coffee as well.'

Mick paused, then replied, 'Sounds like a fair deal.'

Rob reached for his wallet.

'No sweat. We can do a transfer later when we know exactly how much,' Mick said.

'Thanks, mate. You're a trooper.'

Georgia had been listening to the conversation and was stunned that Rob could think of eating at a time like this. She made her feelings known.

'It appears your stomach is more important to you than Zoe, Rob. How can you even think about eating at a time like this?' Rob wanted to comfort her, but he needed to focus if he was going to achieve anything.

'Look, I can tell how upset you are but I'm sure Zoe will be all right. She hasn't been missing for long. Why don't you check in with the local Health Hub and call me back if you still haven't located her in, say, an hour? If I don't hear back from you, I'll call in and see you tonight. Now, I really do have to get back to work.' With the sound of Georgia still sniffling, Rob said goodbye and ended the call.

He sat back and sighed as he thought about the conversation he'd just had with Anna ... Georgia. She sounded so upset and what was with that name change? What was Georgia embroiled in? Could Zoe be in real danger? What if Georgia was right and someone removed Zoe's chip and then she was never seen again? He had Zoe's chip code written on the pad in front of him. He could choose to do nothing or act now and suffer the consequences. *Fuck it!* He thought. *If I'm not willing to take a hit for the woman I love, what sort of man am I?*

Rob sprang into action. He pulled on a pair of disposable gloves and stuffed the box of alcohol wipes sitting on his desk into the top drawer. He sat back and pressed the NEXT CLIENT button. Once the young woman was seated, he looked around the room before suddenly standing up.

'Sorry. I appear to have run out of alcohol wipes. I just need to grab some from the storeroom. I'll be back in a jiffy.' He flashed a smile before leaving the room then slipped discreetly into Mick's office next door. His mate was still logged on. The computer hadn't timed out yet. Rob hurriedly accessed the chip trace function and punched in Zoe's code.

Rob stared at the blip on the screen. He couldn't believe what he was seeing. What was Zoe doing there? He left Mick's computer logged on and went back to his office. It had taken him less than one minute.

'Now, where were we?' he said, giving the young woman another smile as he placed the handful of alcohol wipes he'd taken from Mick's desk onto his own.

In the surveillance unit an alarm sounded. An employee had accessed a chip code trace without authority. Level 10. Room 58. Michael Nightbridge.

Around ten minutes later, Rob heard Mick and a security guard arguing in the corridor. He could hear Mick proclaiming his innocence, no doubt offering the coffee and dumplings as his defence. Rob ignored the commotion and continued to work with his client. He needed a solid alibi, so couldn't afford to appear distracted. It wouldn't take them long to crosscheck Mick's story with camera surveillance. He wasn't in his office when the breach occurred. Once Mick's alibi was confirmed Rob could become the next suspect. Rob became anxious as he realised that he might be in real danger. Using Mick's computer to access Zoe's chip location had bought him some time—but not much. He needed to get out of the tower and then decide what to do.

Rob tried to stay composed as he completed the chip insertion, but his heart rate was up and he was breathing way too fast. The client began to look concerned. She noticed his hands shaking and detected a level of agitation. Mick had been taken away for questioning and Rob could hear the security guards combing through his office. *Sorry, mate,* thought Rob. Once the chip insertion was finished, Rob showed the client to the door. She seemed relieved and left quickly. Rob gathered his belongings then pulled the door of his office shut, for what he thought would be the last time.

60

It was Tuesday night at the desert community. Daniel and Ellen were thoroughly enjoying the night gathering. Large campfires kept the participants toasty warm on this crisp desert evening. The dark cloudless sky spread a spectacular display of the Southern Hemisphere stars above them. It was as if they could see into the very depths of heaven itself. Daniel and Ellen were lying flat on their backs, snuggling close, as Mindy attempted to point out some of the most prominent constellations. There was the emu: its head began in the

Southern Cross, while its body and legs were formed by the shape of the Milky Way. The three brothers in their canoe catching kingfish were found within Orion. Daniel was finding it hard to concentrate. He kept tickling Ellen and kissing her. They were like a couple of loved-up teenagers, without a care in the world.

Since midmorning, whole cleaned animal carcasses stuffed with organically grown vegetables had been buried to slowly roast on hot rocks in fire pits. Wrapped in layers of aluminium foil, held in place by chicken wire and covered with green foliage, these parcels were now lifted out of the ground. Once unwrapped, they revealed steaming hot flesh, so tender it could be pulled directly from the bone. The aroma of roasted meat, vegetables and herbs wafted through the air. Ellen's thoughts immediately drifted back in time to Sunday roast dinners at her grandparents' home.

The entertainment was varied and included traditional dancing. Guitars and handcrafted bush instruments provided the music. Everyone joined in the singing and dancing. The festivities were well underway when Francis spotted the lights of a helicopter heading towards them. It landed and he walked across to meet the occupants. Ellen observed Francis speaking with the two police officers before he escorted them back in their direction.

'Are you Mr Daniel Grant?'

Daniel stood up to face the officers. 'Yes, I am.'

'We are arresting you for the murder of Sarah Baker and the attempted murder of Zoe Ashmore. You do not have to say or do anything but anything you say or do may be used as evidence against you.'

'On what evidence are you arresting me?' Daniel asked with a look of disbelief. 'I won't be leaving here without some reasonable explanation. Surely you're aware that the media are harassing me. Whatever has been reported to police is most likely a complete hoax.'

He paused as the police officers looked at each other. The senior officer spoke.

'Mr Grant ...' he paused. 'We have CCTV footage that clearly shows your direct involvement in the incident that ultimately led to Ms Baker's death.'

'Do you, now?' Daniel pursed his lips and breathed out slowly as he glared at the officers.

'The facial recognition experts have confirmed it to be you ... Mr Grant.' The junior officer said, before his senior colleague instructed him to stop talking.

'I'm sure they have.' Daniel raised an eyebrow as he sucked in air between his top teeth. Not only had Vaughn shafted him, now Gum had joined in. She was the only person capable of doctoring digital footage to be undetectable by even the best experts.

'You'll need to come with us, Mr Grant.'

The senior officer nodded, and the junior officer moved behind Daniel and handcuffed him.

'I don't understand,' Ellen said as she endeavoured to process what was happening. 'What are they on about, Daniel? Tell me you had nothing to do with Zoe and Sarah being harmed?'

Daniel didn't reply. He just stared straight through her as if she were invisible.

'Speak to me, Daniel,' she insisted.

He remained silent.

Ellen turned to the senior officer and asked, 'Can I go with him?'

'No, sorry, miss; there isn't room in the helicopter. You'll need to find your own way back to Melbourne.'

Francis looked across in her direction and mouthed, 'I'll take you later.'

As the officers escorted Daniel towards the helicopter, Ellen followed and called out to him, but he didn't respond or even look back in her direction.

Standing away from the fire pits, she started to cry. She felt abandoned, completely powerless. Her long hair swirled and mingled with the sand being blown about as the helicopter blades gained momentum. She stood shivering and staring into the darkness, as the helicopter lights grew smaller and smaller and eventually vanished. A few seconds more and the sounds of the rotors could no longer be heard and—just like that—Daniel was gone.

Mindy brought a blanket across to Ellen, wrapped it around her shoulders and walked her back to the fire pits. A hot toddy was required. Breastfeeding or not, this new mother needed something to reduce the shock.

Just when Ellen was feeling slightly more relaxed, her mobile rang. She quickly rummaged in her pocket and glanced at the screen, desperately hoping it was Daniel. It wasn't. It was Georgia with more bad news, adding to an already distressing evening.

'Georgia, slow down,' Ellen instructed. 'What do you mean, Zoe has been missing since this morning?'

In loud, rapid-fire words, without pausing to take even the smallest of breaths, Georgia gave Ellen a scrambled explanation.

'Zoe left home and Oliver called and she didn't arrive and she missed the lecture and now no-one can find her and the cameras don't work and no-one saw her enter or leave the building and Rob won't help because he's too hungry.' By now she was shouting down her mobile. 'Don't you understand Ellen? Zoe's gone—just like those other girls—gone. Whoever took them has also taken my Zoe.' Then she burst into tears.

Ellen shook her head and blinked as if her brain had been shaken like one of Pat's rattles.

'You're not making much sense, Georgia. We live in Australia. Those crimes were committed in New Jersey not here, okay? You need to try and calm down. Your blood pressure must be through the roof. Listen to me. Go and get a big glass of water and take one of your anti-anxiety tablets. Then I want you to put on your VR mask and select the bottle-feeding baby mammals program. Just focus on getting all those babies fed. I'll ring Oliver, then call you back, okay?'

'Okay,' she said sniffling. Sensing Georgia's complete hopelessness, Ellen's voice took on a mellow tone. 'I'm positive everything will be okay.'

'Hope so,' Georgia replied.

Ellen ended the call. In reality, she didn't believe everything would be okay. Georgia couldn't be right? Surely there wasn't a connection between the New Jersey disappearances, Zoe's disappearance and AMDAT. There couldn't be ... could there? Then again Daniel had been arrested, accused of trying to harm Zoe. She didn't want to panic Georgia by supporting her conspiracy theory, but a conspiracy couldn't be ruled out.

Why does the shit always hit the fan at the same time? First Daniel. Now Zoe. That was two people she loved in trouble. *They say that bad luck always happens in threes. Who or what will be the third?*

Ellen tried Oliver's mobile several times, but it went straight to message bank. She called Georgia to let her know.

'Any idea yet when you might be coming home?' Georgia asked.

'I'll be home earlier than expected; by Friday, I think.'

She glanced at Francis. He confirmed her plan with a thumbs up.

'Yes, I'll definitely be home this Friday. Francis can't fly me back until then.'

'Who's Francis?' Georgia asked as she blew her nose.

'He's a friend,' she paused momentarily. 'Never mind; I'll explain later.'

'I'll be *soo* relieved to have you home,' Georgia said. 'I really need you.' She paused then added, 'would you like me to cook supper for you and Daniel?'

'No—just me. Daniel won't be with me.'

'What? Why not?'

'It's complex. I won't fill you in over the phone. You have enough to worry about at the moment. Fingers crossed, Zoe will have been found safe and well before I get back. Anyway, stop worrying and get back to feeding time.'

61

Officers from the AFP, FBI and Victoria Police met at Melbourne's police headquarters to finalise the details of the AMDAT raid. Detective Scallioni listened intently as the commander outlined the progress to date. Zoe Ashmore had been missing for seventy-two hours. She was the final girl to disappear of the six children conceived in Doctor Dawson's second round of banned cytoplasmic transfers. An AMDAT employee, Rob Davies, had tracked her location on the day she disappeared, last detecting the chip signal on Level 41 of AMDAT Tower. Rob was now assisting police computer experts with the investigation. With his help, they had managed to hack AMDAT's system and ascertained that Zoe's chip was no longer transmitting. This was a worrying development, but Tony was well aware that transmissions could be blocked. He needed to remain hopeful. None of this information had been made public.

It hadn't taken Lauren long to recognise Georgia. It was the mannerisms that gave her away: the way she walked, how she flicked her hair from her face and how her voice lilted upwards when she was talking seriously. Tony had expected Lauren to work it out. She was very observant, and they had been to school together for twelve years. Georgia was not in any danger. Her true identity was no longer an issue.

Lauren called Tony daily, describing Georgia's deteriorating mental state. Tony couldn't tell Georgia where Zoe had been taken. He did, however, continue to reassure her that the investigation was progressing well and that the police had some promising leads.

Patrick was now working with the Special Operations Group. Their plan for the raid was sound. If anyone was going to breach security, it would be them. Nevertheless, Tony found himself praying for a good outcome, and he wasn't even religious. This case had become far too personal. He had let it get to him and uncovered a weakness. He knew it was too late to withdraw from the case. He needed to step up and refocus. It was essential that he put his fears for Patrick and Zoe to one side and scrutinise the plan to eliminate any chance of failure. He took in a deep breath and turned his attention back to the speaker, as she continued describing to the group of commanders what was to take place over the next twenty-four hours.

The plan to raid AMDAT Tower was well advanced. Level 41 was the target. It would take skill to access the building on this level without alerting the security guards or other employees. No doubt Vaughn Lambert had an emergency response worked out if Level 41 was ever breached. He would not want his research to be revealed. He would, at all costs, want to avoid being arrested with the possibility of jail time. The information gained by Rob Davies and local authorities was vital to the success of this operation. Proceeding strategically was the key.

For the last six months, communication intercepts had been placed on Lambert by the Australian Federal Police. Tony had been pleasantly surprised to discover the level of investigative work already undertaken by his colleagues on the other side of the world. AMDAT had been under surveillance for quite some time.

Several members of the public had been recorded organising the purchase of embryos with enhanced immune systems. A million dollars was the cost of each embryonic transfer. A child who could better navigate a world dominated by super microbes was virtually guaranteed within three IVF cycles. Surrogacy was also available at an even higher price. Following Zoe's abduction, the chatter recorded between Lambert, Lin, and his research team had increased.

The girls were uniquely valuable commodities: it was unlikely that Lambert would be prepared to harm them—at least until all their ova had been harvested. Investigators believed that Bridget Patterson's death was an unfortunate and unexpected consequence of the fertility drugs she would have taken to allow her ova to be harvested. They had interacted with her abnormal blood-clotting factors causing the formation of the clot that killed her. It was impossible to determine if she had formally consented to the treatment that caused her death. Hopefully the other girls were all still alive. It was imperative that as many as possible be located and saved.

62

'Bougainvillea has sharp thorns, so it's imperative that you wear protective clothing and strong thornproof gloves. I presume your tetanus vaccinations are all up to date?' enquired the tutor as he peered over his reading glasses. Everyone nodded in confirmation.

Patrick would be happy if the only threat he faced in the next twenty-four hours came from a plant. Thorns were the least of his worries, but he knew that to pull off the raid he needed this horticultural lesson. Patrick felt sorry for the tutor. Mr Talbot was doing his best to spark their enthusiasm, yet the eight people in front of him were clearly not interested in the topic and he hadn't been given any plausible explanation as to why they required his expertise.

It had been a lame idea to tell Mr Talbot these students were unemployed and retraining to join the public service Green Corps. The six men and two women were in the peak of physical health. Two of the men were Terminator lookalikes, most definitely not the usual type to be interested in learning about plant pruning. He had probably never taught such an uninterested bunch before.

Patrick scrolled through the newsfeed on his mobile then checked the time: only twenty minutes of the agonising lesson left. As the teacher paused and flashed a glance in his direction, he pocketed the device and smiled as if to say, 'Sorry'. Patrick made a mental note to fill the man in sometime, one day when it was all done and dusted, and life became normal. When he could reveal to his family and friends that he was alive.

He couldn't wait to hold his son. He longed to feel the softness of Pat's baby skin against his own rugged face. He looked forward to smelling the distinct scent of a baby or even the less attractive odour of a soiled nappy. And then there was Ellen. Would they ever kiss again? Would they ever lie as lovers do, lost in the heat and sweat of passion until the overwhelming sensations could be contained no longer?

The blurred image of Ellen with Daniel suddenly shattered his pleasant daydream and thrust him back to the present, just as the teacher raised his hand and pointed towards the back of the room and issued instructions.

'Please take a pair of secateurs and move across to the mock window-pruning stations I've set up for each of you. Now try to remember and apply everything you've been taught. Clients generally prefer the foliage to be cut well back from the windows to allow for plenty of growth in between prunings. Some prefer their windows to be artistically framed. It's imperative that you know exactly what each client's expectations are before you start snipping.' He opened and closed his fingers as if working a pair of invisible secateurs.

'Your brief today is to prune and artistically frame each window. Any questions?'

In unison the group moaned, 'No.'

63

The crew gathered at the pub. They felt lost without Zoe, who had been missing for three days. Oliver, in particular, was displeased with the lack of progress the police were making. Quite frankly, they appeared to be doing nothing at all. He decided to take matters into his own hands, and he hoped to enlist the help of his friends.

'I think we should check out Level 41. Zoe might be being held there and I, for one, am not prepared any longer to just sit on my hands and do nothing.'

'It must be hard, mate,' Felix said. 'We all know how much you love Zoe, but we're just powerless students. Think about it for a moment. What can the five of us achieve that the police can't?'

'I know it appears hopeless, but are we all prepared to just do absolutely nothing? Is that really the sort of people we are? No backbone. Just a shoal of spineless jellyfish.'

'A smack,' Kobi offered.

'A smack? What are you on about, Kobi?' Oliver replied quite rudely, shaking his head and frowning at her.

'A group of jelly fish is not called a "shoal", Oliver, it's called a "smack",' Aiza glanced across at Kobi and giggled.

In an attempt to relieve the tension, Kobi continued, 'I, for one, would love to help if you had a decent plan,' she said, confirming that she was just as frustrated as Oliver. 'A plan that actually has a chance of working, not just one that gets us all expelled, or perhaps something much worse.'

'Okay, then. Well, what if you or Aiza seduce Lambert at drinks tomorrow night. When he tries to take you up to his apartment, we all follow, knock Vaughn out in the lift and then use his fingerprint to gain access to Level 41?'

'That's Zoe's stupid plan. We've already given that idea the thumbs down,' Charlie reminded the group as he pointed both his thumbs down towards the floor.

'I realise it's not the greatest of ideas, but I just can't think of anything better.'

'It's not that bad a plan,' Aiza interjected. 'I'm up for it, as long as the rest of you make sure that Lambert doesn't succeed in getting me alone in his apartment.'

'Can't we get him really pissed at drinks?' Kobi suggested. 'Maybe then he could be talked into taking all of us up to check out his apartment view. That will at least ensure he doesn't have a chance to entrap Aiza on her own.' Kobi continued in a soft, slow, mysterious voice as if relishing the idea of plotting Vaughn's downfall. 'Once in his apartment we could drug him. Then we can do whatever we like with him. My father is a nurse and he says diazepam is quite a good sedative, especially when mixed with alcohol. We could grind up some pills and mix them into a few of Vaughn's creamy cocktails. He won't suspect a thing.'

'That's not a bad idea,' Charlie said, nodding. 'Does anybody know where we can get some?'

A smile crossed Oliver's face.

'Yep, I know exactly who can provide us with some diazepam, or, perhaps even better, some extra strong sleeping pills. A big dose could keep him asleep for a few hours.'

'Can you trust them to keep quiet, though?' Felix asked.

'Yes, I can trust them, and I'll make sure they know exactly what we're planning just in case something goes wrong and we all disappear as well.' Oliver paused. He looked quite satisfied with himself. 'Well, now; that's settled. Let's focus on the details.'

64

The helicopter landed on the tower helipad late on Friday afternoon. The Green Corps team disembarked and were greeted by two security guards.

'Why are you so late? The day is nearly done!' one asked.

'My apologies,' answered the team commander. 'We had some unexpected chopper trouble. No matter, it's daylight saving so we can start the job and work until late to make up the ground.' He patted his helmet light to reassure them that his team was equipped to work after sunset.

'Well, you'll need to keep the noise down after ten. Although it's Friday, so the boss will probably be awake later than usual. He has Friday drinks with the students, you know, but still likes to be in bed by midnight to get his beauty sleep.'

The two security guards smirked at each other. They were well aware of Vaughn's vanity and his relentless search to turn back the clock with an ever-increasing age gap between himself and the students he enjoyed fucking. In reality, his physical appearance would never matter. There were plenty of women turned on simply by his possessions and the power he wielded.

'Rest assured, we won't be pruning after ten-thirty' the commander said. *What happens after that time is a different matter,* he thought to himself.

Before leaving the crew to get to work, the security guards checked their identification papers. The eight pruners and their handlers set up their equipment.

The tower's exterior columns had been purpose-built with metal attachments and footholds that allowed pruners to climb around with ease. Two pruners could work on each side of the building where the thick spring growth of bougainvillea had begun obscuring the light entering the windows.

Pulley systems enabled the four rooftop handlers to manage the safety ropes and raise the baskets of prunings upwards to be packed. The large hessian sacks containing the foliage could be removed later. Once the signal was given, eight Special Operations Group officers would be perfectly positioned to enter Level 41. The remaining four would ensure that no-one exited via the roof and provide sniper cover if required.

65

Friday night drinks were well under way. Aiza flirted outrageously with Vaughn. He was pleasantly surprised at how animated the usually quiet, shy girl became after a few glasses of wine. He had barely noticed her lightly tanned face and perfect white teeth before. Yet it was her large sultry brown eyes that really lured him in, bedroom eyes. Eyes that suggested intimacy without a word. He felt himself harden as she chatted. Why had he never noticed her before? Vaughn had just suggested he show her the view from his apartment, when the rest of the hovering crew moved in.

'Hi,' Aiza said as she gave them all a welcoming smile.

Felix was finding the situation intense. Hoping to tone down her seduction technique, he moved in close and whispered in her ear, 'Don't you think you're overdoing it just a teeny bit?'

Aiza simply smiled at him then turned away to focus her full attention back on Vaughn: 'Vaughn was just suggesting I go with him to check out the view from his apartment. Apparently, it's quite spectacular.' She paused for a moment then, as if the idea had never entered her head before, proceeded excitedly, 'Perhaps he'll let us all come?' She threw her sultry eyes at Vaughn, squeezed his arm affectionately and then asked him to include her friends. 'Oh, pleeease let them all come too, Professor. You did just say your personal bar was very well stocked. A drink in your apartment would be sooo wonderful.' She ran her hand fleetingly over the outside of his trouser zipper.

Felix flinched. In his opinion Aiza was enjoying this role far too much.

'Can we all come, then?' Oliver asked, quite matter-of-fact. He had little time for Lambert.

Sensing he'd been taken off guard, yet too relaxed to care, Vaughn reluctantly agreed. With the whole group present, a fuck with Aiza was unlikely. But there was always tomorrow. The shy ones often required extra grooming.

Aiza grabbed Vaughn's hand and pulled him towards the lift. 'Let's go, then. I've been dying to see your apartment since I started the course.'

As the group left with Vaughn, Fleur looked up. She didn't care. Vaughn didn't own her, and she didn't own him. In fact, she expected him to move on sooner or later. It had always been just a matter of time.

Vaughn entered the three-digit code and the lift doors slid open. Drinks in hands, the group entered, chatting excitedly. He pressed his index finger on the smoked-glass panel, and selected Level 42. In no time at all they were in his apartment dancing, drinking and partying. Charlie nominated himself as the barman and Oliver placed himself in charge of Vaughn's vintage record collection. It was quite impressive. First, he chose an original AC/DC recording of 'Jailbreak', and in no time the party was in full swing.

Aiza maintained Vaughn's interest by dancing provocatively and touching him at every opportunity. With his tie now removed and shirt button undone, he appeared more chilled. He planned to make the most of this unexpected situation. Maybe this group of students were into swinging. He certainly was. It might not be such a boring evening after all.

Charlie continued to spike Vaughn's drinks. However, the drugs were having minimal effect. He certainly had a high tolerance to benzodiazepines. By ten-thirty, Vaughn's eyelids finally began to droop, while his body became uncoordinated. Aiza was having trouble keeping him upright. Felix and Oliver intervened to help her. They walked him into the bedroom.

Vaughn waved his arms about dismissively. 'I'm jussh fine. I wanna dance; lemmy dance summor,' he said. Then he yelled out 'Aiza ...

Aiza'. To pacify him, she lay down on the bed with him. In less than a minute he rolled over and, with his head nestled on her chest, went to sleep.

Oliver went through the plan while they waited for the drugs to take full effect. Aiza and Kobi would stay with Vaughn. They were to strip him and tie his hands and feet to each of the bedposts and then undress down to their underwear. If anyone entered the apartment, they should pretend to be having a threesome. With Vaughn's reputation the scene would be credible.

'Okay, then; I guess it's time,' Oliver said.

Felix and Charlie pulled the unconscious man off the bed. They dragged him across the room and down the two shallow thickly carpeted stairs to the lift. Vaughn's head bounced on each.

'That's one for Sarah and one for Zoe, you fucking bastard,' Oliver said with each thud.

If the grog and drugs didn't give him a bad headache in the morning, those two cracks to the head certainly would. Vaughn moaned but didn't open his eyes.

Charlie had filmed Vaughn entering the lift code. He now punched in the three digits and the doors parted. Working together they heaved Vaughn's limp body upwards until his index finger reached and pressed the glass panel. Iridescent green light encircled the number 41. It glowed brightly then dimmed, as if beckoning and challenging them to take the ride.

Oliver held the lift open, while Felix and Charlie dragged Vaughn back to the bed. Kobi and Aiza stripped him down to his underwear and tied his legs and arms tightly to the bedposts. Felix hurried over and gave Aiza a hug. Returning to the lift, he blew her one last kiss just as the doors closed.

The girls stripped down to their bras and underpants and sat down on the bed next to Vaughn.

66

The lift stopped abruptly and the doors slid open. The boys peered out into a dimly lit area. A soft light was emanating from translucent shell shapes attached to the walls. No laser beams were evident. They stepped out of the lift and stood silent and motionless, deciding which of the corridors to explore first.

Oliver could feel that his senses had heightened. Charlie's heart was thumping. Felix was breathing so hard it was audible. Their level of nervousness ratcheted higher when the lift reactivated, startling all three. It had been called to another floor. They looked at each other, knowing that there was no turning back. Nothing left to do but investigate. Hopefully they would find Zoe safe and well and get the hell out of there.

'I hope we haven't risked our medical careers for nothing,' Charlie whispered.

'Zoe is worth any risk,' Oliver replied.

'Shhhhh, you two,' Felix said sternly. 'Element of surprise, re-member.'

They made their way down the corridor directly ahead until they came to a double set of locked steel doors. Charlie punched in the same code as the lift and was pleasantly surprised to hear the lock click open. On entering they found themselves in a large dimly lit laboratory. The lab had white walls, ceiling and floor. It was immaculately clean. The strong smell of a citrusy disinfectant made Oliver sneeze violently several times.

Labelled specimen jars, illuminated by display lights, were set in niches in the outer perimeter walls. The jars contained what appeared to be human fetuses preserved in formalin. Arranged in the centre of the laboratory were rows of clear thick plastic pouches filled with a pale yellow fluid. They were about the same size as a twenty-litre tub and hung from the ceiling about a metre off the floor.

A complex network of electrical cables and tubes across the ceiling seemed to be transferring power and substances to and from the pouches. The pouches were blood temperature to the touch and the external strip thermometers confirmed a setting of 37.5 degrees Celsius. The screen on a central computer danced endlessly with figures. It appeared to be monitoring and maintaining a network.

Each plastic pouch contained one human fetus. They were all at various stages of development. Some were small, no more than the size of a large broad bean; others appeared to be fully formed. Charlie estimated these were between thirty and thirty-eight weeks gestation. The room contained over fifty of these artificial pouches or wombs. The lab was a baby factory.

Felix pressed his face directly against one pouch and peered into the fluid. He tapped the plastic lightly with his fingertips. The fetus within sensed his tapping and the movement of the fluid. It wriggled and squirmed around before lifting its head and opening its eyes. Felix stepped backwards. The eyes staring at him weren't normal. The pupils were oval, more like a cat or a bird. No, it wasn't either of those—something about the eyes was familiar. His hand went instinctively to his mouth as he realised exactly what was staring back at him. These weren't human pupils. They were the pupils of a bat.

The boys could barely comprehend what they were seeing. The fetuses were some kind of human–bat hybrid. The digits on their hands were linked with a thin film of flesh. They appeared to be partially webbed. The skin colour was quite pale, rather than the expected baby pink.

'That mad bastard has blended human and bat genes? Why would anyone even attempt such a thing?' Felix said, clearly disgusted.

At that precise moment the lab doors were flung open and three androids entered.

Caught with nowhere to retreat, the trio stood still and held their breath.

Nothing happened.

The three androids walked past them as if they were invisible. No acknowledgment of their presence whatsoever.

Charlie breathed out. 'Phew. Just bloody TODs.

'Christ, that scared the shit out of me,' Oliver said.

'Me too,' Felix added.

The task-orientated droids, or TODs, seemed to be ensuring everything was working as programmed. They began checking each individual pouch.

Felix waved his hand in front of one TOD's eyes. The android momentarily paused then continued working once his hand was removed.

'I wouldn't mess with them, mate. You might set off an alarm,' Oliver warned.

Charlie moved across to a desk and began thumbing through one of two leather-bound logbooks. The black one had tattered corners and was the older of the two. The navy blue one was less worn and still smelled faintly of leather. He read for a few moments then spoke.

'The researchers are trying to breed humans with better immune systems. I believe their aim is to make the human germline more resilient to microbial attack. Research results have been recorded manually in these logbooks. In the black logbook the experiments go back seventy years. These days it's unusual to keep hard copies of research, but computer systems can be hacked, catch a virus or crash. The High Court still maintains all legal decisions in the judge's own handwriting, you know. Handwriting is less vulnerable to tampering and harder to forge.'

Oliver joined Charlie at the desk. Several of Vaughn's e-mails were printed out, lying in a tray. He picked one up and read it.

'It looks like some sort of IVF black market, with disease-resistant ova being offered for sale at exorbitant prices.'

'Selling ova?' Felix repeated, shaking his head as if trying to make some sense out of the torrent of information.

'I think so. It looks like a single IVF embryonic transfer costs one million dollars. You can also arrange surrogacy, or even adopt a full-term baby.'

'You have got to be kidding me!' Felix responded as he began fiddling with the controls on a high-resolution screen on the rear wall. The screen sprang to life and images of healthy babies and young children faded in and out of view. The last frame froze and a motherly voice beckoned the listener to find out more about how AMDAT could help them to design the perfect healthy family.

Felix pressed the glowing red button. Immediately several spheres hovered above their heads. One by one, each grew in size and delivered a statement before bursting and releasing thousands of rainbow-coloured stars:

Stop stressing about pandemics and vaccine development.

Ensure your child has an immune system second to none.

As your child plays, their temperature will rise and kill pathogens.

The coughs and colds of childhood will become a thing of the past.

No more illness to spoil your recreational and holiday plans.

Don't become another grief-stricken pandemic parent.

Relax and let AMDAT do the designing for you.

Don't miss this once-in-a-lifetime opportunity.

Throughout the presentation, the screen displayed images of healthy adults and vibrant children playing and working in luxurious surroundings. All genders and races were represented in this multi-coloured, multicultural presentation. When the display finished Oliver was the first to speak.

'That was some sales pitch,' he said.

'Not sure how they intend to produce children with a higher basal temp, though,' Felix added.

'Bat mitochondria,' Charlie said, jumping to his feet. 'Remember that bats harbour many pathogens but don't get sick because they have a higher basal temperature than ours, and when they fly their temperature climbs even higher.'

'Do you think that's why they're blending human and bat genes? But you can't blend genes of one species with another. It just doesn't work. Nature won't allow it,' Felix replied.

Charlie continued. 'You're right, nature won't, but that's definitely what appears to be happening here. I'd bet they're blending DNA from humans with bat mitochondria. I don't know how they are achieving it, but it appears they have found a way.'

'They must have switched off the usual DNA coding rejections? Perhaps gene clipping has succeeded in an edit that achieved that outcome? CRISPR has been around for decades,' Oliver suggested.

'Could be, yet the hybrid adults would be sterile, wouldn't they? Like the mule?' Felix asked.

'I don't know,' Charlie answered. 'There's still much we need to find out. All I know is that most of the female students in our group would go ballistic if they knew their donated ova were being used for this type of unethical experimentation.'

'I'm so glad that Aiza, Kobi and Zoe all declined to donate their ova,' Felix added.

Oliver paused as if reflecting, then spoke: 'I wonder if Zoe's refusal to donate ova has anything to do with why she's gone missing.'

'I don't see a connection,' Felix replied. 'There are lots of women willing to donate their ova, even if it is for experimentation. They get their best ova stored for free, so that is a good incentive.'

'I know, but a number of Zoe's school friends have also gone missing. And the other day, Anna told me that the girl who died seemed to have had all her ova removed. She was worried that whoever has taken Zoe might do the same thing to her.'

'But didn't that happen in New Jersey, Oliver, not here?' Charlie asked.

'Yes, it did. I guess a link of that sort is a long stretch. Anyway, we've spent enough time here. Let's push on and try to find Zoe. If we get caught by real security guards, I can't imagine what might happen to us.' Charlie stuffed the two logbooks along with a bunch of e-mails into his backpack. He then snapped some images.

Back in the corridor once more, the young men paused to listen for other signs of occupancy. A small cough came from somewhere to their left. It sounded like a baby.

'Croup,' Felix said instinctively. 'My little brother was always getting croup. It's a very distinctive cough with a high-pitched whoop at the end.'

'Droids don't cough, so it's a real baby,' Charlie added.

They proceeded down the corridor, making their way towards the source of the sound. A baby's cry came from the opposite direction and a light flicked on in that location. Level 41 was far from vacant. Oliver made a decision to speed up their search.

'You two go down that corridor and check out where that baby's cry is coming from. I'll go this way and check out the croupy cough.'

As Oliver neared the lit doorway a voice came from within.

'Is that you, Vaughn?' a woman's soft voice enquired.

Thinking quickly, and in a formal tone that he thought one would expect of a professional security guard, Oliver replied. 'It's just security undertaking a round, ma'am.' He grimaced. He hoped security actually made rounds on that level. He knew they did on every other floor.

'You're a bit early, aren't you?' she replied in a familiar American accent. 'It's not quite eleven.'

'A silent alarm was activated, ma'am, but there's no need for you to be concerned. Oliver stood in the doorway. Inside was a young woman around Zoe's age, pretty with dark hair and green eyes. She was nursing a newborn. Every few moments the infant coughed.

'Tilly has a cough,' she said. 'I called Vaughn earlier. He promised to check on her before he retired. Her cough doesn't seem to be getting any better. He must have turned off his mobile. Can you contact him for me, please?'

'Sure, I can do that for you. Who will I say requires his assistance?'

'Kasey,' she replied. 'But don't you know who I am?'

Oliver paused for a moment. 'Sorry, err, Kasey. The lights are so dim. I didn't recognise you. I'll try to find Vaughn. It might take me a while. He wasn't feeling the best. I think he's gone to bed.'

'Well, Tilly needs to be reviewed tonight. It simply can't wait until morning. I'll call Gum. She'll just have to wake him if he's already asleep.'

Oliver watched, helplessly, as Kasey called Gum and began explaining that Vaughn really needed to assess Tilly.

'Gum will contact Vaughn for me. Thanks anyway.'

'Hopefully help will come soon Kasey. I'll complete my rounds, if that's all right with you.'

Oliver moved briskly down the hall and found Felix and Charlie with another young woman. She was trying to comfort a distressed baby, in a room full of what appeared to be sleeping infants. Two TODs were at the back of the room mixing formula and folding linen. Just as the previous androids had done, they ignored their presence.

Looking up at what she believed were security guards, the heavily pregnant young woman spoke: 'I think Holly is in pain. Poor little mite has been quite upset since her hand operation this morning. It's probably very sore. I've just given her some baby pain medication so she should settle soon.'

The boys could see that the baby's tiny hands were wrapped in clean white gauze. She was screaming and waving her fists in the air as if she were a fighter wearing white boxing gloves.

'Where's the baby's mother?' asked Charlie.

'Her mom's Louise Stuart. She's just taking a break before Holly's next feed.'

The woman laid the baby back in the crib, and with the comfort of a dummy, Holly, still sniffling, began to settle.

'I'm helping here in the post-operative nursery, at least until my daughter is born. These children have all undergone hand operations to remove excess flesh. They'll go home in a couple of days.' She hesitated before adding, 'but you should already know all about what happens in this nursery.'

The woman suddenly realised that none of the young men had security ID. She looked over to her mobile on the bench. It was out of reach. Her eyes flicked across to the alarm button on the wall. Charlie saw her arm start to lift. He manoeuvred in and grabbed her wrist just in time to stop her pressing it.

'There's no need for that ... err.'

'Alice ... my name is Alice—and would you please let go of me or I will scream.'

She pulled a determined face at Charlie as she wriggled, trying to free herself. Charlie held firm and explained what they were doing.

'We aren't here to hurt anyone, Alice. We're just looking for a friend. A young woman called Zoe. Do you know if she's here?'

'I did know a Zoe once. I went to school with one. That seems like a lifetime ago. Vaughn said a new woman was joining us and that she wasn't well. If she is here, she's probably resting in one of the private suites. I don't know if she's the person you're looking for, though.'

'If you tell us where these suites are, we'll be on our way.'

'They're at the very end of this corridor, on the left.'

The three men had only taken a few steps down the corridor when they became aware of a loud buzzing noise. It was as if a swarm of cicadas were trying to eat their way into the building.

67

It was nearing eleven. The crew had been clipping bougainvillea for hours and were now all located outside Level 41 windows. It was quiet and dark inside the building. The commander gave the five-minute warning. Containers with glass-scoring tools were lowered to the designated agents on each side of the building.

On the signal, Patrick and three colleagues began simultaneously scoring one-metre-wide circles in the hardened-glass windows. They used portable diamond water-jet scorers, especially designed to work on bulletproof glass. The machines were noisy, yet the sounds on all four sides made it difficult to ascertain exactly where they were coming from. The glass scores were completed in one minute and, using miniature explosive orbs, the circular entry points were imploded and access ready. The Special Operations Group climbed in and began their systematic sweeping of Level 41. Within ten seconds their presence was detected and the tower alarms activated.

DXDXDXC

Susie was jolted awake by the loud buzzing. She had been responsible for security on Level 41 for more than five years and never had an incident. Complacency had set in.

She dressed, clipped her black hair back into a short ponytail, put on her helmet with its infrared visor and secured her gun belt. As she exited her room, two security droids joined her. Pistols drawn, they made their way down each corridor, kicking doors open and undertaking a sweep of each room. They needed to locate and determine the level of threat as quickly as possible.

The loud buzzing suddenly ceased. Ten seconds of silence were quickly followed by a series of small explosions, then the deafening sounds of security alarms. The whole of the tower was on red alert.

The fluorescent lights began to flicker then went out, leaving Level 41 in complete darkness. Shouting and screaming came from all directions. Infants were crying. Shots were being fired.

The boys heard voices heading in their direction. Somebody was coming towards them. They decided to retreat and make their way back to the lift. Oliver was frustrated they hadn't found Zoe. He was determined not to leave until he had checked out the suites. He made a snap decision to separate from the others and make his way to the lift via the corridor that led past the suites. Charlie tried to talk some sense into his friend.

'I think we should just focus on getting out of here in one piece, Oliver. We can inform the authorities straightaway.'

'They have guns, Oliver. We really need to leave,' Felix added.

'I just want to look for Zoe in those suites. It won't take me long. You two hold the lift and I'll be back before you know it.' Without hesitation he turned and sprinted away from them.

Charlie and Felix arrived at the lift. It came without a code. Felix held the lift open and they waited for Oliver. The gunfire seemed to be getting closer. Where was he? They needed to get out of there. Charlie activated his mobile torch and shone it into the darkness, just in time to see Oliver turn the corner. Oliver glanced to his left and then paused momentarily. A look of horror crossed his face as a volley of bullets hit him in the chest. He shook violently before crumpling to the ground, where he lay motionless.

Charlie stood still. He felt numb with fear. It was as if he'd been frozen to the spot. He sensed Felix pushing him inside the lift and could hear him frantically pressing the glass panel. The lift didn't respond. He heard Felix whisper 'Run!' and in a blur his friend grabbed him by the front of his shirt, pulled him out of the lift and down the corridor, away from the section where Oliver had been gunned down.

Felix knew they needed to hide: a room, a closet—anywhere to get out of the line of fire. Oliver was an unarmed student, for God's sake. These security guards weren't messing around. The stakes must be extremely high if they were prepared to kill an unarmed man just to maintain their secrecy.

A small hatch door about sixty centimetres square was visible on one wall. Felix lifted the hatch door and pushed Charlie in before climbing in himself. The opening flipped closed. They slid in the dark for about five seconds before falling headfirst into something quite soft and rather smelly.

Sweating and breathless, Felix lifted his head and was pleased to discover that they had landed in a vacant laundry collection room. A basket of soiled laundry had broken their fall. Charlie was still too stunned to speak. His teeth began to chatter as the shock of what he just witnessed set in.

Felix suddenly remembered the girls. He needed to warn them that Gum was probably on her way to Vaughn's apartment. He sent them a text. He couldn't risk calling. He had no idea what was happening at their end.

68

Aiza and Kobi heard the loud buzzing noise emanating from the outside of the building, followed by small explosions and a deafening alarm. Kobi, who had been sitting cross-legged in an armchair playing on her mobile, jumped to her feet. Her heart began to thump and her breathing rate increased. Strange sounds were emanating from Vaughn's lounge room. Flashes of coloured light were bouncing in and around the bedroom entrance.

Aiza had been resting on the bed. She sat up and turned towards her friend. Kobi held up her hand in a stop motion and shushed her friend with a finger across her closed lips. Kobi then proceeded cautiously towards the bedroom door and peered around it. The smoked-glass panels that lined the lounge room walls had sprung to life. The whole room was packed floor to ceiling with CCTV monitors. The screens that had given the appearance of decorative blank glass walls had activated and were now streaming live.

Kobi concluded that they must be part of some automatic surveillance system. Each bank of monitors was arranged to match key areas of the tower. The outer perimeters of several screens were glowing a pulsating red. She suspected these red zones indicated the source of the security breaches. From this location Vaughn could monitor most of what occurred throughout the building.

Kobi discovered that she could touch a screen to zoom and listen to specific areas by unmuting individual screens. Level 41 was very dark, but from the sounds and lights it was clear that a firefight was taking place. She began scanning for the boys. Felix had texted something about them landing in a laundry collection room.

Before she had time to undertake a thorough search, the lift shaft activated. Just as Felix had warned, they were about to have company. She ran back into the bedroom and alerted Aiza. The time had arrived for them to put on a convincing performance. Gum Lin would be there at any moment.

Gum was on her way to Vaughn's apartment when the tower alarms began sounding. She would check out what was happening with Vaughn and use his security cams to identify the source of the problem. Gum entered his apartment with a security guard and two droids. She scanned the room. Loud music was playing. Empty glasses and snack packets lay on tables. Chopped fruit, cream, liqueurs and mixers were strewn across the bar – nothing unusual. Gum continued through the lounge and into the bedroom. Vaughn was tied up in a bondage pose. He appeared to be asleep. A young woman in her underwear was sitting cross-legged on the bed next to him, sipping a lime green cocktail. Another, dressed only in underpants, was dancing provocatively and pulling weird faces. She appeared to be drunk or on drugs, or maybe both.

'Get dressed, you fucking sluts,' Gum yelled, picking up and throwing their clothes at them. Both girls ignored her. Gum went across to Aiza and pushed her off the bed. The contents of the glass splashed across Vaughn's torso. Concerned for Aiza's safety, Kobi approached Gum.

'Hey,' she said. 'No need to get so rough with my friend. If you want to join in the action, honey, you only had to ask.' She grabbed at Gum as if trying to dance with her.

Gum lost her footing under Kobi's weight and fell back against the wall before slithering onto the floor. Pushing Kobi roughly to one side, Gum turned and issued an order to the guard.

'Untie Vaughn, get these two sluts dressed, and chuck them off the premises.' She stood up, smoothed down her clothing and determined that Vaughn was of no use to anyone in his current state. With a wave of one hand she summoned the droids. 'You two follow me.'

Gum left the bedroom and paused momentarily in front of the security monitors before heading towards the lift, with the droids in tow.

The guard attempted unsuccessfully to dress the girls. They began toying with him. He wasn't being particularly forceful, believing the two attractive semi-clad girls were simply drunk and playful. Aiza planted a kiss on his mouth, just as Kobi raised Vaughn's solid gold statue of the champion horse Winx and hit him firmly over the head.

He fell motionless onto the bed, landing on top of Vaughn.

'Shit! I hope I haven't killed him,' Kobi said as she used Vaughn's shirt to rub the blood and fingerprints off the statue before placing it carefully back on the bedside table.

'He's still breathing,' Aiza said, watching the guard's chest rise and fall. 'We'd better roll him on his side.' The girls turned him over. Leaving him where he was, they tied his hands and feet together and attached them to the bedposts. Dressing quickly, they checked once more that the two men were firmly tied before leaving the bedroom.

Kobi and Aiza scanned the security system once more, determined to locate their friends. The chute they had slid down most probably collected laundry from the Grants' penthouse, Vaughn's apartment and Level 41. Kobi surmised the laundry chute was probably located somewhere on Level 40 or below. She located the Level 40 monitors, zoomed in and scanned for dark areas. She texted Felix to flick his mobile torch light on and off as if it were a beacon until she found them. It worked. They were located in the facilities zone on Level 40, just behind the visitors' toilets. If they could get the lift working maybe they could go and pick up the boys. Kobi texted Felix:

Ideas to get lift going?

Code 666.

OK Comin 2 pik u 3 up now

Kobi thought, *666—you have got to be kidding me,* as she punched in the code and called the lift. When the lift doors opened, however, she and Aiza found themselves looking directly down the barrel of a Glock.

69

The lift shuddered to a standstill. Before exiting, Gum set the lift doors to close the moment she re-entered. Shattered glass crunched beneath her boots as she stepped into the darkness, then stood still and listened. The silence was broken only by gusts of wind blowing through one of the smashed windows. As the strong air currents blew inwards the blinds tossed around, then sucked back against the metal frame with a loud crack.

The tower had been breached from the exterior. Gum crouched down to examine the abandoned cutting tools. She hadn't seen anything like them. These were professionals. But who were they? Disgruntled clients? Dissatisfied staff? Police? She wasn't sure who or what she was dealing with. And where was Susie?

Although it was unlikely, Gum had planned for this event. She drew her pistol and instructed the droids to do the same. Shots had begun emanating from the eastern corner of the floor. They proceeded in that direction.

The trio hadn't taken more than a dozen steps before they came across a body. Gum rolled the man onto his back. He groaned. She recognised him. It was Zoe Ashmore's boyfriend. So, they were dealing with a pack of students. Nevertheless, very smart students who had managed to breach the most secure floor in the tower.

She was determined not to underestimate this risk to their operation. Students or not, they needed to be eliminated. She placed a gloved hand across Oliver's bloodied mouth and tightly pinched his nose until the young man's chest ceased heaving. *That takes care of one troublemaker,* she thought as she stepped over him.

Motioning the two droids to follow her, she continued on towards the rear corridor. Gum wanted to check that Zoe was secure. Oliver must have worked out that his girlfriend was being held on Level 41, but she had no idea how. Gum heard someone running towards them. She threw her hand in the direction of the droids and they immediately retreated. Tucking herself back into a doorway, she prepared to strike. As the intruder passed, she launched the full force of her body forwards, expecting to collide with a student, only to find herself in a struggle with a fully kitted member of the Special Operations Group. They wrestled for twenty seconds before she determined she was losing and yelled for the droids to intervene.

Patrick heard two thuds, the unmistakable sound of gunfire hitting a body. As he approached, he saw two armed droids leaning over one of his colleagues. He retreated behind a wall to get his breath back. The sweat beading on his forehead began to trickle slowly down his face. He wiped it away with the back of his gloved hand. He hadn't expected to encounter armed droids. The team weren't prepared for this threat. He needed to think and to think fast.

Task-orientated droids were used extensively throughout society. They were commonplace. TODs were designed primarily to relieve humans from monotonous, repetitive, unclean, unsafe jobs and the sleep disruptions of night shift. The use of droids in security, carrying weapons, had been considered a risk to humanity. As long ago as 2015, several leading experts including Stephen Hawking and Elon Musk had presented to the United Nations Security Council their detailed evidence on the dangers of designing artificial intelligence as killing machines. Following years of debate, armed droids were finally outlawed in 2040.

AMDAT had clearly flouted the law. A Special Operations Group member had been wounded or killed by droids. Destroying droids was complicated. Their central processors needed to be disabled, and those weren't easily located.

Patrick's belt held six exploding magnetic orbs. He knew nothing else in his kit would be effective against droids. He had to try—but not now, not with an officer down. He would have to wait until the droids moved on.

Gum was relieved to find Zoe still in her suite and unharmed. The teenager's eyes were closed, and she mumbled the occasional word as she rocked her head from side to side, as if caught in a bad dream. There was not enough time to relocate her, so Gum decided to conceal her instead. She pushed the bed to the back corner of the room, pulled the bedding up and around Zoe's head—taking care to leave her some breathing space—then piled pillows and blankets loosely on top. Satisfied that the bed now looked unoccupied, Gum exited with the droids and made their way back along the corridor.

Patrick dragged his colleague to the safety of a vacant room and assessed her condition. Her pulse was strong and she had no critical injuries. The force of the bullets hitting her armoured vest appeared to have knocked her unconscious. He dragged her behind a lounge suite then rolled her onto her side to ensure her airway stayed open. Patrick was about to leave the room when he heard footsteps approaching. Droids' night-vision beams were bouncing around the corridor walls outside, their colour unmistakable. He pinned back the door, crouched behind it and waited. When he was sure the droids were close, he reached forward and fired six rounds upwards before running across into the adjacent corridor.

Gum was in front of the droids when the bullets struck. She shuddered, staggered, then slumped to the floor. The droids stepped over her and immediately started firing as they combed the dark corridor in search of the threat. Light didn't matter to droids. The warmth emitted by human bodies was easily detected. The droids propped, sensing Patrick's body heat emanating from the adjacent corridor.

Patrick grimaced, then closed his eyes and visualised the droids. Grabbing an orb from his belt, he activated it and tossed it. He then rolled a second orb down the corridor. He had approximately five seconds to get to cover before they detonated. He sprinted towards the lift and leapt inside just as the doors closed and the debris from the explosion flew past.

Gum felt the bullets enter her arms, legs and chest. Critically injured, her body didn't register any pain. The shock set in quickly. She staggered for a few seconds before slumping to the floor. Gum struggled to breathe as her lungs slowly filled with blood. She clutched her chest and felt her heartbeat slowing. Her vision became blurry and her mind floated away.

Looking up, she saw her mother smiling down at her. They were back in their little kitchen in Carlton. With her left hand Mumma was rolling out small balls of dough then pressing them into perfectly round shapes. Dumplings. She was making pork and vegetable dumplings, her favourite. She could smell the aroma of the garlic and ginger frying. Her mother blew on a freshly fried dumpling before handing it to her. Little Gum took a big bite and her milk teeth crunched through the crispy cabbage and water chestnuts. It tasted so good. She devoured it quickly and licked the sweet soy sauce off her tiny fingers. Her mother smiled.

'You must be hungry, my little princess. Your father is on night shift tonight; he won't be home until morning. Come to the table and you shall have as many dumplings as you can eat.'

She held her hand out and little Gum grasped it tightly. It felt warm and soft. She nestled it against her face then pulled it towards her lips and kissed.

'I'm coming, Mumma. I'm coming.'

Gum's heart beat for thirty more seconds before stopping. As it ceased pumping a ticking sound could be heard. The sound grew louder and faster before her heart—and a bank of computers that contained incriminating evidence—exploded.

At the back of the baby laboratory, pages started to emerge from a printer.

70

Georgia's coconut cream curry was as delicious as always, but Ellen found herself pushing the gold-coloured vegetable chunks around the plate. Familiar home-cooked food could be so comforting during times of stress but even this dish wasn't helping all that much. Georgia couldn't stop talking. She was going over and over the same old ground and getting absolutely nowhere. Blabbing on and on about Oliver looking for Zoe because he thought the police were useless. To give them both a break from Georgia's monotonous dialogue, Lauren asked Ellen to tell her what had happened with Daniel.

Ellen explained everything. Georgia couldn't concentrate, but Lauren was quite enthralled to hear about the desert community and the story of the two brothers both falling in love with the same woman; she wondered who would turn out to be Daniel's father. She was sad to hear that, just when Ellen and Daniel had found happiness again, it had been cruelly snatched from them, as if the devil himself enjoyed toying with them with no intention of giving them their Happily Ever After.

Lauren tried to offer comfort to both her friends. Georgia wouldn't listen, so she focused on Ellen, reminding her that Daniel was innocent until proven guilty and that just because he hadn't talked to her since his arrest didn't mean any of the charges were true or that he had stopped loving her.

'Some men just have a great deal of trouble expressing their emotions. Perhaps Daniel went into some kind of psycho shock,' she offered as one possible explanation.

'Maybe he just didn't know what to say and felt too embarrassed to speak,' Lauren continued as she paced around the room, jiggling baby Pat in an attempt to get him to sleep.

Ellen knew Lauren was simply trying to help but she felt totally exhausted and completely numb inside. It was as if something or someone had extracted all her feelings, sucked them out completely, leaving nothing but an empty shell. Her chest felt tight, her muscles ached from constant tensing and her breasts were sore.

As a medic, she knew that her lack of emotional response was most probably just her defence mechanisms kicking in. She had, after all, had quite a number of shocks over the last few days and she had barely recovered from the birth of Pat. Zoe was still missing, Daniel had been arrested, and on top of everything else James had called to inform her that their mother had aspiration pneumonia and was not expected to see the week out. The emotional rollercoaster was simply too much for anyone to bear. She knew that she had to rally, so she just kept shovelling the curry into her mouth and going through the motions of chewing and swallowing. Not eating simply wasn't an option. Pat needed his mother.

Georgia paced around the apartment as she waited and hoped to hear news of Zoe. Ellen was finding her restlessness annoying. She suggested to Georgia that a lavender bubble bath might help her relax.

Despite the bubble bath and Lauren's debriefing, both Ellen and Georgia were unable to sleep. In an attempt to distract them, Lauren switched on the television and opened a box of chocs. It was around midnight when a breaking news story interrupted the usual programming. Footage from AMDAT Tower beamed live into the lounge room.

The reporter was a handsome young man named Miles who appeared slightly anxious and quite out of his depth as helicopters flew overhead and heavily armed police entered the tower through the ground-floor entrances. Miles was joined within minutes by the station's lead news anchor, Gloria Sondameyer.

The unfolding action centred two floors down from the Grants' penthouse. Explosions and gunshots could be heard and flames could be seen lapping out of a window at the southern end of the building.

'And to think it's only a few weeks ago that we were in that very building,' Ellen said. 'Just goes to show how quickly things can change.'

Georgia turned pale and began to tremble. 'Oh no. This can't be happening. My Zoe, Oliver, those poor kids.'

'What's wrong, Georgia? What kids? What are you on about? Talk to me,' Ellen asked.

Georgia's mouth gaped momentarily, then began opening and closing like a fish out of water. It was as if all the oxygen in the room had suddenly been replaced with noxious gas. Not a single word escaped. She was hyperventilating.

'Quick, Lauren, fetch me a brown paper bag from the bottom drawer in the kitchen.'

Ellen supported Georgia and asked her to breathe into the bag. She began speaking to her in a slow, firm tone.

'Breathe in and out slowly. I need you to be able to speak to me. I need you to focus and tell me everything. What about Zoe? What about Oliver? Who are these other poor kids you're so worried about?'

After a few minutes Georgia was able to speak. Mumbling into the paper bag, she explained how Oliver had asked for some of her sleeping pills. That Oliver had an idea where Zoe might be and that he and his friends planned to drug Vaughn Lambert at Friday drinks and use his fingerprint to gain access to the level where she had photographed the toddler peering out of the window.

'What else, Georgia? Tell me what else you know.'

'I think they were planning to do it fairly soon. Perhaps even tonight.'

'Did you tell anyone about this plan?' Ellen asked, taking the paper bag from Georgia.

'Oliver told me not to tell anyone. I thought they wouldn't go through with it. Just silly kids making stupid plans they wouldn't be able to execute.'

'Focus, Georgia; I'll ask again. Did you tell anyone about Oliver's plan?'

'Yes, yes, I did. Like I said, I wasn't supposed to, but I told Rob just before you arrived home tonight, about eight thirty. Yes, it was definitely eight thirty because my favourite show was just starting when I hung up.'

'So Rob knows?'

'Yes, Rob knows.'

'Okay, dial his number.' She handed her the mobile.

It rang out. Ellen left an urgent message to call back asap.

Georgia could not stop crying. Ellen placed her arm around Georgia then turned her attention back to the media coverage. Gloria was now transmitting from the news helicopter. Her immaculately styled hair stayed totally rigid despite the obvious wind gusts. The camera zoomed in onto the tower roof where an evacuation was well underway. Women and infants were being loaded into police helicopters. When one helicopter was clear another landed.

Gloria spotted Margaret Grant and another woman carrying a baby. 'It appears Margaret Grant is currently being evacuated from her penthouse. She's accompanied by another woman of a similar age. It could be ...' Gloria grabbed her earpiece. 'Yes, we have confirmation that the woman is in fact her first cousin, Louise Stuart. The baby is most likely her new baby daughter.'

In an attempt to miss the swarm of media drones, one helicopter veered dangerously close to the tower before the pilot corrected and flew it safely into the distance.

Gloria's report continued: 'As was reported three days ago, Daniel Grant is currently in custody so was not in his penthouse when this raid began. We aren't sure why AMDAT has been raided by the police.'

The coverage passed back to Miles outside the front of the building. AMDAT night-shift employees were being evacuated with the assistance of unarmed police droids. Suddenly Ellen spotted Felix, Aiza, Charlie and Kobi exiting via the main reception area accompanied by officers. Reporters and drones attempted to move in closer to gain clearer footage, but the four teenagers were shielded and escorted rapidly to waiting police vehicles.

'No Zoe or Oliver,' Georgia said anxiously, still peering at the screen as if it might make them magically appear.

'Hopefully they're together somewhere,' Lauren suggested in an attempt to offer a positive spin on what appeared to be an increasingly hopeless situation.

'Let's just try to stay positive. I'm sure they will both be okay. They just have to be,' Ellen added, but she knew it didn't look good for either of them.

Ellen redialled Rob's number. 'Come on. Come on. Pick up,' she muttered under her breath.

Rob sat with the police computer expert in AMDAT's main control centre. He felt his mobile vibrate in his pocket for the second time, but didn't have time to acknowledge the caller. He was required to use his knowledge of AMDAT computer systems to assist the police as they hacked into various databases.

He was surprised just how calm he was. Georgia had told him about Oliver's plan but by then the police raid was already well underway. He never expected the group of teenagers to succeed in infiltrating Level 41, let alone choose the same night as a police raid. He had tracked the teenagers' chips and police assistance had been sent to Levels 40 and 42. He had just observed four of the teenagers exiting the building, but neither Oliver nor Zoe was among them. Oliver's chip was no longer transmitting, and under the circumstances, that could only mean one thing. Anyway, he needed to keep his emotions in check and focus on the task at hand.

The remand centre guards had allowed Daniel Grant to view the tower action from his cell. He was, after all, one of AMDAT's founders.

Perhaps he might have insight as to why the corporation was being raided. Maybe they could sell any extracted information to news-hungry journalists and make some extra dosh.

The day after his arrest Daniel, had been denied bail. The magistrate felt that, with all his power and money, he was an unacceptable flight risk. Daniel had been granted the obligatory one phone call. Under the circumstances, one might have expected that he would call Ellen. He didn't. Daniel called his lawyer and asked him to contact the one person with the most influence and power to help him—Maggie.

Kenneth had engaged two of the leading barristers in the country before he visited Daniel. The lawyers had been instructed to wait outside while the billionaire had an off-the-record chat with his estranged son-in-law.

'You're one lucky man, Daniel. Margaret still adores you despite your dalliance with that Hancock woman. She has informed me that you and she are actually first cousins. Apparently you're the spawn of my brother Francis and one of his many girlfriends whose name, I'm afraid, escapes me.'

'Annette; my mother's name was Annette Ward,' interrupted Daniel, feeling the need to protect his mother's reputation from the bastard who had seduced her and ruined her life.

Kenneth completely ignored the comment and proceeded as if no-one had spoken.

'So let me tell you how things will play out now, if you don't want to spend the rest of your life rotting in a jail cell. I have the original footage of the bat-zone incident. If you do exactly as I say, it will be used to ensure all the charges against you are dropped. If you don't agree then the footage will be destroyed, and you'll be convicted of murder. I'm prepared to give you one opportunity. Did you hear me Daniel? One opportunity to save yourself.'

'So what do I have to do?' Daniel asked in a tone that signalled that he had little choice other than to submit to Kenneth's demands.

'Much to my dismay, my daughter has decided she wants you back. Despite you being first cousins, your marriage remains legal. When you're released, you'll resume your role as head researcher and return to the marital bed.'

'But ...' Daniel started to speak but was immediately shut down by Kenneth.

'No "buts" Daniel. You will publicly reconcile with Margaret and ensure you're a good and faithful husband in every respect from this point onwards. You'll never contact Ellen Hancock again. Do you hear me? *Never!* Finally, you must have nothing to do with your biological father. I've been more of a father to you than Francis has ever been and that's the way it's going to stay. If you agree to these terms my lawyers will start work on your case immediately.'

Daniel didn't speak. He simply nodded.

'Speak up, man,' Kenneth insisted.

'I agree, Kenneth.'

'Now, what do we say when people do nice things for us, Daniel?' continued Kenneth condescendingly.

With his head drooped, Daniel spoke up as requested, as if he was Kenneth's pet rather than his son-in-law.

'Thank you, Kenneth. Thank you very much for all your help.'

Daniel tried to push the memory of Kenneth's visit to the back of his mind as he sat with the guards and watched the tower raid unfolding. Their AMDAT empire was unravelling before his eyes and he was powerless to act.

71

Despite the level of drugs Zoe had been administered, the sounds of the raid entered her subconscious brain. In a dreamlike state, her mind blended memories and reality, almost as if she were surfing through television channels trying to find a program to watch, but never quite managing to make a choice. Every noise was translated into something tangible, something familiar.

Gunfire became the sound of balloons bursting, recalling childhood birthday parties—fairy bread, popcorn, brightly coloured cakes and pass the parcel. Explosions pushed her back to the clearing of an old high-rise apartment block near her school in New Jersey. The whole school community had stood at a safe distance, watching and cheering as an expert team imploded the derelict building to make way for the school's new sporting ground.

She heard someone shouting at her. What had she done wrong this time? Was it one of her cousins teasing her? It sounded just like Archie. Yes, she was sure it was Archie. He was always bossing her around. If he didn't shut up, she would whack him.

'In here, in here,' a voice beckoned.

In where? Where does Archie want me to go now? I just want something to eat. I'm so hungry. Its dinnertime, isn't it? Mom, what's for dinner? I'm really hungry.

Zoe felt someone touching her.

'Leave me alone, Archie, or I'll tell Mom. Go away, find someone else to torment.'

The tugging didn't stop. She started to yell and flung her hands forward to give her cousin Archie a big shove.

'She's pretty agitated,' said the junior paramedic.

'No wonder, with all that stuff piled on top of her. It's lucky she could even breathe,' replied his senior.

'Should we give her a sedative?'

'No, we don't know what she already has on board. Can't risk it.'

All aboard the choo choo train, Frank yelled.

'Daddy—is that you, Daddy?' Zoe called out.

Yes, my little princess. Climb on my back; I'll take you for a train ride.

'For some reason she's settling,' the paramedic commented. 'Get her strapped to the stretcher while we can.'

Zoe could feel the movement of her train ride. Daddy lifted her high and low, leaning left and right, up and down. 'This is the best train ride ever.' She giggled with excitement. 'This is so much fun, Daddy. I've missed you sooo very much.'

The paramedics heard the comments.

'Whatever she's on, it's sure giving her one hell of a ride.'

Zoe was carried down the fire escape to Level 12. The paramedics pulled the sheet up over her face to prevent anyone from taking images, then two parobots floated her down to the foyer and into a waiting hovercraft.

72

It was now five in the morning. Lauren had fallen fast asleep in the rocker recliner. Her head was slumped sideways and her face was half covered with strands of blonde hair. She was snoring softly. Although completely exhausted, Ellen and Georgia had stayed up, glued to the screen. Despite taking a sedative, Georgia remained trembling and teary throughout the ordeal. Her eyes were bloodshot and swollen and her face was red and blotchy. She rocked backwards and forwards, talking to herself and asking question after question that no-one could possibly answer. Ellen had ceased responding hours ago.

Georgia felt so incredibly guilty for not doing more to discourage Zoe's friends. She didn't really think it through when she gave Oliver her medications. She had made a stupid decision. Could she ever forgive herself if any of them had come to harm?

'Please, please let them all be okay,' she kept muttering over and over.

By six in the morning the raid appeared to have ended. Each time a stretcher was carried from the building, Georgia's emotional state would escalate. She would move in closer to the screen, trying to identify the victim. If their faces were covered Georgia would scream, 'Look, they're dead, they're dead!'

Ellen tried to reassure her. 'Camera drones are everywhere. It's common practice these days to cover faces to maintain privacy and dignity, Georgia. It doesn't always translate to people being dead.' Although she knew in her heart that it generally did.

By now several stretchers had been carried from the building, but there had been no sign of either Zoe or Oliver.

Rob hadn't returned any of her calls, so Georgia went down to his apartment. He was either a heavy sleeper or he wasn't at home. She stood outside the door, knocking intermittently for five minutes, until his next-door neighbour threatened to call the police if she didn't move along. 'I'm sick of people knocking on that bloody door,' she said. 'Piss off the lot of ya!' *How rude,* thought Georgia—obviously she wasn't the only one looking for Rob. Where could he be? Just when she needed Rob most, he seemed to have vanished off the face of the planet.

Georgia returned to the apartment to find two police officers speaking with Ellen.

'Anna, come and sit down next to me,' Ellen said patting the couch.

'I knew it. My Zoe's dead, isn't she?' Georgia said. 'Police only ever want you to sit down when a loved one is dead.'

She started shaking and her legs began to give way. One of the officers moved swiftly across the room and assisted her back to the couch.

'It's okay, Ms Taylor,' he said, 'Zoe's not dead. She has been found safe and taken to hospital. She's under the influence of some strong drugs that the doctors are yet to identify. However, it doesn't appear that she has any life-threatening injuries.'

'What about her boyfriend, Oliver? Is he okay?'

'I'm afraid I don't know anything about any Oliver, Ms Taylor. We were only asked to collect you and Ms Hancock and transport you to Zoe. The doctor believes it's important that her mother is there when she wakes up.'

'But how do you know—'

The officer interrupted her. 'We know all about your temporary change of identity, Ms Taylor. We know you're really Georgia Ashmore. Any threat to you has now been eliminated. There's really no need for you to be in hiding anymore.'

'Does that mean they've found and arrested Detective Patrick O'Connor's killer, then?' Ellen enquired.

'I'm afraid I don't know anything regarding the death of any detective, Ms Hancock, but I'm sure you'll find out more details as the full picture of what has occurred overnight unfolds. Are you able to get ready? We'll transport you both directly to Zoe. Could you please pack some clothes and toiletries for her?'

Twenty minutes later, Ellen and Georgia were sitting on each side of Zoe's hospital bed. She was asleep and appeared to be unharmed. Her wrist was bandaged. The doctor had informed them that her chip had been removed sometime within the last few days. Her captors had ensured—not soon enough!—she couldn't be traced via that method.

Zoe remained heavily sedated, so the medics were providing fluids only while they waited for the pathology results. All her vital signs remained stable, so the doctor believed that she would wake up once her system eliminated the sedatives.

Ellen and Georgia could do nothing but wait. Totally exhausted, the two women eventually fell asleep. Ellen was slumped in the lounge chair on one side of the bed. Georgia was sitting rather awkwardly on a vinyl-covered chair on the other side with her head flopped on the bed. She had a tight grip on one of Zoe's hands.

Zoe smelt antiseptic before she noticed the firm pressure on her left hand. She gripped at the hand in hers. It must be Oliver. She was so lucky to have found him. Her head really ached. Did she get drunk again last night? She searched her brain to recall what had happened and tried to open her eyes. They felt unusually heavy, as if lead weights had been sewn onto the lids. She could only manage to half open them for one second before they snapped tightly shut and she drifted back to sleep.

73

It was eight in the morning by the time the forensic team was granted access to Level 41. The tower safety systems had worked effectively, ensuring that damage was contained to the one floor. The engineers determined quite quickly that the structure was sound. Tony Scallioni accompanied the forensic experts as they examined the scene. As yet, no bodies had been removed from the building.

Level 41 was still without full power. Many areas remained dark, although the early morning sunlight was now beaming through the windows, casting shadowy shapes and glinting as it bounced off metallic objects. Carpets and vinyl were wet underfoot. The large volume of water spewed out by the high-tech fire-sprinkler system had extinguished the fire, but left quite a mess. Shattered glass and debris from the destroyed droids littered the once-immaculate facility. Pools of congealed blood were visible around a young man's body.

Oliver's corpse lay still and cold. His injuries were extensive. Even if help had been immediately on hand, he would never have survived. The brave young man had put his life on the line, attempting to save his girlfriend. *If only he had trusted the police to handle the situation,* thought Tony, as he observed the tragic scene. Perhaps the police should have done more to keep Oliver updated. But any information might have compromised their operation.

With each flash of the camera, Oliver's body lit up as if he'd been caught napping in an unexpected thunderstorm. Image by image the details of his wounds were mapped. Samples were swabbed from his clothing and body and placed into long clear plastic tubes. Items that had fallen by his side, including his mobile, were bagged for further examination. Nearby footprints were traced. Shell casings collected and bullets prised from walls. Tony wished he'd been given the opportunity to get to know Oliver. He was one brave but unlucky kid. What a waste.

Further down the corridor, in the once-pristine laboratory, the 'baby factory' remained operational. Generators had kicked in an emergency power supply. The three TODs were busily at work as if nothing untoward had occurred. They had been joined by cleaning droids attempting to mop up and dry the sodden floor. Programmed to continue with designated tasks and devoid of all emotion, their routine was unaffected by the raid. The commander had sent for the maintenance crew to deactivate the droids before they mopped up any more evidence.

It was a challenging scene for even the most experienced personnel. Felix had described the hybrid creatures to police, but that hadn't prepared anyone for what they were now viewing. On entering the laboratory, the overpowering odour of rotting flesh had assailed their nostrils. The warm environment had accelerated the process of decay. Everyone was gasping and struggling to breathe. One of the junior police officers had to leave when he simply couldn't stop retching and eventually vomited into his face mask. There was a short delay as extractor fans were sourced.

Several pouches had been pierced by stray bullets, causing the fluid to drain directly onto the floor. Without the protection of their life-sustaining habitat, the fetuses had rapidly died. The damaged pouches and their lifeless contents hung from the ceiling like discarded meat in an abattoir. In the heated room the exposed white flesh had begun to dry out. Some body parts had adhered to the thick plastic, and a deep purple colour had formed around areas where the blood had pooled.

Opinions on what to do with the remaining live hybrids rapidly polarised. The responses that arose in the laboratory on that day only hinted at what was to become one of the most hotly debated ethical issues of the twenty-first century.

At the southern end of the building the body of an Asian woman lay in the corridor. She was quickly identified as Gum Lin. Her chest had been blown open. The injury was causing quite a distraction, as it closely resembled the type frequently encountered by Ripley in the classic *Alien* series. The forensic team could not agree on how the wound was inflicted. It was too small to be caused by a Special Operations Group orb, but too large for a bullet wound.

On Ms Lin's arm was tattooed an intricate blue and maroon serpent, now distorted and splattered with blood. A fake chip was found dangling from her other wrist. *What about the other AMDAT executives,* thought Tony. *Are they chipped?* He knew Daniel was. That's how police had tracked him to NATGRID East, but what about Vaughn Lambert and Kenneth Stuart? *Bloody hypocrites the lot of them.*

At the rear of Level 41 were a number of one-bed suites. They were fully furnished and well stocked. Three women, including Zoe, had been located in these suites. They had been transferred to the nearby Health Hub for further assessment and hospitalisation if required.

Gum's confession had been found strewn across the wet floor next to a printer at the back of the laboratory. It was a lengthy document in which she attempted to deflect all the blame away from Daniel Grant and Vaughn Lambert. Tony didn't believe a word of it. Still, it would take considerable time to piece together the full picture of what had really occurred.

All hard-copy records and computer systems were dusted for prints before being removed for further examination. Charlie had already surrendered the two logbooks, e-mails and images to police. These would prove to be invaluable.

74

Around midday Zoe finally awoke. She found herself lying in a bed located in a sparsely furnished hospital room. The only sound was the shushing of oxygen as it flowed into her nose via nasal prongs. She looked down and discovered it was her mother holding her hand, not Oliver. Her mom and Auntie Ellen were both there, both asleep.

What had happened to her? She couldn't remember a thing. She didn't feel hurt anywhere, so she couldn't have been in an accident, although her wrist felt a bit sore where it was bandaged. Whatever happened must have been serious. Perhaps she had a head injury, which must be why she couldn't remember. Her head really ached and she felt very drowsy.

The nurse who had been observing Zoe on the monitor from the nurse station turned and spoke to the two police officers.

'She's awake. I'll just page the doctor. He'll need to make sure she's fully orientated before you can proceed with an interview.'

Zoe squeezed her mother's hand and Georgia began to stir.

'Ouch,' Georgia said as she lifted her head off the bed and moved her stiff neck from side to side to loosen the tense muscles. 'I don't think it was a good idea to fall asleep in that position.'

Ellen woke as Georgia's voice penetrated her dream. Pity, it was a very nice dream. She had been quite enjoying throwing bread chunks to the ducks in Bakewell.

Georgia stood up, yawned and stretched both arms above her head before leaning forward to hug her daughter. She kissed Zoe lightly on the forehead then began gently stroking the young woman's cheek as tears of joy welled in her eyes.

'Don't cry, Mom. I'm okay. I feel tired and I have a headache, but otherwise I'm fine. What happened to me, anyway?'

'Don't you remember?'

'I don't remember anything,' she replied with a gentle shake of her head.

'Well, you were found in AMDAT Tower last night. Whatever did happen to you, I'm never letting you out of my sight again,' Georgia blubbered.

'Yes, you will,' Ellen said, as she stood on the other side of the bed, smiling down at Zoe.

'Where's Oliver, anyway? I thought it was him holding my hand.'

Georgia shrugged. She had no idea where Oliver was. Ellen didn't know either. They both presumed, or at least hoped, he was with his friends at the police station. Before they could discuss his whereabouts the doctor and two police officers entered the room. The doctor moved across to the bed and introduced himself to Zoe.

'I'm sorry to interrupt, ladies,' Doctor McDermott said, 'But these police officers insist that they speak to Miss Ashmore before she talks to anyone else.' Doctor McDermott then proceeded to flash the beam from his penlight into Zoe's eyes. Her pupils were both the same size and both reacted normally to the bright light. Next he checked that Zoe knew her full name, date of birth, home address, mobile number, the correct month and year and the name of the President. Lastly, he uncovered and checked the wound on her wrist before stepping back with a satisfied look on his face.

'There, she's all yours, officers. If Mum and Auntie can come with me, I'll take you both to the visitor lounge where you can get yourselves a nice strong cup of coffee. You both look like you could do with some caffeine.'

By late afternoon, most of Zoe's pathology tests had come back and she was cleared for discharge. Ellen and Georgia escorted her home. They remained unaware of Oliver's fate. They believed he was still being interviewed by the police along with the other teenagers. They had, after all, committed a number of offences. Georgia thought she might get charged for supplying Oliver with medications intended to sedate Vaughn Lambert, but with Zoe back safe and well even that impending problem could not dampen her mood.

ᗪᗝᗝᑕ

They arrived at Ellen's apartment to find Tony sitting on the couch next to Lauren. Baby Pat was asleep, she informed them. He'd been no trouble at all and had taken the expressed milk via the bottle like a champion. Ellen went across to her room to take a peek before Lauren intervened.

'He's only just gone back to sleep, Ellen, and your bedroom door has developed a dreadful creak. Give him a bit more time to fully settle.' Ellen backed away from the door and sat down.

'Tony has just been filling me in,' Lauren said. 'He was in on the raid last night but, of course, he couldn't tell us.'

'Oh, thank you so much for helping Zoe,' Georgia said.

'It wasn't just me,' he replied. 'I wasn't actually at the raid, just involved in the planning phase.'

'I don't understand,' Ellen said as her already tired and drawn face screwed up, producing even more wrinkles. She pointed her index finger from left to right as she slowly continued to speak. 'How and why does a detective from New Jersey end up planning a raid on AMDAT Tower in Melbourne on the other side of the world?'

Tony reached into his pocket and pulled out an envelope.

'Here,' he said, handing it over, 'why don't you read this? It might help to explain a few things.'

Ellen stared at the grubby envelope with her childhood home address handwritten across the front.

'Somebody has already opened it?'

'That would be me,' Tony replied. 'I thought the letter might contain information relevant to the investigation into the missing Jersey girls and, as it turned out, my instincts were correct.'

Ellen pulled out the letter and unfolded it. The handwriting was familiar, but she couldn't recall to whom it belonged.

'You don't have to read it out loud,' Georgia said with a pleading look that hoped for the complete opposite.

Ellen paused for a moment to check who the letter was from. 'How nice,' she said with a genuine sense of warmth. 'It's from old Doctor Dawson. I worked for him one summer, years ago. His scandal was such a shame; I really liked him. It's okay, Georgia; you can stop giving me those begging eyes. There's nothing that he could have to say that I wouldn't want any of you to hear.'

Georgia's face turned from pleading to smiling.

Ellen cleared her throat, took a sip of water and began to read:

Dear Ellen,
If you are reading this letter, I am no longer alive and it's high time you knew the truth.

   I was thirty-five years old when I started working at the IVF clinic and met your mother Beatrice. She was having difficulty conceiving. To gain background on Beatrice's case, I read her mother's file. Elaine had undertaken IVF unsuccessfully for years. My mentor, Doctor Hughes, had tried a new procedure ... cytoplasmic transfer. He used mitochondria from a second female to correct deficits in your grandmother's mitochondria. Doctor Hughes had used cytoplasmic transfer before, and sixteen healthy babies had been born. Elaine became pregnant after the first transfer and Beatrice arrived nine months later. She was baby number seventeen.

   Doctor Hughes explained to me that the scientific community became concerned that cytoplasmic transfer might cause genetic changes that could be passed on to future generations ... that the human germline could be permanently altered. Imagine his disappointment when, in 2002, the government withdrew all funding and banned the procedure.

I suspected that Beatrice had the same infertility issue as Elaine, so despite the ban, I used cytoplasmic transfer. It worked on the first transfer and you were conceived. I recorded the results but didn't tell anyone. Twenty years later I found out you were studying medicine, so one summer, I invited you to work at the clinic. On my suggestion you decided to harvest and store some of your ova.

Your friends Georgia and Frank Ashmore joined my IVF program that same summer. Frank was sterile, from chemotherapy to treat childhood leukaemia. I suspected that a mitochondrial defect with Georgia was also adding to their infertility. Although I should have sought the permission of all parties, I made a decision to use your ova as the third DNA donor and use cytoplasmic transfer.

In my lab, I noted that the cells divided more rapidly than when you were conceived. I was excited but knew I was acting illegally. I used your ova successfully with five other infertile couples that summer. I recorded my findings but didn't tell anyone what I had done. I closely followed the progress of the six children. I sent them all birthday cards and they often wrote back to me. Their health was exceptional and they all survived the 2064 pandemic.

Unfortunately, one girl was involved in a car accident and blood tests revealed the two sets of mitochondria. The authorities were called in to investigate. My medical licence was revoked and my reputation ruined. Despite everything, I still firmly believe that cytoplasmic transfer leads to humans with superior immune systems. My experiments supported this hypothesis but no-one was interested.

When I became ill, I decided to send my research to an Australian doctor. He had designed the insertion of the health chip and I felt that, in the future, Doctor Vaughn Lambert might find a use for my research. I hope that Doctor Lambert uses

the information to enhance the human germline. Humans need to evolve much faster to survive climate-change challenges, compete with superbugs and even populate other planets. I sincerely apologise for using your ova without your consent and I hope, dear Ellen, that you can find it in your heart to forgive me.
 Yours Sincerely,
 Keith Dawson

Ellen paused to reflect on the contents, then wafted the letter in the air as she addressed the group.

'You're right,' she said looking up at Tony. 'This letter does sort out quite a few issues, but it almost raises more questions than it answers. It most definitely points the finger in AMDAT's direction—and trust that bloody Lambert to be involved.'

'I know it will make more sense to you once we have the outcome of the AMDAT raid,' Tony replied. 'I do have a copy of the ledger with me and I'll show it to you later, but I really can't say anymore until we have all the facts, Ellen. In my opinion, Doctor Dawson was both grandiose and delusional if he thought sending his research logbook to Lambert was in any way a good idea.'

'Does that letter mean that you're actually related to me?' Zoe asked Ellen.

Ellen sensed that Georgia was a bit put out by the question. It was one thing to think of Ellen as her pretend auntie, and she was already aware that her beloved Frank wasn't Zoe's biological father. Ellen needed to tread carefully.

'In a biological sense I am related, but Georgia will always be your real mom. My egg was simply used to repair your mother's unhealthy egg, that's all.'

'I don't understand what that all means. It sounds like your egg was used, not mine,' Georgia replied with a worried expression.

'Well, in a way it was, Georgia.' Ellen paused to give herself time to think of a sensitive way to explain. 'Look, it is complex, but I'll try to explain how it works. Two eggs are harvested, one from the mother and one from the donor. The nucleus of both eggs is removed and the donor nucleus is destroyed. The mother's nucleus is then transferred into the donor's egg and then fertilised with the father's sperm. The nucleus is the most important part, Georgia, and Zoe has your nucleus. The nucleus determines what a person looks like and their personality. The mitochondria only contain a small number of genes compared with thousands in the nucleus. The mitochondria is best described as the energy supply or battery. Georgia's battery was faulty, so they replaced it with one of mine.'

'But what is this cytoplasmicish stuff, and what does it have to do with anything?' Georgia asked.

'I can answer that one,' interrupted Zoe. 'Cytoplasm is the jelly-like substance that contains both the nucleus and mitochondria. So they put your nucleus, Mom, into the cytoplasm that contained Auntie Ellen's mitochondria with her nucleus removed. That's why it's called cytoplasmic transfer. They just switched the nucleus.'

Zoe paused as if reflecting on this news. 'You know something, Auntie Ellen, in a way I already knew we were related. We've always had a very close bond. I can't think of anyone else whose extra DNA I would rather carry than yours.'

'Strangely, I think I knew it as well,' Georgia piped up. 'You two are just so alike and I've always thought Zoe had your ears.'

'You're so funny, Mom. The process wouldn't have any effect on my ears,' Zoe said with a giggle.

'I think she's right, though,' Lauren said as she scrutinised the two women closely. 'You two do have the same shaped ears.'

Everyone laughed.

A knock on the door interrupted them. Georgia leapt to her feet, opened the door and found herself face to face with Rob. Her smile morphed into a smirk.

'Oh, it's only you,' she said. 'Well, I guessed you'd show up sooner or later. Been hunter-gathering for more food, have we?

You've missed *all* the action and, *no* thanks to you, Zoe is home safe and well.'

Tony stood and turned towards Georgia, who appeared to have no intention of inviting Rob in.

'Actually, Georgia, Zoe may never have been found without Rob's help. It was Rob who first located her and who helped police to track the other teenagers' chips last night so that we could send police help to them,' he said.

Georgia looked gobsmacked and her face turned red.

'Can I come in now, Ms Georgia Ashmore?' Rob asked with a grin. Without waiting for a reply, he slipped under Georgia's outstretched arm that was blocking the doorway and seated himself with the other guests.

While everyone listened, Rob outlined how he had assisted the police.

'Every time we get more information, the pieces start to fall into place,' Ellen said. Here, Rob, read this letter.' Ellen held the letter out to him.

'Thanks, Ellen, I haven't read it, but I was filled in as to what it contains.

'Why would anyone tell you what was in a letter to me?' she asked.

'Well … as you've already heard, I informed the police that I'd tracked Zoe's chip to Level 41. I also told them about Georgia's theory—that Zoe's disappearance could be linked with the other Newark girls. The police then asked me to assist them to hack into AMDAT's core systems. When Detective Scallioni—Tony—found out I used to live with Ellen and Zoe and was now dating Anna, I mean Georgia, he felt the information in Ellen's letter might help me feel more comfortable about betraying the AMDAT Corporation. The letter certainly links Doctor Dawson to Vaughn Lambert and I can understand why he became the prime suspect in the disappearances of all the girls, including Zoe. As it turned out, Georgia's belief in a connection between the missing girls and AMDAT was spot on.'

As if on cue, Pat began crying. Ellen stood up and moved towards the bedroom door, eager to see and feed her son. His crying had triggered her milk to 'let down'.

'Wait for it, Ellen,' Lauren said, holding her hand up in a stop motion. 'I predict young Pat will stop crying right about … *now*,' she said dramatically.

Silence.

'O…kay,' Ellen paused. 'How did you do that?'

'Magic, Ellen, pure magic,' Lauren said, grinning mischievously.

A puzzled Ellen opened the bedroom door. Pat's baby face was peering at her over the back of a man's shoulder. He was sniffling and his little face moved up and down with the man's gentle bounce. She felt annoyed that Lauren had allowed a stranger near her baby and then she smelt the familiar odour of … Kouros aftershave. The same aftershave that …

The man turned to face her. Ellen couldn't believe who she was seeing. She braced herself against the wall.

'You're dead,' she said.

'Clearly I'm not,' Patrick replied.

'Oh God,' she gasped. 'Please tell me you haven't been watching any ViewTube clips lately.'

'Only the occasional porno clip. There was this really hot redhead a few weeks ago.'

Ellen couldn't maintain eye contact. She bowed her head and buried her face in her hands.

Patrick kissed his son on the forehead and laid him back in his cot. Then he moved across to Ellen, pulled her hands away from her face and wrapped them around his waist. He lifted her chin and looked into her eyes. Ellen's bottom lip began to tremble, and she started to cry.

'Shhhh … It's all going to be okay,' Patrick said as they hugged. 'I'm really sorry that you had to face everything on your own. I promise that, after tonight, I won't ever leave you alone again.'

Ellen held Patrick tightly—too tightly.

'Careful of my chest,' he grimaced. 'I suspect a couple of my ribs are broken.'

He breathed out hard to cope with the pain. After Pat was fed and changed the reunited couple lay down on her bed together, kissing and hugging until they both felt ready to rejoin the others.

Patrick and Ellen sat close together on the couch as he explained his role in the investigation to the group. Ellen hardly heard any of it. She was just so surprised to be sitting next to a man she thought was dead. She couldn't stop looking at him and kept touching him just to be sure he was real, as if at any moment he would vanish in a puff of smoke.

Georgia was just as perplexed and annoyed. She had been with Patrick on that fateful day and was positive he'd been blown into smithereens. She could have been trusted to keep her gob shut. She could have done without the shock of believing Patrick was blown up, and all those unnecessary police interviews where she was accused of murdering him. Not to mention the change of identity, even if it was only temporary. But then again, if it hadn't happened as it did, she wouldn't have met Rob. She just needed to focus on the fact that Patrick and Zoe were both alive and well. In the end, that was all that really mattered.

'Show Patrick the letter,' Georgia urged.

Ellen reached into her pocket and held it out to him.

'Oh, that letter,' he said. 'I've already read that.'

'Have you, now?' She turned and faced Tony. 'Is there anyone who hasn't read my private correspondence?'

'I don't think the drug squad have,' Tony offered.

'Yes, they have,' Patrick said, nodding his head.

'What about the marine division?'

'Yep, they circulated it at their last meeting,' Tony replied.

The two men started laughing and Ellen raised her eyebrows.

'Okay, you two, stop pulling my leg.'

'All jokes aside Ellen, if you come into the kitchen, I'll show you the ledger,' Tony said. 'It's very interesting and will help you to understand why I felt the need to open and read your private correspondence.'

Ellen understood why Tony was reluctant to discuss the ledger in the group situation. It did after all contain private and confidential information.

Together they combed through the pages that related to Ellen. Finding out that she was biologically related to the five missing girls was quite a shock. But an even bigger shock was the realisation that a DW ... Daniel Ward, was the biological father of both the dead girl, Bridget, and Zoe. Ellen completely understood why Tony had wanted to keep this information from Zoe—for now at least.

'I think Zoe needs to be fully recovered before she has anymore shocks, don't you?' he said. Ellen agreed.

The gathering of the lost and found continued well into the night. The reunited group of friends traded raid stories and caught up on the last six months. They sent out for gourmet food, more champagne and bottles of cabernet sauvignon. Hangovers and sleep-ins all round tomorrow.

Let them have fun, Tony thought. By tomorrow Oliver's body would have been formally identified and his next of kin notified. Zoe would need to be informed that Daniel Grant was her biological father before DNA testing revealed it anyway. That revelation would not be an easy pill for any of the women to swallow. At least Patrick and Ellen had already processed that one. The way forward was not going to be smooth, but until then everyone deserved some downtime.

The theory of natural selection is grounded on the belief that each new variety, and ultimately each new species, is produced and maintained by having some advantage over those with which it comes into competition; and the consequent extinction of the less-favoured forms almost inevitably follows.

CHARLES DARWIN
"ON THE ORIGIN OF SPECIES"

75

One month later, social media platforms showed a world divided over what to do with the hybrid children. An emergency meeting of the World Health Board recommended that all children with bat mitochondria in their DNA be located and terminated. They were considered a threat to the 'purity' of the human race. Human rights campaigners, including Mindy, had intervened to save them.

Kasey was the only girl who chose to remain in Australia. She gave a compelling speech in defence of the hybrids to the World Health Board.

'These children didn't ask to be genetically engineered. Humans designed them and, as the biological mother of many of them, I must also be held responsible for giving them life. It is up to me to protect these children, regardless of their DNA. Someone needs to embrace, love and care for them despite their differences. I implore everyone else to do the same. To destroy them is to commit murder and I, for one, am not prepared to have their blood on my hands.'

A human rights court case was under way to decide if the hybrids had the same rights as humans, or if they should be classified as a new species. It was still not known if they could breed or interbreed. However, their reproductive organs were found to be intact. If the current case failed to allow legal termination of the hybrids, a state-enforced sterilisation case was already in the pipeline.

Locating all the children was proving difficult. Gum had ensured many of the records were destroyed. The designer babies all belonged to wealthy families and, having paid between one and twelve million dollars per baby, the families had no intention of giving them up without a fight. Those who had been found and assessed were all normal happy kids. They had all required excess flesh to be removed from between their digits, but they fought off human pathogens with an almost constant basal temperature of forty degrees Celsius.

DNA profiling showed the children all carried at least one strand of the CCR5 Delta 32 gene passed down through the centuries from ancestors who had survived the bubonic plague pandemic.

The community was polarised. Many people believed that altering the human germline had been a positive step for humanity. Was Lambert a bastard or a genius? Or was he simply a mad scientist? Was this a backward or a progressive step? Some even suggested that the professor had just sped up an evolutionary process that was simply too slow to compete with rapidly evolving superbugs.

Like the slippery eel that many of his students knew him to be, Lambert slithered out of all charges.

Georgia was horrified. 'How can they not lock him up for life?' she had said on hearing the news. 'Can't they see that he's the one behind this whole operation?'

'People only see what they want to see, Georgia,' Rob had told her. 'Even blindness is a commodity that, for enough money, can be bought.' He had also found the outcome disappointing.

In the confession that Gum left behind, she took full responsibility for the destruction of the IVF clinic and the murder of Patrick O'Connor. She confessed to the religious brainwashing of the New Jersey girls and claimed to have reprogrammed AMDAT's droids into killing machines. She had been adamant she acted alone, and that Lambert and Grant were unaware of her actions.

Lambert stated that all the young women had happily lived at the tower and had freely given their ova to science. He had been honoured to father their children. Lambert was adamant he was not involved in the death of the New Jersey woman.

'I have no knowledge whatsoever of a Bridget Patterson, let alone how the poor woman died.'

Without any proof, once again, he avoided conviction.

Lambert insisted that the breeding of bats with humans was '... a unique research project that I never expected to work. Believe me, I was *just* as surprised as the rest of you that the embryos thrived.'

In the current climate of pandemics and rapidly mutating microbes, few could argue that his intentions weren't for the good of the human race. In any case, the original illegal cytoplasmic transfer experiments were undertaken by a deceased American doctor, not by him. Once again, the charges fell away. He was labelled 'Professor Teflon' as each and every allegation he encountered failed to gain traction. Nothing stuck. Kenneth's lawyers had ensured all additional charges against Daniel Grant were dropped, and in no time at all the two AMDAT executives were back in control.

Despite the legal system failing to gain any convictions, the public backlash had begun. AMDAT's reputation began to slide from the high moral ground it had once enjoyed into the murky swamps below. No amount of spin could hide the ever-widening cracks. It was only a matter of time before systemic changes would be forced upon them.

Daniel had kept his word and hadn't spoken with either Ellen or Francis since the day of his arrest. He had refused to take any of their calls. Once Daniel was properly medicated with lithium, his mood stabilised and he became his usual reclusive self. He settled back into his old life at AMDAT.

Margaret wasn't accused of anything. When you're the daughter of a billionaire you don't give more than one police interview in the company of the finest barristers in the country. AMDAT was proof that, with enough power and money, anything, no matter how unethical or illegal, could be made to simply 'go away'. Any remaining loose ends—including the death of Oliver—were blamed on Susie Long. Within twenty-four hours of the raid she was found hanging in Gum's apartment. 'Suicide' was the coroner's finding. No suspicious circumstances. He speculated on two probable causes for her actions: guilt from killing Oliver—ballistics had matched the rounds found in Oliver's body to her weapon—or grief from the death of her life partner Gum Lin.

'No suspicious circumstances,' Ellen said as she repeated the reporter's words verbatim. 'What an absolute *fucking* load of crap.'

She snatched the remote from Patrick and the screen went blank. 'If I have to listen to anymore lies, I'll lose my breakfast.' She tossed her bowl into the sink and stormed out of the room.

Zoe, on the other hand, was a complete mess. Ellen and Georgia had banned her from surfing the internet. She had no hope of defending herself against the tsunami of negative comments designed to destroy her. Few people believed that Zoe couldn't recall anything that happened to her during those missing three days, or that she didn't consent to being with Vaughn on Level 41. Her reputation was trashed at each and every turn.

Students came forth to sign statements that Zoe had gone willingly to Lambert's apartment on a number of occasions and had once become so drunk she had stayed overnight. Several other men claimed that she often become intoxicated and flirty at the Friday gatherings. One-night stands were her normal habit. Anyway, didn't she live with that doctor woman who screwed Daniel Grant and nearly broke up his marriage? Hadn't everyone watched slutty Ellen Hancock seduce and attempt to destroy one of Australia's most eminent scientists? No doubt the 'witnesses' were given financial incentives, but naturally no monies were ever traced. The all too common trial by social media destroyed Zoe's reputation. To those who didn't know her she was nothing more than a lying whore.

As the days rolled by, Zoe sank into a deep depression. She was upset to discover that Daniel Grant was her biological father, and that she had been tricked by Maggie and Daniel into donating her ova. The couple had never intended to have a child by IVF. The plan all along had been to give her ova to Lambert for use in his sick experiments. But Zoe had no proof of this deception. Margaret Grant's lawyers had produced the consent to extract ova and Margaret claimed that, once the couple found out Zoe was Daniel's biological daughter, the ova were used in research, as authorised by the contract she had signed. Zoe had simply failed to read the small print.

Zoe was furious with Margaret and Daniel Grant.

'I don't care about the blood that runs through my veins, Mom. Frank will always be my one and only father. I want nothing to do with that liar Daniel Grant. I never want to see or speak to him or Maggie again as long as I live.' Then she pulled the bedcovers back over her head and the sobbing started again.

Zoe's heart had been broken when she learned of Oliver's death. The online criticism only added to her despair. She had barely eaten since the crisis. Kobi, Aiza, Felix and Charlie had visited a number of times, but had been unable to rally her.

'We all know the truth,' Kobi had said as the five of them sat together in Ellen's apartment. They were all finding it hard to believe how widely such unfounded lies could circulate. 'If we take this shit on board, we'll only hurt ourselves. You can't convince fools to change their minds.'

Aiza smiled at Kobi as she spoke, and then added her own advice.

'We just have to let go and move forward with our lives. Control our own thoughts. Keep them as positive as we can. That's really all we can do. We can't control the thoughts of others.'

Charlie and Felix nodded. They remained traumatised after their own brush with death and having witnessed Oliver's murder. They were both receiving counselling. The police had dropped all charges against the teenagers.

Zoe was grateful for her friends' help and everyone assured her the pain of losing Oliver would diminish. Regardless, she felt like her soul had been ripped from her body and she wished her life would end. Georgia stayed with her day and night to ensure she didn't have the opportunity to harm herself. Ellen was also attentive to Zoe's health. The young woman was fragile and vulnerable. The past could not be changed. Helping Zoe to learn to live with what had happened and move forward was imperative.

Francis had contacted Ellen after he received positive confirmation that he was indeed Daniel's biological father. He hoped to reunite with his son but, for the moment at least, Daniel was avoiding him. Margaret had spoken with Mindy on Daniel's behalf and asked her to pass on a message to Francis.

'Daniel doesn't want a reunion to take place, now or in the future. Daniel and I are fully focused on the most important things—repairing our marriage and getting AMDAT back on track.'

It appeared Daniel Grant wanted to put everything he had experienced with Ellen and Francis behind him, as if none of it had ever happened. Ellen struggled to understand his attitude. She felt betrayed. Despite Daniel refusing to take her calls, she hoped one day to talk to him. She wanted to understand how he could have put his own daughter in harm's way. She was angry he had manipulated Zoe into donating precious ova just to foster an illegal, unethical and dangerous research program. Why would he do such a thing?

Ellen would have liked to find closure with Daniel, but was more than satisfied that Patrick—the love of her life—was alive. The Huntington's cloud had finally been lifted. They looked forward to a long life together raising their son.

Even though his son had been found and then lost again, Francis was hoping to at least meet his granddaughter. He was sad to hear how unwell Zoe was. He and Mindy invited everyone to visit the desert community and to stay for as long as they liked. Ellen decided that a change of scenery might do them all good. Tony and Lauren would be returning to New Jersey next week and they were keen to see the community, so they all accepted the kind invitation. Looking forward to the visit, Francis and Mindy immediately began planning a desert feast in honour of their new-found granddaughter. They hoped that Zoe and Georgia might even consider staying with them until the young woman fully recovered.

The group had been at NATGRID East for only a couple of days before Zoe began to show signs of improvement. She'd recognised Mindy as the woman she had seen at the protest march outside AMDAT Tower all those months ago. Mindy was a colourful character and a passionate advocate of human rights. Zoe enjoyed checking out all her protest images and media releases. Mindy was truly an inspiration.

Mindy's nephew Dorak was only two years older than Zoe. His mother—Mindy's sister Rachel—had been taken by the pandemic. Dorak was a quiet, intelligent, softly spoken young man. He had taken Zoe under his wing, showing her around and outlining the philosophy behind NATGRID. Zoe had begun to rethink many of her own belief systems in the light of the community that her grandfather and Mindy had designed.

The desert feast had been fantastic. The homemade cider had everyone chirpy and the roasted food didn't disappoint. Impromptu performances followed. Trent and his recycling mates played on mass digeridoos, while Scout beat out a rather strange rhythm on his homemade kettledrum. Mason sang bush ballads with Mindy. Travis told a scary ghost story that had everyone laughing instead of being spooked. Skye taught Lauren a few traditional dance moves and Lauren showed the younger kids how to do cartwheels and backflips. The festivities lasted well past midnight.

The next morning, Ellen heard Zoe vomiting in the bathroom. Ellen knocked on the door and called out, 'are you okay in there?'

Zoe came out a few moments later. 'I'm fine.'

'I didn't think you had that much to drink,' Ellen said.

'It has nothing to do with alcohol. I know exactly what the problem is.'

Zoe paused and took in a deep breath then looked directly at Ellen. 'I'm pregnant.'

'But I thought the doctor was checking your bloods regularly, to make sure your hormones had normalised? A pregnancy would have been detected weeks ago.'

'It was. I've known I was pregnant for some time. Apart from any formal pregnancy test, I haven't had a period since before the incident.'

'Does your Mom know?'

'No-one knows.'

'Well surely you aren't going to keep it?'

'I know you mean well Ellen, but I'm not a child anymore. I've been through a lot these past few weeks. Oliver is dead, but I think I'm carrying his baby.' Ellen now understood Zoe's dilemma. With Oliver dead she wouldn't want to forego her only chance at having his child. But had the young woman considered that Oliver might not be the father?

'There's no need to look so concerned Ellen. I'm fully aware that it could be someone else's, or … something not totally human. Don't you think I haven't already thought of that?'

76

Ellen made it clear to Zoe that she needed to consider termination as soon as possible if she wanted it to be an option. While Zoe had been enthusiastic about carrying Oliver's child, she was concerned at the prospect of Vaughn being the father or something far worse. On hearing news of her dilemma, Francis decided to invite Zoe's girlfriends Kobi and Aiza to stay for the weekend. All the adults in his granddaughter's life had been offering her advice and he and Mindy felt that she needed the perspectives of her younger set before she could make such an important decision. DNA testing was another possibility to help her decide, but Zoe would need to consent to specialist testing of the embryo by a trusted laboratory—

definitely not AMDAT. She was considering this course of action, but it would be very costly and not without risk.

Kobi lay on her stomach at the bottom of Zoe's bed with her ankles crossed and her legs swinging back and forth, listening to her friend throw up in the bathroom.

'I know what decision I'd be making if I was as sick as you,' she called out. 'You're a terrible colour and that's the third time you've spewed in the last fifteen minutes.'

'I do understand your point of view,' Zoe said as she returned and climbed back onto the bed. 'I've heard it all before. I'm young, with my whole life in front of me, rah rah rah. But you're not in my shoes, Kobes; it's a really hard decision.' Zoe paused mid-sentence to run to the bathroom and throw up again.

The sound of vomiting finally put Aiza off her blueberry smoothie. She placed it on the bedside table and spoke up. 'I think that we should just work through the alternatives one by one and examine the pros and cons until your decision becomes clear. Although you're young, having a baby at your age isn't the end of the world, and you do have a very supportive family—and us.' She held her arms open and looked directly at Kobi for a response.

'Aiza, you're so measured and logical about everything. I'd just get rid of it. It wasn't planned and Vaughn might be its father. Zoe would never be rid of him if that was the case.'

'Well, it isn't an it and it's not our decision. Our job this weekend is to help Zoe make the right decision for her—not the right decision for us.'

Zoe smiled at Aiza as she headed once again to the bathroom. She brushed her teeth and washed her face before returning to continue the discussion.

'I think I like Aiza's plan. Let's go with that.'

Kobi decided to get the ball rolling with a question. 'Okay, would you want to keep the child if Oliver is the father?'

'Yes, definitely,' Zoe answered without hesitation. 'It would be a child conceived in love by the man I miss every day.' Her eyes flooded with tears. There was a short pause as she blew her nose and composed herself before continuing. 'I expect his parents would be very supportive. They would probably be more than happy to help me raise their grandchild.'

Aiza posed the next question. 'What if *Vaughn* turns out to be the father?'

Zoe took in a deep breath then expelled the air rapidly between her lips. 'Well, that would be a bit trickier,' she said.

Kobi frowned and shook her head in disbelief. 'That would be more than a bit trickier. What if Vaughn convinced the courts that you consented to sexual relations with him? He could be granted access. You might have to share the child with Vaughn for *the rest ... of ... your ... life.*'

'Well, at least until one of us dies,' Zoe added.

Kobi rolled her eyes and let out a whimsical sigh.

Zoe looked from one friend to the other. 'Regardless of whether the baby is Oliver's or Vaughn's, or, God forbid anyone else's— which doesn't even bear thinking about—there's one thing I do know.'

'What's that?' the girls asked in unison.

'I'm the baby's mother, and I don't think I can kill my own child regardless of who the father is. It isn't the child's fault. Why should an innocent child be punished?'

A smug look crossed Kobi's face. 'What if you're not the biological mother? What then?'

'I think I'd have to be biologically related, wouldn't I?'

'Not if you've been impregnated with a designer embryo. The child might be no relation to you *whatsoever.* It could even be a hybrid baby. It is Vaughn we're discussing here and that fruitcake

Gum. They both have—or in her case had—the potential to do something that warped.'

'I agree, but I doubt they did. They only had a three-day window. It's highly unlikely. I slept with Oliver quite a few times before I was abducted. The child is most likely his.'

'Anyway, if Zoe isn't biologically related to the baby she wouldn't have to keep the child, would she?' Aiza added.

'Valid point,' Kobi acknowledged.

'So have we all circled around back to me being the mother regardless of who the father is?'

'It appears so.'

⋈⋈⋈

By Monday morning Zoe had decided that she would keep the baby. She was the child's mother and it was her responsibility to provide all the love and care he or she needed. Naturally she hoped the child was Oliver's. That would be the best outcome for everyone who had loved him.

Zoe made an appointment to see an obstetrician in two weeks. Her mother and Ellen would accompany her to provide support. In the meantime, she was enjoying the rest at NATGRID East and wasn't ready to go home anytime soon.

⋈⋈⋈

Doctor Marilyn Kyte slid the scanning wand across Zoe's stomach. Immediately, Ellen and Marilyn saw the unexpected contents of the teenager's womb. They glanced at each other before Doctor Kyte broke the news to Zoe and Georgia.

'Twins.'

'You're expecting twins, Zoe.'

Zoe looked stunned. Georgia didn't speak. She just looked towards Ellen for guidance.

'I really think that you should check the twins' DNA, Zoe. What do you think?' Ellen asked.

'No,' said Zoe emphatically. 'I want to stick to my original plan. My mind is made up. Anyway, I'm sure that the child—children—will be Oliver's. I just know they will be. They simply have to be.'

77

Vaughn sat in his rocker recliner, smoking a cigar and surfing through the zones of his elaborate camera surveillance system. He looked quite unkempt. His hair was uncombed and greasy and he sported a five-day growth on his normally clean-shaven chin. The AMDAT Corporation had required him to step down from lecturing. Although Vaughn had managed to avoid any charges, the community weren't buying his total innocence. AMDAT was deep in damage control. More than fifty companies had already withdrawn funding and many more were expected to follow. The government had immediately introduced tighter licensing measures and monthly facility inspections. Ethical approval pathways were strengthened and all embryonic experimentation banned until further notice. Kenneth had suggested to Vaughn that he take at least a year off. Find something else to keep him occupied for twelve months or so, just until all the fuss died down.

Vaughn ignored the knocking on his apartment door. Kenneth waited a few moments then entered without invitation. He was worried about Vaughn and wanted to check on him. The room was thick with smoke and for one brief moment Kenneth thought there was a fire. He quickly determined the smoke was emanating from a cigar.

'Pppfftt … you'll set the fire alarm off,' he said, coughing and wafting the smoke away from his face with both hands.

'I've disabled it.'

'I didn't even know that you smoked.'

'Only after sex,' he answered, grinning.

At that moment Kiera came out of the bedroom. She was one of Vaughn's regular sex workers—from the same agency Kenneth sourced his.

'Hi, Mr Stuart.'

'Hello, Kiera; you're looking well.'

'You too, Mr Stuart.'

Kiera turned to Vaughn. 'Same time next week?'

'No, I'm going away for a while. I'll give the agency a call when I get back.'

'Okay … well, enjoy yourself and I'll wait to hear from you.'

She held her mobile next to Vaughn's. There was a ding signalling a successful financial transfer.

'Thanks,' she said.

'See you later, Mr Stuart.'

Kiera slung her brown leather bag over her shoulder and sauntered towards the lift. Her long jet-black hair lapped against the waistband of her tight blue jeans. Kenneth's eyes lingered on her until the lift doors closed, then he turned his attention back to Vaughn.

'Have you checked out the offers yet?' Kenneth asked.

Vaughn didn't reply. He wiggled his index finger up and down in the direction of one of the surveillance screens.

'See that storeroom? It gets more action than me these days.'

Kenneth looked up. A couple of researchers were locked in a passionate embrace between the test tubes and the microscopes.

Without commenting, Kenneth continued to press Vaughn. 'Have you even read them?'

'Nope,' Vaughn answered in a clipped manner that emphasised the *p* sound.

Kenneth picked up the folders on the coffee table.

'Let's go through them together, then, shall we?'

Vaughn didn't reply, so Kenneth proceeded anyway.

'Space Genesis looks okay. Apparently procreation on Mars is only about a decade or so away and all the embryos must be genetically engineered and screened here on Earth. They want you to undertake research to determine the effects of zero gravity on embryonic development. How does that sound?'

'Bor...ing. I'm not interested,' Vaughn responded.

'Okay. What about the offer to set up a CRISPR program in South Africa to increase the elimination rate of inherited diseases? You would have to agree that project would be very good for your public image.'

'I like my image just the way it is,' Vaughn replied, as he yawned and took another drag on his cigar.

Kenneth started to speak before Vaughn butted in.

'Save your breath. I've already accepted an offer.'

'Who with? Doing what?'

'I'm leaving for North Korea next week. I'll be setting up a presidential IVF laboratory. Apparently there are some royal infertility issues that no-one has been able to overcome. Unlimited budget, suite in the palace grounds and free rein to do whatever experimentation I desire.'

The furrows on Kenneth's forehead deepened as a look of concern washed across his face.

'You'll need to be very careful, Vaughn. Cross the North Korean president and you might never be seen again.'

'I can look after myself,' Vaughn replied dismissively. 'I've been doing so for as long as I can remember.'

'I know you can, but there are very strict codes of behaviour in North Korea and you won't have the same legal rights as you have here. You will need to behave yourself—and no womanising.'

Vaughn flicked his hand dismissively in Kenneth's direction.

'I'm not *stupid*. Stop worrying.'

'Well, keep in touch and don't outstay your welcome. You are needed here, you know.'

Kenneth turned to leave. 'Oh … by the way, Maggie was talking to Louise Stuart the other day. Apparently Zoe Ashmore is pregnant with twins.'

'Twins,' Vaughn replied. 'Are you sure it's twins?'

'Yes.'

'Well, that's the most interesting news I've had all week.'

78

Zoe's labour was expected to be complex. Doctor Marilyn Kyte would have preferred to undertake a caesarean section, but with the reduced effectiveness of antibiotics she hoped a natural birth was achievable. Zoe knew the twins were boys. Their gender had been difficult to conceal from a medical student watching an ultrasound. Marilyn had refused to take on Zoe's case unless she consented to undertake all routine obstetric testing, including fetal DNA. Doctor Kyte wanted to avoid any surprises, even if the young mother chose to remain ignorant.

Ellen and Marilyn both knew what was to come. Zoe had given consent for Doctor Kyte to discuss her case with Ellen but no-one else, especially not her mother. Georgia was a total basket case from the minute Zoe's pregnancy was announced. She couldn't even follow the instructions of a simple bootie knitting pattern, and had unpicked them at least five times.

Dorak, on the other hand, had been terrific. It was obvious he had feelings for Zoe but she seemed oblivious to them. He fussed around, making sure she had everything she needed, cooking anything she desired to meet her endless cravings and massaging her back and feet as the due date drew near. Everyone but Zoe knew he was completely besotted with her.

The day of the delivery had started out quite normally. Dorak had popped in with freshly cooked blueberry bagels to give her breakfast in bed. He had been sitting on the lounge chair next to Zoe, watching the morning news show, when her labour pains began. For the last three months Francis had kept his private helicopter fully fuelled and on standby. Within fifteen minutes they were in the air, headed for St Julia's maternity hospital.

At precisely six that evening the first little chap was born. Marilyn announced that he was in fact Oliver Adams's son. With this information Zoe named him Oliver Frank Ashmore-Adams.

Around thirty minutes later the second baby boy slid into the world. The theatre went quiet. It was as if everyone had been left mute. The medical staff just stared at the infant and waited for someone else to take the lead. One staff member let out a nervous giggle before excusing herself and leaving the room.

The silence was suddenly broken by the piercing screams of the newborn. Marilyn lifted the crying infant onto his mother's chest. He looked nothing like his brother Oliver. He was larger, paler in colour and had small webbed fingers. Zoe was completely overwhelmed. She didn't speak, but began whimpering. Not one to cope well with surprises, Georgia took one look at her grandson and fainted.

Ellen had been planning for this moment since Marilyn had shown her the DNA test results. It was one thing to plan, but another to watch the perplexed expression wash across Zoe's face. Ellen had hoped to offer comfort and reassurance that everything would be okay. Now that the actual moment had arrived, she was, for once, speechless.

As well intentioned as Zoe had been, she had never really anticipated that her babies could be hybrids. Once baby Oliver was born it seemed only logical that her first love would be the father of both infants.

Zoe trembled as she continued to peer down at the baby boy in her arms. Finally, she spoke. Her voice quivered.

'Is it mine?'

'Yes, Zoe, you're his biological mother,' Marilyn replied.

'Is Vaughn its father?'

'The biological father's DNA file is locked. Now that your son is a live birth, I can request that the file be opened and the information released for you to place on his birth certificate.'

'Okay. How long will that take?'

'I'll complete the e-forms today, but it generally takes a week for them to be processed.'

Attempting to move Zoe's thoughts in another direction, Marilyn asked. 'Do you have a name in mind?'

'I'm not naming him until I know exactly who his father is.'

'Fair enough.'

'Could someone please take it away.'

Marilyn looked over to Ellen with her eyebrows raised and handed her the baby. Ellen looked down at his small pale face. His tiny oval eyes stared back at her. He appeared to be checking her out. After a few moments his face screwed up and turned a bright red as he began screaming loudly once again.

Georgia had regained consciousness and was sitting on a chair with her head between her legs. An orderly fanned her with a folder and a nurse was encouraging her to drink some water. Her face was white. Georgia took one sip then immediately threw up. The nurse escorted her from the room: she was of no use to anyone in her current state.

Daniel looked down at the mobile vibrating in his hand. It was a private number and usually he would ignore it. Something, intuition perhaps, made him say *Accept*. He placed the device to his ear and heard a familiar voice.

'Daniel?'

'Ellen?'

After a short pause he continued, 'How are you?'

'I've been better, but this is not a social call.'

'Is everything okay? You sound upset.'

'I am upset ... very upset.'

'What's wrong with you?'

'There's nothing wrong with me Daniel ... it's Zoe.'

'What's happened to Zoe? Maggie did tell me she was pregnant. Has she had the babies? Are they all okay?'

'Zoe has just given birth to twin boys and one is a hybrid, as if you didn't already know.'

'Oh.'

'Is that all you can say ... *Oh!*'

'I don't know what else to say. I'm shocked.'

'*Really?* ... You're shocked. Well, how do think Zoe is feeling right now?'

'You don't think I had anything to do with this, do you?'

'Well, did you?'

'No! I would never hurt Zoe. She's a part of you and me, Ellen. A really good part.'

'I don't want to go there, Daniel. We had our time and now it's over. You threw us away the night you stopped talking to me. The night I found out exactly what sort of man you really are.'

'I'm sorry I hurt you, Ellen, but thinking we could be together wasn't realistic. It was never going to happen.'

'Well, I wish you'd figured that out before you made the promises you did. Anyway, I didn't call to discuss the past; it's the future that's important now. I'm only calling because I need you to fast-track something for Zoe.'

'You know I'll do anything to help her. Tell me what you need.'

'The hybrid twin's paternal file is locked. I need the DNA file unlocked, Daniel. I need the file unlocked *today*! Zoe needs answers, and she's far too distressed to wait seven days.'

'Okay. What's the file code?'

Ellen read it out. There was a short pause before Daniel responded.

'That's Vaughn's.'

'I thought as much. That man is pure evil, Daniel, and you and Maggie are not much better.'

'I don't know anything about this, Ellen. Please believe me.'

'*Believe you!* I will never believe anything you tell me ever again.'

'Okay … I can tell you're very angry at the moment, so I'll go now. Please take care.'

'Care of what, Daniel? The mess you and that insane bastard have put us in?'

Daniel started to speak but Ellen had already hung up. She was simply too furious to continue the conversation. She didn't know what she ever saw in him, and to think that all these years she had put him up on a pedestal like some bloody god.

Zoe tried to be a mother to both boys but it was clear she had only bonded with baby Oliver. On hearing the child was Vaughn's, she named him Vincent. She wasn't sure what surname to use, but still had time to consider her options. Within twenty-four hours she said Vincent wasn't breastfeeding properly and he was placed on the bottle. She wouldn't hold Vincent for more than a few minutes and kept leaving him to cry in his cot.

'It's called controlled crying, Ellen.'

It was clear by the end of the first week that Zoe found Vincent repugnant. The situation couldn't be allowed to continue. Ellen decided to convene a meeting to discuss the problem with Georgia, Francis, his daughter Louise and son-in-law Dale and his wife Mindy. Dorak said he was happy to stay with Zoe until they returned.

'I've invited you all here to discuss what we can do to support Zoe and ensure that Vincent isn't neglected. We all know that depriving a child of physical affection can lead to permanent psychological damage and simply being a hybrid will be tough enough.'

'She'll warm to him, won't she?' Georgia asked.

'I don't think that she will. Zoe's a kid herself, and she seems to have rejected Vincent. We could send him to his father, but he's rumoured to be in North Korea of all places. Despite Zoe's lack of affection for the infant I don't think she would be agreeable. After all, she's still his mother.'

The whole room erupted with objections at the mere suggestion of giving custody of Vincent to Vaughn.

'Dale and I would like to take him.' Louise looked towards her husband. 'We've been giving this a lot of thought since you called this meeting. The thing is, Holly is a hybrid so if we raise Vincent as her brother then at least they will have each other. Our friends have been quite strange since Holly was born. Most of the play dates I've arranged have been cancelled at the last minute, and when I took her to a mother's group one anxious woman grabbed every toy that Holly touched and cleaned them all vigorously with alcohol wipes. It was as if she thought her child might turn into a bat if she swallowed any of Holly's saliva. I found it most uncomfortable. I'm still breastfeeding Holly, so I could wet-nurse Vincent as well. It wouldn't take long for my milk supply to increase. The hybrids are different, and we all know that society doesn't like different. If Holly and Vincent have each other, then at least they can be different together. They can look into someone else's eyes and see the same shape as their own.'

Louise became quite emotional. It was clear that raising a hybrid was not what she'd expected. Dale put his arm around his wife and Francis came across and gave his daughter a hug.

'That's a really generous offer. It has my approval, but in the end it's up to Zoe.'

The proposal was outlined to Zoe, who agreed. Louise and Dale were her relatives and it would be good for Holly. And so Vincent was to be raised with Holly, Louise and Dale. Big brother Sam was quite excited at the prospect. He thought having two hybrid siblings would be cool. Vincent couldn't be formally adopted because that would require Vaughn Lambert's consent, but Zoe and Oliver could visit him whenever they chose.

The next three years flew by. Holly and Vincent not only survived, they thrived. They were highly intelligent and physically strong, reaching all the standard milestones months before expected. Their future, however, was full of unknowns.

Melbourne
New Year's Day, 2078

79

Ellen's extended family, including her brother James and his wife Joanne, gathered at her apartment to celebrate New Year's Day. Patrick had boned and stuffed the large trout he'd caught at Lake Toolondo a month earlier. Rob and Georgia had prepared a number of delicious salads and Mindy had made an enormous tiramisu and a mixed-berry pie. Louise and Dale had arrived with lots of chocolates and other delicious homemade treats and Francis had brought some rather nice bottles of wine from his extensive personal wine cellar.

'I've been saving these for a very special occasion,' he had told them proudly as he wiped the dust off the labels with a damp cloth.

Rob and Patrick were looking up each of the vintages on the net and from the excited sounds they were making were most impressed with his offerings. They selected a bottle of red, opened it and set it aside to breathe.

As usual, Ellen was organising everyone.

'Just put the two trestle tables together please Dorak; if you gather up all the chairs you can find, along with the folding ones under my bed, we should have enough.'

Dorak smiled at Zoe then went off on the chair hunt.

'Smells good,' Zoe said as she sat on the floor with Louise and Sam playing with the four children. The coffee table had been set up for the kids with lots of healthy snacks for them to nibble on. Regardless, Holly kept asking for the chocolates she knew her mother had brought to the party.

'After lunch you can have a chocolate,' Louise said. 'Just eat a few more of the non-sugary things first. Okay?'

Holly pulled a grumpy face that showed her mother that 'No', in her opinion, it was not okay. She wanted chocolate right now.

'I'm in charge,' she yelled at the top of her voice.

'Not today, little Miss Bossy Boots,' said Dale. Holly's face crumpled and the tears that followed indicated that the end of the world was clearly imminent.

Further screams rang out. Ellen looked up just as young Pat snatched his toy cars from Oliver and ran off to his room to hide them. Sharing—something else to work on.

As Zoe watched Vincent playing, she wondered if she had made the right decision, allowing Louise to mother him. A red-eyed Oliver looked quite left out as Holly and Vincent chattered away to each other. They were close.

Over the years her memory had provided some insight into those missing three days. She had remembered being in an operating theatre, which was when they must have undertaken the embryonic transfer. She had a vague recollection of Vaughn being sexually inappropriate with her and she shuddered to think what might have occurred. 'Not today,' she said to herself, breathing in deeply and out slowly. 'Remember to focus only on the moment. Not the past. Not the future.'

'Focus on the here and now, Zoe. That's the secret to happiness,' her therapist had stressed at each visit.

Zoe snapped back into the present as the vid-link commenced beeping. The large screen filled with the image of Tony standing next to a heavily pregnant Lauren. The couple were expecting their second child any day now.

Patrick raced over to talk to them. 'Hope you two are geared up for another few years without sleep,' he said, laughing.

Rob and Patrick chatted to them until Ellen signalled with two loud claps that lunch was now served.

The meal was scrumptious. The wines lived up to everyone's expectations and Holly eventually stuffed her face with chocolates. Her little pink cheeks were now smeared with what looked like dried brown paint that crinkled every time she laughed.

A midmorning shower had settled the city dust and refreshed the surrounding gardens. It was a warm sunny day, so after lunch they decided to go down to the local park for a game of cricket. As Ellen watched her extended family enjoying the day, she wondered when would be a good time to give Zoe the letter. Vaughn had almost been forgotten. Then, last week, a letter had arrived. It was addressed to Ms Zoe Ashmore and looked rather official. Zoe was no longer living with Ellen so, thinking it might be important, she had opened it.

No-one had heard from Vaughn for three years. Then out of the blue he'd formally applied for access to his son Vincent. Just when Zoe was becoming emotionally strong, Vaughn had popped up with the potential to wreck her life yet again. Louise and Zoe would be devastated. Without mentioning the letter to anyone, Ellen had slipped it into the kitchen drawer. *We will take on this fight later*, she had decided, not wanting to spoil the upcoming family gathering.

New Year's lunch was a roaring success. Ellen couldn't recall feeling as happy and satisfied as she did that evening. Once everyone had left, she poured herself a drink and began to tidy up. Ellen quite enjoyed cleaning up after a successful function. She didn't drink much during an event but then always had a few while she washed the dishes. As she polished the crystal wine glasses her thoughts drifted to each of her loved ones. It had been such a wonderful day.

Georgia had moved in with Rob twelve months ago and they still appeared to be going strong. Rob was just what her best friend needed. Someone decisive who could make her feel secure and loved.

Zoe now lived at NATGRID East. She had become quite the little rights agitator and had put her medical studies on hold indefinitely. Ellen was sure Zoe would return to Melbourne University one day. Francis was still keen on that desert hospital and Zoe would be just the person to run it—with Dorak's help, of course.

The children were all doing well and, until now, Vaughn had not made contact with either Zoe or Louise. Why now? Why did he want access to Vincent after not seeking any contact since his birth?

Patrick sat on the floor playing with Pat junior. Francis had given him an enormous fully restored train set for Christmas. The two boys in her life were having a wonderful time setting it up on the now freshly cleared floor.

'Put on the six o'clock news, please, darling.'

Patrick reached for the remote and flicked on the World News channel.

A tsunami had rolled in across two Pacific islands—fortunately they were no longer inhabited. A new immune system–enhancing drug was expected to prevent more deaths from flu in the coming decade than any other advancement in years.

'That's welcome news,' Patrick commented.

Ellen agreed as she scrubbed away at the fish skin adhered to the large baking tray.

The news broadcast continued in the background: 'An Australian citizen living in North Korea has been killed. Reports have been flooding in over the last hour that Professor Vaughn Lambert is dead.'

When the reporter said the victim's name Ellen froze. She turned to face the screen and began listening intently.

'He moved to North Korea three years ago to undertake research for the president. Yesterday he was tried and convicted of treason. Social media sites are reporting that he was executed by firing squad at dawn today.'

Ellen felt quite light-headed. She put down the scrubbing brush and sat down. Blank-faced from shock, she stared at the screen in front of her as the reporter continued to give a potted history of Vaughn's life. Images of Vaughn with Daniel and Gum at AMDAT attending the chip launch filled the screen. Three promising young scientists who had offered the world new hope. Footage of Vaughn the lecturer, researching with his students. A beautiful wedding portrait of Vaughn as best man, standing proudly with Maggie, Daniel and Kenneth. Finally, the reporter outlined the hybrid designer-baby program that had polarised the world and effectively ruined his career. Ellen shivered as footage of the AMDAT raid forced her to revisit that dreadful night. Patrick, sensing her anxiety, sat next to her and placed his arm around her shoulders.

It all seemed so surreal. Could Vaughn really be dead? Could the man who had hurt so many of the people she loved have actually taken his last breath? After a few minutes it began to sink in, and a smile slowly spread across her face. Ellen rose from her seat and walked over to the kitchen drawer. She lifted out the letter, stared at it, then began ripping it into shreds.

Patrick watched her. 'What's that you're murdering?'

'Just something I don't need anymore. I'll explain later,' she replied as the rubbish bin lid snapped tightly shut.

EPILOGUE

The Kent
1677

E lizabeth Hancock stood on the deck of the Kent with her two sons and together they watched the English coastline fade from view. The decision to leave England had come easily to Harold—but not to his mother. He dreamed of a new life, a family of his own. He longed for adventure. She wanted simplicity—a roof over her head, enough food and ... to never dig another grave. Ten-year-old Henry just wanted to sail on a ship. The three had boarded the Kent up north in the Port of Hull. Others had boarded in London. 'There's more than two 'undred souls on board now,' she had overheard one passenger say.

Henry looked up as loud slapping sounds cracked through the air. The last of the sails were unfurling and getting caught by the wind. The vessel lurched sideways and picked up speed. Master Gregory Marlow watched his crew: sweaty, tattooed men with thick beards and black stumps in place of teeth. They grunted, yelled and climbed like monkeys while seagulls squawked and circled overhead. Henry pointed at them, then slipped from his mother's hand. He ran to the stern and leaned over to watch the ship's hull slicing through the waves. Seagulls flying up and around the foaming wake, diving for fish.

'Keep well back laddie!' yelled a sailor, 'If tha falls in, tha'll be drownded!' A startled Henry scurried back to the safety of his mother.

Elizabeth had insisted that they visit Eyam before journeying to Hull.

'I need to say goodbye,' she had explained to Harold, 'And, I want young 'enry 'ere to get sum idea of where he's cum from.' She ruffled the boy's auburn curls.

It had been overcast on the day of their visit and it took some time for them to find their dead. Elizabeth rummaged for the markers with her feet through the tall grass and wildflowers that hummed with insect life. Each grave was marked with a stone: Alice, Ann, John, William, Oner, Elizabeth and their father John. They stayed overnight at the Reverend's house— after a meal and a hurried christening they set off once more for Hull.

Life on board the Kent was harsh. Canvas screens provided little privacy for conversations and copulations. These sounds along with the smells of human excrement mingled with those of the animals housed in the decks below. Salted meats and dry bread created a thirst that was never quite quenched by the daily ration of stale water. The preserved eggs were rubbery and maggots grew fat in the grains and flour.

'Just stop lookin for 'em 'enry,' Harold laughed, as he watched his little brother screwing up his face and picking out the maggots. 'They're more scared of you! Just eat 'em!' Elizabeth didn't examine her ration of food. She shoved whatever she was given into her mouth. She chewed, swallowed then gave thanks to the Lord. Eating only had one goal at the moment and that goal was to survive.

On a bone-dry wooden vessel, fire was the greatest fear. Sailors told stories of ships that had caught fire, burned and sank.

'The fire on my ship was started by a tipped oil lamp,' one sailor had said, 'Someone's carelessness could have killed us all.' That tale made everyone extra careful not to knock over their oil lanterns, and to nip out the flame at bedtime.

They had been at sea for only five days when the fever struck. In the crowded conditions the illness spread like fire. Elizabeth found herself nursing the sick and dying—an all-too-familiar role. Henry helped spoon feed the sick with salted pork chunks dunked in yellow lentil soup. 'It's called pease puddin',' the ship's cook had told him. Harold assisted those well enough to move up onto the deck for some fresh sea air.

Eventually the sickness ran its course and life on board became more settled. On days when the weather was warm and the sea calm, the men would catch fish. Female servants would wash the well-to-do passengers' clothes in large tubs of salt water, bashing the garments against the wooden rails to try and remove the stains. The children would skip with ropes, play knuckles and hopscotch. It was on one of these days that the children noticed the birds. Five seagulls were sitting on one of the masts, all in a neat row, as if they had flown out to meet the ship and were too weary to fly back.

'Land!' came the cry from the crow's nest. Harold ran to fetch the others. Elizabeth stood with her lads and fellow passengers, as they crammed onto the deck. In the afternoon light, they all looked much the same. Tired, wrinkled and sunburnt, with greasy unkempt hair. They wore clothes that *had once been white or coloured, now faded shades of grey. But, despite everything ... they were alive. They had survived months at sea. They had crossed the Atlantic Ocean ... a voyage that only the brave or oppressed dared to take. Elizabeth wondered what would become of them. Her time was near, but she hoped her sons would thrive in this new place. Harold had met a delightful Quaker family. The father had convinced Harold to turn to their faith and join their party of settlers. They could use a good cutler. Harold had agreed and flashed a smile in the direction of the man's youngest daughter.*

The Kent docked first in New York, where some of the passengers left the vessel. The ship then sailed up the Delaware River where two hundred and thirty Quakers disembarked. A meeting place for worship was set up within a few days—it was a large tent made from the sails of the Kent. Harold, Elizabeth and Henry joined them. They, like many European migrants, carried with them Delta 32. This genetic mutation would pass down through the generations providing plague immunity to many of their descendants, including Ellen Elizabeth Hancock.

Dedication and Acknowledgments

I dedicate this novel to my parents Henry and Miriam Priestley. In the nineteenth century, my father's branch of the Priestley family moved from their farm in Derbyshire, England to Sheffield in search of work. Henry, Harold, Leonard, Beatrice, Edith and Irene are family names shared by *Germline* characters. My red-headed father, Henry, was born in Sheffield in 1925. He and his six siblings were raised in abject poverty, much like the Ashmore family depicted in the novel. Henry told me of his squalid living conditions, constant hunger, sleeping with his brothers under overcoats and burning bugs off the walls at night. Henry's eldest brother, Harold, survived the evacuation of Dunkirk. His wife was Edith. Henry's youngest brother, Leonard, died of diphtheria in his childhood: he wasn't vaccinated. Beatrice was one of Henry's sisters, a name also shared by his mother, my grandmother. Irene was my mother Miriam's sister-in-law.

Germline is fiction, although some aspects are factual. Elizabeth Hancock did live in Eyam during the plague outbreak of 1665-66. Her husband and six of her children died of the plague; Elizabeth buried them. The final resting place of Elizabeth's family is now known as the 'Riley Graves'. A scientific study of the descendants of Eyam plague survivors demonstrated that a high proportion carry the genetic mutation called Delta 32. Whether the bubonic plague or another disease caused this genetic mutation is inconclusive.

Several babies were conceived in New Jersey in the late twentieth century via an IVF procedure called cytoplasmic transfer. DNA from three people—a male and two females—corrected infertility issues. Cytoplasmic transfer was banned to prevent the possibility of DNA changes passing to future generations. It is fiction that these children have super immune systems.

I would like to sincerely thank the following people for reading my manuscript and providing feedback: Kasey Craig, Marc Edwards, Travis and Caroline Edwards, Jim and Helen Fitzgerald, Jane Miller, Rebecca Munnings, Teresa Northam, Georgia Pyke and Harry and Kerrie Virs. My husband Mark needs a special mention. I have lost count of the number of drafts he patiently scrutinised. He is the love of my life!

Thank you to the editors: Dr Catherine Heath who taught me a great deal about plot and character development, grammar and political correctness; and Elizabeth Spiegel for teaching me that there are infinite ways to improve a manuscript even when you think it's finished.

Thanks also to the team at Forty South Publishing: Lucinda Sharp and Chris Champion, for manuscript assessment and encouragement; Kent Whitmore, for internal book design; and Ella Michele, for book cover design.